MEDICAL

Life and love in the world of modern medicine.

Paramedic's Reunion In Paradise
Alison Roberts

Healing The Baby Surgeon's Heart
Tessa Scott

T0362973

MILLS & BOON

PARAMEDIC'S REUNION IN PARADISE
© 2025 by Alison Roberts
Philippine Copyright 2025
Australian Copyright 2025
New Zealand Copyright 2025

First Published 2025
First Australian Paperback Edition 2025
ISBN 978 1 038 94051 3

HEALING THE BABY SURGEON'S HEART
© 2025 by Tessa Scott
Philippine Copyright 2025
Australian Copyright 2025
New Zealand Copyright 2025

First Published 2025
First Australian Paperback Edition 2025
ISBN 978 1 038 94051 3

Published by
Harlequin Mills & Boon
An imprint of Harlequin Enterprises (Australia) Pty Limited
(ABN 47 001 180 918), a subsidiary of HarperCollins
Publishers Australia Pty Limited
(ABN 36 009 913 517)
Level 19, 201 Elizabeth Street
SYDNEY NSW 2000 AUSTRALIA

MIX
Paper | Supporting
responsible forestry
FSC
www.fsc.org
FSC® C001695

Cover art used by arrangement with Harlequin Books S.A.. All rights reserved.

Printed and bound in Australia by McPherson's Printing Group

Paramedic's Reunion In Paradise

Alison Roberts

MILLS & BOON

Also by Alison Roberts

Therapy Pup to Heal the Surgeon
City Vet, Country Temptation

A Tale of Two Midwives miniseries

Falling for Her Forbidden Flatmate
Miracle Twins to Heal Them

Alison Roberts has been lucky enough to live in the South of France for several years recently, but is now back in her home country of New Zealand. She is also lucky enough to write for the Mills & Boon Medical line. A primary school teacher in a former life, she later became a qualified paramedic. She loves to travel and dance, drink champagne and spend time with her daughter and her friends. Alison is the author of over one hundred books!

CHAPTER ONE

OH, NO…

Not now.

Please…

Maya Thompson had been heading for the biggest space amongst the resort buildings—the dining room and conference area that made a U shape around the largest swimming pool.

She knew there would be a buffet breakfast laid out and she'd been really looking forward to that first taste of some of her favourite fresh tropical fruit like mangos and pawpaw but she had just lost her appetite completely.

Maybe it was because it hadn't happened for so long that it had caught her unawares. Or maybe it was because this was the last place she would have expected it to happen.

Ten years ago, it had been so frequent Maya had almost come to expect it. She'd see someone in a crowded street, or getting on a plane, or amongst the audience at a conference that would remind her of Eli—the same height or with the same dark hair or that wide smile, perhaps, and she'd quicken her pace or simply stare at them until it became quite clear that it wasn't him. And then she'd have to cope with a wave of heartbreak that was an actual physical pain.

But...*here*...?

On a small South Pacific Island right on the outskirts of the Fijian archipelago?

A *private* island?

It wasn't possible.

Except...it kind of was, if you took into account that Reki Island was about to host a camp for children with complex medical needs who couldn't attend the usual holiday camps for kids and that qualified volunteers, like Maya, came from all over the world to take part in the ten days that were life-changing for the children that were lucky enough to get chosen to come here.

And that Eli Peters was still—as far as Maya knew, anyway—a doctor.

It didn't matter how unlikely it was; in this moment Maya needed a few minutes to herself and she knew exactly where she needed to go. She took a left turn onto a different track that led past a string of round *bures* with thatched roofs that provided individual sleeping and bathroom facilities, and she kept walking until the paved pathways that were designed to cater for wheelchairs or walking aids gave way to soft sand and the occasional coconut that had fallen from the palm trees that lined a perfect crescent of white sand and a lagoon that was still tinged with the pink of a fading sunrise.

Maya took off her white slip-on canvas sneakers and held them in her hand as she walked to where the tiniest waves barely lapped the firmer damp sand. A soft tropical breeze made her curly hair tickle the nape of her neck and she took in a very deep breath and then closed her eyes as she let it out slowly.

Was she going to let an unexpected mental hiccup sabotage something that only happened once a year? Something that Maya looked forward to more than Christmas, New Year celebrations, her birthday or...pretty much everything else put together?

Of course she wasn't.

Reki Island was not only a physical paradise, with its warm sunshine, perfect beaches, lush forests and both sunrises and sunsets that belonged on postcards, it brought together everything that mattered most to Maya. Her job, friendship, children, adventure and...the joy of belonging. Being needed, in fact. This was a place and time where both her profession as a highly trained paramedic and her skills in the leisure activities she loved made her the perfect fit as a volunteer for Reki Island's sought-after camp experience for children with special needs.

'Maya?'

Her eyes flew open and she turned her head sharply but it wasn't a ghost walking towards her from the shadows of the palm trees.

'Mike...' Maya could feel her smile reaching as far as her eyes. 'How good to see you.'

Their hug was full of genuine warmth. Mike might have made it clear years ago that he hoped for more than friendship but that had never been an option and Maya felt completely safe with him. She had encouraged his dream of setting up the camp and hadn't hesitated to become a part of it herself.

'I'm sorry I wasn't still awake when you arrived last

night,' Maya said as she stepped back. 'I didn't even hear the chopper landing.'

'I'm sorry I wasn't here to welcome you earlier. I had no intention of getting caught up in a management crisis back in my hospital in the States, but there you go. I knew Team Reki were more than capable of putting the finishing touches on the months of setting up and I promised that nothing was going to stop me getting back in time for the first day of camp. Not when it's our fifth anniversary.'

Mike Davis shaded his eyes against the rising sun as he gazed out towards the reef and he echoed the way Maya had taken a breath and let it out in a sigh. 'I feel like we're established now,' he said. 'This place is exactly what I wanted it to be. And it can grow. The income from the resort is more than enough to fund expansion and we've got waiting lists of kids who are desperate to come. We're going to look at running a second camp very soon.'

'It's an amazing achievement,' Maya said quietly. 'I'm very glad that there are some people in the world who use their wealth to do something this special. You can be very proud of what you've created and how many lives you've changed for the better. Not just for the kids but for their whole families.'

Mike shrugged off the praise. 'I got lucky. It was past time for my family's fortune to do some good in the world. Going to camp was the best thing in my life as a kid, but it would have been so much better if my brother had been able to come as well.'

Maya nodded. She knew the story. Mike's younger brother had been too sick to ever be considered for a summer camp and his death as a teenager had left a scar deep enough to motivate Mike to train as a doctor and become a paediatrician. Wealthy enough to buy a private island with an existing resort, he'd added a state-of-the-art medical facility and then collected a passionate team of medics and other helpers who were prepared to volunteer their time and skills. He'd been the driving force behind creating a unique camp for a very special group of children and young people who were facing serious health challenges.

'How many campers do we have this time?'

'Thirty, if they're all still well enough to make it. We've got volunteers meeting some of them at the airport in Nadi this morning to bring them out to the island, but most have got a carer with them.' He glanced at his watch. 'Breakfast should be done by now. I want to get our briefing out of the way so we can all get ready for a busy day. Coming?'

'Of course. You go ahead, though, Mike. I'll need to get the sand off my feet and put my shoes back on. There's bound to be a dozen people who are waiting to talk to you before the staff meeting begins.'

Mike nodded and was gone with a smile and a wave. Maya stayed where she was for just another breath, watching the island's owner and camp director stride towards the tracks where glimpses of thatched roofs could be seen amongst the lush greenery. Shifting her gaze towards the end of the crescent beach, she could see the rocky outcrop that was the bottom of their very own mountain and out to sea were the tiny islands whose only inhabitants were huge sea turtles and a rainbow of tropical fish.

Maya realised she was still smiling as she turned her back on the view. Moments later, she balanced herself against the trunk of a palm tree as she brushed sand off her feet and then put her shoes back on.

And why wouldn't she be smiling? This was her happy place.

Maya had been a part of this since well before the very first camp. She'd even helped to choose the name of the island. *Reki* meant 'something joyous' in Fijian and it was also part of *ka rekitaki*, which meant 'delight'—the provision of which was exactly what Mike's mission was for the children who came here during the part of the year that the resort was closed to other clients. She'd also been involved in designing the uniform she was wearing that was comfortable and practical, with the sneakers, a pair of navy-blue shorts that had a cuff just above knee level and a white polo shirt that had her name badge on one side and an embroidered 'Star of Life' symbol on the other. She loved the bright red, blunt-pointed star with the white snake wrapped around the staff in its centre that was an internationally recognised badge of qualification for someone in an emergency medical service. She was proud to wear it.

Maya straightened her spine. She was proud of everything about Reki Island and her part in its history and purpose.

The blip of memory of a relationship that had failed in such a hauntingly spectacular fashion was not going to change anything. It was so far in the past now it was irrelevant, anyway.

Just like Eli Peters was.

'Are you listening, Simon?'
'Look at *this*, Dad...'

The young boy was lying on his stomach. Open in front of him on the floor was the information booklet for the Reki Island Children's Camp—a thick volume of laminated pages full of instructions, explanations and photographs. The page Simon was pointing to had children wearing helmets and harnesses, abseiling down what looked like a sheer rock cliff.

'That's so cool,' Simon said. 'I want to sign up to try that.'

'No.' Eli Peters shook his head. 'Sorry, Si, but that's not going to happen.'

'Why not?'

'You know why.'

'But it says in here that the people who take these activities are able to let every child experience them safely within their level of capability.'

That a nine-year-old could read this well gave Eli a glow of pride but he had to make something very clear.

'We talked about this and you know the rules. Some things are going to be too dangerous for you and anything like rock climbing or abseiling are at the top of the list.'

He wasn't about to try and scare Simon by reminding him that it wouldn't take much of a bump from some sharp volcanic rock to cause internal bleeding that could be life-threatening. And yes, he'd brought Factor VIII and tranexamic acid himself to boost the medical supplies they had available here for children with haemophilia A but…they were in the middle of the Pacific Ocean and even with a helicopter on the island and Mike's private jet in Nadi they were a hell of a long way away from the kind of hospital Eli would be happy for Simon to be getting any major surgery done.

'But, *Dad*...'

'No buts,' Eli said firmly. 'Now...I'm about to go to a staff meeting. Someone should be here any minute to look after you, okay?'

'I don't need looking after. I'm nearly *ten*.'

'*Bula*...' The cheerful greeting was coming from the *bure's* veranda. 'I'm Ana. Are you Dr Peters?'

The young Fijian woman was wearing a bright pink and white dress and had a matching pink flower tucked behind her ear. She was also wearing the widest, brightest smile Eli had ever seen. It was impossible not to smile back.

'I am. Come in, Ana. Simon's in here.'

'You're lucky,' Ana told Simon when she saw what he was looking at. 'You're the first one here for camp so there'll be lots of space for you to choose which activities you want to do first when we go over to the big room later.'

Eli caught Simon's gaze. He didn't have to say anything. They'd already been through the huge list of available activities. Simon would be able to go swimming, snorkelling, sailing, kayaking and paddle boarding for water sports. He could go on forest walks and boat trips to see the turtles. He could join in games like balloon tennis and mini golf, and then there were all the art and craft sessions, dance, music and cooking classes, a scavenger hunt and a talent show to take part in. Pony riding had been a major concession on Eli's part but he was assuming that any animal chosen to interact with medically fragile children would be completely safe.

Simon might be scowling back at him but he really couldn't complain about being banned from high impact activities like rock climbing, abseiling or water sliding. The next ten days were probably going to be packed with more excitement than he'd ever had in his life.

Ana looked up at Eli. 'You'll be busy all morning, yes?'

'Yes. There's a staff meeting and then the tour of the medical facilities. I'll get a break a lunchtime, I expect.'

'Don't worry about Simon,' Ana said. 'I will take very good care of him. He can come and help greet all the campers that will start arriving on the boats soon and I'll take him to put his name on the lists for tomorrow's activities.' She smiled at Simon. 'Did you know that there's a huge bonfire tonight? And a barbecue dinner to welcome everybody to Camp Reki. There'll be lots of singing and dancing. And drumming. Can you play the drums, Simon?'

He shook his head.

'Would you like to learn?'

Simon's nod was eager.

'There's a class for that,' Ana said, 'but if we get time I'll take you to meet my little brother, Tevita. He's about your age and he can teach you some drumming today. That way, you could come and help welcome the boats when they arrive.'

'Yes, *please*... Can we go and see him now?'

Simon's eyes were shining and he'd clearly forgotten any resentment about the banned activities. Eli gave Ana a grateful glance as he left. He needed to hurry now and find the way back to where they'd had breakfast to be in time for the staff meeting that everybody involved with the medical side of the camp was required to attend.

It looked as if most of the huge medical team were already gathered by the time Eli reached the space where tables had been cleared away and replaced by rows of chairs. There was a whiteboard at the front of the room and Mike was clearly trying to get his laptop connected to deliver a presentation.

Eli looked around the room, trying to find a spare seat, but people were still moving, leaning over the backs of chairs to shake hands or hug people they obviously knew well. He couldn't tell what chairs were about to be used or who intended to sit beside those already seated. How many of these people had been here before? There was a lot of chatter and laughter going on and for a moment Eli felt as if he didn't belong.

He'd loved social gatherings once, though, hadn't he? Had he shut himself off so much from normal life in recent years that he'd turned into some kind of recluse? He really did feel a bit like the new boy at school at the moment.

Almost...vulnerable?

He hadn't expected quite this many people.

And...

No...

It couldn't be. Could it...?

Eli could feel his brows almost meeting at the top of his nose, in a mix of a downward frown and an upward question. He couldn't see the woman's face because she was at the front of the room but that wild, dark curly hair made him think instantly of Maya.

And the feeling in his gut was just the same as it always had been whenever he thought of her.

That hollow sensation that was all about loss.

Regret.

And okay…maybe there was still a bit of anger some-where, if he dug deep enough.

Which he wasn't going to do, of course. What would be the point of that?

It was ten years ago, for heaven's sake.

Eli couldn't imagine why his memory had ambushed him quite like this, but it wasn't hard to dismiss. It was, after all… What was the word he was looking for?

Oh, yeah…*irrelevant.*

The hum of conversation in the conference room faded as Mike Davis moved to stand beside the whiteboard, holding a microphone in his hand as he looked at all the people in front of him.

These were the specialist dieticians, psychologists, physios and occupational therapists, paramedics, nurses and doctors that had come here to take care of the special requirements of children with complex medical needs.

'First of all,' he said, 'as the medical director and founder of Camp Reki, I want to welcome you to the island and to extend my heartfelt thanks to you all for giving so much of your time and expertise to this project—without you, none of this would be possible. Many of you have been here before—some have been a vital part of the operation since the very beginning.' He was smiling as he looked straight at Maya, who was sitting at the side of the front row. 'Others are here for the first time, so I want to give you a special welcome.'

There was a wave of applause as Mike lifted a hand in a gesture towards someone who was at the back of the room. Maya turned her head but there were a couple of latecomers moving to empty seats and she couldn't see anyone acknowledging his mention.

'We'll do some introductions later,' Mike continued, 'but let's crack on. We want to get through all the house-keeping stuff and a tour of the facilities before our camp-ers are all here by this afternoon and are coming in for their initial check-ups. I know you've all received infor-mation on anyone who's been flagged as needing your particular areas of expertise but I'd like everyone to be fa-miliar with the group as a whole. You may well be asked to get involved with other children, so we'll run through a quick overview of medical histories for the kids we're expecting this time.'

Mike tapped a key on his laptop and the whiteboard filled with a montage of pictures. One was a child on the back of a pony with a helper on either side to support them. Another was holding up shells they were collect-ing on a beach. Some were on surfboards or in the sea with snorkels and facemasks on. There were wheelchairs deep in the forest and children in special harnesses on a zipline. The activities portrayed were all different but what every photo had in common was the expression on the faces of the children.

Sheer joy…

'As you know,' he began, 'the children can't come to camp unless they've been given a recent all-clear from their own doctors that they're stable and don't have a con-dition or potential complications that might endanger the health, safety or emotional well-being of themselves or other campers or any of the staff but, as you also know, accidents or unexpected medical events can happen any time or anywhere and there's no denying that the range of experiences we offer here increases the risk factors, no matter how well we aim to manage them.'

He tapped again and the image changed to one of a girl with long brown hair who was sitting on a beach, helping to make a sandcastle—holding a bucket despite having no hands.

'This is Hazel,' Mike said. 'Eleven years old and this will be her fourth time at camp. Meningitis as a toddler left her a multiple amputee, losing both hands and feet. She also has some hearing loss, so it helps to make sure she can see your face when you're talking to her. She's medically stable and very independent.'

Independent and as keen as mustard to try anything. Maya had fallen in love with this little girl when she'd been here as an eight-year-old, determined to have a go at the climbing wall with the help of a harness, ropes and Maya dangling behind her. She wouldn't be at all surprised if Hazel intended to try out a real cliff this year.

Mike moved on swiftly through the group of children who, like Hazel, were stable and confident enough to be here without a personal carer. Amongst others, there was Mason, who was a badly scarred burns survivor, and Scarlett, who was currently in remission from her cancer.

Mike was clicking through the case histories that detailed any medications the children were on and what was needed in the way of routine monitoring.

'This is William,' he said. 'He was born with a heart defect and had a cardiac arrest during surgery as a baby which left him with mild cerebral palsy and epilepsy. And this is Simon, nine years old, who's also a newbie this year and is a type A haemophiliac.'

The photo showed a boy with dark spiky hair, a delicate elfin face and a happy smile.

'Simon's here with his dad,' Mike continued, 'who also happens to be a new member of our medical team. We're very lucky to have an emergency medicine consultant who has a special interest in paediatrics. Eli, stand up for a sec, will you? Let's give you a proper welcome this time.'

Maya turned with everybody else but the movement was no more than a reflex because the chill that was rushing through her entire body was freezing her ability to even think, let alone direct her body to move. She certainly wasn't making the slightest effort to contribute to the welcoming hand clapping.

Eli...

It hadn't been simply a physical similarity that had conjured up the ghost from her past.

It really *was* Eli.

And he had a *son*?

A nine-year-old?

Her brain might be frozen but it could still do some maths. Eli had walked out on her ten years ago. Straight into the arms of another woman who'd become instantly pregnant?

Or was this kid closer to turning ten and discovering he was already a father had been the real catalyst, rather than the accident and its aftermath?

How ironic would that be?

The second round of applause faded and everyone was turning back to the front of the room as Mike carried on with the thumbnail medical histories of this year's campers, but for a long moment Maya still couldn't move.

Because as people turned and settled again she found she had a clear line of sight to the back corner of this group of people. To where Eli Peters was still standing.

Staring back at *her*...

He looked just as shocked as she was feeling.

As if this was the last thing he had expected. Or wanted. He almost looked...good grief...*angry*?

That snapped something back into place for Maya and she was back in control as instantly as she'd frozen. She was the one to break the eye contact and turn away. She probably looked as if she was completely focused again on Mike's presentation, but that couldn't be further from the truth.

She was being sucked back in time. Ambushed by a kaleidoscope of memories and emotions. Wounds that should have been long healed felt as if they were being ripped open again and...and it hurt.

More than she would have thought it possibly could after all this time.

CHAPTER TWO

THE INTRODUCTORY TOUR of the medical facilities was more for the benefit of newcomers who needed to know basic things like where the defibrillators were kept, the rules for accessing controlled drugs and the protocols for emergency evacuations of any children who needed more intensive care than the clinic could provide.

'I'm going to give this session a miss,' she told Mike, having hung back as the group of people left the conference room after his briefing. 'I'd like to be there for the first boat coming in. I don't want to miss the chance to give Hazel her first hug of the year.'

Mike knew there was no real reason for Maya to tag along when she was just as familiar with the medical side of running this camp as the doctor and senior nurse who were going to help him lead the tour.

'Give her one from me, too,' he said. 'I'd come down to the jetty myself but I haven't seen the new ultrasound and X-ray equipment that got set up while I was in the States. I'll catch up with you soon.' Mike was smiling but there was a hint of a frown on his face at the same time. 'Are you okay, Maya? You're looking a bit pale.'

Maya managed a smile but it was an effort. 'I'm fine,' she assured him.

She couldn't tell him that she was still reeling from seeing the man that at one time she'd been so sure she was destined to spend the rest of her life with. Or that she was even more shocked that he had a child whose conception or birth might even overlap somehow with the time that she'd been living with Eli.

Trusting him.

Loving him with her whole heart and soul.

Staff were busy around them now. They were shifting tables and setting up photo boards and decorations. Like a mini conference, this would be where the camp attendees and their carers would come this afternoon to choose the activities they wanted to try and to talk about how they might need to be adapted to cater for any special needs.

As Mike left he pointed at a poster of a child with obvious cerebral palsy, dangling halfway down a cliff. The person in another harness right behind the child, helping him every step of the way, was Maya and they both had wide grins on their faces. Mike threw a grin of his own and a 'thumbs up' signal as he disappeared in the wake of the group, but this time Maya couldn't find one in response.

To her horror, she felt like she might even be close to tears and that was hardly going to reflect the joy that this camp promised to deliver. She knew she needed to get her head back together as soon as possible because she would be back here this afternoon to take charge of the area devoted to abseiling, rock climbing and the climbing wall which had custom holds and a system of harnesses that made it possible to give almost every child the experience of a vertical adventure.

Somehow, she had to face the explosion of memories

that were threatening to overwhelm her and make a plan of how she was going to deal with this, and maybe the best first step she could take was to remind herself of why she was here.

The first boat carrying a group of the children and their carers from the main island could be seen approaching Reki Island as Maya arrived at the jetty. The local staff members, who had their own village on this private island, and jobs within the resort all year round, were gathering on the shore to greet the very different guests they would be helping to look after for the next ten days.

The women wore their uniform bright pink and white patterned dresses and the men had equally bright shirts and plain pink shorts. They all had colourful hibiscus or fragrant frangipani flowers tucked behind their ears and some had flower and shell necklaces draped over their arms, ready to be bestowed on the new arrivals as they came ashore.

One of the older women brought a yellow and white frangipani flower with a stem and went to tuck it behind Maya's right ear, but then she raised her eyebrows and grinned at her.

'Maybe it needs to be the left ear this time?' she asked. 'Did you get engaged or married since last year?'

'No...not this year, Moana.'

Oh, man... Could she blame the bright sunshine for how much she was having to blink?

Moana tutted. 'I don't understand why a gorgeous girl like you is still single.' She slipped a shell necklace around Maya's neck for good measure and gave her a hug. 'It's so good to see you.'

Maya let herself sink into the warmth and softness of

the hug. Pacific women gave the best hugs ever. She felt
better already, she decided as she moved to one side of the
welcoming committee as they got ready. A couple of men
were holding guitars and a few more had drums. Maya
wasn't surprised to see a younger boy amongst them because, as always, there were plenty of children running
around. What did surprise her was that this child wasn't
Fijian. And that she recognised the delicate features of
his face and the spiky hair over big dark eyes.

This was Simon.

Eli's son.

He was with Tevita, who was Ana's younger brother.
Ana wasn't far away, watching them rather than the boat
coming closer to shore so Maya knew she must have been
tasked with looking after Simon. He looked…happy, she
thought. He also had a shell necklace on and a flower
behind his ear and his smile suggested he was very excited to be a part of the singing and dancing that would
start as the boat tied up at the jetty. He qualified as one
of the campers while he was here, because of his medical condition of haemophilia, but being on this side of
the equation right now made him special.

Not that it was going to his head. Maya saw him look
up at the bigger boys he was standing with and could see
the way he took in a deep breath, proud to be one of them.

He looked like an adorable child.

He also looked very like his father.

It was Maya's turn to pull in a deep breath. She closed
her eyes for a moment as well, willing herself to put the
past back where it belonged, but it was harder than she
expected. Because it was still hurting.

How could she not remember that first time she'd met

Eli, when it had been so dramatic, both professionally and personally? She'd gone into the emergency department of a New Zealand hospital as part of a frontline ambulance crew to find the new English locum in the trauma response team ready to take over the management of a critically injured patient.

Maya had been riding the stretcher because she couldn't afford to take the pressure off an arterial bleed caused by a penetrating abdominal wound. The team had worked around her, stabilising the man's airway, breathing and IV access for fluid replacement before rushing him to Theatre so Maya had a central stage position to watch the most gorgeous man she'd ever seen at work. He'd noticed her, too. And he'd been the first person to notice, as they'd walked back to the ED after helping to get their patient to the surgeons, that some of the blood on her arm was coming from a deep scratch she hadn't realised she'd received.

'What have you done to yourself?'

'I have no idea. I did have to crawl under the car wreckage to get a line into him. I must have got a bit too close to some mangled metal before the firies could cut him loose.'

Maya had liked how hard-core it made her sound. Or rather, she liked how impressed Eli had looked.

'It might need stitches. Let me look properly.'

It wasn't that serious. Maya was pretty sure this cut didn't need more than a spot of skin glue and a dressing at most and she was up-to-date with her tetanus booster, but Eli had held her arm gently in one hand as they rode the lift back to the ground floor and by the time he'd examined the wound they both knew it had begun.

And it felt like it could be the love story of the century.

They'd moved in with each other within three months. They were making plans for the rest of their lives.

As if they were providing a track for the movie of her life, Maya heard the joyous singing start around her— the strumming of guitars, the wonderful harmonies of voices and the heartbeat of the drums keeping the rhythm. It was the sound of the islands. A sound that Maya loved so much it was enough to make her smile through any pain her memories were trying to rekindle.

She'd been too young to know that flames that burned that brightly couldn't last. That even the glow of the embers could be completely snuffed out. They'd gone full circle, hadn't they? It had all ended just as dramatically as it had begun. With her being injured in the course of doing the job she was so passionate about, only this time it wasn't something that could be fixed with a bit of skin glue.

No... This was not the time or place to be thinking about *that*...

Maya snapped her eyes open, deliberately widening her smile as she saw the first passengers coming off the ferry Someone in a wheelchair being pushed by their carer was first and then a young girl came around them, almost running on prosthetic lower legs and feet, holding out arms that ended in points rather than hands.

'Maya... I'm *here*...' She raised her voice to be heard over the background singing.

'Hazel...' Maya didn't need to put any effort into smiling now. Even better, any unhappiness her brain had been trying to wrap around her was obliterated the instant she had this child in her arms. 'I'm *so* glad you're here, sweetheart. We're going to have *such* fun.'

But not quite yet, it seemed. Someone was running towards the jetty from where they'd parked an electric golf cart.

'Maya? Can you come, please? You're needed up at the helicopter pad.'

The call that led to the dispatch of Reki Island's helicopter to Nadi Airport had come in while Eli was touring the clinic, infirmary and minor procedures theatre that were all part of the island's impressive medical facilities.

'One of our first-time campers had what sounds like a syncopal episode after getting off a ten-hour flight from San Francisco. Fourteen-year-old who got a heart transplant three years ago and is travelling alone. The staff member meeting him got him to the first aid room and says he's got a rapid heart rate and seems a bit short of breath, but he's more distressed at the thought of missing camp than how he's feeling. It's a quick trip by chopper so I said I'd send one of our doctors to make the call about whether he needs to go to hospital and get checked out. Our pilot's standing by. I'd go myself but I can't abandon this introductory tour. Are you happy to go?'

'Of course.' Eli was already following Mike out of the clinic buildings. 'I'll need a life pack so I can get a twelve-lead ECG and monitor vital signs like his pulse oxygen level.'

'We've got a full resus kit, including a defibrillator, on board, just in case. And our paramedic is an experienced helicopter rescue crew member. She's going to meet you at the helipad. Her name's Maya. Come on, I can introduce you.'

Eli opened his mouth to confess how well he actually knew Maya but no words emerged. It wasn't as if it was going to make any difference to his ability to work with these children so there was no real reason for Mike to know that he might have decided not to come to Reki Island if he'd known Maya would be here. Or maybe he was processing the fact that she *had* ended up working on helicopters.

Of course she had.

The echo of his own voice from so many years ago felt like a reprimand. A familiar guilt trip that he'd been the cause of the wheels beginning to fall off the most significant romantic relationship of his life.

'You want to work on a helicopter crew? Are you kidding? Don't you think your job is dangerous enough already?'

'It's my dream job, Eli...this is what I do...it's who I am... You can get killed crossing the street, you know— why are you so paranoid about things that might never happen?'

'You know why...'

He could almost feel an echo of Maya's reassuring touch on his arm as well.

'Lightning never strikes twice in the same place, Eli. Nothing bad is going to happen...'

Except it had, hadn't it?

And maybe Eli was only beginning to realise how bad it had really been because he'd thought it was so far in the past it was completely buried. Until that moment in the conference room when he'd made eye contact with

Maya for the first time in ten years and he'd felt a kick in his gut that was so powerful it felt like his heart had stopped beating for long enough to be alarming.

It was a punch of sensation that was a tangle of emotions he had no desire to try and untangle, but Eli could recognise the pain of loss, the struggle to get past something overwhelmingly huge and...and, *dammit*...there was also a unmistakable twinge of what he'd felt the very first time he'd laid eyes on Maya Thompson.

Unforgettable, irresistible, bone-deep sexual attraction.

How was he going to cope with that happening repeatedly for the next ten days? Or had that gut-wrenching reaction only happened because seeing Maya again had been so unexpected?

Unwanted...?

He was about to find out. A bright red electric vehicle was approaching the helipad behind the medical wing of the resort. Even from this distance he could see the wild dark brown curls of Maya's hair. He'd already felt the effect of making eye contact with her and that had been across a huge room crowded with other people. How much more powerful was it going to be when they were within touching distance of each other?

It had been like that from the first moment they'd met. An actual physical pull that had been like nothing Eli had ever felt before.

Or since.

Eli pulled in a deep, deep breath.

There was a professional reason they were about to be breathing the same air. He just needed to focus on that.

* * *

It was good that there was no time for anything but the briefest of introductions from Mike.

'Eli, this is Maya—a brilliant paramedic who can cope with anything. Maya, this is Eli—HoD of one of the largest emergency departments in London, with a special interest in paediatrics.' He grinned at them as the rotors on the helicopter were gaining speed. 'You guys are the A team for Reki Island's medical crew, that's for sure.'

She had to look at him as she nodded acknowledgment of the introduction. It was the briefest graze of eye contact but it was enough to notice that ten years had barely changed him. Maybe there were a few more crinkles at the corners of his eyes and deeper lines from his nose to that mouth, but those dark blue eyes were just as bright and there was no hint of grey in that thick brown hair that he always pushed back from his face if he needed time to think about anything.

Just like he pushed it back right then, as his polite smile faded almost instantly.

Maya's heart did an odd little flip at the familiarity of the gesture.

Or was it sinking like a stone because reading that gesture without having to translate it had suddenly opened the door to that private nonverbal language that was uniquely hers and Eli's? And she could feel the pull to walk closer to the door. To step through it, even?

How could she be that stupid?

She knew what lay beyond that door.

Heartbreak, that was what.

Her own equally polite smile also vanished and she

reached for one of the helmets that the co-pilot, James, had ready for them as soon as the medical kits had been stowed. She jammed it on her head and climbed into her seat and hooked the straps of the safety belt over her shoulders and clicked the central locking system together. They were airborne within seconds.

'We've got a flight time of just under fifteen minutes,' Danny told them. 'The patient's in the first aid room and someone will be waiting to show you where that is. If necessary, we can transfer them to Nadi Hospital. Air traffic control will give us priority for landing and take-off.'

'Is it possible to get an update of whether there's been any change in the patient's condition, please?'

Oh, help... Maya had underestimated the effect of hearing Eli's voice through the inbuilt communication system in her helmet. It sounded as if he was close enough for his lips to be tickling her ears. How could it feel, after all this time, as if she'd heard that voice *that* close only yesterday?

'Sure thing.' Danny radioed through to the airport authorities.

'Do we have any history?' Maya's voice sounded oddly rough and she had to clear her throat. 'This is a first-time camper, isn't it? A heart transplant recipient?'

'I've got his notes.' Eli's voice was crisper now. Focused. He was looking down at his phone. 'Carlos Hermandez. Fourteen years old. Received a heart transplant two years ago due to heart failure caused by cardiomyopathy. Possibly hereditary—his father died suddenly four years ago at the age of thirty-five, leaving his mother with five kids to raise on her own. Carlos is the oldest. He's down to six-monthly checks by the transplant team and they've been delighted with his recovery. There's a note on his pre-camp check-up form to say he's an exceptional boy, responsible and independent. They can't see any problems with him coming to camp on his own and he deserves the privilege, given how much he does for his younger siblings.'

This was better. Maya was getting used to the sound of Eli's voice again. It helped that she had something else to focus on.

'And he had a syncopal episode?'

'At the luggage carousel. Apparently, he got too dizzy to stay standing. We don't know if he actually lost consciousness. The airport first aider reported a rapid heart rate and breathing and said he looked pale and sweaty.'

'Where did he fly in from?'

'Direct flight from San Francisco.'

Danny's voice broke into the conversation. 'Sounds like he's feeling better. Just scared he's going to have to go to hospital instead of camp.'

'Let's hope he doesn't,' Maya said. 'Have we got a list of his meds?'

'Yep.' Eli was scrolling the file he still had open. 'Immunosuppressant drugs, as you'd expect. An anti-hypertensive, lipid-lowering medication and…that's about it. No known allergies.'

Maya could see the shape of Fiji's main island coming into view. They would be landing soon.

'Fingers crossed it was nothing more than excitement causing a vagal reaction. Or nervousness, if he's never flown by himself before. Or maybe his anti-hypertensive has lowered his blood pressure a bit too effectively.'

'Could be an arrhythmia,' Eli said. 'The scar tissue

from a transplant can create a pathway for re-entrant arrhythmias like atrial flutter.'

'We'd have to send him to hospital if there's any sign of infection,' Maya said. 'We can't afford to risk spreading something through a whole bunch of vulnerable kids.'

'No.' Eli's tone was sombre. 'Any sign of rejection is something else I'd be worried about. What happens if he's too unwell to come to camp?'

'The camp has insurance to cover an international medevac air ambulance service if it's necessary to send someone back to their own medical team. We've never had to use it in the five years we've been up and running, though.'

Maya could feel the surprise in Eli's gaze on her. 'Have you been involved all along?'

'Yes.' She didn't meet his gaze. 'I met Mike about nine years ago when he was on holiday in Australia. He'd just bought the island but he was full of the dream of using the success of the existing resort to set up the camp one day.'

The silence told her that Eli was reading way too much between the lines but she wasn't going to say anything else. She couldn't, when the thought occurred to her that she must have been with Mike around the time Simon had been born.

Anyway…for the sake of her pride as much as anything, Maya would much rather he thought she was—or had been—in a relationship than knowing she'd been left so broken when he'd walked away that it had always been an impossibility—with Mike, or anyone else for that matter.

Yes…let him think that she had got over him and

moved on fast. That she had a life that wasn't going to be derailed by knowing he'd left her for someone else— and his baby.

An incoming international flight that had just landed was being held on the runway while the helicopter landed close to the terminal buildings. The empty arrivals hall made it easy to follow their guide as they carried their equipment and they were in the first aid room very quickly.

A tall, lanky teenager sat on the edge of a bed. His Spanish heritage was evident in his olive skin and mop of black curls. His distress at being kept in this medical facility was just as evident.

'Hey...' Eli put the backpack of medical gear he was carrying down on the floor, as if he knew it wasn't going to be needed in a hurry. 'Carlos? I'm Eli. Pleased to meet you.' He held out his hand in greeting and Carlos looked surprised but took his hand to shake it. 'I'm a doctor,' Eli told him. 'And this is Maya, who's a paramedic. We're both working at Camp Reki and we've been sent to see how you're doing. You had a bit of a dizzy spell, yes?'

Carlos shrugged. 'I guess... I'm fine now, though. You're not going to make me go to the hospital here, are you?' There was a plea in his dark eyes that told them it was the very last place he wanted to go.

'Not unless there's a very good reason to do so,' Eli said. 'How are you feeling now?'

'I'm good.'

'Can you tell me exactly what happened?'

'It was just hot in the baggage claim area and...I was looking around because I wasn't sure what to do and then

I felt a bit sick and…I dunno…next thing I knew, I was on the floor and there were all these people staring at me.'

Maya had moved closer to put a life pack on the end of the bed. The machine beeped as she turned it on. She unzipped one of the pouches on the side and pulled out a blood pressure cuff. She smiled at Carlos.

'Can I check a couple of things while you're talking to Eli? Like your blood pressure and temperature—you know the drill, don't you?'

Carlos gave a resigned nod. Eli quizzed him about how the flight had gone and how he'd been feeling in the last couple of days and had a quick look at his hands and ankles to see if they were puffy.

'Have you been having any joint pains?'

'No.'

'Any chills or feeling shivery?'

'No. Bit hot here, but I knew it would be. It's a tropical island, isn't it? It's supposed to be hot. I can't wait to go swimming. And diving around the reef.'

Maya was working quietly beside him. She clipped a pulse oximeter onto one of his fingers, swiftly wrapped the cuff around his upper arm and held his other wrist to take his pulse while the cuff inflated. She pricked his finger to get a drop of blood to test his glucose levels, and then pointed a thermometer at his forehead by the time the cuff was finishing deflating and figures were settling on the screen of the life pack.

'Temperature's thirty-six point five,' she said. 'BP's one zero five on sixty, heart rate's ninety-six, resp rate's twenty and pulse ox is ninety-eight on room air.'

Oh, wow… Had Eli forgotten just how efficient and calm Maya was when she was doing her job?

'That's all good, isn't it?' Carlos still sounded anxious.
'It is,' Eli said.

He could see that Maya was unravelling the wires required to do an ECG and see whether there was anything
of concern in the heart rhythm or function, but that blood
pressure and oxygen level in the blood was reassuring.

'Maya's going to stick some dots on you for the ECG
and I want to listen to your breathing.' Eli turned to open
the pack but Maya handed him a stethoscope. 'Deep
breath,' he instructed as he positioned the disc on various areas over the lungs. 'And another one... Okay...lie
back now and Maya can put the extra dots on your chest
for that ECG.'

Carlos pulled up his tee shirt as he lay back on the pillows. The long scar down the middle of the teenager's
chest was still in the process of fading.

Eli could feel how lopsided his smile was, but it was
impossible not to think of how he'd feel if Simon had un-
dergone such a major surgery.

'That's a pretty impressive war wound,' he told Carlos
quietly. 'You've won a big battle, haven't you?'

Carlos grinned back at him with the same kind of
cheekiness that Simon would have. 'I'm tough,' he said.

'You are,' Maya agreed. 'Keep really still for a moment, though. I need to print out a copy of just how well
that heart of yours is behaving.'

She handed the printout to Eli. It felt as though both
Maya and Carlos were holding their breath as he examined each section of the twelve-lead ECG. When he
looked up, it was Maya's gaze he caught first and...he
knew she was reading his thoughts.

Like she had almost always been able to do...

When she smiled, it was impossible not to smile back at her. A real smile this time, because this wasn't about them. It was about a boy who was desperately keen to have some fun that he really deserved to have. They would need to keep an eye on him for a day or two but there was nothing to suggest he needed to go to hospital.

They both turned to Carlos and Eli's smile widened. 'How would you like a private helicopter ride to get to camp?'

CHAPTER THREE

BY LATE AFTERNOON all the camp attendees had arrived on the island and the registration process was in full swing.

Camp uniforms with the sky-blue tee shirts and baseball caps were distributed. They had a logo of a bright yellow circle for the sun framing a palm tree, Camp Reki and the year printed beneath. Best of all, the tee shirts were personalised by having the name of the child embroidered beneath the right shoulder with a small smiley face beside it.

There were queues in the conference area for the uniforms and welcome packs that had all the information needed for the medical facilities available and how to contact staff members. Children and their carers were also lining up to peruse all the activities available and sign up for what they most wanted to do on their first day tomorrow.

Maya was standing beside the photo montage of climbing activities with an electronic tablet in her hands and a smile on her face as she entered the name of a young girl who wanted to try the 'wall with the pretty bumps on it'.

'It's called a climbing wall,' Maya told Aliesha. 'And it's great fun.'

Aliesha nodded, as if she already knew that. 'I'm going to make friendship bracelets too,' she told Maya. 'I could make you one, if you want?'

'That's very sweet of you,' Maya said. 'And I'm happy to be your friend, but I think you should keep your bracelet. You could make one for your mum, too, maybe?'

As Aliesha skipped away with her mother, Maya turned to see a boy who was staring at the photos on the board with such an expression of longing that it tugged at her heartstrings.

She knew who he was. She'd seen him earlier today, playing a drum amongst the island boys down at the jetty.

She'd also seen his face on the screen at the meeting this morning where the staff had been briefed on the range of medical conditions this year's campers represented.

'You're Simon, aren't you?' she asked. 'You come from London, don't you?'

'How did you know that?'

'I know heaps of stuff,' Maya said. 'I know that you're nine years old and that you're here with your dad.' She frowned. 'I don't know if you've got any brothers or sisters, though.'

Simon shook his head. 'It's just me and Dad.'

Maya blinked. 'What about your mum?' As soon as the words left her mouth she knew she'd stepped over a boundary, but Simon wasn't bothered.

'I've never had a mum,' he said. 'Do you know that my dad's a doctor?'

'I do.'

'And that the hospital here looks like a tropical island? It's got palm trees and turtles on the walls and the rooms look like the huts. There's even a big tank in the waiting room that's got fish in it that are all different colours.'

'I do know that.' Maya nodded. 'I've been here before and I help out in the clinic sometimes.'

'Dad's there now. He's on duty till bedtime so he's going to miss the bonfire and the barbecue.'

'I'm sure he'll be able to come and have some dinner with you if nobody needs him. And everybody has to be there for the s'mores. It's like a camp rule.'

'What's a s'mores?'

'It's an American thing,' Maya told him. 'Mike, who's in charge of the camp, says it's not a proper camp unless you have s'mores. They happen when the bonfire has burnt out until it's just hot coals and everyone can get close enough to toast marshmallows. You get a cracker and put a piece of chocolate on it and then the roasted marshmallow and then another cracker goes on top of that and it makes a delicious, crunchy and squishy sandwich.'

'S'mores.' Simon nodded. 'Got it. I'll tell Dad he has to come for that bit.'

'Do you want to know why they're called s'mores?'

Simon nodded again.

'It's because they're so delicious that when they were first invented at a Girl Scouts camp, everybody wanted "some more" and it got shortened to "s'more".'

'If I tell Dad that and that it's a camp rule, he'll have to come, won't he?'

'Unless someone needs him,' Maya agreed.

But she was aware of a wash of relief that she wouldn't see too much of Eli on this first evening at camp. Even with something professional to focus on, like they'd had in their time with Carlos this afternoon, being that close to Eli had had its moments—like hearing his voice inside her helmet and the way he'd smiled at her when they'd both known there was no reason not to let Carlos come to camp.

Oh, *man*...she'd felt that smile right down to her bones.

'Hey...' Maya needed to stop any echo of how that smile had made her feel. 'I saw you playing the drums today. You're very good at it.'

Simon ducked his head but his smile was proud. 'It was Tevita who showed me how to do it. He's Ana's brother. Ana's looking after me while Dad's busy. She's gone to get my tee shirts for me.'

Oh...it was a smile that came with the ease of being well-used, but that didn't dilute any of its warmth.

It was a smile so like Eli's...

With an effort, Maya crushed that persistent line of thought. She noticed that Simon was staring at the photos again.

'Do you want to try one of the climbing activities?'

He shook his head sadly. 'I can't,' he said. 'I've got haemophilia A. Do you know what that is?'

Maya nodded. 'It means that your body doesn't make enough Factor VIII, which is a protein that makes the blood able to clot.'

Simon nodded. 'So I can't do stuff like climbing mountains because, even though I get infusions all the time, if I hit something sharp like a rock I could still get bad bleeding. I've got a port, too, so I have to be careful not to bump it.'

'I understand,' Maya said. 'And I wouldn't suggest going anywhere near the real cliffs until you knew what you were doing, but the climbing wall is very safe. See those bumps and ledges? No sharp edges anywhere like real rocks. You'd be wearing a helmet and gloves, knee and elbow pads and you're in a harness and on a rope so you can't fall. The harness should cover your port and protect it, but if it doesn't we can sort that out. You've got someone right behind you, too. Someone like me, who's had lots of practice keeping people safe.' She grinned at the way Simon's face was lighting up. 'It's my favourite thing to do, teaching people how to climb safely.'

'I really want to do it.' Simon's voice was just a whisper.

'I've got one space left tomorrow morning in the first session,' Maya said. 'Shall I put your name in there? You can check with your dad later and make sure it's okay.'

Simon was sucking in an excited breath as he nodded. 'What time does it start?'

'Half past ten. After breakfast and the first swim for the day. It's easy to find. There's a signpost where the tracks cross near the front doors to the clinic building, but if you get lost it's on the outside of this building—round the back. You can't miss it—it's a huge wall covered in a rainbow of lumps and bumps.'

Bonfire nights were special. There was one on the first night for everyone to meet each other and any new children were shy and wide-eyed at the excitement of it all, the smell of food being cooked, the sound of drums in the background and the flicker of real flames from the fire in the central pit and the torches on tall poles that outlined the large grass circle.

There would be another bonfire on their last night at camp and Maya knew how different that would be, with children who'd gained so much more confidence, made friends for life and were ready to put on a performance and show off the songs and dances they'd learned.

Mike Davis was in his happy place, mingling with the guests, both children and adults, many of whom were catching up with friends from previous camps. Maya saw Mike spend extra time with Carlos and, judging by the way the teenager was shaking his head and smiling, he was being reassured that the medical incident at the airport had not been repeated. He then took Carlos to where a group of boys had gathered to watch the fire being stoked. Mason was there. And William, on his crutches. Maya found her gaze drifting, wondering where Simon was and whether he would like to be part of the group. She spotted him with Hazel and some of the younger children. Ana and another local woman were teaching them a dance near where the music was happening.

Maya had been busy in the last hour, shut in the supply rooms, double-checking that every emergency pack was fully stocked, that oxygen cylinders were full, that bags of fluid had not gone past their expiry dates and that the drug kits had everything she might need if she was called to an accident. Adding ampoules of tranexamic acid, a medication used to help control severe haemorrhage in trauma patients, had made her think of Simon.

Thinking of Simon made her think of Eli.

And thinking of them both made one question only get louder.

What had happened to Simon's mother?

'Penny for them?'

Maya turned swiftly to find that Mike was beside her. He held out a glass of what looked like fresh juice.

'Thought you might like a mocktail.'

'Thank you.' Maya accepted the drink. 'I was thinking of going to join in the dancing over there but I suspect the kids won't want big people taking over.'

Mike followed her line of sight. 'Ah…that's where Simon got to. I told Eli I'd keep an eye on him. I also told him to bring his pager and come down to the circle, but he's determined to go through the detailed medical background of every kid in camp.'

'Ha…' The word was more like a huff of breath. 'That sounds like Eli. Overcautious.'

She could feel Mike's steady gaze on her. 'You know him?'

'It was a long time ago.'

Mike was silent for a long moment. 'When I met you, I got the feeling that you'd been burned enough to put you off even thinking about a long-term relationship.' He cleared his throat. 'Would Eli Peters have had anything to do with that?'

Maya was silent long enough for it to be the answer to the question and Mike's next words were quiet.

'You okay with him being here?'

'As I said, it was a long time ago. It's ancient history.'

'That doesn't answer the question.' But Mike's gaze was gentle. 'I'm sorry I didn't know. I could have at least given you a heads-up. I only met Eli a couple of months ago—at a paediatric conference in Paris. I gave a talk about the benefits of medically complex kids being able to do normal stuff like going to camp and it came up in conversation when I met Eli at a dinner. Seemed like a match made in heaven when I heard about Simon.' His glance was quizzical. 'Did you know about Simon?'

Maya shook her head. 'That was more of a shock than

seeing Eli again, I think. Do you know what happened to his mother?'

'What do you mean?'

'He told me he's never had a mum. That it's just him and his dad.'

Mike shrugged. 'I don't know anything about that. And what did you mean about being overcautious?'

'Eli's not a risk-taker,' Maya said. 'Which is partly why he's such a good doctor. He had adrenaline junkie parents who got killed by an avalanche when they went cross-country skiing in Switzerland. He was only about fourteen and his sister was even younger. They got brought up by grandparents. When he ended up working in emergency medicine it just reinforced his opinion that so many accidents were due to recklessness and I suspect that made him even more cautious.'

Mike was shaking his head. 'You're another adrenaline junkie,' he said. 'And I can't imagine you letting anyone clip your wings with the job and sports you love so much. I get why it didn't work out.'

Maya made a sound that acknowledged how unlikely a couple they'd been.

But it had never felt like that.

Quite the opposite. Even when she had indeed felt like her wings were being clipped, she'd been so sure they could work things out. That nothing could blow them apart.

And Maya had believed that until she'd fallen down that cliff. Literally and emotionally.

At eleven o'clock the next morning Eli Peters looked up from reading the repeat ECG he'd done on Carlos after giving him another thorough check-up.

'Thanks for coming back in this morning. I know it meant missing your first activity session, but we needed to make sure you were over whatever it was that made you unwell yesterday. I'd hate to think we'd missed something but, as far as I can tell, you're in great shape.'

'It's okay. Someone's going to get me some flippers and a snorkel and they're going to take me out in the lagoon. Just me...' Carlos looked as if he'd grown an inch since yesterday. 'They're really nice people here, aren't they?'

Eli nodded, smiling. 'They are. This is my first time here, too, and I'm really impressed. Did you enjoy the bonfire last night?'

'Yeah...it was great.'

'I only got there towards the end—when everyone was making those sticky marshmallow things.'

'S'mores.' Carlos nodded. 'They always have them at summer camps.'

'So I heard. We don't have them in England, but I might have to learn how to make them. My boy, Simon, thought they were the best dessert ever invented. Now...' He grinned at Carlos. 'How 'bout you get out of here and have some fun?'

Eli could get out of here for a while now, too, and he was planning to have a wander and see where some of the various activities were happening. He had a rough idea from the tour he'd done yesterday but it was information that he would prefer to have in greater detail. The tracks might be well signposted, but if there was an emergency like an accident he'd want to be able to get to the exact location as fast as possible.

He'd end his walk down at the beach and maybe he could find Simon, who might still be collecting shells.

Or had he said something about going fishing after his swim?

Eli glanced at the pile of patient notes on the edge of the desk in this consulting room that he still needed to put away after going through them all last night. Simon had been disappointed that he'd missed most of the first night celebrations but the effort of getting really familiar with the medical history of every child at camp had been valuable. He'd felt as if he already knew everyone who'd come to the clinic this morning for routine checks or the administration of their long-term medications, some of which were done by IV infusion. Knowing what normal was for these children who needed more intensive monitoring meant that he'd be more likely to notice any change that could be the first indication of a serious problem.

Or was he justifying something he'd done for more personal reasons? Like avoiding spending any more time than necessary in Maya's company? That was hardly a strategy that he could keep up for ten days, was it? At some point, they were going to have to talk to each other.

How good would it be, Eli thought, as he clipped on his pager and headed towards the reception area of the clinic, if he and Maya could actually agree to forgive and forget and put the past behind them? If they could leave this tropical paradise having recaptured something of the friendship they'd once had, even?

Eli stepped out of the medical wing and stood for a moment looking at the signpost at the intersection of tracks near the front door. One yellow arrow was pointing towards the beach. Straight ahead was a forest walk loop and the opposite direction to the beach led to the climbing wall he'd seen on his tour yesterday. He'd go there first, he decided, and see how long it took to get there from the clinic because it was exactly the kind of location that you could expect an accident to happen.

He arrived to see a lively session in action, with each of the rainbow-coloured tracks of hand and foot holds reaching from the ground to the roof—a good ten metres in height—being used. A solid steel structure went up the sides of the wall and across the top, anchoring at least a dozen ropes. Children and instructors were attached to the ropes, wearing harnesses that looked as though they'd been specially designed to cope with any disabilities a child might have. They were wearing helmets and elbow pads and there were mats on the ground. The safety measures being taken were more than impressive enough to satisfy Eli.

Until he saw who was almost at the top of the wall.

Simon...?

Eli could feel the blood draining from his face as his heart rate accelerated. Fear morphed into anger. Where the hell was Ana? How had this been allowed to happen? Someone was responsible for this and he was going to find out who it was. They shouldn't be allowed anywhere near vulnerable children again.

Frozen to the spot, he watched as the instructor hanging beside Simon coached him into stretching his leg to find a foothold as they began their descent. The instructors and some of the older children were controlling their own belay devices. Adults on the ground were controlling the release of the ropes keeping other children safe. They were also clipped onto new metal fastenings on the wall every time they moved far enough, but that didn't stop Eli's heart dropping like a stone as he saw Simon lose his grip and swing away from the wall.

He could hear Simon's laughter, as though swinging in mid-air far enough off the ground to potentially kill him if he fell was the best fun he'd ever had. The instructor reached out a hand and Simon caught it. He was drawn back to the wall and found a hand grip. As the instructor turned to point to the ledge he needed to get his feet onto, Eli could see the face beneath the helmet.

Maya...

Of course it was. How had that not occurred to him as soon as he'd realised someone was breaking rules around here and being unacceptably irresponsible?

By the time Maya and Simon reached the ground, Eli was absolutely furious. He kept it hidden as he watched helpers unclip Simon's ropes and help him out of his harness and the safety gear. Maya kept her harness on and coiled a rope to hang from one shoulder, clearly ready to help the next child who was waiting for a turn on the wall, but Eli was walking towards her as she gave Simon a high-five hand-slap.

'Good job, buddy. It wasn't that scary, was it?'

'It was so *cool*.' Simon was grinning from ear to ear. 'Can I try it on the real cliff next time?'

'We'll have to see about that,' Maya said.

'Yeah...' Eli's tone was dry. 'That might be a good idea.'

Simon's head swivelled. So did Maya's.

'Hi, Dad...' Simon's voice was as small as he suddenly seemed. Guilt was written all over his face.

Maya looked from Eli to Simon. 'When I asked you

this morning if your dad was okay with you doing this, you said he was.'

Simon scuffed the ground with his foot. 'I just said it was all good.' The look he sent his father made it clear that he blamed Eli for spoiling his fun. 'It *was* all good,' he muttered. 'Maya said it was safe and...' he was scowling now '...and I wanted to do it. More than stupid fishing...'

'Okay...' Eli kept his tone calm but it was an effort. 'Do you know where Ana is?'

'No.'

'Can you find the way back to our *bure*?'

'No.'

'I can take him.' The volunteer who had been helping Simon take off his elbow and knee pads looked up.

'Thanks. Could you please take him to the reception area in the clinic? Simon?'

'What...?'

'You can wait for me in the room with the big fish tank.' It was an instruction rather than a suggestion. 'I'll come and find you in a few minutes and we'll have a talk about what activities you can do after lunch. Or, in fact, whether you deserve to be doing any at all.'

Maya watched how Simon's shoulders slumped and his head hung down as he was led away. He'd been so happy only a minute ago. So proud of his achievement of getting to the top of the wall. She flicked a glance at Eli, preparing to turn away.

'He was perfectly safe,' she said.

'He knew perfectly well he wasn't allowed to be doing a high impact activity like climbing. I'm going to go and find out what Mike thinks about this. You had absolutely no right to give him permission.'

'I didn't.' Maya was indignant. 'I explained how much safer the wall was than being out on a real cliff, but I told him he needed to talk to you about it.'

'You are aware that Simon has severe haemophilia?'

'I checked his notes,' Maya said, her tone cool. She resented the suggestion that she wasn't doing her job properly. 'I noted that he has a port-a-cath in place and that he's on infusions three times a week to boost his clotting factors. Our helmets are the best available and I gave him a padded harness and joint protection pads. I've had children who are a lot more medically fragile than Simon climbing this wall.'

'I'm sure you have,' Eli snapped. He'd lowered his voice so no one else could hear their exchange. 'But do you have any idea of how repeated bumps and bleeds into joints in a child with haemophilia can lead to life-limiting arthritis and the need for major surgery? Or how little it takes to cause an internal micro-bleed that can go unnoticed until it suddenly becomes a serious issue? Do you, in fact, ever take into consideration the possible consequences of *your* actions?'

Maya stiffened. He still blamed her for what had happened so many years ago, didn't he?

And why wouldn't he?

She'd never stopped blaming herself.

Maya took a steadying breath and spoke quietly.

'Has it occurred to you that you can't stop people doing something they really want to do for ever?' She risked making eye contact. 'That it might be a better idea for children to learn how to problem solve and do things safely than to put themselves in real danger by having a go at something like climbing when no one's watching?'

But Eli was glaring at her and she had to look away.

'Nothing's changed, has it?' His voice might be quiet but it was raw. He sounded disgusted. Or disappointed? 'Except that it's not enough for you to be doing what you want to do and flirting with danger when you're working—now you're using your time off to encourage kids to be just as irresponsible with their own safety.'

Maya's self-control was slipping. Okay, maybe she had good reason to regret some of her choices in the past and Eli had equally good reason to hate her for how they'd affected him, but this was more than unfair. It was a direct attack and she had to stand up for herself.

'You're being a helicopter parent,' she replied in a low voice. 'And you're still trying to wrap people in cotton wool and stop them being who they are. Or who they *want* to be. But you're quite right…'

She turned her back on Eli and began to walk away. 'Nothing *has* changed.'

CHAPTER FOUR

THE NIGHTMARE WAS always the same.

But this was the first time Maya had experienced it in more than a year and it had never happened on the haven of Reki Island as she slept beneath her mosquito net, her windows open so that she could hear the distant sound of waves washing onto the coral reef.

It was the sound that was the worst part of this recurring dream—the cry of a newborn baby. Maya could hear it so clearly but she could never find it as she ran from room to room in a building that felt like a deserted hospital, with long, long corridors that had too many doors on each side. The nightmare ended, as it always did, when she opened a door to find there was no floor behind it. She could still hear the cries of the baby as she fell, tumbling down the cliff, knowing that when she hit the bottom it would be the end of everything.

She woke with a cry of her own and sat bolt upright in her bed, wrapping her arms around herself in the hope that it would hasten the return of reality. She knew there was no hope of getting back to sleep so she got up, made a soothing cup of herbal tea and went outside to sit on the tiny veranda of her *bure* with its view onto the beach and the moonlight-gilded lagoon.

It was no surprise that the nightmare had found her again here.

Because the baby she could never find was her own.

Hers...and Eli's.

The fall had happened when she was at work. They'd been sent to a track that wound through a pine forest, up in the hills surrounding the city, to a mountain biker who'd come to grief on a steep downward slope and needed the assistance of the ambulance service. Maya loved calls like this that took her somewhere different and presented unique challenges. The biker had a badly broken leg and backup was needed to help carry him out of the forest when they'd splinted the fracture and given him pain relief. Maya had gone to pick up the pack she'd carried in. She'd stepped off the track without thinking, forgetting how slippery a thick layer of dry pine needles could be on a steep slope. It wouldn't have mattered because they should have cushioned her fall, but who could have known that beyond the screen of the trees to one side lay an enormous drop into what had once been a quarry?

Maya had been lucky to survive. A helicopter crew was called in to rescue her and she was transported to the emergency department where Eli was on duty. He wasn't allowed to treat her—only to hold her hand as she was assessed and stabilised. He'd been holding it tightly when the surgeon came in to give them the results of the CT scan that had added a significant injury to her spleen to the list of bumps and bruises and a few cracked ribs.

'We need to take you to Theatre to fix that laceration before you lose any more blood,' he'd told Maya. 'You're going to be fine but...I'm so sorry...you've lost your baby...'

Maya closed her eyes tightly as she remembered it, as if that might help her not to see the look on Eli's face as he'd heard those words. She felt herself curling her fingers into a fist at the same time—as if that could help her not feel the echo of the way his hold on her hand had loosened.

She could hear her own whisper. The words she hadn't really believed herself.

'It was an accident, Eli...it wasn't my fault...'

Simon wasn't smiling.

He wouldn't even look up at Eli as they went into the treatment room at the medical centre the next morning.

'Hop up on the bed here, Si,' Eli said. 'Do you want anaesthetic cream on this time?'

'No. I don't need it.'

'Okay...' Eli put a mask on the pillow of the bed and then moved to the bench area. 'I'll be ready in just a minute.'

He prepared his tray as Simon climbed onto the bed, took his camp tee shirt off and put his mask on.

They might be in a new place today but this routine had been a part of their lives long enough for it to become as commonplace as getting dressed in the mornings. The regular infusion of a product that replaced the function of Factor VIII could prevent or reduce the frequency and severity of bleeding episodes in people with haemophilia A and it was a huge advance in treating the condition. Simon had had his port—a device that lay under the skin and connected to a vein—inserted when he was only twelve months old, which meant it was far less stressful to get IV access.

That didn't mean that care had to be taken, however. And Eli was always careful. He prepared a sterile tray with everything he needed, including the port needle, factor product and sterile syringes with saline and heparin. He could feel the silence behind him as he ripped open packets and dropped items without touching them.

A heavy silence. The kind you got when someone was far from happy. The talk he'd had with Simon last night about how he was only trying to keep him safe because he loved him so much had clearly not had the desired effect.

He mixed the factor product and filled the syringe. Then he carried his tray to put on the end of the bed that Simon was now sitting on.

'All set?'

'When can I start doing this by myself?'

'You already do some of it yourself. Like pushing the syringe plungers and putting pressure on afterwards so you don't get bleeding under your skin.'

'I want to do it *all* by myself. Other kids do.'

Ouch... Eli could feel the rejection.

'Other kids are older. They have their ports removed and they can inject themselves into a vein in their arm. The youngest person I know about who does that is thirteen years old.'

'I'm nearly ten,' Simon muttered. 'I could do it.'

Eli cleaned the skin over where the port was situated under his right collarbone. He anchored the device with two fingers of one hand and held the wings of the port needle with his other hand, ready to insert it. Simon didn't even flinch when the needle went through the skin.

He probably was just about ready to learn to inject himself. But Eli wasn't.

He attached the saline syringe. 'Want to pull back and make sure we're in?'

Simon's head was down. He wasn't even watching. 'Nah…I don't feel like it.'

Eli confirmed access, flushed the line and attached the factor syringe to inject the product slowly.

'So what's first on the agenda today? You're going kayaking, aren't you? And snorkelling? Or is it the boat trip out to see the giant turtles?'

Simon shrugged. 'I don't care. It's not what I really want to do.'

Eli let his breath out in a sigh. 'You know why the climbing wall isn't a good idea, Simon. There are so many other amazing things to do here. Why are you so determined to make not being able to do this one thing such a big deal?'

'Because…' Simon shrugged again and then his voice wobbled. 'Because it makes me happy…'

It was Eli's turn to be silent. He flushed the line again and then injected the heparin which would prevent the line clotting and causing a problem next time. He could hear Maya's voice in his head now, telling him he was being a helicopter parent. That he didn't let people be who they were, or wanted to be.

Had he always been like that?

He couldn't deny he'd worried about the risks that Maya faced in her work as a paramedic. He'd been the same with his younger sister, Sarah, when he'd become the protective older brother after the death of their parents. She'd been an adrenaline junkie, too, and that love of extreme sports had been responsible for her death, albeit indirectly. She hadn't been stupid enough to be sky-diving herself, days after giving birth, but she couldn't stay away from her parachute club's exhibition of a group halo formation performance. Having parked on the road-side, she'd got out of the car to get the best view of her friends joining up in freefall, with Simon still tucked into his safety capsule in the back seat, and it was when she went to open the driver's door to head home that a speeding drunk driver had sideswiped the car and hit her, causing catastrophic injuries.

He could never forget that bolt of fear when he'd heard that news. It was automatic to clench a fist when he felt even an echo of it, as if it could prevent his fingers shaking the way they had when he'd scribbled that note to Maya in the midst of trying to find the quickest way he could to cross the world to be with his sister.

He'd written:

It's Sarah. It's bad. I'm sorry—I wanted to be here when you woke up but I have to go.
I'll call you. I love you...
Eli

It wasn't often these days that Eli felt a pang of the grief of losing Sarah but he felt it now, as he removed the needle from Simon's skin and pressed a wad of gauze onto the puncture site. It always came with the sadness of knowing that, in her induced coma, she wouldn't have been aware of how he'd sat beside her in the intensive care unit, day after day, with baby Simon in his arms. That she wouldn't have heard his promise that he would do everything in his power to keep her son safe. To make him happy.

He wasn't happy right now, though, was he?

'How 'bout we make a deal, Si?' Eli said quietly. 'You go on the activities you're signed up for today and I'll ask whether it's okay for you to do the climbing wall again tomorrow?'

Simon's head jerked up. 'Really? You'll let me do that?'

'You're growing up,' Eli said. 'You'll be able to take care of your own infusions before long and I know I'll be able to trust you to do it as carefully as when we do it together. I already trust you to be careful when you're at school or out with your friends. It shouldn't be any different just because we're at camp.'

'I knew you'd be mad at me,' Simon said with a grimace. 'But I thought the climbing wall was safe. Maya was looking after me.'

'I know, buddy.' Eli pulled off his gloves and ruffled Simon's hair. 'I wasn't angry with you. It just gave me a bit of a fright. Do we have a deal about today?'

'Yes...' Simon slid off the table. 'I've got to go and get ready. I can't wait to go and see those turtles.'

Eli watched him haul his tee shirt back on. He might not have been angry with Simon yesterday but he certainly had been with Maya. He'd blamed her entirely for what, if he was being really honest, was his problem.

He had been unreasonable.

He needed to apologise, didn't he?

The day had started badly for Maya, having not been able to get back to sleep after the nightmare and painful memories being stirred up.

It got worse that afternoon when her pager sounded, and she ran from the climbing wall session she was taking to arrive at the doors of the medical centre to find one of the resort's most popular workers looking very unwell as he was carried inside.

'Timi... What's happened?'

'He was sick,' one of the men told her. 'He said he had terrible pain in his chest.'

'Follow me.' Maya looked towards the reception desk. 'Who's on call?' she asked Moana.

'Dr Peters. We've paged him.'

'Okay... Tell him we're in the treatment room.'

Maya braced herself for the moment that Eli would come into the room. She had managed to avoid being anywhere near him since that unpleasant encounter at the climbing wall yesterday. She knew it was inevitable that it was going to be awkward having to work together, but by the time Eli came in, ten minutes later and rather out of breath, Maya was completely focused on her patient and, remarkably, it was easy to ignore any personal issues. She gave Eli a brief glance before turning back to the twelve-lead ECG trace that was emerging from the machine in front of her.

'This is Timi,' she told Eli. 'He's forty-six years old. He had sudden onset, ten out of ten, central chest pain radiating to his left arm and back that started about twenty minutes ago. He was diaphoretic, hypertensive and tachycardic when he came in and...' She walked towards Eli and for a long moment they both looked at the recording in her hands of the electrical activity in Timi's heart.

'Inferior STEMI,' Eli murmured. 'That's some impressive ST elevation in leads two, three and aVF.' He caught Maya's gaze. 'Do you have a Code STEMI protocol?'

'Yes.' A myocardial infarction that needed urgent intervention had a very clear pathway of treatment. 'I've already got IV access and he's had a bolus of five milligrams of morphine for the pain.' Maya stepped back towards Timi. 'How's the pain now?' she asked.

'Bit better,' Timi said.

'Score out of ten? It was ten out of ten when you arrived. What is it now?'

Timi closed his eyes. 'Maybe six?'

'We'll give you something more for that in a minute.' She took hold of his hand. 'It looks like you're having a heart attack, Timi. This is Dr Peters, who's going to look after you here, and then we're going to get you to hospital as quickly as we can so they can fix you up properly, okay?'

Timi was reluctant to let go of her hand. 'Will you come with me?'

'Yes. It's my job to go with people if they need to go to hospital. We've got a few things to do here first, though.' She turned back to Eli. 'Would you like me to activate Code STEMI and transmit this ECG to the hospital in Suva? I can get our pilot on standby as well. We'll need to transfer him by helicopter.'

'Has he had GTN and aspirin already?'

'Yes.'

Eli was looking at the oxygen saturation level and the blood pressure reading on the monitor. 'He's got a saturation of ninety-five percent on room air so we don't need any oxygen on, but we'll need to get a beta blocker infusion started to get that blood pressure under control. We'll need additional antiplatelet and anticoagulation therapy, too.' He picked up a stethoscope as he stepped towards the bed. 'Hi, Timi. I'm Eli. Can I listen to your chest, please?'

Timi nodded. He had his eyes tightly closed. Eli turned his head to speak to Maya. 'Let's top up that pain relief.'

Maya listened to Eli's questions as she flushed the IV line and administered the first of several medications Timi was going to need. It felt as if she'd stepped back in time to when it was normal to be working alongside Eli. Something to look forward to because, even though they maintained a perfectly professional distance at work, it felt as if it was knitting their lives closer together.

It didn't feel like that today.

Working with Eli might not be as awkward as Maya had feared but that professional distance was only a fraction of the personal distance between them. They might as well still be on opposite sides of the world.

Eli was finishing quizzing Timi on his medical history.

'Have you had any broken bones or major surgery in the last six months, Timi?'

'No.'

'Been to the doctor for anything recently?'

'No... I'm healthy. I've been off the smokes for a year now, Doc.'

'That's great.'

'I'm trying to lose a bit of weight, too. But it's not so easy when you've got a wife who's such a good cook...' Timi was smiling now as the pain relief began to kick in.

Eli was running through an extensive checklist of any contraindications for any of the standard medications for starting to dissolve the clots blocking Timi's coronary arteries when Mike arrived.

'I heard you called a code,' he said. 'The chopper will

be ready to take off in a few minutes and I can go with
Maya to help monitor Timi.'

Maya felt a wash of relief, knowing she wouldn't have
a return trip with Eli when there wasn't a patient to focus
on, which would only make that personal distance even
more painfully obvious.

'What can I do to help now?' Mike asked Eli.

'We're going to need another IV line. Maya's already
done a great job with the initial assessment and treatment but I'd like to get the fibrinolytic therapy underway ASAP.'

The praise was unexpected.

So was the look Eli gave Maya after Timi's stretcher
was loaded onto the helicopter and Mike was already
on board.

'See you later,' he said. 'Come and find me when you
get back? Please?'

Maya nodded. 'Of course. You'll want to know how
Timi's doing.'

She turned to get into the helicopter but felt Eli touch
her arm and turned her head. He didn't need to say anything because she could still read his eyes. It *felt* as if she
was reading his mind.

He wanted to talk to her about more than how Timi
was doing. It looked as though he wanted to apologise.

And suddenly that personal distance seemed to have
shrunk. Because Maya wanted to talk to him, too. She
had an apology of her own that was long overdue.

The beaches of Reki Island were stunning at both sunrise and sunset, and when Maya met Eli by the jetty the

light was just beginning to fade and the first hint of a pink blush was staining the sky.

'How's Timi?' Eli asked.

'Fine, thank goodness,' Maya responded. 'He went into VF en route and we had to defibrillate him but we got him back into sinus rhythm on the first shock.'

Eli whistled silently. 'I can imagine how tense the rest of the flight was.'

'We waited until he was out of the catheter lab. No neurological deficit. He's got two stents, one of which fixed a total blockage in the left anterior descending artery, and he was feeling very happy to still be alive.'

'I can imagine. He's a lucky man to get a second chance at life.' Eli looked up at the darkening hues of the sky and the reflection of the colour on the still waters of the lagoon. The beach was deserted. 'Fancy a walk?'

'Have you got time?'

Eli nodded. 'Mike's on duty at the medical centre. He'll only page me if there's a real emergency. And Simon's at movie night with his mates and what looked like an endless supply of popcorn. He couldn't be happier.'

For a long time, they walked in silence along the stretch of damp sand, close to the tiny waves uncurling beside them. When the sun had sunk low enough to make them need to shade their eyes as they looked up, they spoke at the same time.

Only two words.

'I'm sorry...'

There was another moment's silence. Maya wanted to say more. Too much, perhaps, because she couldn't find the words she needed to even begin. Eli broke the silence.

'I'm sorry about the way I spoke to you yesterday,'

he said. 'I *am* overprotective of Simon. I have been ever since he was a baby and it only got worse when I discovered he had haemophilia.'

'How old was he when you found out?'

'He was in the accident that injured my sister Sarah so badly. The paediatrician who examined him thought the bruising was odd, given the protection of the car seat he was in. By the time I got there from New Zealand, they'd done the tests.'

Maya was frowning. 'Why was your baby in your sister's car?'

'Because Simon was Sarah's baby.' It was Eli's turn to frown now. 'He's not *my* baby. I'm his uncle.'

'But he calls you Dad.' Somewhere in her confusion was a wash of relief. He hadn't walked away from her to be with another woman. To be a father to his own baby.

'I adopted him to try and keep him safe legally, although I don't believe his biological father even knows of his existence.'

'You never told me that Sarah was pregnant.'

'I didn't know. I hadn't seen her, except in video calls, since I went to New Zealand and she'd gone off to go backpacking around Europe and there were always good reasons that she didn't call often. I guess she didn't want to tell me because she knew I'd be worried about her. Maybe she wanted to prove she could live her own life without her helicopter brother hovering over her.'

Maya bit her lip. She shouldn't have said that. It was perfectly understandable that Eli was overprotective. Simon had needed special care ever since he'd been handed to Eli as a tiny baby when his mother was too sick to care for him.

'I spent more than a week sitting in the intensive care unit by Sarah's bed,' Eli added. 'But she never woke up. I often had Simon in my arms. I felt like his dad from the moment they gave him to me. The first thing I did after they turned off the life support for Sarah was to go and pick him up and hold him. I told him that I was always going to look after him.'

'Oh, my God...' Maya could picture Eli sitting there, holding a baby as he was grieving the loss of the baby sister he'd been protecting ever since their parents died. She could feel the prickle of tears at the back of her eyes. 'I'm so sorry, Eli. I...didn't know.'

It felt like no excuse at all. She hadn't been there when the man she'd loved so much was going through something so awful. And then it struck her.

'That was why you left New Zealand in such a rush. And why you never came back? Why didn't you *tell* me?'

'You'd just been taken to Theatre—after that awful row we'd had about you still working even though you were pregnant—and suddenly I was trying to get through to the hospital in London to find out what was going on and trying to book flights that would get me there as soon as possible. I barely had time to get home and grab my passport and pack a bag.' He shook his head. 'But I did tell you. I left you a note. I said something bad had happened to Sarah.'

She remembered. She'd read that note a thousand times.

'You said you'd call,' Maya said quietly.

'I did call.' Eli's voice was expressionless. 'Whenever I could, which wasn't that often, I admit, because I was trying to learn how to care for a baby and spend as much time as I could with my sister, and then I had to organise a funeral and try and make plans for the future. I left voice mails. I texted. Until I couldn't even do that because all I got was some automated network voice telling me that the number was not in service.'

'Of course it wasn't. It had been lost somewhere on that cliff I fell down. The battery would have died. Why didn't you call the hospital?' Maya hadn't forgotten what it had been like to come round from the anaesthetic to find that Eli wasn't there. To wait and wait for a visit that never happened. The pain, both physical and emotional, had been horrible. The grief—and guilt—she was feeling about the loss of their baby only made it a hundred times worse.

'I did,' Eli said. 'But you'd been discharged by then. I got hold of a friend in ED and he found out that you'd gone up north to stay with your family while you recuperated. He said he could try and get the number but...' Eli pushed his fingers through his hair. 'There was too much I had to deal with and...and I was still shocked about you losing the baby. About that fight we'd had. It felt like a mess I didn't have the energy to deal with right then. When I hadn't heard from you by the time I needed to resign from my locum position remotely and arrange to have personal stuff shipped back to the UK, I guess... I don't know... I was hurt. Angry. I felt kind of powerless. My life had been completely derailed.'

Maya understood all of that.

Maya remembered feeling exactly like that herself. Arriving home after more than a month away, recovering from the accident and surgery, doing well but still nowhere near a hundred percent, to find any trace of Eli had been removed from the apartment they'd shared. The life she'd thought she would have for ever had been simply erased.

'I had to focus on what really mattered,' Eli said. 'And that wasn't how I was feeling. It was Simon.' He blew out a long breath. 'You didn't try and call *me*...'

'No.' Maya stopped walking. She stared at the final, bright halo of the sun sinking swiftly below the horizon, sucking the colour from the sky as it disappeared. 'I...' she cleared her throat '...I didn't think you'd want to hear from me. I knew it was my fault...'

'The accident?'

'No. Well, yes...but that *was* an accident. I'm sorry about the baby. I'm sorry I didn't listen to you when you said I needed to step back from working on the road. I thought it was far too early to worry. Maybe I needed more time to just get used to the idea—it wasn't as if we'd planned on having a baby. I'm sorry, Eli...' The tears Maya had been holding back were finally escaping. Hot, slow, painful tears. 'I'm sorry about everything. About the baby and Sarah and not calling you...'

'I'm sorry, too. For everything that happened all those years ago. And for taking it out on you when I found that Simon had managed to sneak into a climbing session. He...um...wants to come again tomorrow, if that's all right with you?'

Maya looked up, startled. 'You're okay with that?'

'It's what he wants,' Eli said. 'And I know, from personal experience, that it's not a good idea to stop someone trying to be who they are. It can end in tears.'

Maya swiped at the tears on her cheeks but she found

a hint of a smile. 'That's true. I'd be happy to see him back. I'll take good care of him.'

'Thanks.' Eli looked around them. 'It's getting dark. Mike's probably wondering where you are.'

Maya's eyebrows rose. 'Why would he be? Oh...' She was remembering something else now—being okay with letting Eli think that she was in a relationship. Being less than completely honest with this man had led to a decade of guilt and self-recrimination and it simply wasn't acceptable to let history repeat itself.

'Mike and I are just friends,' she admitted as she began walking to the nearest track leading away from the beach. 'I've never...' Her voice trailed into silence. What could she say? That she'd never found another relationship? That she'd never found anyone that could have taken Eli's place? That she'd never found the courage to trust anyone that much again?

Eli was close behind her, otherwise she might not have heard his soft words.

'Neither have I...'

CHAPTER FIVE

MAYA DIDN'T HAVE any bad dreams that night, but she didn't sleep particularly well either.

Why hadn't she tried to call Eli all those years ago?

She could—and had—excused herself by the fact that she had been badly hurt, both physically and emotionally, but even during the worst period of her life she'd been aware that she was being selfish. She'd made it all about her. *Her* surgery, *her* miscarriage, *her* being abandoned by her boyfriend…

She hadn't even tried to find out what had happened to Eli's sister.

She'd pushed aside the fact that Eli was the other parent of the baby that had been lost.

She'd simply refused to tap into the heartache of knowing that Eli was probably feeling just as hurt and confused and sad as she was.

Instead, she'd endlessly replayed snatches of the awful interaction that had been the last time they'd spoken before he'd vanished from her life. They'd had to wait for an operating theatre to become available. Her physical discomfort had been under control but the silence in that private room as Eli stared out of the window was full of a level of pain that the medication couldn't touch.

'This...this is why I hate you doing such a dangerous job. You could have died, Maya. Our baby did die...'

'You're blaming me? It was an accident, Eli. Accidents happen.'

'It didn't need to. You knew you were pregnant but you decided it was way too early to worry about it. You decided to take the risk—even when I said it wasn't just your safety you were risking. You didn't really care, though, did you?'

'Are you saying I don't care that I lost the baby?'

'I'm saying you don't care about the risks you take. And that makes me wonder how much you care about anything. Yourself. Our future. Me...?'

Maya had turned her face into her pillow.

'Go away, Eli. I really don't need this right now.'

It was a new shock to discover why Eli hadn't contacted her and it reignited that awareness of how badly she had treated him. He had been going through more than the pain of a physical injury and the loss of an unplanned and very early pregnancy. He'd had to cope with the stress of getting back to the other side of the world as quickly as possible and then the loss of his sister. On top of that, he'd had the overwhelming responsibility of a tiny, vulnerable human put into his hands at the same time. And he'd done it without her support. She'd told him to go away and he'd done so wondering how much she really cared about him. She wouldn't have blamed him for hating her enough to not try and contact her at all.

But he had. Again and again. He must have assumed, as she had, that her phone was still clipped to her belt in the bag of patient property along with all her other clothing. He must have decided that she didn't want to talk to him. That she really *didn't* care that much.

Had it changed anything for him to learn that she hadn't received any of the text messages or voice mails?

As much as learning what Eli had had to deal with had changed things for Maya?

They both needed time to process that intense conversation they'd had last night, but when Maya walked into the dining room a short time later she saw Eli and Simon at the buffet table, choosing their breakfast food. She picked up a bowl and headed for the fresh fruit salad that was always her choice to start the day and as she turned she found Eli watching her.

And smiling.

'Hi, Maya.' Simon was beaming at her. 'Dad says I can come and do the climbing wall again this morning if it's okay with you.'

'It's more than okay,' Maya told him. 'I think it's a brilliant idea.'

She smiled back. At both of them.

Unexpectedly, it felt as if it might be a good thing that her path had crossed with Eli's again like this. As if it might be possible to find forgiveness—on both sides—and make peace with the past. To heal enough to be able to rekindle some kind of friendship?

More than friendship...?

Maya sucked in a shocked breath. What was she thinking?

It had been bad enough recognising that connection was still there between them—the one that had created a whole nonverbal language. Did she need to remind herself again that getting her heart broken once had been more than enough?

Of course she didn't. So why on earth was she having to push away something that felt like…longing?

Maya reached for some coconut milk yoghurt to spoon onto her fruit, giving an imperceptible shake of her head to complete the process of dismissing that line of thought.

Feeling at peace when it came to Eli Peters was all that she needed to find. That would be life-changing enough in itself.

Eli knew that Maya was expecting Simon at the climbing wall session but the way her face lit up when he arrived suggested that she was genuinely delighted that he was being allowed to do it again.

Clearly, she hadn't expected Eli to come as well. He saw a flash of wariness in her eyes that was disturbing. Did she think he had come along in order to watch her every move in case she made a mistake and Simon got hurt? That he was here to rain on Simon's parade the way he probably had on hers when they'd been together, despite—or perhaps *because* of—being so much in love with her, when he'd criticised her choice of a career and her even riskier preferences for hobbies and exercise?

He raised his hands in Maya's direction, palms up, in both greeting and a gesture of submission. 'I'm just here to watch,' he said. 'Simon wants me to see what he can do.'

'I have to go and get my helmet and harness on now, Dad. And my elbow and knee pads. I'll be back soon. Don't go away, will you?'

'Not going anywhere, buddy. Do you want some help with the safety gear?'

'We've got plenty of helpers who know what they're doing,' Maya said.

Were her words mild encouragement to step back and let Simon be more independent? If so, it was fair enough. Eli gave a single nod.

During the long hours of a broken night, Eli had been sucked back into the past and, with the benefit of hindsight, he could see that, to Maya, it would have felt like he was holding her back from living her best life. He couldn't blame her for accusing him of being overprotective with Simon either. But, in his defence, he hadn't realised it at the time. Maybe it had been woven into every breath he'd taken, thanks to the trauma of losing his parents and being too young to take on the frightening responsibility of keeping his little sister safe.

Simon was already heading towards the equipment area but he turned back. 'Can I try the blue route today, Maya? Or the green one?'

'You did the orange one last time, didn't you?'

'Yes…and you said I smashed it.'

'You did.' Maya was grinning again. 'How 'bout we go up one level and do the red route today? Maybe the blue one next time.'

'Okay…' Simon ran off happily to get ready.

'What colour is the easiest?' Eli asked.

'Yellow. You can see that there are handles to hang onto and steps for easy foot positions. They're the routes that we use for the more disabled kids and there's an option to go sideways and not get to any real height. We can actually use it for children in wheelchairs. Or who need to be on oxygen.'

Eli could see a little girl skipping towards them. 'And for kids like Hazel?' He shook his head, more than a little surprised that a child with no hands or feet would have climbing down as a choice for camp activities. But he was smiling as well. 'How amazing is her attitude to life?' he added quietly.

'She's an inspiration all right,' Maya agreed. 'But I don't think she did Yellow more than once. She gives climbing the same determination she does everything else in her life. I wouldn't be surprised if she conquers Black eventually.' She held her arms out for an enthusiastic hug and then sent Hazel off. 'Simon's over there,' she told her. 'I think he likes climbing as much as you do.'

Eli was looking up at the wall. 'Who's doing the black route at the moment? It looks like Carlos.'

Maya nodded. 'Turns out he's been climbing for a year or so at his local gym. He's wanting to practise his abseiling so he can come on the real cliffs later this week.'

'Who's that doing Red?' Eli shaded his eyes. 'Oh… it's Alice. I've seen her at the medical centre a few times. She comes in to do her respiratory exercises with the physiotherapists.' He could feel himself frowning. 'She's frail, isn't she? Looks like just a bump would break her arms or legs.'

'She's been struggling with her cystic fibrosis for the last couple of years. We almost didn't accept her for camp this time but her family said she was desperate to come and they're afraid it might be her last chance.'

Eli could remember scanning her notes. 'She's on the waiting list for lung transplant, isn't she?'

'Not yet. She put it off for as long as possible. She's recently had the work up tests and counselling but she would have had to stay within a certain distance of the hospital in case donor lungs became available and that would have meant she couldn't come to camp. She made a deal with her family that if she was allowed to come here she'll go on the list as soon as she gets home. That's her older brother, Jake, who's on the wall beside her. He's come as her carer. He's nineteen and planning to go to medical school.'

'That doesn't surprise me. Growing up with siblings who need complex medical care is often the catalyst for a career choice.'

Her sideways glance at him was almost shy—as if Maya wasn't sure if she should broach a more personal subject? 'Like it was for you after your parents died?'

Eli shrugged. 'They were killed instantly in that avalanche so that should have encouraged me to become a paramedic or search and rescue expert.' He offered Maya a wry smile. 'Guess I knew I would prefer a nicely controlled indoor environment for my work. If anything, my choice was influenced by Sarah's penchant for ending up in Emergency when she'd fallen over rollerblading or got thrown off the naughty pony our grandparents bought for her.'

But it was food for thought. Had he chosen his specialty knowing that he might be able to prevent other families going through the grief of losing someone who hadn't been careful enough? To save someone like Sarah who couldn't resist the adrenaline rush of fun that had an edge of danger?

Maybe, one day—if they could ever get that close

again—he could tell Maya how his relationship with his own sibling might have contributed to breaking what he and Maya had found together.

'You don't need to worry about the ponies we have here if Simon's going on one of the forest or beach treks. They're all totally bombproof.'

'I thought they would be. I think he's got that on his programme for tomorrow.' But Eli was clearly thinking about something else as he stared up at Alice. 'Is she okay?'

Jake had his arm around Alice, who seemed to be hanging in her harness, making no attempt to move her hands or feet to new holds.

But Maya was no longer beside him. Climbing the wall like a spider, she had reached Alice's level within seconds. They were only about halfway up the wall but, to Eli, it still seemed a long way to be off the ground without a safety harness and rope.

It was impressive. It also reminded Eli very strongly of that single-minded focus on someone in trouble that had first attracted him to Maya Thompson and he could feel a much stronger flash of that attraction that had been so disconcerting when he'd first seen her again on the island. This time, his body responded in a way he hadn't felt in years.

About ten years, to be precise...

So long, he'd forgotten how powerful it was to feel every cell in his body coming alive like this.

Her confidence was just as sexy now as it had been then and Eli could see, with the benefit of being older and wiser, that it wasn't that she was throwing herself into something without thinking it through. The intense expression on her face advertised her lightning-fast assessment of every move she was making. When she stopped, she had her feet on two different holds that protruded from the wall, was hanging onto a higher lump with one hand and, with the other, he could see her taking Alice's pulse as she was talking to Jake. On top of planning her own movements on her way up, she had probably been thinking about how to approach her assessment of Alice, hadn't she?

Wow...

Had he forgotten just what an impressive person Maya was?

How proud he had been of her?

He hadn't forgotten any of it, of course. He'd just buried it to protect himself from the pain attached to all those memories. It should have been easier than it was to bury it again now as he watched Maya helping both Jake and Alice down to ground level as swiftly as possible.

'Alice had a bit of a dizzy spell,' Maya told Eli. 'And some muscle cramps.'

Eli could hear the wheezing sounds of her breathing that suggested a level of airway obstruction that needed attention.

'Let's get you to the medical centre,' he said.

Jake was looking very worried. 'She seemed okay when we did her breathing exercises this morning. She did say she had a bit of a headache but she still wanted to do the climbing. I should have realised something wasn't right...'

Eli's heart went out to the teenager. He could remember all too easily what it was like to feel this protective of a younger sister. As if sometimes the weight of the whole world was resting on your shoulders.

'You're doing an amazing job of looking after Alice,' he told Jake. 'This isn't your fault, okay?'

'Have you got your inhaler with you, sweetheart?' Maya asked.

'I've got it.' Jake pulled the device from his pocket. He was clearly practised in helping Alice use it and doing something to help was the best way to distract him from blaming himself.

'We'll get the harness and all the pads off you, too.' Maya was already undoing fastenings. 'Being overheated won't be helping. Have you had plenty to drink in the last couple of days?'

Alice nodded, too focused on her breathing to say anything.

'I've been trying to make sure she's getting plenty of fluids,' Jake said. 'I know that people with CF are at a much greater risk of dehydration because they lose so much more salt in their sweat. But maybe I miscalculated how much she needs. It's hotter here than at home and Alice is doing more physical stuff, isn't she?'

'The symptoms could be caused by dehydration,' Eli agreed. 'But we need to rule out any kind of infection.' He crouched and held his arms out to Alice. 'Best way to get you inside quickly is for me to carry you. Are you okay with that?'

Standing beside Alice, Maya caught the full force of the smile that Eli was giving the young girl as he reached out to lift her into his arms. It was genuine and caring and irresistible because it was so warm. She could *feel* it, all the way down to her toes.

She knew what it would feel like for Alice to be swept up and held like that, too. It might have only been in fun, when Eli sometimes picked her up and carried her into their bedroom but she knew exactly how strong those arms were.

How safe they could make you feel.

The sigh she could hear beside her seemed to echo exactly what she was thinking as she watched Eli carry Alice around the corner of the building, heading for the medical centre. She looked down to see the disappointment on Simon's face.

'Dad's not going to see me climbing, is he?'

'Maybe not this time,' Maya said. 'He needs to help Alice. She's not feeling very well.'

Simon's nod was resigned. 'He likes looking after sick kids.'

'He's very good at it,' Maya said. 'He's good at looking after anybody,' she added. 'Kids or grown-ups. People who are sick or have had accidents and hurt themselves, sometimes very badly. And you know what the best thing about him is?'

'What?' Simon was scuffing the ground with his foot.

'He really cares about the people he looks after.'

Maya had known that about Eli from the first time she'd seen him at work and she'd never seen that level of care slip. He'd always been particularly good with kids and that was one of the things she loved most about him.

Had loved, she corrected herself instantly, but the damage had been done.

Had she really just reminded herself of how much she'd loved this man?

Or felt a pang of yearning for something more than friendship to be rekindled?

Bad idea...

Because it was confirming a fear she'd held at bay for the last ten years. A fear that she had never really got past that breakup. That she never would. And if she had been too afraid to go into another serious relationship ever since, surely it was a no-brainer not to get any closer to the man who'd done the damage in the first place?

The man who'd left her waiting...

Hoping against hope for something that was never going to happen?

Maya knew exactly how disappointed Simon was feeling. She put her arm around his shoulders. 'He said to say sorry. And he told me to stay here and make sure you had fun.'

She had offered to go to the medical centre and help with Alice's care, but Eli had already picked Alice up and she knew that Mike would be there to assist and they could call in any other staff they needed, like physiotherapists to help try and clear Alice's lungs.

The glance Eli had given her as he declined her offer and told her to stay and help Simon with his climbing session had said a lot more. She knew he was trusting her to look after his son and, no matter that the echoes of the past were making themselves felt, she wasn't about to let either of them down.

'Tell you what,' she said. 'Why don't I give my phone to my friend Josefa, who helped you get your safety gear on, and ask him to take some photos and videos of you climbing and then we can show your dad later?'

'Oh…can we?' The glow was back on Simon's face. 'That's a *great* idea, Maya.'

Maya took Simon to the dining room after the climbing wall session but let him sit at a table with other kids, including his friends Hazel, Carlos, Alice and Mason, to eat. There was a rest period after lunch when Ana took him back to his bure because Eli was still busy at the medical centre, but when she went to the beach to help with the sand sculpture competition that afternoon, he turned up a short time later.

She handed Eli her phone to let him catch up on Simon's achievements on the climbing wall that morning. Being on a section of the beach that was shaded by palm trees made it easier for him to see the videos and photos.

He was impressed.

Simon was as proud as punch.

So was Maya.

'Look at that,' she said. 'The way he's feeling for the holds and making sure he's secure before he shifts any of his body weight. And there…that's called a bump. He's a natural.'

Oh…she'd had to lean rather close to Eli to point to the small screen. She could smell his aftershave. Except that this smell was *so* familiar and he'd never used aftershave that she knew of. This scent was simply Eli.

And it gave her a sudden curl of sensation deep inside her body that was more than a little disconcerting, especially when it came with an awareness that she was only wearing a bikini beneath the sarong tied in a knot over her shoulder and tucked in at her waist because she was planning to have a swim when the sand castle competition was finished.

Thank goodness Simon broke the moment and pushed closer to try and see what they were talking about.

'What's a bump?' he asked.

'It's where you get a hand hold but you can tell it's not really going to work so you reach for another one straight away.' Maya nodded at him. 'Look…I'll start it again. You're good at this stuff, Si.'

His dad was also nodding. 'I'm proud of you,' he said. 'Maybe we can find a place for you to keep doing this when we get back home.'

Simon's grin couldn't have been wider and Maya caught her breath. She felt oddly proud of herself now as well. She'd been the person who had introduced Simon to this activity and contributed to the pleasure—and confidence—he'd gained from it. And if she hadn't stepped in his father might have banned the sport as being too dangerous and he wouldn't have this record of his efforts this morning, which would be a memory he could treasure and show off to his friends at home.

She tapped the screen of her phone. 'Put your number in,' she said to Eli. 'I'll forward the album.'

The thought occurred to her that she would have Eli's number then and they could keep in touch, but she pushed it aside. Why would either of them want to do that?

'Are you going to help with our sandcastle?' Simon asked his father.

'Sure.' But Eli raised an eyebrow as he looked down at the odd shape on the damp sand they were standing on. 'It's a castle…?'

'Sand sculptures can be anything,' Maya said. 'Simon's decided to make an octopus.'

'And adults are allowed to help?'

'Yes. It's kind of a family thing because some campers need more help than others. There are staff members to help the kids that are here without family or carers. Or they gang up together, like Carlos and Hazel over there. Looks like they're making a boat. Are you sure you don't want to join them, Si?'

'Not now that Dad's here.' Simon was still smiling. 'But you can still help, too, Maya, if you want to.'

Eli caught Maya's gaze as he handed back her phone. 'That would be great,' he said softly. 'If you don't have other stuff you have to do.'

'Not at all.' The invitation was giving Maya a wash of something warm. A feeling of being welcome? Wanted, even? Whatever it was, she liked it. A lot. 'I'd love to help.'

For the next hour, they carried buckets of water to keep the sand damp, collected a lot of shells and some sticks to use as tools and then sculpted a head for the octopus and long, tapering legs radiating outwards. The overall effect was that of a rather misshapen starburst.

Simon stood back to look at their creation. 'He's a bit wonky.'

'He's fabulous,' Maya declared. 'And see these cockle shells we found?' She held up a round white shell. 'If you stick those on his legs, upside down, they'll look just like tentacles.'

Simon pushed a shell into a sand leg. 'Hey...you're right. But we'll need an awful lot of them.'

'We'd better get on with finding them, then. I think we've only got another half an hour and then the judges will be coming to look at everybody's sculptures.'

Eli watched Simon race off with his bucket to find more cockle shells and then he smiled at Maya.

'You're good with kids,' he said. 'Have you got any of your own?'

She avoided looking at him as she shook her head, reaching for another shell to push into the sand of the closest leg. 'Never felt ready, I guess.'

There was a beat of silence.

'Because of the miscarriage?' Eli's voice was soft. 'I'm sorry, Maya. I…should have tried harder to reach you. I was so caught up in my own life going belly-up that I didn't think enough of how hard things were for you. And—'

'It's okay,' Maya interrupted. She didn't want to be reminded of how many reasons he'd had to feel angry with her. 'Let's not keep apologising. We were both young. We made mistakes.' She looked up to catch his gaze. 'It would be nice if we could put it behind us.'

Eli held her gaze. 'It would,' he agreed. And then he smiled. 'We're both older and wiser now. I can recommend having a kid. It felt like a bomb had gone off in my life to start with, but I wouldn't be without Si now. He makes everything…worthwhile. Special. It might only be the two of us but it…feels like family.'

Maya simply nodded and smiled back. She couldn't say anything else because Simon was already on his way back, his bucket brimming with the common shells.

'I found these big, long curly ones, too,' he said, holding out one of his treasures. 'How cool would they be for his eyes? Like kind of laser beams or something.'

'Exactly like laser beams.' Eli admired the shells. 'You're a genius, Spider-Man.'

Maya sat very still for a minute, watching as Eli and Simon threw themselves into decorating the octopus, crawling around on their knees, their dark heads close together as they positioned the eye shells.

They were a family, these two, and she could feel just how special their bond was. She'd been honest when she'd told Eli that she'd never felt ready to have children. Maybe she hadn't even given it much thought, what with focusing on her career and her sports. She got her fix of being with kids every year when she came to this camp, too. But being here, like this—as part of the Peters' octopus creation team—had changed something. Maybe it was because of what Eli had said about Simon making his life worthwhile. Or, more likely, it was due to feeling like she was part of the family after being included in that bond, even for a short time.

This was something important that was missing from her life.

Maybe she *was* finally ready to move on. To find a new relationship and have a child. To have a family— and a bond like that—of her own.

CHAPTER SIX

THE NEXT DAY dawned as blue and sunny as the last and the sea breeze that ruffled the hibiscus and frangipani flowers on the bushes near every bure was as warm as always, but the camp staff members, gathered for their daily briefing before breakfast, were talking about a weather system brewing in the South Pacific Ocean that was threatening to turn nasty.

'It's being closely monitored by the Fiji Meteorological Service,' Mike told them. 'It was noted as a low-pressure area northeast of the Solomon Islands last week but it's been upgraded to an off-season tropical cyclone this morning and has been named Lily. Currently, Vanuatu is on high alert and preparing for the cyclone to arrive in around seventy-two hours, but it's not expected to affect any Fijian islands— even those of us closest to Vanuatu. We might get some wind and rain and bigger waves but I'll keep you posted on any warnings.'

Eli walked out of the meeting area with Maya.

'Have you been here on the island in bad weather before?'

She shook her head. 'I think Mike's a bit more worried than he's letting on. Not that we couldn't keep the kids entertained if we got shut indoors for a day or two. It's more the problems it could bring if we needed to evacuate someone for emergency treatment. Bad weather would ground the helicopter. Even transport by boat could be cut.' She was frowning now. 'How's Alice this morning, do you know?'

'I'm just about to find out. She'll be in the medical centre for her respiratory physio about now and I'm heading over to give Simon his factor infusion.'

'Do you think her symptoms yesterday were due to just dehydration?'

'She certainly responded to some fluids. It would explain why her oxygen levels and forced expiratory volume had dropped noticeably. Dehydration thickens the mucus and makes it difficult to clear the lungs. We gave her bronchodilators, anti-inflammatories, antibiotics. She was feeling—and looking—a lot better by the time I got to the beach to help with the octopus.'

Eli threw a quick grin in Maya's direction. 'I know it was for the kids but I haven't had that much fun in quite a while.'

'It *was* fun,' Maya agreed. 'Simon was so happy with his prize for the most artistic sculpture.'

'He was. But I think he was even happier when he was invited to sit in the sand boat with Carlos and the other kids when the tide was coming in. I got some great photos while you were swimming.'

'Show me?'

He opened the images on his phone and watched her smile as she scrolled through them. It made him smile, watching *her*.

He'd been watching her yesterday afternoon, too. Brief glances at first as they'd worked together helping Simon build the octopus, but after the judging she'd announced that it was time for a swim and had untied the sarong she was wearing to reveal her bikini.

Eli had been unable to politely avert his gaze. Maya's body didn't seem to have changed at all, despite the years that had passed. He knew every inch of that gorgeous, tanned skin that was suddenly on display. He knew what every curve felt like. *Tasted* like… He'd never found anyone else that turned a sexual encounter into so much more. He'd had sex since being with Maya—of course he had. But he'd never truly made love, had he?

And until that moment he hadn't realised how much he'd missed it.

At least Maya didn't seem to guess what he'd been thinking when she dropped her sarong into the basket where she had her phone and pager safe from the sand and looked up, straight at him. She'd simply asked him to give her a wave if he heard her pager go off.

She handed him back his phone. 'Brilliant photos,' she said. 'Can I keep this one to go in the Camp Reki newsletter?'

Eli looked at the row of children in the boat, laughing as they continued the game of leaning over the sides to scoop handfuls of seawater to throw at each other.

'Yes, of course,' he said.

He took another glance at the photo as Maya tapped in her phone number and forwarded the photo. All the kids, including Simon, had such incredibly happy faces that it brought a lump to Eli's throat. Simon was going to remember this camp for ever.

So was he. For more than the good times he was sharing with his son. He would never think about this camp without remembering reconnecting with Maya. Hopefully, they were undoing some of the emotional damage they'd both been living with for the past decade so those memories wouldn't be tinged with regret.

He had her number in his phone now. He could easily add it to his contacts, but did he want to do that?

To stay in touch?

Yes...if it was possible to retrieve some kind of friendship from the fragments of what they'd once had together, how could he resist?

'You'll get some more great photos this afternoon.' Maya was turning to head down another track. 'The pony trek in the forest is very photogenic. I hope Alice is well enough to do it. She's horse mad—just like I was at her age.'

Like Sarah had been, too.

Eli found himself thinking about his sister as he headed for his morning clinic in the medical centre. Remembering being Jake's age and living with that fear that he might lose the person he was trying so hard to protect because they were the sunshine for *his* world. He'd stepped back as they got older and began to go their own ways. Sarah had been desperate to go travelling and he'd taken the opportunity to have an adventure of his own. He'd gone to work in New Zealand, where he'd met Maya. Had part of the attraction been that she had that adrenaline junkie gene like Sarah? Like his parents?

His protective instincts had become divided as he'd fallen more and more in love with Maya. In those first, terrible days watching over Sarah in the intensive care unit, Eli had wondered if it would have made a difference if he'd stayed more focused. If he'd kept watch over her more carefully instead of being persuaded that she was more than capable of looking after herself.

She had promised to keep herself safe. She'd said—like Maya had—that what she chose to do for her work or hobbies wasn't really any more dangerous than anything else in life. How ironic was it that she *should* have been totally safe when she'd only been watching the sky-diving?

However unjustified it had been, that hadn't stopped a small part of Eli's grief—anger, even—being directed at Sarah because she'd been so passionate about a high-risk sport. And laid at Maya's feet for not only feeling the same way about taking risks in life but having distracted him from what had been so important when he'd been Jake's age—watching over his little sister. If he hadn't been in New Zealand, he could have been with her that day. He would have been, if he'd just become an uncle and wanted to make sure that both Sarah and her baby were being looked after. She might have been uninjured if she'd been opening the passenger door of the car instead of stepping out onto the road.

Eli pushed the overly-familiar thought away. 'What ifs' never helped.

Like the one that had resurfaced so strongly after talking to Maya. What if he'd tried harder to get hold of her?

But he couldn't, could he? Not when he was in the middle of experiencing what he could be setting himself up for in years to come by being with Maya—a repeat of this agony of losing someone he loved this much.

It had seemed so much wiser to let it go. And so much easier because he had a tiny baby who needed his full attention.

* * *

The serious young man was with his sister in the treatment room of the medical centre when Eli arrived. Jake was watching Alice as she did her positive expiratory pressure exercises.

'Breathe in through your PEP,' he encouraged her. 'Now blow out. Harder...bit harder...keep the blue bobble between the lines... That's better... Okay, one more time...'

'How's it going?' Eli asked.

'Peak flow's down on yesterday,' Jake told him. 'We're doing some extra physio to see how much Alice can clear her lungs.' He picked up a small plastic cylinder. 'You ready to huff now?'

Alice nodded, not speaking to save her breath. She took the cylinder and closed her lips around it. Jake held a strip of tissue in front of her. Alice took in a slow, deep breath, held it for a few seconds and then breathed out as hard as she could, making the tissue flutter. She bent her arm to cough into her elbow.

A short time later, Alice tested the strength of an expelled breath again, blowing as hard as she could into the peak flow meter.

'Better than it was,' Jake said, but he didn't sound happy.

'Any more headaches?' Eli asked.

Alice shook her head.

'Dizziness?' The query elicited another head shake. 'Temperature?'

'Normal,' Jake said.

'Not feeling sick?'

'No.' Alice was biting her bottom lip. 'I'm okay to do

stuff today, aren't I, Dr Peters? I really want to do the pony riding this afternoon.'

'Let me have a listen to your chest,' Eli said. He was frowning as he put the earpieces in place, remembering something else from Alice's notes. 'Aren't you allergic to horses?'

'It's only a mild allergy.' Alice was scowling at him. 'I'm fine if I take some antihistamines.'

Eli caught Jake's glance and he could understand all too well that note of helplessness he could detect. There was good reason to stop Alice going on the pony trek, but they would be stopping her doing what she desperately wanted to do and…it was possible that this was going to be her last camp. Her last opportunity to do something that brought her so much joy.

'Our camp paramedic will be there,' he reassured Jake. 'She's got a kit that can cover any airway issues. I'll be there, too. My son Simon is really looking forward to it.'

Maya loved the pony treks and always put her name down to assist. She loved the reminder of her teenage years with grooming and putting the tack on ponies of all different sizes. There were special saddles, including one that was almost a chair for children like Eliana who had been born with severe spina bifida and had a passion for all animals, but especially turtles and ponies.

There were extra staff and volunteers involved, with up to three people for each child and pony—one to lead it and another on each side to help any children who had issues with balance or hanging on, like Hazel or William with his cerebral palsy, but there was never a shortage of helpers. There was a particular magic in vulnerable children interacting with large, gentle animals that was always a highlight of an already rewarding camp experience for adults and children alike.

Amongst about fifteen children in the group, Simon was riding a brown pony called Toffee. Ana was holding the lead rope but Simon had said, very firmly, that he didn't need people walking on either side. Behind him, Jake was leading Alice on a shaggy grey pony called Smoke. Having been asked to keep a close eye on Alice, Maya was walking not far behind her. She had a pack on her back that was heavier than usual because she'd added a small oxygen tank to the usual range of trauma gear like dressings, splints and bandages.

Eli fell back far enough to walk beside Maya along the wide track that had been carefully woven through the forest. It was deliciously cool in the shade of enormous trees like kauri and mahogany and so green with a mid-level layer of palm trees and ferns covering the ground. The pop of colour from wild orchids was pretty and the sound of children's laughter and excited squeaks was just as musical and joyous as any birdsong it was drowning out.

When Maya looked sideways, she caught the expression on Eli's face.

'Gorgeous, isn't it?'

'Unbelievably so.'

'It's my happy place,' Maya said. 'Well, the whole island is—especially when it's full of kids.'

The smile they shared gave that happiness a dimension that Maya had almost forgotten existed. She knew that sharing an experience with someone you knew made it special because it somehow made it more real when it was going to become a shared memory. But sharing an experience with a soul mate—which was what Eli had once been for her—took it to a whole new level. It forged bonds. Or reinforced them.

Could it be capable of mending them, too?

Would she want that?

That flash of longing she'd had when she'd seen Eli for the first time after they had talked on the beach that night was there again, squeezing her heart, but Maya didn't get a chance to even think about it before it evaporated. The pony trek was coming to an end and it was when Jake lifted Alice from Smoke's back that they could hear her breathing. A wheeze that was audible from too far away.

But Alice was smiling as she threw her arms around her pony. 'Take a…photo, Jake… I want to…remember today…' She pressed her cheek against Smoke's neck. 'That was…so…cool.'

Being unable to speak more than a few words before trying to grab another breath had both Eli and Maya walking towards Alice.

'Have you got a nebuliser mask and salbutamol in your kit?'

'Yes. And oxygen.'

Alice gave Smoke another kiss before he was led away but then she seemed relieved to sink to the ground. She leaned forward, clearly in respiratory distress. Jake had gone pale.

'If you kneel behind Alice, you can support her to sit up and lean forward,' Eli told him. 'That will help make breathing easier. We're going to set up a nebuliser mask to give her some bronchodilator medication. Did she take the antihistamines and use her inhalers before coming on the trek?'

'Yes. I made sure she took everything.'

Maya filled the chamber of the nebuliser mask with medication and attached it to the oxygen cylinder.

'I'm just going to put this over your face, Alice,' she warned. 'It should help make your breathing a bit easier.'

'Is it her CF?' Jake asked. 'Or is it asthma from her allergy?'

'Doesn't matter right now,' Eli said quietly. 'We need to treat the symptoms, not the cause.' He'd unrolled the IV kit from Maya's pack and tightened a tourniquet around Alice's arm. 'I'm going to pop a needle into your vein,' he told her.

'I shouldn't have let her come on the trek,' Jake muttered. 'I knew it was risky.'

Alice pulled the mask off her face. 'I don't…care…' she said, with difficulty. 'Best…day…ever…' She held the mask to her face again and Maya pulled the elastic band back into position.

Ponies and other children were being taken away and someone arrived in a golf cart. 'Do you need to get Alice back to the medical centre?' they asked.

'In a sec.' Eli nodded. 'Sharp scratch, Alice…' He slipped the cannula into a vein and removed the needle seconds later.

Maya handed him tape and then a clear plastic covering to secure the IV access.

'Thanks.' By the time he'd flushed the line, she had removed any air bubbles from the tubing attached to a bag of saline and it was ready to provide fluids and keep the line open.

This time, Eli thanked her with no more than a graze of eye contact but it was as clear as him having spoken aloud and it took Maya straight back to times they'd worked together in an emergency in the past. Back to the first time he'd ever made eye contact with her, in fact—when she'd known that the world as she knew it had just tilted on its axis.

Right now, it felt as if nothing had ever come between them.

They travelled together with Alice on one electric vehicle, with Jake following in another. There was no improvement in Alice's breathing by the time they arrived at the medical centre. Mike came to assist Eli and they started a continuous salbutamol infusion and began administering other medications including adrenaline. Maya put electrodes on Alice and monitored her vital signs at regular intervals. Her heart was beating too fast, her attempts to breathe were too rapid and shallow and the oxygen levels in her blood were too low.

An hour later, there was still no improvement and it was obvious that Alice was becoming drowsy. And confused.

'Where's… Smoke?' she asked. 'Did I…fall off?'

'No, sweetheart.' Maya squeezed her hand. 'You didn't fall off. You're a great rider. You did the whole trek without even looking like falling off.'

Alice's eyes were drifting shut but she was smiling. Her lips were starting to look a little blue as the level of oxygen in her blood decreased further.

'She sounds a bit better,' Jake said. 'I can't hear her wheezing now.'

Eli took him further away from Alice and Maya knew he was explaining that not hearing the wheezing was not a good thing in this case. It meant that Alice was getting too tired to keep struggling to breathe and was in danger of a respiratory arrest, which would necessitate intubation and mechanical ventilation. She needed to be in an intensive care unit as quickly as possible.

Maya stayed with Jake as he made contact with his parents, ready to answer questions or take over the call if he became too emotional to speak. Her heart was breaking for this big brother who was trying so hard to hold things together when he was clearly terrified that he might be put in a position to make decisions that were too huge to do alone. He had tears rolling down his face by the end of that call.

The only decision that had been made in the wake of the shocking news was that Alice and Jake's parents were going to head to the airport immediately and wanted to be called again in an hour when they got there to see what flights might be available. If possible, they wanted to speak with Alice's doctor at that point.

By then, Mike and Eli had Alice intubated and ventilated. The helicopter was waiting to transfer them to the biggest hospital available in Fiji, but they were already talking about having to medevac Alice to New Zealand which, at less than four hours flight time, was the closest country to get more expertise and advanced intensive care facilities. Eli and Maya would accompany Jake and Alice and stay until the next decisions were made. Mike and the other medical staff on the island would work extra shifts and cover everything needed on the island. Ana would be with Simon at all times to care for him.

As they settled Alice onto the helicopter's stretcher and arranged all the equipment they needed to ventilate, monitor and keep on top of the medications their patient required, they could hear Mike talking to her parents.

Jake caught Maya's gaze as she was checking the IV lines on Alice's arm that were connected to the bags of fluids. 'What is he talking about?'

'ECMO,' she told him. 'It stands for Extra Corporeal Membrane Oxygenation.'

'It's a machine that can take someone's blood and oxygenate it and put it back in their body,' Eli added. 'It would be an option if Alice was getting worse despite mechanical ventilation and intensive care but it's not available here. That would mean taking her to New Zealand or Australia.'

Jake looked horrified. 'She wouldn't want that.' His voice broke. 'She told me she didn't even want a lung transplant. She was only going to go through it because it was what Mum and Dad wanted.'

Maya knew that it was emotion that was making Eli's eyes so dark. She could almost feel his touch herself when he reached out to grip Jake's shoulder.

'It might not come to that, mate. Let's just take this one step at a time, okay?'

'You're coming with me, yeah?'

'Yes. We'll be with you the whole time.'

They were with Jake as Alice was cared for in the ICU in Suva as each hour passed and her condition didn't improve. They were there when his parents found flights that could get them to Fiji by late the next day. And they were there when Alice's body finally gave up because it wasn't getting enough oxygen and she went into cardiac

arrest and died despite the best efforts of everyone involved, including Eli and Maya.

They sat with Jake as they waited for his parents to
arrive and it was the most heartbreaking experience in
Maya's life. Alice's big brother was absolutely devastated.
He was also afraid that his parents might blame him for
allowing her to do the pony trek that had caused the allergic reaction that had been enough to tip Alice into a
downward spiral that couldn't be reversed.

'Tell them,' Maya said softly. 'Tell them what Alice
said to you.'

Jake had his head in his hands. 'What? That she
thought she'd fallen off Smoke?'

'No.' Maya put her arm around Jake's shoulders but
her gaze was holding Eli's. They both had tears falling.
'That it was her best day ever...'

It was late by the time they arrived back on Reki Island
the next day. Mike told Eli that Simon was already asleep
and that Ana was in the bure with him.

They went into the medical centre and talked Mike
through everything that had been done for Alice. That her
parents had, of course, been devastated not to have been
with their daughter but they could take comfort in knowing that Jake had always been her favourite person in the
world and she would have known he was there with her.
They'd sent a message for Mike to thank him for giving
Alice such a magical time at camp over the years. They
were going to send him a copy of the last photograph
taken of Alice—when she had her arms around her pony's
neck and the happiest smile imaginable on her face. They

would be holding that image in their hearts, they said, for the rest of their lives.

There were tears. Comforting words and hugs. And then Eli walked with Maya as she finally headed to her own *bure*, one of the closest to the beach. They could hear the whisper of waves breaking and the rustle of the wind in the leaves of the palm trees.

They got to the steps that led up to her small veranda, but Eli didn't turn away to go to his own *bure*. He could see Maya's face so clearly in the moonlight and how could he leave when he could see just as clearly that she was utterly exhausted and so deeply saddened by what had happened?

But he didn't know quite what to say to try and comfort her either.

In the end, he simply opened his arms and held her when she instantly stepped into them. He kept holding her until he could feel the tension in her body start to subside, breathing in the scent of her hair as she softened in his arms.

And then she looked up at him and he could actually feel himself falling.

Back into a space he knew as intimately as his own body. A space that had—and *could*—only be there if Maya was sharing it.

It was *their* space. Where there was nothing to keep them apart—physically or emotionally. Where they could give, and receive, what had often felt like everything anyone could possibly need.

It felt as natural as taking his next breath to press his lips against her hair. Against her forehead as she raised her face. And then she tipped her head back even further and he thought it was so that she could look up at him, but she had her eyes closed and her lips parted—just a little—and he could *feel* that she wanted this as much as he did. So he kissed her lips.

Just softly. Briefly.

But he couldn't quite lift his head again and his lips hovered over hers, not quite touching but close enough to feel them. Or perhaps he was feeling the crackle of electricity between them, just for a heartbeat. And then another.

That infinitesimal gap was suddenly gone and this kiss wasn't going to be nearly as soft. Or brief.

This was a *real* kiss. A kiss that took Eli back, not only into that space that could only be there with Maya, but back in time, as though the last ten years had simply evaporated.

Except that he knew they hadn't.

That this kiss should not be happening.

So he broke it, trying to move far enough away this time to not feel any irresistibly magnetic pull.

Maya's whispered words jerked him to a halt. 'Don't go… Please…'

She needed him. He could hear it in her voice and see it in her eyes. He could feel it in his heart, or possibly in his soul.

And there was no way Eli was going anywhere.

CHAPTER SEVEN

THE NEWS ABOUT Alice spread like wildfire through the camp.

Maya could almost feel it happening as she walked on the beach as dawn was breaking the next morning. Shocked whispers as staff members and caregivers were informed. Gentle conversations with the children that were cushioned with cuddles and tears.

There were clouds on the horizon this morning but they only made the sunrise more dramatic. The sea breeze was strong enough that it should have made it a nuisance to have to keep pushing her hair out of her eyes, but Maya found it comforting. Because it reminded her of how Eli had brushed tears from her face last night and buried his fingers in her hair as he'd kissed her for the first time in ten, oh, so long years and yet it felt *exactly* the same.

Well…not exactly. They'd both gained a decade more experience of life, including the pain of their own failed relationship, and that had added a depth to this physical touch that could never have been there otherwise. This was so much more significant than it ever had been, too, because the comfort of intimate human touch, even in the wake of an overwhelmingly emotional experience, had to be based on trust. For Eli and Maya to trust each other this much had made that first kiss, and the slow, tender lovemaking that came later, something extraordinary.

Maya turned to face out to sea and closed her eyes as she took a deep, slow breath. The wind kept her hair off her face now. She could smell the salt of the sea in the air and hear the sound of waves crashing on the reef outside the lagoon. She still felt sad and emotionally drained after being so involved in the tragic loss of Alice yesterday, but surrounding those feelings—like a huge internal hug—was the comfort she had found in Eli's arms.

More than that even, because twinkling like small stars amongst it all was something that felt like astonishment.

How amazing was it that the love she had felt for Eli had apparently never died, even though it had been so deeply buried? That it was still there, like the tiny embers of a fire that could, if she wanted it to be, quite possibly be reignited. That unique ability to communicate without words had made her think that Eli had been just as astonished, but nothing had been said aloud. Maya didn't want to say anything that could potentially break something so new and fragile. Or perhaps it was because she couldn't allow herself to even hope that this meant something when she knew how much it would hurt if Eli didn't feel the same way.

Or maybe the real problem was that he would feel *exactly* the same way. As they'd both said—or rather, fired as verbal weapons at each other—nothing had changed. Even if Eli did feel the same way as she did right now, getting too close might mean they were setting themselves up to be reminded of how incompatible they actually were. And that might hurt even more than this rekindled attraction turning out to be only one-sided.

The distraction of remembering every moment of last night, before Eli finally left her *bure* so that Simon wouldn't wake to find himself still under Ana's care, wasn't going to help Maya face a difficult day ahead. Or maybe it was, because she would be able to tap into the strength of knowing that, even if it was unwise, or Eli wouldn't—or *couldn't*—acknowledge it, he still loved her.

He had told her that with his body last night.

The sound of a helicopter getting ready to take off made Maya turn. She hadn't realised that Eli's *bure* was so close to the nearest path down to the beach until she saw him on his balcony. He lifted a hand in greeting and by the time she walked closer to the fringe of palm trees he had come down onto the sand.

They both looked up as the helicopter flew overhead, still gaining height. Maya raised her hand to farewell Mike, whom she knew would be on board and possibly looking down at the beach. She touched her hand to her heart, too, hoping that he would take the gesture as a sign that she would be thinking of him today, while he was in Suva to assist Alice's family with arrangements for the sad journey they would be making to go home.

'Are you okay?' Eli asked.

Maya was about to give the automatic response that she was fine, but she could see something in Eli's face that made her change her mind.

'Those poor parents,' she said softly. 'They've lost something so precious. They'll be devastated.'

Even having lived with the knowledge that their daughter had a terminal illness couldn't lessen the grief for Alice's parents at losing one of their children.

But Eli knew that she was talking about something

else as well. That she was opening the door to a discussion that neither of them had probably ever imagined they would have.

'At least they have each other,' Eli said just as quietly. 'I'm sorry I wasn't there for you, Maya.'

Eli and Maya had lost their baby. Being so early in the pregnancy hadn't seemed to lessen that impact enough. They'd never shared that grief and maybe that *had* made it harder for both of them. They'd lost their relationship as well. Grief upon grief.

'I'm sorry, too, Eli.'

'It's a long time ago.'

She nodded. 'But sometimes—for me—it feels like yesterday.'

Eli's half-smile was poignant. 'Me, too.'

He pulled her into a quick hug and then, with his hands on her shoulders, he bent his head and kissed her.

It was nothing like the kiss that had escalated into passion last night but it was slow. And so tender it broke Maya's heart.

'I'd better go,' Eli said as he broke the kiss. 'Simon should have got himself dressed and ready for breakfast by now.' He turned before she had time to say anything, striding off as if he needed to escape.

Maya didn't follow him immediately. It had been a huge subject to broach. A huge thing to acknowledge that they had both let each other down by not offering support. Maybe they both needed at least a bit of space.

She watched him walking back towards his *bure*. Catching movement from the corner of her eye made her glance up to see that Simon had come out on the balcony and he was also watching his father.

Her breath caught as she realised that Eli's son was close to the age their own baby would have been if things had been very different. It was also a reminder that Eli had a whole new life that not only didn't include her, it was on the other side of the world.

They had a past that had destroyed the trust they had once had with each other. Could an apology and amazing sex be all it took to wipe the slate clean?

How unlikely was that?

The medically fragile children at Camp Reki might be better equipped than most to handle this kind of shock because, sadly, most of them had dealt with the tragic loss of friends made during hospital admissions or members of the support groups they belonged to, but this was camp. Their happy place. The hardships and pain of real life were not supposed to intrude on their time here any more than was absolutely necessary to keep them safe and not disrupt their long-term treatments.

Maya didn't eat any breakfast herself. She moved from table to table, offering both children and their caregivers the opportunity to talk about how they were feeling and to have any questions answered. She was also offering hugs and encouragement to go to all the activities that they wanted to do today—both as distraction and to make the most of the fine weather. While the cyclone was still on course to bypass Reki Island, there was rain and some stronger winds forecast for the next few days.

Hazel was Maya's small shadow as she moved through the dining area and, while her trademark smile was as bright as ever, it was obvious that she was struggling. The blunt end of her arm, where a hand should have been, was constantly seeking the comforting touch of Maya's hand.

'Have you had any breakfast, sweetheart?' Maya asked.

'I'm not hungry.'

'Is that because you're feeling sad about Alice?'

Hazel's eyes filled with tears that overflowed as she nodded. Maya scooped her up into her arms and cuddled her.

'Why couldn't you make her better?' Hazel's voice was muffled against her shoulder.

'We tried,' Maya told her. 'We tried so hard. But Alice has been sick for a very long time and her poor, tired lungs had been having a hard enough time with just ordinary breathing. Having an asthma attack as well was too much for them.'

'Did it hurt?'

'No. She was asleep. I think she might have been dreaming about the pony ride she'd had because it made her so happy. She told us that it had been her best day ever.' Maya could feel tears gathering in her own eyes. 'And you know something?'

Hazel rubbed her nose on Maya's as she shook her head.

'Alice would want you to have the best day ever. Every day while you're at camp. What were you planning to do first this morning?'

'I'm supposed to be doing baking this morning. And dancing. And this afternoon is the scavenger hunt.'

'Ooh, I love scavenger hunts. Do you have any ideas about what you might have to find?'

'No.' But Hazel sounded more interested. 'Maybe a special sort of shell? Or flower?'

'Shall we go and see if we can find out any clues?'

Maya turned to walk towards the table near the door that was being set up to provide details for all the activities being offered for Day Six of this season's camp but she didn't move any further.

Because Eli, and Simon, were standing right in front of her.

Eli's glance told her that he was over any need for space. It was almost as if he was thanking her for having found a way to mention the elephant that had been in the room and, as he held her gaze, Maya felt her whole body start to tingle. It felt as though she was being held in his arms, not standing in front of him. As though he had the power, just by looking at her, to hold her upright. To give her strength?

This was not the time to think about the significance of what had happened between them last night or this morning. Or to try and see into the future. This was about taking everything, including what was likely to be a difficult day, one step at a time and, right now, Maya could be very grateful for this feeling of having someone by her side. Someone who cared enough to want her to be okay.

'Simon's planning to do the scavenger hunt, too,' he said. 'Can we come with you?'

Hazel wriggled out of Maya's arms. 'Yes,' she said. 'We can do it together.' She smiled at Simon but he was staring up at his father.

Frowning.

Oh, help…

Had Simon sensed something in the way Eli and Maya had been looking at each other so intensely? Was it possible, when he'd been out on the balcony of the *bure*, that he had seen them kissing on the beach? She knew how protective Eli could be. If there was any chance of Simon being upset by Maya getting too close to his father, that would be the end of whatever seeds that might have been sown last night.

She tried to sound as if she was imparting a secret. 'I think Ana and Tevita will know all about what you're going to have to look for in the scavenger hunt. He might give you some clues and you can keep an eye out for things this morning.'

Hazel and Simon took off to the other side of the room to where Ana and her brother were unpacking boxes of small baskets that had cards attached to their handles.

'I heard some of what you said to Hazel about Alice,' Eli said quietly, as they followed the two excited children. 'Is she okay?'

'I think so. We need to support them and let them process things in their own way. How's Simon taking the news?'

'He didn't say much. Mike was in the clinic when we went in to do his factor infusion and they had a bit of a chat.' Eli shook his head. 'I think Si might have taken advantage of me wanting to make sure he was okay, though.'

Maya's steps slowed. 'What do you mean?'

'He said that he was feeling really sad about Alice but there was something that might make him feel better.'

'Which was?' They had both stopped walking, creating a human island in a room that was getting steadily busier.

'Being in the group that you're taking abseiling on the cliff this morning.'

Maya let out a huff of laughter. 'You didn't fall for that, did you?'

Eli grimaced. 'I kind of did.' His face softened as he caught her gaze again. 'Keep him safe for me? I've got a clinic this morning so I can't come and watch.'

He was asking *her* to keep Simon safe for him?

Wow…

It was almost like telling her that he could trust her again.

And that felt even bigger than being able to talk about the shared loss of their baby.

'I promise,' Maya said quietly. She couldn't look away. 'And you know you can trust me. I never break a promise.'

The longing to be in his arms was so powerful it almost brought tears to her eyes. It was just as well they were in a crowded space and it would have been totally inappropriate to even think about touching each other.

The brush of skin on her hand didn't come from Eli, of course. And it was familiar enough to recognise without looking down—a gentle reminder that she was needed elsewhere.

'Okay, Hazel… I'm coming…'

Carlos was waiting outside the medical centre when Eli arrived.

'Are you not feeling well, Carlos?' Eli asked.

'I'm fine. But I'm going abseiling this morning and Maya said she wanted me to get a check-up.' Carlos shrugged. 'I guess she doesn't want me getting dizzy when I'm halfway down a cliff, which is fair enough.'

'No worries,' Eli said to Carlos. He was impressed

with Maya's diligence in following up the dizzy spell Carlos had experienced at the airport when he'd first arrived. 'We'll do a quick check of your blood pressure and heart rate and rhythm and if they're okay you'll be good to go. Come on in—you'll be back with the group before you know it.'

A glance over his shoulder showed him the group, including Simon, gathering around Maya to put on their harnesses and other safety gear. He raised a hand and Simon waved back. They exchanged 'thumbs-up' signals.

Maya waved, too, and smiled. Eli went through the doors of the medical centre wrapped in the warmth of that smile. He could still see the look in her eyes when she'd promised to keep Simon safe. When she'd reminded him that he could trust her to never break a promise.

He knew he could trust Maya.

As much as he could trust himself.

He might have believed that trust had been broken but he'd been wrong, hadn't he?

Last night had proved that.

They had both been exhausted, physically and emotionally, having finally returned from such a heartbreaking day. They'd been deeply affected. Fragile enough to be utterly vulnerable. But when they were alone in Maya's *bure* there were no barriers to the comfort they could both give and receive because the solid foundation of that absolute trust was still there.

It hadn't changed.

It was also instantly recognisable. Eli had never found anything close to it with anyone else and he knew instinctively that it was a connection so rare he never would.

He would also never forget last night.

What was the dividing line, he wondered, between trust and love?

Was that what turned sex into making love?

Neither of them had said anything out loud last night but that was what they'd been doing, that was for sure.

Making love...

Oh, no... He couldn't let himself go any further down a mental track that had kept him awake for far too long after he'd finally gone back to his own *bure* in the early hours of this morning. He wasn't going to step back into a space that held the risk of heartbreak.

Because it wouldn't just be a risk for himself, would it?

Simon already thought Maya was amazing. Imagine if he and Maya did get back together. Simon would adore her. She'd be a mother to him and he'd have to worry that, one day, she might not come home from her work or a hobby like abseiling down cliffs and then he'd lose his mother all over again. It would be devastating for him.

Even if he didn't have Simon to put first in his life, Eli wasn't at all sure he could take that risk for himself. He certainly didn't have enough evidence that, despite giving in to the pull towards Maya, anything fundamental had really changed to stop history ending up repeating itself. Last night was simply a product of having gone through a traumatic and very emotional experience together, combined with a past relationship that had made it too easy to get too close, too quickly.

'Okay, Carlos. Sit on the side of the bed for me and I'll take your blood pressure.'

Eli wrapped the cuff around the teenager's arm and put the disc of his stethoscope on the inside of his elbow, waiting to hear the sound of the pulse starting and then finally fading as he let the pressure out of the cuff. It was during those moments of silence that he could feel that something was different about Carlos today.

'You okay, mate?' he asked quietly as he unwrapped the cuff. 'I know it's a bit of a tough day for everyone.'

Carlos didn't respond, other than giving a shrug. He lay quietly back on the bed when Eli stuck on the sticky electrode patches needed to monitor heart rate and rhythm for a few minutes and then he suddenly spoke.

'She didn't want it.'

Eli raised his eyebrows.

'The lung transplant. We talked about it and Alice told me she really didn't want it.' The words were tumbling out now. 'She was so scared of the pain and all the complications and she said she didn't want to live longer if it might be even worse than it was now. She said she was sick of being sick. I'm glad she doesn't have to do it… that she's not scared any more.'

His voice broke and then he cleared his throat.

'There's nothing to stop me going to college, is there, Dr Peters?'

'No, not at all. There are lots of people out there who had heart transplants more than thirty years ago and the medicine to help, like new anti-rejection drugs and monitoring, is getting better all the time. There's nothing to stop you doing whatever you want to do with your life, Carlos, and every reason to go for it.'

'Do you think I could become a doctor? And help kids like Alice?'

Eli took a deep breath as he printed out a rhythm strip to go in Carlos's notes. It wasn't the first time a patient had given him pause for thought. When he looked up, he smiled at the courageous young man in front of him. It was his turn to clear his throat so that he could say something.

'I think you'll make a great doctor, Carlos. Now…your heart is behaving itself perfectly so how 'bout you get out there and do whatever it is that will make you feel better today?'

Carlos nodded. 'Thanks, Doc.'

'Any time.' Eli took the strip of graph paper from the ECG monitor to attach to the patient notes as Carlos left the room, but for a long minute he found himself deep in thought.

Thinking about Carlos. And Alice.

About Simon and Sarah.

And Maya.

Life was precious. Too often, it was too short but the people who made the most of it and wanted to help others more than simply looking after themselves were the ones who made their time infinitely valuable.

People like Carlos.

And Maya.

Eli was aware of something else, too. He needed to be inspired by Carlos's attitude and let Simon follow whatever dreams he might have for his future.

Maybe he needed to think about his own future as well. He'd been so focused on his life with Simon that he hadn't realised what was missing. How lonely he was sometimes.

Until last night.

When he'd held Maya in his arms and realised just how much he had missed her. How much he still cared about her.

The weather began to change late that afternoon, with ominous-looking black clouds crowding the skies and the gusts of wind were strong enough for a warning to be issued not to go near the palm trees on the beach in case coconuts were falling. Not that anyone wanted to spend any more time on the beach today.

Tired children gathered in the main room before dinner to compare the contents of their scavenger hunt baskets. There were shells and pieces of coral, flowers and sticks and feathers amongst the natural objects and small plastic toys and wrapped candy treats that had been scattered around designated search areas by staff members. There was rather a lot of sand on the floor as well.

There had been a list of about twenty items printed on the laminated cards attached to the baskets but Hazel and Simon hadn't been able to get a heads-up on any of the items they might be searching for from either Ana or Tevita that morning.

'They could have told us *something*,' Simon complained as he spread the contents of his basket onto the floor in front of him. 'If I'd known we had to find a ginger flower I could have picked one this morning. There was a bush right beside the bottom of the cliff where we went abseiling, wasn't there, Maya?'

Maya and Hazel were sitting on the floor beside them.

'I should remember,' she said. 'Because they're one of my favourite flowers, but I must have been too busy going up and down the cliff all morning to notice. There are ginger plants growing all over the island, though. Did it have long, spiky red flowers?'

'Yes. Just like the picture on the card of things we had to hunt for. I saw it when I was going up to the top of the cliff for my turn to come down with you. But I wasn't allowed to go back to the cliff by myself this afternoon and you weren't there to help, Dad.'

'No, I'm sorry, Si. Somebody cut their foot on a broken shell on the beach and we had to put some stitches in it. And someone else wasn't feeling very well so I wanted to keep an eye on them this afternoon. But you had lots of helpers, didn't you?'

'I guess…'

'I wish I could have come to watch you abseiling this morning, too. I've seen some of the photos.' They had been a bit hair-raising, to be honest. Simon had been halfway down a craggy cliff with his feet against lumps of sharp-looking volcanic rock, Maya hovering right behind him in her own harness. Maybe it was just as well he hadn't been there watching it. 'Was it scary?' he asked.

'Not really.' Simon shook his head. 'It was just like the climbing wall, but Maya made me go really slowly.'

'We were just being careful,' Maya put in. 'It wasn't that slow.'

'It's always a good idea to be super-careful the first time,' Eli said. 'Sometimes you need to think twice about everything you do to make sure it's safe.'

Maya noticed the shell Simon was taking from his basket.

'That's a fabulous cowrie shell,' she said, touching its smooth, speckled brown surface. 'One of the biggest I've seen.'

'We had to find a big shell. And a curly one. And a piece of coral.'

'I got a big one with spikes,' Hazel said. 'See? I'm going to take it home and put it on my windowsill.'

'That's called a conch shell,' Maya told her. 'It's beau-

tiful. And did you both find the secret I told you about—
when I joked that you might really be going on a bear
hunt?'

Simon laughed. 'You didn't say it was a *chocolate*
bear.'

'I've eaten mine already,' Hazel said sadly.

'You can have mine.' Simon was tipping out the rest of
his basket to find the small, foil-wrapped candy.

Eli leaned over to pick it up and pass it to Hazel. He
grinned at Maya. 'Did this come over from Australia
with you, by any chance?'

'Yeah...so did the chocolate fish. They were my con-
tributions to this year's scavenger hunt. We like to put
different things in every year. The plastic geckos were
Mike's choice this time.'

'How did you know the bear came from Australia?'
Simon asked. 'And that it came with Maya?'

'It's a koala bear. They only come from Australia and
that's where Maya lives now.'

Simon was staring at him. 'Where did she live before?'

'In New Zealand. Same as me. I told you about how I
lived there for a while.'

The look Maya flashed at Eli felt like a question. Did
Simon have any idea that they'd been more than friends?

Hazel broke a silence that had suddenly become a little awkward.

'Can I eat the bear now?' she asked.

'It's almost dinnertime, sweetheart,' Maya said. 'How
'bout you wait and have it for dessert?'

It was Simon who unknowingly answered that silent
query that still seemed to be hanging in the air.

'Was Maya your girlfriend?' he asked.

'Um…' Eli caught Maya's gaze again. He was trying to send a silent apology for opening what might be a can of worms but he was also searching for an indication of how private she wanted their past history to remain. If she wanted it to remain a secret, it would be a problem because he'd always been as honest with Simon as he was old enough to understand. About everything.

He'd never told him about having left a relationship when he'd come to look after Simon as a baby because it had never been relevant to their lives. It felt relevant now, however.

And…dangerous?

Was Maya deliberately not looking in his direction now? She was helping Hazel put her treasures back into her basket.

'We *were* friends,' Eli said uncomfortably, knowing that Simon was waiting for a response. 'It's a long time ago, Si.'

'Yes…' Maya got to her feet, still avoiding his gaze, picking up the basket as Hazel also got up a little awkwardly onto her prosthetic lower legs. 'You were a tiny baby, Simon—that's how long ago it was.' She handed the basket to Hazel, who hooked it over her elbow. 'We need to give your basket to Ana so she can count up how many things on the list you found. You might get a prize.'

Hazel bounced happily. 'I only had three things I couldn't find.'

'I only had one,' Simon muttered as he watched them walk away. 'That ginger flower.'

'You did well,' Eli said. 'I hope it was fun.'

Simon didn't say anything. He was giving Eli an odd look.

'What's up?' Eli asked. 'Are you feeling sad about Alice again?'

Simon started to nod but then shook his head.

'What is it, then?'

Simon ignored the question. He was silent as he piled his items back into the scavenger hunt basket but then his words came out in a rush. 'If you went to live in Australia, would you take me with you?'

Eli's jaw dropped. 'Why would I go and live in Australia?'

Simon's voice was no more than a mutter. 'Because that's where Maya lives.'

Oh, help… Was the electricity between himself and Maya, in the wake of their lovemaking last night, obvious enough that even an almost ten-year-old child could feel it? And feel threatened by it?

As if he would ever let anything come between him and this beloved child that had become the centre of his world.

Eli pulled in a breath. 'I'm not going to live in Australia,' he said firmly. 'But even if I went to live on the moon, Si, I wouldn't be leaving you behind. I would never leave someone I love so much behind. Why would you even think that?'

'Because…' Simon was brushing spilt sand together into a small pile on the floor. 'Because you're not really my dad, are you? You're only my uncle.'

'I adopted you, Si. You *are* absolutely my son.'

'It still doesn't mean that I'm your *real* son.'

Eli felt a shiver run down his spine. How—and when— had Simon even come up with such a notion? What had changed?

Nothing. Except they'd come here to this island.

And he'd, very unexpectedly, reconnected with Maya.

As if to underline Eli's sense of foreboding, there was a sudden flash of lightning from the dark clouds outside, a crack of thunder only seconds later and then the sound of torrential rain began to hammer on the roof.

Maybe that cyclone wasn't as far away as everybody had thought...

CHAPTER EIGHT

MAYA COULD SEE the slump of Simon's shoulders from the far side of the room and the way Eli was bent towards him as if they were having a very serious conversation.

She really hoped they weren't talking about her. Because neither of them looked happy and that was creating a cloud over any embryonic thoughts of this reconnection with Eli going any further. A stormy kind of cloud, even, like the ones that had gathered outside in the last couple of hours. The flash of lightning, followed too closely by a clap of thunder she could feel vibrating in her bones, made it seem as if the universe was issuing a warning not to pin any hopes on Eli wanting—or being available for—anything more than a short excursion down memory lane.

What was it he'd just said to Simon?

Oh, yeah...that it was always a good idea to be super-careful the first time and that you might need to think twice about everything you did to make sure it was safe.

Had he been thinking twice about the wisdom of getting too close to her when she'd seen him talking to Simon so seriously?

Maya didn't have the time to think about anything twice right now because she could see Mike near the doorway. It was the first time she'd seen him since this morning when he'd been flying out to be with Alice's family. Hazel was lining up with all the other children to get her dinner so Maya went out of the room to speak to Mike.

'How did it go?' she asked. 'I can imagine how rough the day's been.'

'Alice's parents are devastated,' Mike said. 'But I was very relieved that they're fully supporting Jake and the decision to let Alice come to camp. They're all on their way home now. I was glad I was there to make all the bureaucracy a bit easier for them.'

'You must be exhausted.'

'Can't afford to be,' Mike said. 'The weather was closing in as we flew back and I was fielding calls from the Fiji Meteorological Service. Cyclone Lily has started changing direction in the last sixty minutes. If it keeps going on its current trajectory, we might end up being a lot closer than we'd want to be. It could potentially make landfall on Reki Island.'

Maya's eyes widened. 'How severe is it now? I heard that it got downgraded from a category four to a three earlier today.'

'It did. And they're hoping it might weaken further in the next few hours.'

'When's that expected to be?'

'Depends on how often the direction changes but we can expect heavy rain nine to twelve hours ahead of it making landfall and it looks like that's started already.'

'Did they give any idea of how long it will take to get past us?'

'Maybe twelve hours.'

'And it could get a lot worse out there than it is now.'
Maya was frowning. A category five was the highest level
for a tropical cyclone, but even at a three it could cause
structural damage to buildings, ruin crops and damage
trees.

'We need to be prepared for that,' Mike agreed. 'It's
likely to blow through fast if it does reach us but I don't
want to take any chances. Can you come with me to tick
off the checklist and make sure that all our emergency
kits are fully stocked at the medical centre?'

'Of course.'

'I've got ground staff out now, making sure that any
outdoor equipment and furniture is secured or put away.
Danny and James are getting the helicopter safely into
the hangar. I'd better find Ana, too, before I do anything
else. I'll call a meeting of all senior staff when everyone's had some dinner and Eli will need someone to stay
with Simon.'

An hour later, however, it transpired that a babysitter
would not be needed.

Mike and Maya had checked that all the medical kit
backpacks in the medical centre were fully stocked and
that drugs and IV fluids were still within their expiry
dates when another call came in from the Meteorological Service. Cyclone Lily had changed direction again
and they were now officially on standby for it making
landfall on the island later in the evening. Mike had some
big decisions to make.

'I want everybody to stay in the main complex overnight. These buildings were made to withstand a cyclone
and we're on higher ground. It's not just the wind damage

or flooding we have to anticipate, it's the storm surge. There are a lot of *bures* that are too close to the beach.'

Maya nodded. 'We don't want to be having to worry about getting medical care to the far corners of the resort either. We've got internal access to the medical centre from here and we don't have to worry about power failure, do we? We've got the solar power batteries and the generators.'

Mike nodded but let out a growling sound. 'I should have been more onto this. I was so focused on Alice's family today. We could have arranged ferries and evacuated people to the main island. We're going to have some scared kids on our hands and that's not going to help anyone who's physically fragile.'

'You didn't know,' Maya reminded him. 'As far as we knew, this cyclone wasn't going to come close enough to do more than give us a bit of stormy weather. By the time things changed it was already too late to evacuate anyone. You only just made it back here yourself.'

But Mike didn't look reassured. 'We've never had anything like this to deal with at camp. It's nowhere near cyclone season.'

'So let's try and make it exciting rather than scary for everyone,' Maya suggested. 'This can be the first ever camp sleepover. We'll move all the tables and chairs from the dining room and bring in their mattresses and bedding and any medical equipment they need. We can keep them entertained and keep everybody accounted for until the worst blows over.'

'Can I leave you to inform caregivers and start getting set up? Get Eli to help you? I need to get down to the village and let them know they can all come up here for shelter.'

'They may not want to leave their houses. Or their animals.'

'They could use the church as an evacuation centre if they prefer. But they need warning about what's on the way—including the risk of a storm surge. I'll get a trailer loaded with supplies like bottled water and torches and take that down with a golf cart.'

Simon looked happier than he had all day.

'We're having a sleepover? All of us? In here?'

'Apparently so,' Eli said. 'It looks like this storm is going to get a bit worse before it gets better and this is the best building for us to be in.'

Several staff members were already clearing tables away to stack in another room and others could be seen outside, putting sandbags along the outside walls as extra protection. The heavy rain had stopped for the moment but, by the look of the clouds, another squall could come through at any minute.

'Stay here,' Eli instructed Simon. 'Ana and the others will be looking after you while we get set up. I think they're going to teach you some new songs, ready for our last night concert. I'm going to go back to our *bure* and get your pyjamas and toothbrush and stuff.'

'Are you coming to the sleepover, too?'

'Sure am.' Eli could see Maya opening one of the outside doors to this area. She had a raincoat on over her uniform but hadn't fastened it and a gust of wind nearly pulled it from her body as she stepped outside.

She was trying to hold her hair out of her face with both hands and…

And Eli needed to be out there too. To find out where she was going and to make sure she was going to be safe.

'I'll be back really soon,' he told Simon.

He caught up with Maya as she passed the external entrance to the medical centre.

'Hey…where are you going?'

'I need to get a change of clothes that I can wear under protective overalls.' Maya's hair was whipping around her head in the wind. 'My steel-capped boots are under my bed, I think. And I need to find a hair tie and enough clips to stop my hair blinding me when I'm outside.'

A small frond from a palm tree hit Eli's shoulder and he heard the sound of something crashing onto the path ahead of them.

'What was that?'

'Probably a coconut. They're lethal in this kind of wind. I should have grabbed a hard hat before I came out. I'd better hurry.'

'I'm coming with you.' Eli put his arm around her shoulders, as if that was enough to protect her from whatever the rising wind could throw at them.

Maya grabbed what she wanted from her room and then they both ran back towards the main complex, but Maya slowed as they got closer. 'I need to get into our storage shed,' she told Eli.

He followed her in there and the roller door went up. The shed was lined with deep shelves and large enough to have a four-wheel all-terrain vehicle with a trailer attached parked in the centre of the space. He could see large items in the trailer, like a hard-shell basket rescue stretcher, coils of rope, blankets, tools like a chainsaw and shovel and...

'What are those metal things?' he asked.

'Struts,' Maya said. 'They're a fairly vital part of technical rescue equipment. For stabilising and lifting in case of someone being trapped under a collapsed building or a vehicle or something.'

She climbed onto the two-person seat of the ATV. 'I need to check that this is ready to go. Just in case.' She turned the engine on and revved it. 'Sounds good to go. Fuel tank's full. I'll leave the shed doors open.' Maya got off the bike to head to a rack where overalls were hanging. A shelf above the rack housed bright yellow hard hats with torches attached and a board to one side had portable radio transmitters hanging on hooks.

'I can't believe how well set up you are here,' Eli said. 'It must have cost a small fortune.'

'We've got sponsors that are happy to help keep the camp running. And Mike fills in any gaps. This is his passion.'

'Have you got a pair of those overalls that would fit me?'

Her head turned sharply. 'You don't want to be out in a cyclone, Eli. It's dangerous. We'll need you in the medical centre if we run into any trouble. And Simon needs you nearby. I...' Maya sounded hesitant. 'I saw you talking to him after he asked you if I used to be your girlfriend. He...didn't look happy. Is everything okay?'

Maya wasn't looking happy either and Eli could feel a knot in his chest that was heavy enough to make it hard to take a breath. Without really thinking about what he was doing, he walked to Maya, took her in his arms and held her close.

He wasn't sure if this was intended to be an apology or he simply wanted her to know that, whatever happened next, he was never going to regret what had happened between them last night. When Maya lifted her chin to look up at him, he bent his head and kissed her softly. He lifted his head but then dipped it again to give her another kiss—he just couldn't help himself. Then he rested his chin against Maya's curls as he pulled her close again.

'I think Si might be feeling a bit confused,' he admitted. 'Threatened even, perhaps? He's never seen me in any kind of meaningful relationship so maybe he was a bit shocked by the idea I've had one in the past.'

'Oh, no...' Maya's eyes had widened.

'What?'

'I didn't think about it at the time but...it's just possible he might have seen us on the beach this morning. He might have heard the helicopter leaving and gone out to watch and then seen us talking and...'

'And kissing,' Eli finished for her. He let his breath out in a sigh. 'I'll have to explain that kissing someone doesn't automatically mean you're in a significant relationship.' He shook his head. 'I know he's old enough to realise how much things could change if there was someone else in our lives but...but he seems to have the crazy idea that I'd walk away from him if that *was* the case. He asked if I'd take him with me if I went somewhere else. Like Australia.'

'What?' Maya pulled back, looking shocked herself. 'Why on earth would he think you wouldn't?'

'I've always been honest with him. He knows he's adopted and that he's actually my nephew. I didn't think it mattered until he said something about not being my "real" son.'

He could read her thoughts in her eyes. She knew that Simon was the most important thing in his life and that he would never do anything to damage their relationship. He could see that she was dismissing the idea that she could ever be as important in his life as she had once been.

And he thought he could see—though it might be him projecting what felt almost like a fear of his own—that last night was already being parcelled away as a one-off. Something they probably shouldn't have done because it was a reminder of what they'd once had together but were never going to have again.

'It'll be okay,' Maya said quietly. 'He won't be upset if we're just friends. If we keep in touch after camp's over. Hey…maybe you could bring him out to Australia for a holiday some time. It's a brilliant country to visit.'

'And we'll be back for camp next year,' Eli added. 'If we get another invitation, that is.'

Maya smiled. 'I'll have a word with Mike. I don't think that'll be a problem.'

For a long moment, they held eye contact. As if they were letting go of what might have been, if things were different. As if Maya was trying to echo what he'd hoped he was silently communicating—that she had no regrets about last night.

It was Maya who broke the eye contact, turning away to pull down a pair of overalls. 'There's some bigger sizes on the other end of the rack,' she said. 'It's probably not a bad idea if you have some on hand. Just in case. You are the most highly qualified person here to deal with a trauma case if we get one.'

Above the noise of the wind outside, they could both hear something else. Someone calling.

'Help...we need help...'

Eli was right behind her as she ran outside. He recognised the big Fijian man as Sione—one of the gardeners at the resort. He had another man in his arms who was bleeding from a head wound and looked semi-conscious.

'Follow us.' Eli led the way to the medical centre. 'Can you tell us what happened?'

Maya flicked on the lights in the treatment room as Sione carried his friend Ma'afu to the bed.

'He was trying to get his boat out of the water,' he told them. 'I was running to help but a big wave caught it and he was underneath it when it came down on the beach.'

Eli was checking Ma'afu's airway and breathing, but when he put his stethoscope on his chest the injured man tried to push him away with a loud groan.

'Does that hurt?'

Ma'afu nodded.

'Does it hurt to breathe?'

He nodded again. Blood was running down his face from the cut on his forehead and Maya grabbed a dressing and pressed it against the wound. 'Sione, could you hold this for me, please?' She took his hand and showed him how hard to press.

Eli was cutting Ma'afu's tee shirt to expose his chest and observe his breathing. If a lot of ribs were broken he might have a flail segment that would be visible and also a warning that his breathing could be significantly affected. The sharp ends of broken ribs could also cause bleeding that would accumulate in the chest cavity and affect the function of both the heart and lungs.

'Can we tilt the bed up to a forty-five-degree angle?' he asked Maya. 'And let's get some oxygen on. Ma'afu? If a really bad pain was a number ten and no pain at all was zero, what number would you give your pain at the moment?'

Sione had to shift his hand as he was translating the question, so that Maya could slip the elastic band of an oxygen mask over Ma'afu's head. With the bleeding now under control from the pressure, she could see the head wound was superficial. It would need stitches but that could wait.

'He says it's bad,' Sione reported. 'A number ten.'

Maya switched on the monitor beside the bed, wrapped a blood pressure cuff around Ma'afu's arm and put a pulse oxygen clip onto a finger. Eli was gathering supplies to insert an IV line.

'I'm going to give you something for the pain,' he told their patient as he put a tourniquet around his arm. 'I know how painful it is for you to breathe at the moment. You'll feel better soon, I promise.'

They would also be able to do a secondary survey as soon as they had the pain at a more tolerable level. A thorough head-to-toe examination was a priority because there could well be other injuries to find.

'Are you allergic to any medications that you know of?' Eli asked.

Sione had to translate that question for Ma'afu and then he shook his head. 'He doesn't think so.'

As Maya stuck some electrodes onto his chest so they

could watch his heart rate and rhythm, she watched Eli's swift, easy movements to insert the cannula, flush the line and then draw up and administer some morphine.

Sione reported that the medication had brought the pain level down to maybe a six and Eli topped the dose up a little.

'Do you want me to set up some fluids?' Maya asked him.

'Yes, please.'

An upward glance as Maya unravelled a giving set and pushed the spike into the port of a bag of saline revealed how focused Eli was on his task as he began the secondary survey, carefully examining Ma'afu's skull for any evidence of more damage than the laceration, like a skull fracture and potential brain injury. Then he shone a torch briefly into his eyes, checking for foreign objects like bits of shell or splinters and evidence of haemorrhage or an irregular iris shape, and swiftly moved to check their patient's ears for any sign of a CFS leak or blood. She knew he would be thinking ahead to any potential repercussions of the injuries that were already obvious and how they could handle them this far away from a fully equipped emergency department. They had no surgical facilities available and, for the moment, there was no backup of being able to evacuate a patient.

It was that familiar vertical line of utter focus between Eli's eyes that gave Maya a hard squeeze in her chest.

Or was it a tingle on her lips that clearly didn't want to let go of those kisses he'd given her so recently?

Whatever it was, it was enough to distract her from what she was doing for just a heartbeat as a wave of something that felt like sadness washed over her.

She still loved this man.

But it seemed as if their paths had crossed only to part again. Within a few days, they would be heading to opposite sides of the world.

That they could part as friends after so many years of unresolved pain they had caused each other should make it easier this time, shouldn't it? It was all Maya had been hoping for initially, after all. Was it only such a short time ago that the idea of anything more than friendship had been almost unthinkable? That taking the risk of being hurt again was too much to even consider?

Maya had the horrible feeling that walking away as friends might actually make it harder.

Not that this was the time to be thinking about it at all. Maya pushed it aside as she turned to check the current information they were receiving on the monitor screen.

'Sinus rhythm,' she said aloud. 'Tachycardia at one twenty.' The rate had increased. Was it because of a lack of oxygen? She pushed the button to inflate the automatic blood pressure cuff and as she waited for it to deflate again she couldn't help one more glance at Eli.

As if he felt the glance, he looked up to catch her gaze, unhooking his stethoscope earpieces. 'I'll top up the pain meds,' he said. 'And do an ultrasound.'

Had he heard diminished breath sounds? The pounding of the rapid heart rate? He didn't need to tell Maya that he was concerned about internal bleeding that might be happening.

'What's the blood pressure?' Eli checked as he turned to set up the portable ultrasound machine. 'And oxygen saturation?'

The figures had just stopped changing on the screen.

'Blood pressure's dropped a bit. It's now one zero five over sixty. SpO2 is ninety-five.'

He caught her gaze again, just for a heartbeat, and she knew they were thinking the same thing—that it was now urgent for them to find out whether there was enough blood or air, or both, in the chest cavity to impede the function of the lungs or heart.

Them...

Part of that silent communication had made Maya feel that they were doing this together, as a team, and there was a poignancy there that reminded her too much of having been a team in their personal lives as well.

Was Eli feeling that, too? Was that why he sounded so professional as he put some gel on the side of Ma'afu's chest and got Sione to translate the reason he was doing this examination.

'It will let us see even a small amount of bleeding. An ultrasound can detect small amounts of bleeding far better than an X-ray. As little as ten mils—that's only two teaspoons. You'd need at least a hundred mils for it to show up on an X-ray.'

'What will you do if he is bleeding inside?' Sione asked.

'We'd put a tube in to take the blood away and make it easier for Ma'afu to breathe well. Can you ask whether this is hurting him?'

Thanks to the pain medication, it didn't seem to be too painful for the probe of the ultrasound to be positioned on the right side where the ribs were fractured, above the liver and just under the diaphragm. Maya watched as Eli angled it up to see into the thoracic cavity. He sensed that she was also watching the screen.

'That's the liver in the middle of the screen,' he said quietly. 'And that white line is the diaphragm. You can see it moving with each breath. And that dark patch there beside the liver? Can you see that?'

'Yes. Is that fluid?'

'Yes.' Eli moved the probe to examine the area more closely. 'Blood.'

'What's the odd-shaped bit that's waving?'

'Part of the lower lobe of the lung. It's compressed into that shape by the pressure of the amount of blood that's collecting.' Eli put his hand on Ma'afu's arm. 'We do need to put a tube into your chest,' he told him. 'I'm going to give you some local anaesthetic so it doesn't hurt, but you might feel some poking and pushing. Sione, can you help him stay as still as possible, please?'

'Yes, of course.'

'And, Maya? I'll need your assistance.'

'Of course.' Her words were an echo of Sione's agreement but they felt as if they were saying much more.

That Eli could ask her for anything and she would be there, by his side, without hesitation. Even if it had nothing to do with a professional situation like this. A tiny piece of her heart was breaking as she remembered how unlikely it was that he would ask.

She watched Eli's hands as he swiftly identified the landmarks he needed, like the tip of the scapula and the line of the twelfth rib to mark where the diaphragm was. Maya prepped and draped the skin and Eli worked fast, making a small incision and doing a blunt dissection and making a track for the tube that he inserted carefully, held in the teeth of a clamp.

Maya had the suture ready for Eli to secure the tube,

with stitches in the skin and multiple knots, before winding the suture around the tube and making more knots. They covered the area with a gauze dressing, taped into place. Blood was already collecting in the drainage bottle hanging on the side of the bed.

'All done,' Eli told their patient. 'Well done for staying so still. We want you to rest now, okay?'

Ma'afu was drowsy. 'Thank you,' he mumbled beneath his mask.

Within a short time his vital signs were improving, with oxygen levels increasing and his heart rate slowing. By this time, other staff members were gathering in the medical centre and were ready to take over monitoring Ma'afu's condition.

When Maya left the treatment room to dispose of the soiled drapes, she found Mike had just returned from his visit to the village. He had a portable radio clipped to his belt.

'I've left a radio with Petero in the village,' he said. 'He'll call if there's any problems. We're on channel three.'

Maya nodded. Pete was another one of the groundsmen at the resort, a friend of Sione's and just as sensible and reliable. He was a good choice as the village contact.

'I'll go and get a radio for myself so I'm in the loop,' she said.

The rain had started again and the wind was getting strong enough to be howling across the roof. A gust was almost enough to knock Maya off her feet as she headed back to the storage shed and she felt an apprehensive shiver run down her spine. This storm was coming in harder and faster than they'd expected. She could only hope it would blow past and dissipate just as quickly.

Dressed in her overalls and boots, Maya had no sooner turned on another fully charged radio and set it to channel three when she heard a panicked voice.

'Mike... Mike... Can you hear me?'

'I'm here, Pete.' Mike's voice was calm. 'You're coming through loud and clear. What's happened?'

'It's a tree...' The radio crackled. It sounded as if there were people screaming in the background. 'It's come down on a house. We can't get in and...and I think there might be people inside.'

Maya pushed the button on her radio. 'I heard that, Mike. I'll head to the village straight away. Pete? Can you hear me? Pete...?'

There was a crackling sound loud enough to make any words incomprehensible. And then it stopped. Mike's voice came through to break the ominous radio silence.

'Go and see what we need to deal with, Maya. But be careful, okay? I'll get a team on standby for backup.'

Maya clipped the radio to her pocket and reached for a hard hat. She started the ATV and was driving it out of the shed when she had to stop.

Eli was right in front of her.

'You're not going there alone,' he said. 'I'm coming too.'

CHAPTER NINE

IT WAS A NO-BRAINER.

Simon was safe. He was inside. Tucked up in a building designed to withstand the destructive force of a tropical cyclone, with a thick cushion of sandbags as extra protection against a possible storm surge. There were any number of people available to keep him safe.

Maya was about to head out into the storm and put herself in danger to help others.

Alone.

Eli couldn't have stayed in the safety of the resort, knowing that Maya was out there in danger. He had to go with her.

It would be too hard to stay in safety here and imagine what might be happening because that would tap into too many memories.

Of being at home and hearing the news that his parents had been killed in that avalanche.

Of being in New Zealand when Sarah had been so badly injured.

It was possibly a timely reminder that he didn't want to go back to where he had to live with that kind of fear on a regular basis but he was here and this was a crisis and…

And it was almost as if he could try and make up for

not being anywhere near the people he had loved, and lost, in the past.

He might not be able to prevent disaster but at least he wouldn't be able to beat himself up for not being there.

And having made sure the island villagers had shelter and supplies and a means of contact, Mike needed to stay in the medical centre and near all the children and their caregivers that he had taken responsibility for when he'd accepted them into this camp for children with complex medical needs. There were plenty of medical staff who could care for the only, now stable, casualty so far but there could well be others in the village and Eli was the most highly qualified medic on the island to deal with traumatic injuries. Another no-brainer.

He kept Maya waiting for less than a minute, grabbing a radio, dragging on a pair of overalls made of strong protective fabric to cover the clothes he was wearing and jamming a hard hat on his head after he climbed on board the ATV, fastening the strap as they took off down the track that led to the village. The sheets of water from the torrential rain were being driven off the visors of their helmets by the wind but the visibility was still only a few metres ahead at most and the further they went from the resort, the rougher the track became.

Eli had to hand it to Maya. She could handle this vehicle with apparent ease and she was taking them to where they were needed as fast as possible. There were safety belts but Eli still needed to hang onto the bar of the anti-roll protection frame to try and stop himself bouncing against Maya when they hit any bumps or potholes. This should have been terrifying but, strangely, it wasn't. Not only because he was so focused on what they were heading towards.

It was also because he had complete faith in Maya.

She'd been doing this kind of thing for years. She knew what she was doing, and she wasn't about to take any stupid risks. This had nothing to do with an adrenaline junkie who was looking for thrills. This was a courageous woman who was prepared to put her own safety at risk because others were in danger.

He was proud of her.

Okay…he hadn't coped that well with the background anxiety of her working in a profession that could put her in danger and, worse, having hobbies that were even riskier, but that was because it tapped into the tragic loss of his parents at a vulnerable time in his life and how protective he'd been of his sister afterwards and that mistrust of tempting fate had continued, thanks to being reinforced by the accident victims he treated in the emergency department who hadn't been careful enough.

But Maya had been right when she'd said simply that 'accidents happen'. That she hadn't been to blame for what had caused the tragic loss of their unborn baby.

Mike had said something similar in that introductory staff meeting.

'Accidents or unexpected medical events can happen any time or anywhere…'

He'd always known how much he could trust Maya— right from the first moment he'd met her.

But had he pushed that knowledge away so many years ago? Had it been buried by the fear that the worst was happening? Had allowing himself to ignore that faith in Maya contributed to the way they'd been pushed apart by events and emotions spiralling out of control? And was it why, despite finding each other again, it felt as if it could be too late to undo enough of the damage that had been done ten years ago? Or was the real problem that there were new barriers to them being together?

Like a boy on the cusp of adolescence who didn't feel secure enough?

It was just as well that Maya had instantly understood the implications of Simon asking if Eli would go to Australia without him. That she had made it clear that she believed their night together had been no more than a one-off. For old times' sake.

He'd always loved the way they could communicate silently like that.

And that she'd always had his back.

A snapped branch bouncing off the roll bars of the quadbike, catching his helmet as it dropped, was enough to jolt Eli's thoughts back to the present.

'You okay?' Maya had to shout to be heard over the shriek of the wind.

'Glad I'm wearing a helmet.'

'We're almost there.'

The small church was the first building they got to. Sturdily built, it was where the villagers were gathering for shelter and there were people holding torches and carrying armloads of supplies heading inside. Others were waiting for this help to arrive and they ran beside the vehicle as Maya kept going.

'This way...this way...!' they yelled.

There were *bures* still standing but on the edge of the village an enormous tree had come down, crushing a house beneath it.

'Whose house is it?' Maya asked. 'Is anyone missing?'

'We can't find Tevita.' Pete, the groundsman who'd made the call for help, was here. He'd managed to push into a section of the foliage but there were thick branches blocking him from getting any further. 'I've called someone at the resort to see if he went to find Ana, but someone else thought he was with his grandparents, Lani and Josefa, helping them pack what they needed to go to the church. We can't find them either. They never made it to the church. And...this is their house.'

The tree was massive, a Pacific kauri that was probably over a hundred years old. It had been growing on the outskirts of the village but it was tall enough for the mass of foliage and branches on the top of a clean trunk to totally engulf the house.

The headlights of the quadbike were shining on broken branches creating sharp barriers within a mass of the leathery, dark foliage. Or were they the beams that might have been holding up the roof of the *bure*?

'I've got a chainsaw in the trailer,' Maya told him.

Pete had it going only minutes later. He started cutting sections of branches and there were willing hands to carry the logs away. These were people without any protective clothing or hard hats on and they should be seeking shelter in the church with the other villagers, but how could Eli order them away?

There were people they loved somewhere under that tree, potentially injured amongst the wreckage of their home.

And one of them was a boy who wasn't much older than Simon.

'What can I do?' Eli asked Maya. 'How can I help?'

* * *

More people had gathered, including Jackie, one of the nurses from the medical centre, who held a raincoat around herself as she braced against the relentless wind and rain.

'Mike said to tell you that Ma'afu's doing well.' She had to raise her voice above the noise of the extreme weather and the chainsaw being used. 'The bleeding has slowed down and his breathing is better. The oxygen levels are almost normal.' She watched Maya fastening the knee pads around her legs. 'Do I need some of those?'

Maya shook her head. 'It's not safe out here,' she told her. 'You can be more help by going into the church and looking after anyone in there who's injured. I imagine there's quite a few people with cuts and bruises by now. We're trying to carve a passage through the tree branches to get to this house and I'll probably need to crawl so that's why I need the pads. I've got Eli here if we need to treat anybody, but if you find anything you're not comfortable to deal with yourself, send someone to let us know and he can come and help.'

'Take one of the first aid kits for now,' Eli added, handing her a small backpack. 'There are plenty of bandages and dressings in here.'

'Where's the church?'

Maya could see someone she recognised coming towards them, leaning into the gusts of wind.

'Timi can show you.'

But Timi had something to say first. 'They're in the church,' he said. 'Lani and Josefa.'

'Oh, thank goodness for that. Are they okay?'

'Josefa has cut his hand, that's all.'

'Take Jackie back to the church with you. She can look after him. What about Tevita?'

Timi shook his head. 'They don't know where he is. Lani thinks he might have gone to try and find Ana at the resort.'

The sound of the chainsaw stopped as Timi and Jackie turned to run back down the track. Pete emerged from the remaining foliage a few seconds later.

'I can see into part of the house,' he told them. 'But I can't get closer. There are big branches that come straight from the trunk and if I cut there might not be enough to stop it all coming further down onto the house.'

'It's good that you stopped,' Maya said. 'We may not need to do any more here. Josefa and Lani are safe at the church.'

'Are they?' Pete looked surprised. 'When I stopped the chainsaw, I thought I could hear someone calling. Maybe it was the wind?'

Or maybe it was Tevita.

Maya radioed Mike to update him on the situation and to ask if there'd been any sign of Tevita at the resort.

'No,' he said grimly. 'Ana thinks he would have stayed with his grandparents.'

'He might be trapped in the house, then,' Maya said. 'I'll have to go and have a look. We can't give up until we know where he is.'

'Be careful...' Mike sounded worried.

'Roger that.'

Maya tightened the strap on her hard hat and clipped her radio back to her belt.

Looking up to make sure Eli also had his radio, she caught the look on his face.

The fear…

For her?

It gave her heart a squeeze that hurt. But it also gave her a strength that was more than she could ever have found on her own.

'I know what I'm doing,' she reassured him. 'I've done a lot of search and rescue training.'

Not that it had covered an event precisely like this, but she had learned about how to approach a building collapse or other situations where the safety of rescuers depended on the stability of structures or vehicles. Maybe the branches of this enormous tree were working like the struts that protocols might have called for and they would keep her safe.

Oddly, it did feel safer as she went into the tunnel Pete had created. It was suddenly a little quieter in here. More sheltered. But it was still frightening. She could hear the creaking of the branches high above her and feel the snap of something breaking under her boots. At any moment she knew she might hear the cracking sound of a huge branch unable to take the weight of what it was supporting and it was highly unlikely she would have enough time to avoid being crushed. She glanced behind her, to reassure herself that she had an escape available, but what she saw was anything but reassuring.

'Eli…what are you *doing*?'

She didn't want Eli to be involved in what could be an unpredictably dangerous action. It was unthinkable to imagine him being seriously injured. Killed, even?

'Go back,' she ordered sharply. 'I have no idea how safe this is.'

'Keep going,' was all he said. 'There's no time to waste.'

But she hesitated for just another heartbeat. Because she remembered the fear she'd seen in his eyes only moments ago. The fear for her safety. The fear she was feeling for him because...because she loved him *this* much.

Did this mean that Eli loved her that much, too?

The thought barely formed before it was gone. They both heard the faint cry of someone calling for help.

'Tevita?' Maya pushed forward. She got to the big branch that Pete had told her about, but she could see that there was enough of a gap to squeeze underneath it. Just. Then there were smaller branches to push past and she felt one of them flick back against her cheek hard enough to make it sting. There was something different underfoot now, however, and the torch on her helmet showed her that it was the thick, thatched plant material used for the walls and roofs of the local *bures*. Ahead of her, amongst more broken pieces of thatched panels, she could see the colours of a flower-patterned fabric and it looked like a sarong being used as a bedcover. Beside the mattress, hunched on the ground, she could see the lanky limbs of a boy barely into his teens, his face tear-streaked and completely terrified, but at least he was conscious and alert.

'Tevita...' She was beside him in moments. 'It's okay... we're going to get you out of here.'

She needed to check that he wasn't hurt, but she took a moment to put her arm around his shoulders to comfort him because she could see him shaking with fear. 'It's okay,' she said again. 'Eli's here too.'

He was. Right here beside them, and it almost felt as if he'd put his arm around her shoulders.

'Does anything hurt, Tevita?' Eli asked.

Tevita nodded. 'My leg,' he said. 'I can't move it. I fell over when…when the tree came down.'

He had his leg bent and his lower legs were bare beneath his shorts. Maya could see a large, distinct lump on one side of it.

'Looks like he's dislocated his patella,' she said. 'I don't think it's a knee dislocation, though. There's no gross deformity of the knee joint.'

Eli nodded. He was using his torch to scan the rest of Tevita's body as well, however. 'Did you hit your head?' he asked.

'No.'

'Can you take a deep breath? Does it hurt?'

'No.'

'What about your tummy?'

'It's just my leg. It really hurts…'

'Can you wriggle your foot?'

'No.'

'Can you feel me touching it?'

'Yes.'

Maya caught Eli's gaze. 'We can't move him with his leg bent and knee locked like this.'

'Let's give him some pain relief and see if we can reduce it.'

Maya opened the pack to find what she needed as Eli explained to Tevita what they were going to do.

'You've dislocated your kneecap,' he said, 'which means it's in a place that's stopping you from being able to move your leg. We're going to put it back by straightening your leg.'

'No…' The sound was almost a sob. 'That will hurt even more.'

'Maya's getting something ready for you that will stop it hurting too much. And it will feel a lot better afterwards. We have to be quick, though, Tevita. It's not safe for any of us in here. Can you be brave and help us?'

Maya glanced up to see that Eli had his hand on Tevita's shoulder and the boy's gaze was fixed on his. She could almost feel the bond of trust that had somehow been created between the two of them in the space of such a short time.

'Yes...' Tevita said.

Maya had poured methoxyflurane into the base of an inhaler. 'We call this a green whistle,' she told Tevita. 'You breathe in and out with your mouth on the green bit and it won't hurt when we straighten your leg. Okay? It won't take long.'

Tevita nodded. He closed his lips around the mouthpiece of the inhaler and breathed in cautiously. The second time he took a deeper breath.

Maya looked at Eli. 'Ready?'

He nodded. He held Tevita's lower leg while she palpated the edge of the patella.

'On your count,' Eli told her.

'Suck hard on the whistle,' Maya advised Tevita. She waited until he was taking a really deep breath of the analgesic. 'On three,' she said to Eli. 'One...two...*three*...'

Eli lifted Tevita's foot to straighten his leg. As he did so, Maya pushed the side of the patella to shift it back to the front of the knee where it belonged.

'Take another big breath, Tevita. You're doing really, really well...'

She lifted it slightly to help it over the ridge on the end of the femur and she could feel the clunk as the dislocation was reduced.

'Ooh…' The sound Tevita made was one of relief. 'That feels better.'

'We're going to put a bandage on it,' Eli told him. 'And then we're going to get you out of here. You'll need an X-ray to make sure you haven't broken any of the bones in your knee.'

The sound of something cracking overhead reminded them that the sooner they were out of here, the better. There was no time to try and get better access and use a stretcher but, with his leg straightened and the knee well bandaged, Tevita was able to crawl and they got him out of the wreckage of the house and into the foliage of the tree. It was harder getting under the big branch but there were others in the tunnel now, wanting to help. Eli had radioed Pete to get the scoop stretcher from the trailer and once Tevita was inside it they could slide him out the rest of the way with ease.

They got out into clear space to find that the wind had dropped noticeably and the rain was much lighter.

'It could be the eye of the cyclone,' Eli said. 'Which might mean it'll pick up again soon, but this is good. We can get Tevita to the medical centre.'

Strong men were waiting to lift the stretcher and put it into the back of a four-wheel drive station wagon from the village. Tevita's grandfather was already in the vehicle, his bandaged hand in a sling.

'You go with them,' Maya suggested to Eli, when they'd loaded the stretcher. 'I'll drive the ATV back when I've checked on how Jackie's going in the church. I need to find out whether anyone else is unaccounted for. This will be the best time to look for them if we need to.'

But Eli shook his head. 'I'll come with you. Mike's on

standby to give Tevita an X-ray and check for any other injuries so I'm not needed there at the moment. I don't want you driving anywhere by yourself. We can't know if or when the wind's going to get worse again. Or how bad it's going to be.'

It was over an hour later that they left the church. Every one of the villagers had been checked. Some superficial wounds had been cleaned and dressed. They made sure that people who had conditions like diabetes, asthma or heart problems had any medication they might need on hand. Jackie would stay with the group until morning. Both she and Pete had radios to call for help if they ran into any trouble.

People were anxious but none of them wanted to leave their village and go to the resort for shelter. They were in a well-built, solid structure and they had mattresses and blankets and food and, most importantly, each other. There were animals being kept safe as well. Pet dogs and chickens in crates.

'Where are the ponies?' Eli asked. 'Are they safe?'

'They've been through storms before,' Pete told him. 'Their paddocks are tucked in behind the mountain and they know where to find the best shelter. We'll go and check on them as soon as it's safe. This might get worse before it gets better but I have a feeling it will have all blown over by morning.'

'Let's hope so,' Eli said.

'Call if you need us,' Maya said. 'I'll come back at first light tomorrow, but are you okay for us to go back to the resort now? I think that Simon will be wanting to see that his dad is safe and we both want to check on how Ma'afu's doing.'

'Go.' Pete nodded. 'We'll be fine. Go now, before it gets any worse out there.'

They climbed into the ATV and it was only then, as a fresh gust of wind swept Maya's hair away from her face, that Eli saw the streak of dried blood on her cheek, near her ear.

Oh, *man*...

That knot in his gut that formed faster than the speed of light at the thought of Maya being injured. It should have been a warning but it was too late, wasn't it? He'd known he still cared deeply about her—okay, *loved* her—but he'd shied away from the idea of being *in* love with her so successfully it hadn't occurred to him that it had happened all over again. In fact, he realised, it probably hadn't.

This felt too familiar.

It felt like coming home.

He'd never *stopped* being in love with her, had he?

Whatever had buried that intensity of how he felt about her had simply disappeared. Blown away by the same deadly winds that had blown the tree down onto the house they'd just crawled into together?

'You've hurt yourself,' he exclaimed, reaching up to touch Maya's face.

'It's nothing. Just a scratch.'

But he didn't take his hand away. He leaned closer.

'We should get going,' Maya said. 'Simon needs you.' But she didn't start up the quadbike. She was leaning into his hand, turning her face so that it was cupped in his fingers. She was looking up at him at the same time and it was a look that he could have fallen into if he let himself.

He wanted to tell her that he still loved her.

He wanted to tell her that everything was going to be okay and that they would find a way through this but, right now, it was more important that they got going. They needed to get back to the safety of the resort before the wind and rain picked up again. This was something he could actually do to keep Maya safe.

He took just a moment, however, to grab what could be the only time they might have alone together for a while.

To do this...

To kiss her with a fierceness that might let her know just how much he loved her.

She was kissing him back with a need that felt tinged with something poignant. Sadness, even?

He knew why. He'd felt the tacit agreement that this couldn't be allowed to mean too much when Simon was going to need his dad more than ever as he approached adolescence. When he was already feeling insecure.

No...he couldn't promise that everything was going to be okay, could he?

Not yet...

CHAPTER TEN

ELI SCRAMBLED OUT of the ATV as soon as Maya pulled it to a standstill outside the doors of the medical centre as they got back to the resort.

'I'll be back to join the medical team in a minute,' he said. 'I just need a moment to check on Simon first.'

Maya nodded. Of course he did. She saw him running to the main dining room and conference area that made the U shape around the swimming pool. It was late enough for all the children to be asleep by now but Simon might well still be awake, worried about his father being out in the storm.

While the strength of the wind and rain had increased since they'd left the village, it didn't feel quite as frightening as it had earlier this evening. Was it subsiding into a tropical storm rather than a cyclone? Was she simply getting used to it?

The way she was getting used to the idea that she and Eli could never be more than friends?

That kiss they'd just shared, though...

It hadn't felt like it was coming from nothing more than friendship.

But maybe that was just wishful thinking.

What was it that Eli had said when she'd told him that Simon might have seen them kissing on the beach?

Oh, yeah...

'Kissing someone doesn't automatically mean you're in a significant relationship...'

Seeing Mike through the window of the treatment room, Maya tapped on the door and went inside. Mike was working alone, stitching the cut on Josefa's hand. He glanced up briefly.

'All good?'

'Yes. We've left Jackie and Pete in charge at the village and they've both got radios so they can contact us. Everyone's accounted for, either in the church or here at the resort, and I said I'd go back at daybreak to check on them. I have a feeling that the worst will be over by then.'

Mike nodded. 'Yes...the latest report from the Meteorological Service has downgraded Cyclone Lily to a tropical storm. We're still waiting to see what the storm surge will be like at high tide and we don't want anyone outside sightseeing first thing tomorrow. Okay, Josefa... that local anaesthetic should be working by now. Can you feel me touching your hand?'

'No.'

Mike picked up a suture from the tray beside him, taking another glance at Maya at the same time.

'You okay? What's happened to your cheek?'

'It's nothing. Just a scratch. I'm good.'

'I heard about you rescuing Tevita from under the tree.' Mike was carefully inserting a stitch below skin level in the deep cut Josefa had at the base of his thumb. 'Well done, you. And Eli.'

The swift glance was a silent question. Had she been

okay, working under such fraught conditions with someone that she might find it difficult to be that close to?

Maya's smile was intended to reassure him. She was
strong. She could handle this.

'How's Ma'afu?' she asked.

'Sore, but breathing pretty well. We've done an X-ray
to check that the chest drain is in the best place—and
it is. Eli did a good job. He's got a few broken ribs, but
the internal bleeding seems to have stopped. We'll need
to keep a careful eye on him until we can transfer him
to hospital. We've cleaned up his head wound but we're
watching for any signs of concussion or TBI.'

'And Tevita?'

'He's also had an X-ray. He's lucky—he seems to have
escaped getting an osteochondral fracture. Ana's in with
him now.'

'She's a good girl,' Josefa put in. 'She's been like a
mother to him since they came to live with us here.'

'I remember when that happened. It was our first year
of holding the camp.' Five years ago, when Josefa and
Lani's only daughter, a single mother who'd been living
in Suva, sadly died.

Five years but it felt like yesterday. It was ten years
since she'd felt as if she had a future with Eli but that,
too, suddenly felt as though she'd only just lost sight of
it. She could feel that loss all over again.

Because of that kiss?

Mike was closing the wound at skin level now, with a
few neat sutures. Maya picked up the package holding a
sterile dressing and peeled it open so Mike could take it
when the last suture had been placed and knotted.

Mike was doing exactly that when there was a tap on

the door of the treatment room and it was opened enough for Eli to peer in. His hair was wet enough to be dripping water. Why had he been outside when he could get from the conference area to the medical centre through an internal corridor?

Something didn't feel right.

'Sorry to interrupt,' Eli said. 'But you haven't seen Simon around here, have you?'

Maya's heart skipped a beat at the note in Eli's voice. 'Wasn't he with all the other kids?'

'No.' Eli sounded like he was determined to stay calm. 'He wasn't on his mattress or in the bathroom. Carlos said he hadn't seen him since they all had a game of balloon football in the dining room, before the movie started, but he remembered that he asked one of the camp crew if he knew where I was. Carlos thought he might have come here to see if I'd got back from the village but he's not in the waiting room or the office.'

'Could he have gone to your *bure*?' Maya suggested.

'I'll go there next. I wouldn't have thought he'd want to go out into that weather, though.' He sucked in an audible breath. 'I'd better find Ana. She might know something.'

'She's with Tevita,' Mike told him. He smoothed the dressing on Josefa's hand and picked up a gauze bandage. 'Go with him,' he said quietly to Maya as Eli disappeared. 'He needs you.'

Ana was horrified to learn that Simon wasn't with the other children.

'He was there when I got the news that Tevita and Grandpapa were being brought here. He promised he'd go straight to bed after they had the hot chocolate and

marshmallows that the chefs were making for everyone.'
Ana had tears gathering in her eyes. 'I shouldn't have left
him. I'm so sorry…'

'You needed to be with your family,' Eli told her. 'This
isn't your fault, Ana. Simon knew where he was supposed
to be. I don't understand why he made a promise he didn't
keep. What was he doing when you last saw him?'

'He'd just finished watching the movie they'd put on in
the dining room and he'd been sorting through his scavenger hunt basket again. He was kind of disappointed
that he hadn't found everything on the list, you know?
He thought he might have won a prize if he had.' Ana
bit her lip. 'I think he wanted something special to show
you, Dr Peters. He always tries so hard at everything because he wants you to be proud of him.'

Eli felt a chill run down his spine.

The pieces were suddenly coming together.

The fragments of old fears had morphed into the birth
of new ones. The need to protect the people he loved and
the guilt of not having done it well enough.

And every piece had something to do with Maya,
didn't it?

It had been Maya who had persuaded Eli to let Simon
do the climbing activities he wanted to do. Not just on
the relatively safe climbing wall but on a real cliff.

Simon might have seen him kissing Maya on the beach.

He'd definitely heard that panicked message come
across the radio about the tree coming down on a house
and he'd listened to his father telling him that he had to go
with Maya because people might be hurt and she might
need him to help her. He'd left without a backward glance,

hadn't he? He'd gone to try and protect Maya when he should have stayed here and looked after Simon.

Had Simon been worried that he'd been left behind? Had he somehow convinced himself that an old girlfriend might be more important than a son who didn't feel 'real' and could therefore be left behind for ever? That if Eli could leave him behind at camp so easily, maybe he *could* leave him behind to go as far as Australia?

The prospect of being abandoned would have been even more frightening in the middle of a storm.

Eli turned to Maya. She was pale. Her eyes were reflecting his own fear that he was desperately trying to control.

His voice sounded hollow. 'He might have tried to follow us to the village. He knew that was where I was going with you.'

'I'll get Mike,' she said. 'We'll find him, Eli...'

He started to follow her but had to pause to take a ragged breath. The fear was getting harder to control.

Maybe Simon hadn't gone looking for him at all. Had he, in fact, run away in a different direction because he was convinced that Eli wanted to be in a relationship with Maya again? That he might be in the way?

Why hadn't he taken the time to reassure him properly?

Simon had been his priority since the moment he'd picked him up into his arms after he'd arrived back in London to be by Sarah's bedside. Since he'd promised his sister that he would always look after her precious baby.

Nothing could be allowed to come between himself and Simon.

Not even Maya.

And the only thing that mattered right now was to find Simon.

'I'll contact Pete,' was the first thing Mike said as came out of the treatment room. 'He can start looking around the village. I'll get people here to search the resort.' He held Eli's gaze. 'You need to check your *bure* and...' He was frowning now. 'If he's not there, check the beach. It's close to your *bure* and it's possible that Simon couldn't find his way in the dark. We need to make sure he's nowhere near the waves that might come in at high tide.'

'I'll come with you,' Maya said.

But Eli was already turning away. This was his son. His responsibility. He couldn't let himself be distracted in any way. How could he try and protect Maya and Simon at the same time without being torn in two, knowing how he felt about Maya but knowing that he had to do what was best for Simon?

It was only the commanding tone in Mike's voice that made him turn back.

'Don't go alone,' he ordered. 'Take Maya with you.'

It felt like Eli didn't want her to be here with him.

If she let it, it might feel as if the last ten years had been peeled away to reveal that she was still in love with Eli but he didn't feel the same way, but the fear that she could be facing the same rejection that had nearly destroyed her all those years ago had to be pushed aside. This was about Simon. A gorgeous boy with an adventurous spirit and so much courage. A vulnerable child who might well be in danger.

They *had* to find him.

There was no sign that he had gone to the *bure* he'd been sharing with Eli.

'Nothing's been touched since we came in here to get the things he'd need for the sleepover,' Eli said. 'If he *was* looking for me, he would have come here or to the medical centre.'

'Or tried to get to the village,' Maya added. 'Except...'

'What?' The prompt to continue was sharp.

'It was what he was doing when Ana last saw him.'

'Looking through that basket? Being disappointed that he wasn't going to get a special prize for finding everything in the scavenger hunt?' Eli's voice was raw. 'So that I'd be proud of him and not leave him behind when I went off to Australia with you...'

'We'll find him,' Maya promised, even though she knew she had no right to be so sure. 'What if he's gone off to try and find that ginger flower? So he could get that recognition? The cliff's not that far away.'

'I don't even know where it is.' Eli sounded angry now. 'I should have been with him. For the abseiling and the scavenger hunt. The only thing I've done with him properly was that sandcastle competition. I feel like I've let him down completely.'

'You haven't let him down at all,' Maya said. 'He's had a great time, Eli—and you gave him the freedom to let him try things he's never been allowed to do before. Like the pony riding. And the abseiling. He's loved everything he's done here. He knew you'd see the photos of him on that cliff and be proud of him. He knows how much you love him. It's me that's the problem. He doesn't want to share you.' She caught her breath. 'It's because of me he's run away, isn't it? Because of...*us*...'

The answer to her question was in his eyes. There was something like an apology there as well. Because, even if he did still love her, he would never do anything that could harm Simon in any way. Maya got that. She wouldn't allow Simon to be hurt either. She cared deeply about every child she met at camp but this one was also the son of the man she loved and that took her concern to a whole new, agonising level.

Eli gave a single nod, as if he agreed with her unspoken thought.

'I think you might be right,' he said aloud.

Maya's heart sank even further. This felt like the final blow to any dream she might have had about them being together again. Or the three of them becoming a family.

But Eli was, apparently, agreeing to something else.

'He could have been thinking about that damn flower all evening. Where was it growing? Where is that cliff, exactly?'

'It's part of the headland at the end of the lagoon beach. We need to check the beach anyway so we can go and have a look.'

They made their way to the beach, the light from the powerful torches on their hard hats bouncing as they ran. Eli had a first aid pack on his back that they'd taken from the trailer as they'd left the medical centre and Maya had a heavy coil of rope looped over her shoulder. She sent up a silent prayer that any loose coconuts had already been blown from the trees in the first hours of this storm as they went under the crescent of palm trees that framed the lagoon beach.

The beach couldn't have been any different to her first day at camp this year. The day she'd seen Eli again for the first time after so many years. She'd been walking down here at daybreak with the wind no more than a delightful tropical breeze and the only waves way out on the reef. She'd had no idea what lay ahead of her when Mike had told her that he'd scored the perfect member for their medical team at this year's camp—an emergency medicine consultant who had a special interest in paediatrics. Someone who'd been persuaded to come because his son qualified to be a camp attendee due to his Type A haemophilia. When she'd had no idea that she was about to find herself face to face with the man she'd loved so much and then lost so long ago.

Now, it felt as if her entire world was a very different place, emotionally as well as physically. The wind was still strong enough to make it hard to stay upright and there were waves that were coming so far up the beach from the lagoon that Maya had to jump out of the way of the foam. She stumbled then, on a coconut perhaps or a piece of driftwood, or maybe it was the gust of wind that made her lose her balance and fall. Eli's gesture to hold out his hand and help her up was automatic but he didn't let go of it as they ran along the beach and the squeeze on her heart was just as powerful as the wind.

'Simon…' Maya cupped one hand to her mouth and called again. '*Si*-mon…'

They kept shouting for Simon, although they both knew that even if he was really close he wouldn't hear them. Was the thought that he might hear them—and call back—the real reason for doing it? Because it gave them hope?

'*Si*-mon…' Eli's voice was getting a bit hoarse. 'Where are you?'

They were at the end of the beach now. The tumble of rocks was directly in front of them but Maya knew the track that would take them higher, through trees and shrubs to the side of the rocks and onto the wide ledge that provided such a good base for the cliff they used for their beginner abseiling sessions.

Simon had thought he'd seen a ginger plant growing on the path that continued up the steep slope, on the other side of the ledge, that they used to get to the top of the cliff and then abseil down. In daylight, the start of that path also provided a view down to the next bay past the lagoon. This was a beach that was open to the sea and it had waves so it was used for teaching children who wanted to learn to surf or bodyboard. Maya couldn't see the beach but she could hear waves that were big enough to be crashing onto the foot of the rocky outcrop that formed the barrier between this beach and the resort's lagoon.

Looking down made the beam of light from the torch on Maya's helmet catch the spray from a wave that was reaching high enough to be metres above the hidden beach and it looked thick enough to mimic a snowstorm. If a storm surge made the waves any higher than they were right now, this ledge that they used for the abseiling would be in danger of being undermined and possibly washed away. The edges already looked dodgy...

'Oh, my God...' Maya froze.

'What?' Eli was right behind her. The additional strength of his torchlight made what Maya was looking at even clearer. A small figure clinging onto the rocks below the ledge. The sky-blue camp tee shirt with the yellow circle and the palm tree on the front. A pale, terrified face was looking up at them, but Simon was trying to shield his eyes from the bright light.

The sound Eli made was almost a growl. He tried to step past Maya and get out onto the ledge but she put her arm out to stop him.

'No—' Her tone was urgent.

Her body was awash with adrenaline and it made her thoughts go so fast she could barely catch them.

The thought of Eli going onto that ledge and having it crumble—of him falling onto the rocks and hitting his head or, worse, losing him for ever because he'd been washed into a vicious sea was unbelievably horrific.

Dear Lord…had this been how Eli felt whenever she'd done something challenging enough to be risky? Did he have to fight feeling like that every time he let Simon do something that might not be absolutely safe—like going on a climbing wall? She'd had *no* idea how overwhelming it could be.

The thoughts were there and then gone in the space of a blink.

'You can't go anywhere near the edge, Eli.' Her words were even more of a command than Mike had given him to make sure he wasn't out here alone. 'You're too heavy. You'd end up down on the rocks. Or in the sea.' She tried to aim her torch at Simon's feet rather than directly into his face. 'Simon?' She shouted as loudly as she could, after a wave had broken and before the next could start. 'Can you hear me, sweetheart?'

She could see him nod his head in the edge of the beam of light.

'I'm coming down to get you, okay?'

'No...' Eli sounded distraught. 'I can't just stay here and do nothing.'

'You won't be doing nothing.' Maya was uncoiling the rope she'd been carrying. 'I want you at the back of the ledge, right beside the cliff. Don't go anywhere near the edge. You're going to hold the end of this rope after I find a rock to wrap it around.'

'It's not enough. I need to—'

Maya cut him off. 'This is *the* most important thing you *can* do,' she told him fiercely. 'Just being there, holding on, will be what it takes to keep both of us safe.'

A rope around her waist was nothing like as safe as wearing a harness but it was better than nothing. Maya went over the edge of this flat ledge, well away from being above Simon, knowing that she could be dislodging a shower of small rocks and dirt. She got down to the top of a huge boulder and then stopped to look around in the hope of finding a way down to the next step in this outcrop but, without the proper gear and safety measures, there was nothing she could see that was anywhere near safe enough to try. She looped the rope around a jagged cone of rock and lay down on her stomach to look over the much rounder top of this weathered boulder. She was so much closer to Simon. If she stretched out her arm, she could almost touch him.

But it wasn't close enough.

'It's okay,' she called out. 'I'm going to get you out of here. Are you hurt?'

It looked as if Simon was crying. He said something that Maya couldn't hear but, even though he was clearly terrified, he was listening. He pushed himself to stand up so, if he *was* hurt, at least it wasn't badly enough to stop him being able to move.

'Can you do something for me, Si?' Maya didn't wait for an answer. 'Do you remember that day you first did the climbing wall?'

His nod was dubious.

'Can you see the lump of rock just in front of you? Like a step?'

He was looking in the right direction.

'And just above your shoulder, there's another rock. Can you put your foot on the step and reach up for that rock with your hand?'

Slowly, Simon followed the instructions she was shouting. Maya held her breath. She tried not to imagine how dangerous a gust of wind or a sudden shower of sea spray could be. It seemed as if the wind had dropped, but who knew how long that could last?

'Good job,' she told Simon. 'It's just like the climbing wall. There's another bit that's going to be just right for a step, but don't let go with your hands just yet. I'll shine my torch on where your foot needs to go.'

Simon was hesitating.

'You can do this,' she called. 'Pretend it's the climbing wall, Si, and your dad's watching you. And...' Maya could feel her heart breaking a little '...he's *so* proud of you...'

Yes... Simon was moving sideways. Feeling for the foothold. Getting closer.

'Let go with your left hand and reach up.' Maya was leaning down as far as she could. 'Catch my hand...'

There was a split second where Simon seemed to hang in space and then Maya felt the touch of his fingers and slid her hand past them to wrap around his wrist. He felt so light as she pulled him up. So fragile. So precious. She wriggled them both back from the edge of the boulder so that she could wrap her arms around him. The wind and rain and crashing surf beneath them became almost irrelevant as she focused for just a breath or two on trying to offer this child some warmth. And love. Trying to make him feel safe.

'Does anything hurt?'

Simon was shivering too hard to speak. But he was hanging on to her with a grip that was strong enough to let her know it was safe to try and get them both back to the ledge.

'Don't let go,' she said against his ear. 'Dad's waiting for us. Just up here...'

It had probably only taken five minutes from when Eli had positioned himself beside the cliff to be the anchor on the rope to when he saw Maya and Simon climb back onto the ledge but it had felt like the longest period of time he'd ever had to survive. It was only when his lungs started burning that he remembered to stop holding his breath and fill them with oxygen again.

Maya was putting her life on the line to save his son. He was so afraid for her but so incredibly proud of her at the same time. This was who she was and he wouldn't want to change a thing about this woman he loved so much.

He was so afraid for Simon, too.

And...he was afraid for himself. Because how could he go on without either of the people he loved this much in his life? Nothing would ever feel complete. He would never feel whole.

The moment when he saw them appear almost undid him. When he could let go of the rope and scoop Simon into his arms he had no idea what percentage of the rain running down his face was actually tears. He held Simon close with one arm and used his other arm to bring Maya closer.

He held them tightly. He'd never felt this relieved in his life. This grateful. He never wanted to let either of them go. Ever. And yet hadn't he just realised that he would never want to change a thing about what made Maya the person she was? Trying too hard to protect the people he loved carried the risk of stopping them being who they wanted to be. Who they really were.

It was a moment of astonishing clarity. The way he was feeling in this moment, as if every one of his senses was at maximum capacity, was like nothing he'd ever felt before.

He could feel the warmth of the bodies so close to his own and the chill of the dying wind around them. He could smell, and taste, the sea spray in the air. He could hear the sniffle of Simon trying not to cry and, was it his imagination or could he see—in Maya's eyes—a depth of love that made his heart feel as if it was about to explode?

Was this simply the joy of being alive?

Was the flip side of extreme fear an exhilaration like no other?

And had he, in fact, been stopping himself from being the person *he* really was because he'd given fear too much power? Had his anxiety about the safety of the people he cared most about become a kind of white noise that was stopping him from being able to feel what it was like to be really alive?

To feel like *this*?

Not being able to feel every nuance of the best that life could offer was too high a price to pay for not having to feel the worst that could—but might actually never—happen.

There was a new message in Maya's eyes now. They needed to get back to shelter. Back to the medical centre where they could make sure Simon was really safe. Eli could feel him shivering and being too cold, on top of being on the flip side of feeling far too frightened, could easily be masking the signs and symptoms of injury.

'Let's go,' he said, matching his words with movement.

Simon's head jerked up. 'Maya's coming too, isn't she?'

'She sure is.' Eli hadn't quite broken that eye contact with Maya. 'She's showing us the way.'

CHAPTER ELEVEN

WRAPPED IN THE foil survival blanket from the first aid kit, Simon looked as if he had fallen asleep in his father's arms by the time they got back to the medical centre. Mike had the treatment room ready and well heated.

'I've got a bucket of ice from the kitchens,' he told Eli. 'And the storm's definitely blowing through. If we need to get Simon to the main island for imaging we can't do here, we should be able to have the helicopter available by midday.'

But that was still hours away and Maya knew how worried Eli had to be. She felt sick with worry herself.

'Your Factor VIII supplies are in the fridge here, aren't they?'

'Yes. Could you find the testing kit, please, Maya? It looks like a blood glucose monitoring kit.'

He was putting Simon down gently onto the bed and, to her relief, she saw that he was looking more awake, but she knew that a head injury and brain bleed was the most serious injury someone with haemophilia could suffer. It could be fatal.

Eli wasn't showing any sign of the stress he had to be under, however. He was so warm and reassuring with

Simon that Maya was starting to believe that everything was going to be okay.

Everything.

Even whatever was going to happen—or not happen—between herself and Eli?

She handed the small, zipped pouch to Eli and then helped position the pillows and tuck warm blankets around Simon. He pricked the end of one of Simon's fingers and collected the drop of blood onto the test strip.

'This will let us know what level of Factor VIII he's got on board but we'll need to start an infusion if there's any sign of injury. We'll need to get his levels to at least fifty percent of normal in that case.'

'I didn't know you could do a finger prick test for Factor VIII.'

'And thrombin on this one. We're part of an international trial for home testing monitors. The technology is getting more reliable all the time.' Eli put the test meter down and shone a pen torch across Simon's eyes, to check pupil sizes and reactions.

'Did you get knocked out?' he asked.

'No. I remember everything. I dropped my torch and it rolled over the edge and when I tried to see where it had gone, a big bit of dirt broke off. I was kind of sitting on it as we went down.'

'Like a surfboard?' Maya asked. 'That was a smart move, Si.'

Not that it had been intentional, of course, but the cushioning could well have saved him from far more serious injuries.

'So you didn't hit your head at all?' Eli's fingers were in the damp spikes of Simon's hair that had been quickly towel dried to try and help warm him up. Maya could almost feel that gentle touch herself.

'I don't think so.'

'Does anything hurt anywhere else? Can you take a deep breath?'

Simon pulled in a huge breath. 'My tummy kind of hurts. And my elbow…'

Maya was careful not to let her expression change. Internal bleeding was another big thing to worry about. And bleeding into a joint could have lasting effects on movement and function.

She watched Eli unwrap the blankets around Simon and help take his shorts off. As he passed them to Maya, something fell out of the pocket. Something red.

'Oh—' she exclaimed, stooping to pick up the long, and very squashed, bloom. 'You did find a ginger flower, Si. You'll be the only person who found everything for the scavenger hunt.'

'I didn't get it for that,' he said. 'Ow…that hurts, Dad.'

'Sorry, buddy. You've got a big bruise coming up on your hip.'

Was the blood below his skin there coming from an internal injury—like trauma to his liver?

Eli flattened his hand and pressed gently on the different quadrants of Simon's abdomen. 'Tell me if anything hurts,' he instructed.

Maya could see that familiar vertical line of concentration on Eli's face. She wanted to distract Simon in case he interpreted it as concern that his father was finding something seriously wrong with him.

'You did so well, climbing up off those rocks,' she told

him. 'You remembered everything you learned on the climbing wall, didn't you?'

'It was scary,' Simon confessed.

'Of course it was.' Maya nodded. 'But you were really brave.'

'I'm glad I didn't lose the flower.'

Maya shook her head. 'Why did you go looking for it, if it wasn't to finish off your scavenger basket?'

His eyes looked too big in a very pale face. 'I wanted to find it for you,' he said.

'For *me*?'

'Ana said it was a special flower because it got used when people get married in Fiji. And you said it was one of your favourite flowers.'

'It is. I love that you wanted to get me one, but...' Maya's gaze flew to Eli's. Was this another reason why she could blame herself for Simon hurting himself?

Eli's glance told her not to.

'You shouldn't have gone out in the storm, Si,' he said. 'You know that, don't you?'

'Yes.' Simon's voice was small. 'I'm sorry, Dad...'

'I know...' Eli touched his son's face. 'I'm sorry, too. I should have been there to take care of you.'

But Simon shook his head. 'You were taking care of other people and that's your job. I'm not a little kid any more. I *can* take care of myself.'

'I know you can.' Eli smoothed the spikes of hair off Simon's forehead. 'And you don't ever need to collect any special prizes, you know. I couldn't be more proud of you than I already am.'

It felt like a very private moment between a father and

his son. It was enough to create a lump in Maya's throat that felt far too big to swallow.

Eli looked like he was blinking back a tear himself as he shifted his gaze to Mike. 'Can we get a cold pack to go on that bruised hip?'

'Coming right up.'

Eli moved on with this rapid but thorough initial survey.

'We'll need one for this elbow, too. And a compression bandage.'

Mike had started bandaging the bruised elbow as Eli got ready to set up an infusion. The only other finding had been found a bumped knee that was painful to bend, which would need the same treatment of rest, ice, compression and elevation. With all vital sign measurements stable and normal enough to suggest that Simon had somehow avoided an injury that could be causing serious, unseen internal bleeding, the level of tension in the room was beginning to decrease noticeably.

An hour later, with better levels of Factor VIII, thanks to the infusion, some pain relief and being tucked up in a warm, comfortable bed, all Simon wanted to do was to go to sleep and his eyes were drifting shut.

Mike was back with Ma'afu and Tevita. Danny and James, the helicopter pilots, were in the office, getting updates on the improving weather conditions and planning the first flights to evacuate their patients as soon as they were given clearance.

The first fingers of light in a murky dawn could be seen through the high windows of the treatment room.

'I'll have to go back to the village soon,' Maya told Eli. 'I promised I would.'

'I'll stay with Simon. It's time I refreshed those cold packs on his bruising and I want to check his Factor VIII levels again.'

Maya was trying to make her feet move and take her towards the door but they weren't co-operating.

She wanted to stay with Simon as well. To watch him like a hawk for any sign of his condition deteriorating. To be near Eli because she knew how much of his concern he was keeping carefully hidden.

No...actually, she just wanted to be near Eli.

Taking this step away from him now might be the first of countless steps that would see them on the opposite sides of the world again.

In the end, it was Eli that took a step.

Towards her.

He held out his arms and Maya went into them without hesitation. She felt them wrap around her and pull her close. She could hear—and feel—Eli's heart beating.

'I haven't said thank you,' he said. 'It was you who got him off those rocks. If the tide had come up any further...' His voice trailed off and Maya felt a shudder ripple through his body.

'I couldn't have done it by myself,' Maya said. 'It was Simon who was brave enough to close the distance between us so that I could get hold of him and it wasn't an easy thing to do. He had to find footholds and handholds and make himself move even though he didn't have any safety gear on at all.'

She could feel Eli taking in a deep breath. 'You told me, that day when Simon got into your session at the climbing wall, that it would be better for him to learn how to do something like that safely than to put himself in real danger by trying it when no one was watching. It was only because of you teaching him what to do that he could help get himself off those rocks. You saved his life, Maya. And mine... I would have gone after him if you hadn't stopped me and I wouldn't have known how to do that safely.'

Maya's smile was shaky. 'Maybe you should come to a climbing wall session yourself.'

'Maybe I will. Next time we're here.'

'Are we coming back again, Dad?'

Maya gasped, stepping hurriedly away from Eli, turning towards the bed to find Simon watching them both, his eyes wide open.

'Um...yes, I hope so,' Eli said. 'That is, if you'd like to come back, Si.'

Simon nodded. 'I want to come back. But I'd quite like to go home again, too.'

'We'll go home very soon,' Eli told him. He perched on the side of the bed. 'I need to take you to the hospital and make absolutely sure you're okay. Camp Reki's due to finish soon, anyway.'

'I want to go to Australia, too,' Simon added.

'Really?' Eli sounded cautious. 'For a holiday?'

Simon didn't answer his father. 'Are you going back to Australia, Maya?' he asked.

'Yes. That's where I live.'

'But you used to live in New Zealand.'

'Yes.'

'That's where you lived, isn't it, Dad? When I was a baby?'

'Yes. I've told you that story.' Eli reached out to stroke Simon's hair. 'How I heard about the terrible accident your mum had and I jumped on a plane and came back to England so I could look after you.'

'Did you live with Maya? Because she was your girl-friend?'

Maya could see Eli taking a deep breath. He'd told her he had always been honest with Simon.

'Yes, I did.'

'So why did you leave her behind?'

Maya's eyes widened. So did Eli's. He opened his mouth and then closed it again.

'You told me you'd never leave someone you really loved behind. And...'

Simon was frowning quite fiercely and it reminded Maya of the way Eli looked when he was totally focused on something very important.

'And you really love Maya, don't you?'

'I do.' Eli looked from Simon to Maya. 'I do,' he repeated softly. Solemnly.

She could see the truth of that in his eyes—the glow that was warming her entire body. 'I don't think I ever stopped loving you, Maya.'

Eli's gaze was back on Simon. 'But I love you, too, Si. I always will. That's never, ever going to change, okay?'

Simon ignored that question, too.

'And you love Dad, don't you, Maya?'

'I do,' Maya said. She waited for Eli's gaze to catch her own again. 'I never stopped loving you either.'

'That's why I went to find your favourite flower,' Simon said. 'I wanted you to love *me*, too.'

'Oh, Simon...' Maya went to sit on the other side of the bed so she could hug Simon. Gently, taking care not to bump his bruises. 'You don't have to give me flowers, sweetheart. I *do* love you already.'

'So...' Simon was stifling a huge yawn as he turned to his father again. 'Does that mean I'm going to have a mum *and* a dad?'

Eli caught Maya's gaze over the top of Simon's head. 'I hope so,' he said softly.

Maya couldn't say anything. The words were caught somewhere in her chest but she didn't need to say anything aloud, did she? She could tell Eli just how much she also hoped that was going to happen just by holding that gaze.

And smiling.

They *were* going to find a way to be together. They were going to become a family.

'There's no rush,' Eli added. 'It's a big thing for you to get used to, Si. It's a big thing for us, too. Maybe we'll have that holiday in Australia first.'

'And then we'll come back here.' Simon's eyes were drifting shut again. 'For another camp.'

'We will.'

'And you can get married here.'

'Maybe...'

'Ana says that some people who get married here like to carry a whole bunch of ginger flowers.' Simon's words were getting quieter. 'I might need to find some more...'

He was sound asleep a moment later.

Eli was smiling at Maya. 'Would you like that?'

'A bunch of ginger flowers?' Maya was teasing him. 'Yes, I would. They're one of my favourite flowers, you know.'

'And the rest?' Eli's smile faded. 'I love you, Maya. I

need you in my life. Simon needs you in *his* life. I want to marry you this time. To be with you. For ever.'

This was serious. He was asking about the rest of her life. The rest of *their* lives.

'Oh, yes.' Maya's tone was just as serious. She had no doubt about this at all. 'I can't think of anything I'd like more...'

EPILOGUE

Three years later...

IT WAS THE first night of Camp Reki.

Bonfire night.

S'mores night.

Maya was sitting on the edge of the circle surrounding a bonfire that had burnt down enough to be no more than a pile of embers. Camp staff and caregivers were helping children roast marshmallows on long sticks. There were smiles and laughter everywhere but Maya saw a dismayed expression on one young girl's face as her marshmallow burst into flames, slipped off her stick and fell onto the hot coals. Her carer looked just as disappointed but, before the girl could burst into tears, someone was there to rescue her.

Eli was there. He'd been about to start toasting the marshmallows on his own stick but he'd witnessed the disaster and crouched beside her to not only put a fresh marshmallow on her stick but to show her how to turn it and take it away from the heat before disaster struck again. She had a smile on her face in no time at all.

Maya was smiling as well.

Every day she thought she couldn't love Eli Peters any more than she did already.

And every day she proved herself wrong and she could feel her heart softening enough to get that little bit bigger so it could hold that extra bit of love.

If he wasn't surprising her with what a caring husband and father he was, she could be blown away by his devotion to his work and the concern he had for every person who came under his care. Okay, he still worried too much sometimes but that was just because he cared so much.

She had married a kind man.

They would be celebrating their second anniversary during this year's camp. How many people were lucky enough to be able to celebrate every year in the actual place that both their wedding and honeymoon had taken place?

In a tropical island paradise?

It had been the most perfect day in her life.

Everybody at camp—and in the village—had been invited. Maya had worn a long, floaty white dress, frangipani flowers in her hair and she had a huge bunch of bright red ginger flowers in her hands.

Picked by Simon, of course. And his mate Carlos.

They'd both been online to find out why the colour red was important for weddings.

'It's special all over the world,' Simon had announced. *'It brings good luck for a happy and harmonious marriage—whatever harmonious means.'*

'It's a good thing,' Maya had assured him.

'Apparently it represents love, power, passion and fertility,' Carlos had added. He'd winked at Maya. *'That's a good thing, too, yeah?'*

Maya had simply winked back at him.

They'd been married at sunset, barefoot on the lagoon beach, under an archway of hibiscus flowers that looked like fragments of the sky's colour as the sun slowly sank. Simon and Carlos had been Eli's groomsmen. Ana and Hazel had been Maya's bridesmaids. The party afterwards had been epic, with island music, singing and dancing, an absolute feast of delicious food. And s'mores for dessert. Because it was camp, after all.

Where Maya and Eli had been so unexpectedly re-united after so many years apart.

Where they'd chosen to make public their commitment to each other that would last for the rest of their lives.

Where they fully intended to return every year, not only to celebrate but to be a part of Camp Reki.

The s'mores had been Simon's idea but both Maya and Eli had been more than happy to embrace it.

Because it hadn't been simply a ceremony between two people, had it? It had been the formal recognition of the family they had created. They'd moved, as a family, to live in Australia. They lived near a beach in Sydney, Eli was in charge of an emergency department that was even busier than where he'd been in London and Simon was thriving in his new country and school, embracing every new adventure that came his way.

Maya scanned the crowd around the bonfire, wondering where Simon had got to but not at all worried that she couldn't see him. He was twelve years old now, going on thirteen, although she and Eli often joked that it was more like he was going on thirty because he was so grown-up and responsible.

He looked after his own Factor VIII infusions now and

knew what to do if he had any bleeding episodes. He also made his own decisions about how to keep himself safe enough to enjoy his new passions of surfing and scrambling up indoor climbing walls. Between having his own fun at camp this year with other activities, he was going to be taking Maya's place to help teach the younger children about the challenges and fun of climbing.

Right now, though, he would be with his friends, which was exactly where he should be. What tweenager wanted to hang out all the time with their parents? Maybe Tevita had given him a drum and he was part of the group providing the music this evening that would always take Maya straight back to the joy of her wedding.

A joy that had never gone away but had an intensity here, on the island, that made it feel brand-new all over again.

Maya's gaze sought out Eli and she saw that he was busy toasting his own marshmallows. He'd go to the long table next and get the crackers and chocolate and then he'd bring the treat to where she was sitting. Maya licked her lips. She couldn't wait…

'You look happy.'

Maya turned her head and her smile widened. 'Hey, Mike.' She nodded. 'I couldn't be happier.'

'Happy anniversary.'

'Thank you. It's going to be the best one yet. I was just thinking how lucky we are to be able to come back here to celebrate every year. Especially when I'm not even here in an official capacity this time.'

'Wouldn't be Camp Reki these days without the Peters family,' Mike said. 'I see Eli's getting your anniversary dessert ready.'

'Yes. Maybe I should go and find Simon.'

'He's with Tevita, helping him entertain his wee nephew while Ana's busy with the camp kids.' He grinned. 'Getting in a bit of practice, I reckon. Did you hear that Alice's parents are coming to visit this week? And her brother, Jake?'

'I did.' Maya's smile was poignant. Alice would always be part of her own story. *Their* stories. Hers and Eli's.

Mike's smile mirrored hers. 'They wanted to be here when we unveil the memorial for Alice. They also want Carlos to meet Jake.'

'Oh? Why?'

'They asked if they could do something more than put up a memorial here. I told them about the trust fund that's there to help kids who can't afford to get to camp on their own. I also told them I'm planning to help Carlos if he doesn't get a scholarship. And I told them that helping kids like Alice was why he decided he wanted to go to medical school. They want to make a significant contribution to the trust fund. And Jake wants to encourage Carlos to achieve his dreams. It could be the start of a lifelong friendship.' Mike let his breath out in a sigh. 'That's what camp is all about, really, isn't it? Making lifelong friends?'

'And making dreams come true,' Maya agreed. She could see Eli coming towards her now, with the s'mores on a paper plate. 'It certainly worked for me.'

Mike just smiled again. He lifted a hand in greeting to Eli but then faded into the crowd to carry on with his usual goal of spending time with every camp attendee on the first evening.

Eli sat down beside Maya.

'Better have one of these fast,' he warned. 'Simon's on his way.'

Maya laughed. 'He must have been keeping a close eye on you. He does love s'mores.'

She picked one of the cracker sandwiches and bit into the sticky, chocolatey, sweet and salty treat.

'Mmm...' she said with her mouth full. 'So do I.' She grinned at Eli. 'I think it's my new craving.'

Eli laughed, putting his hand on the impressive bump of Maya's belly. For a long moment, it was simply a moment between them. An exchange of a look that spoke of limitless love. Of gratitude for everything they had and the excitement for what was coming. It was also a look of pure happiness.

'You are eating for three,' Eli said. He pushed himself back to his feet. 'I'd better go and make...' he rolled his eyes to warn of a bad joke '...s'more?'

Simon was right behind him and he thought it was hilarious. 'S'more s'mores,' he said. 'Good one, Dad.'

'Come and help me make then,' Eli said, putting his arm over Simon's shoulders. 'Those ones are just for Mum. They're her new craving.'

Maya watched the two of them walking back towards the dying fire but, as if they'd been reading each other's minds, they both looked over their shoulders at exactly the same time and smiled at her.

She smiled back, of course. But she suddenly found herself blinking back tears.

Happy tears.

She could feel the babies moving inside her. Two girls who were due to arrive in a couple of months.

The Peters family was growing.

And there it was again. That feeling of her heart expanding to accommodate even more love. Maya had thought she'd been perfectly truthful when she'd told Mike that she couldn't be happier.

But clearly there was still more to come…

* * * * *

Healing The Baby Surgeon's Heart

Tessa Scott

MILLS & BOON

Tessa Scott is a lover of animals, nature and happily-ever-afters. She lives in Northeast Connecticut, surrounded by lots of trees, wildlife and a menagerie of pets. A copywriter by day, she enjoys that magical moment when the characters she creates come to life and help take the story in new and exciting directions.

Healing the Baby Surgeon's Heart
is **Tessa Scott**'s debut title.

Look out for more books from **Tessa Scott**.
Coming soon!

Discover more at millsandboon.com.au.

In memory of my mom,
who always encouraged me to follow my dreams.

CHAPTER ONE

CLAIRE DELANEY PULLED her soft cardigan tight around her chest as a breeze rose off the Atlantic Ocean and flitted through her thick chestnut hair. She was walking along a paved path at least one hundred feet inland from the rocky coastline, so the chilled wind caught her by surprise. Still, she welcomed its invigorating caress against her skin.

Two days ago, she had arrived in the small town of Ballyledge on the West Coast of Ireland for a month of...well, she still wasn't quite sure what to call it. Rest and relaxation? Not exactly, given that she had taken an extended leave of absence from Boston General Hospital in order to reevaluate her career as an obstetrician and gynecologist.

It was a chosen profession that meant the world to her. That was until one day seven months ago, when she had lost her own baby daughter as a stillbirth at thirty-two weeks along.

Claire winced as emotions flooded through her, still as raw now as ever. And the words that she had once used to counsel and reassure her own patients who had suffered a miscarriage or stillbirth? Turned inwardly, they brought little comfort as she tried to make sense of her loss.

As a highly regarded double board-certified ob-gyn at the top of her field, Claire knew that it wasn't always possible to pinpoint the reason why a pregnancy ended in miscarriage or stillbirth. An autopsy might have provided some answers, but she hadn't been able to bear to have Ariana's tiny body cut open like that. And she didn't need conclusive evidence to know deep in her heart that her loss had been triggered at least in part by the stress and shock of her then husband Mark walking out on their marriage six months into her pregnancy.

She could deal with the end of her marriage. But the loss of her unborn child? The pain and devastation were so profound that they had extinguished the joy and passion she had once felt for her profession.

You just need some time, everyone had said.

And yet here she was, many months later and seemingly no further along in the healing process. How could she be, when every day in her life as an ob-gyn was a reminder of her loss?

Almost instinctively, Claire touched her lower abdomen, her right hand lingering there for several seconds until she forced herself to lift it away.

Quickening her step along the path, she spotted a smattering of people partaking in various activities on a gently sloping carpet of rich green grass to her left.

It really does look like the color of emeralds, she mused to herself, once again glad that she had chosen Ireland as her getaway destination on not much more than a moment's notice.

It made sense, given that as a proud Irish American, visiting the country had always been on her bucket list. Although she had certainly never imagined that it would be under such trying circumstances.

A smile formed over Claire's lips as she watched a man with two young children—presumably their father—trot across the field as he struggled to control a fluttering kite that was caught in a rip-roaring wind. When he slid on the grass and the kite escaped his grip, twirling upwards until it was little more than a tiny diamond-shaped spot in the sky, she cupped a hand over her mouth as her smile gave way to a chuckle.

It felt good to laugh, to feel the warmth of the sun on her

face as the late-morning clouds began to drift further apart. Maybe she'd get through this after all. Maybe she would still find happiness somehow, some way. Perhaps she could take up another area of medicine that wouldn't be a constant reminder of her loss.

Yes, I could do that, she told herself, pushing aside her doubts that she had it in her to start all over again.

Or maybe there was another profession calling to her, outside of the medical field—a previously unfathomable proposition.

She turned to view the coastline, and the small slice of pale blue water that peeked through the gap between the cliff bluffs and the horizon.

I'll become a painter.

She envisioned herself perched in front of an outdoor easel in a flowing silk scarf and red beret, conveniently ignoring the fact that she could barely draw stick figures.

Or maybe I could try—

Claire's thoughts—and her body—suddenly froze as a woman's agonized shriek reverberated through the air. Catching her breath, she scanned the several small groups of people in the field to her left, her eyes locking in place as they fell upon a woman lying on her back in the grass. A kneeling man hovered over her.

The sight sent a current of ice through Claire's veins. Was he attacking her in broad daylight? And, if so, why was no one rushing to her defense? The kite man was slowly making his way over with his kids, as were several other people who had been walking nearby. But there was no attempt to tackle the man. Something wasn't right.

Wait.

Claire squinted, and then took a deep breath. Even from a distance, there was no mistaking the woman's hugely swollen belly. She was pregnant. And as another guttural scream punctured the otherwise quiet morning, Claire knew one thing for certain.

She's in trouble. I have to help.

It wasn't until she was halfway to the unfolding scene that Claire realized she was running—and fast. It was as if her legs had a mind of their own and her "off" doctor button had been switched back on.

Dropping to her knees beside the woman, she turned to the ashen-faced man who was clutching her hand, his eyes wild with fear. They were both young, quite possibly first-time parents, Claire surmised.

"It's okay," she said breathlessly, her lungs still reeling from her no-holds-barred sprint. "I'm a doctor."

She turned to the woman, equally as pale as her partner, but drenched in sweat, her long dark hair nearly as soaked as if she had just stepped out of the shower. Her light peach cotton maternity top clung to her damp chest. During her quick scan of the woman's body, Claire observed the growing patch of wetness on the inseam of her gray sweatpants. It was all the confirmation she needed that her water had broken.

"I'm Claire," she said, in the soothing tone that was her go-to voice for nervous moms-to-be—and often more so their partners. "What's your name?"

"Margaret," she said in a near-whisper. "And this is my husband, Ted. We were out having a picnic and—" She gasped, grabbing her lower belly, pain gripping her face like a vice.

"Our baby… S-Sam," Ted stuttered. "He's breech."

Two words that cut through the air like a knife.

Claire's throat clamped shut, but he wasn't about to let on that her concern had instantly shifted from medium range to glaring red warning lights.

"We…she has a C-section scheduled in…in…" Ted stammered, unable to say more.

"Three weeks," Margaret managed to say through clenched

teeth. "My doctor said this could happen, but I…" She paused to release a barely controlled yelp as another contraction grabbed hold of her.

"But he said it most likely wouldn't," Ted said, finishing his wife's sentence.

Claire tried to piece together the bits of information being volleyed around. "You mean an early labor?"

"Right," Ted replied, nodding vigorously. "He told Margaret to have an overnight bag at the ready, because if her waters broke before the scheduled C-section it would be an emergency situation. Oh, God. What have I done?" Clasping his forehead with jittery hands, he slowly rocked his upper body back and forth. "It was my idea to have a picnic today. I thought the fresh air would do us both some good—"

Claire grabbed Ted's forearm and squeezed it just tightly enough to pull him back into the present. "Ted, I want you to focus, okay? You need to be strong for Margaret. I know you can do this."

He straightened up, the panic in his eyes giving way to resolve. "Right. You're right. Um…um…what can I do?"

Claire glanced at his phone on the ground next to his knee. "Did you call nine-one-one?" It wasn't until she saw the perplexed look on his face that she realized it might not be the same number in Ireland as in the US. "Emergency. Did you call for help?"

"Yes. They said they were sending the nearest ambulance… about ten minutes out."

No sooner had the pronouncement left his mouth than the sound of an approaching siren pierced the air.

Claire turned to Margaret, clasping her free hand with her own. "You're going to be okay, Margaret."

Margaret's gray eyes were clouded with fear. "Sam…"

"Sam is going to be okay, too."

Don't make promises you can't keep.

Reassuring smile still in place, Claire inwardly winced as the obvious crossed her mind. Breech births *were* safe—in a hospital setting. But the chances of them getting to a hospital in time was iffy at best.

"I told you earlier I was a doctor, but I left out an important detail. I'm an ob-gyn, so delivering babies is my specialty."

By now, a small crowd of about a dozen people had gathered around.

"Oh, thank goodness," an older woman said as she puffed out a sigh of relief.

"What are the chances?" a male voice murmured.

What are the chances, indeed? Claire thought.

"Have you delivered breech babies before?" Ted asked anxiously.

"I have. Many times."

Claire's calm voice and reassuring words masked her significant concern. As the ambulance siren grew louder, she forced her mind to filter out the noise so she could be fully present in the moment.

"Did your doctor ever say what type of breech position Sam is in?"

"Um…uh…frank—is that right?" Ted asked, and Margaret replied with a tight squeeze of Claire's hand.

This was slightly better news than a transverse breech, in which the baby was positioned horizontally across the uterus, but dangers still abounded.

"Margaret, I'm just going to feel on your abdomen now," Claire said as she gently pulled her hand away from Margaret's grip. "It's possible Sam has turned on his own, so what I'm trying to determine is the placement of his head."

"I tried everything," Margaret said through gritted teeth as she bit down on her pain. "Acupuncture, chiropractor, tilt exercises…"

"Our doctor tried to turn the baby as well," Ted said. "He wouldn't budge."

It only took several light-pressure pushes on Margaret's abdomen for Claire to confirm that Sam's head was just under her ribcage. *Damn.* She had witnessed many babies flipping into a head-first position in the final days of pregnancy—sometimes just hours before birth—but it was not to be in this instance.

"Is this your first baby?" Claire asked.

Though she was fishing for critical information, she posed the question as casually as possible, so as not to set off further alarms.

"Yes," Margaret replied, smiling weakly as rivulets of sweat rolled down her cheeks.

"We've been over the moon, waiting for Sam to arrive and starting our family," Ted added.

"That's wonderful," Claire said.

She meant it...but the unspoken flipside of this acknowledgement was that a first-time vaginal birth was riskier, especially with a late preterm baby. Sam's small body pushing through the cervix first meant the opening could still be too narrow by the time his head was ready to pass through. If his head were to become stuck before they could reach the hospital, Claire would need to act without delay, flexing and maneuvering it to help bring him into the world as quickly as possible so that he could take that critically important first breath.

Though her intensive training and expert skillset were made for moments like this, Claire couldn't pretend that her nerves weren't on edge. But, as was always the case in a medical emergency, she knew how to fully suppress her fight-or-flight response while staying fully—and calmly—engaged in the moment.

"Thank God! The ambulance is here," a female voice within the small gathering announced.

Claire looked up. The yellow and red box-shaped vehicle

slowed to a stop on the road that ran parallel to the walking path, but it was a good five hundred feet or more away. She wondered if it would remain there, which meant the EMTs would have to cover a lot of ground on foot to retrieve Margaret on a stretcher, but seconds later the ambulance pulled off the road and slowly rambled down the green field.

Claire discreetly breathed a sigh of relief—then tensed up as a pair of muscular legs in maroon running shorts appeared just inches away. Her line of vision followed them upwards, settling on a rugged, dark-haired man who looked like he had stepped—or jogged—off the set of a commercial after playing the role of "quintessential Irish hunk."

"I'm a doctor," he said as he kneeled down beside Claire.

Claire did a double-take. He could easily pass for a professional rugby player—but a doctor? It most certainly would not have been her first guess. Still, she was grateful that he had chosen this particular morning and pathway to go for a run. She could use all the help she could get to ensure a safe birth delivery for Margaret and Sam.

"I'm an ob-gyn," she said. "Claire Delaney."

He nodded, thick, tousled hair bobbing as he did. "Kiernan O'Rourke."

"The baby is in a frank breech position," Claire said, her eyes meeting his to silently convey the gravity of the situation. "It's her first pregnancy and she has a C-section scheduled in three weeks."

He pursed his lips together, and Claire felt an unspoken understanding pass between them.

This could be serious. Their lives could be in danger.

"They're probably taking her to West Mercy Hospital in Galway. I'm chief of surgery there." He extracted a phone out of the athletic carry belt around his waist. "I'll call my team to make sure they're on standby."

Claire thought he looked too young to be a chief of surgery, but maybe the climb up the surgical hierarchal ladder proceeded at a quicker pace in Ireland than in the US.

As the ambulance pulled up and came to a stop, the back doors flew open and two EMTs emerged. Kiernan stood up to greet them, pulling a hospital ID badge from the wallet in his belt, which he quietly showed to the pair. Claire observed a subtle shift in the demeanor of both EMTs as they glanced at the badge, then looked up and nodded respectfully.

"I've been in touch with my team at West Mercy and they're awaiting our arrival," Kiernan said.

"Got it," said the young female EMT.

"It's a good thing you came out for a run today, eh?" said the other EMT, a thin man in his fifties with a salt-and-pepper goatee.

"Yes, but she was already in good hands when I arrived." Kiernan nodded toward Claire. "She's a doctor as well."

"Wow!" the female EMT exclaimed as she and her partner set the stretcher next to Margaret. "That's one heck of a coincidence."

It was all hands on deck as Claire, Kiernan and the EMTs carefully helped Margaret onto the stretcher.

"You're doing great, Margaret," Claire said as she squeezed her hand.

"I don't know if he's going to wait," Margaret said in a near-whisper.

"We're going to get you to the hospital as soon as possible," Claire said.

As the stretcher was loaded into the ambulance and secured into place, both EMTs stepped back outside.

"I'm going to ride in the back with you," Kiernan said, and the male EMT nodded.

"Me, too," Claire quickly added.

The EMT looked at Claire, his expression hesitant. "Are you a doctor at West Mercy as well?"

"No," Claire replied, "I'm a doctor in Boston." She paused, thinking perhaps she shouldn't assume they knew it was a large city on the East Coast of the United States. "It's in—"

"Boston!" The EMT cut her off. "I've got some cousins living there. Nice city. Cold, but nice."

"Go Celtics!" the female EMT said enthusiastically as she referenced the world-famous basketball team that called Boston home.

Her fervent cheer startled Ted, who had been standing several feet away. "Shouldn't I be with my wife?" he asked, his face dazed and his voice equally shaky.

"You can ride with me in the front," the female EMT replied.

He turned to Claire, wide-eyed with worry, and she nodded reassuringly. "It's okay. We'll be watching Margaret closely."

As Ted followed the EMT to the front of the ambulance, her partner gestured to Claire. "I'm sorry, but only authorized medical personnel are allowed to ride in the back."

"Seriously?" Claire asked, unable to hide her displeasure. She looked at Kiernan, waiting for him to overrule the EMT's well-meaning but—in her opinion—misguided decision.

"I'm sorry, but he's right," Kiernan replied, his honey-brown eyes conveying that he wished it were otherwise. "There was an incident a few years back... A man at the scene with a heart attack victim claimed he was a doctor, so they let him on the ambulance while they transported the patient to West Mercy. Turns out he was an imposter."

"That's putting it mildly," the male EMT said as he raised a squirrelly eyebrow. "One of my colleagues was on that run. The guy went berserk inside the ambulance and the patient almost died because of the ruckus."

"That's terrible," Claire conceded. "But I can assure you I'm a real doctor." She paused, her mind racing. "You can look up my name on your phone. I'm an ob-gyn at Boston General."

Kiernan stepped up into the back of the ambulance, turning to face Claire as the male EMT hopped inside and disappeared from view. "I'm sorry," Kiernan said as Margaret screamed through another contraction. "I really am. But we need to leave *now*."

As he shut the left-side ambulance door and started to close the right, Claire's arm shot out, pulling the door open again.

Kiernan's startled look matched her own.

Did I just do that?

She blinked and swallowed hard. Defying orders was so not her thing, but saving lives *was*. And that took precedence over everything.

"Look," she said in a barely controlled low voice. "I get that you're a chief of surgery. But have you ever delivered a frank breech baby? And I don't mean by C-section. Her water broke and she's having contractions. Maybe you'll get to the hospital before the baby enters the birth canal, but you can't guarantee it. And, depending on how he presents, it might take the two of us to turn and maneuver him safely out."

Claire thought she could actually hear the seconds tick by as her stalemate with the handsome chief of surgery continued.

"Well?" she finally asked, rising adrenaline creating an even louder buzz in her head.

Kiernan stood immobile as he stared at the American doctor who stood just inches away from him. With wavy reddish-brown hair that bounced past her shoulders, porcelain skin and the palest green eyes he had ever seen, she was, without question, one of the most beautiful women he had laid eyes upon. But it wasn't her striking appearance that had frozen him in place. Rather, he had a split-second decision to make—and, in full contrast to his normally resolute, take-charge nature, he wasn't sure what to do.

If he allowed her to accompany this patient and himself to

the hospital—potentially assisting in a breech delivery on the way—he would be violating medical emergency transportation laws. And hospital protocol as well. For a chief of surgery, that could have all sorts of repercussions, and none of them good.

Another second passed and Margaret cried out in the throes of a contraction. It was more than enough to jolt him into action.

"Come on," he said, reaching out and pulling Claire up into the ambulance.

She brushed past him, her silky, fruit-scented hair swiping him on the cheek. As the ambulance suddenly took off and began to roll up the grassy field Claire's knees buckled, and she struggled to regain her balance. Kiernan quickly grabbed her arm and pulled her up, her face just inches away from his own.

"Uh…we have a situation here," the EMT announced loudly as Margaret wailed and called out Sam's name.

Kiernan locked eyes with Claire, but only for a second. Rushing over to Margaret, she pulled away from him with such force that it nearly pushed him into the ambulance doors.

"I need gloves," she said to the EMT, her voice growing sharper as she called, "Doctor? I need you over here."

Kiernan was at her side before the words were fully out of her mouth. Snapping on the gloves handed to him by the EMT, he moved in closer and lowered himself while still giving Claire the room she needed to assist with the delivery.

And then he spotted it. Margaret's umbilical cord was protruding, trapped between her pelvic bone and Sam's buttocks, which were lodged in the vaginal opening. He knew that Claire had to find a way to quickly release the pressure on the prolapsed cord, or the baby would be starved of oxygen and blood.

Kiernan took a deep breath and held it in. Standing idly by while another doctor took action was foreign to him, but for once he had to concede that doing so was in the patient's best interest. He barely knew Claire, yet something told him she was an exceptionally gifted ob-gyn. But were they intervening in time? Had the umbilical cord been compressed before they'd loaded Margaret onto the ambulance?

As Claire briefly turned and looked up at him, concern clouding her light green eyes, he couldn't help but think she was silently asking the very same questions.

CHAPTER TWO

"I'LL TAKE FULL RESPONSIBILITY," Kiernan said as the EMT looked wide-eyed at Claire, his lips slightly parted as though he was about to launch a protest.

Eventually he nodded and said, "Just let me know what you need."

"Can you stay close to Margaret, monitor her vitals and coach her breathing?" Claire said.

As the EMT quickly moved toward the front of the stretcher, Claire slid her gloved hand under the baby's partially exposed buttocks, effectively lifting him off the umbilical cord.

She turned to Kiernan, her voice calm and a steely determination in her eyes. "I need you to replace my hand with your own so that I can free his legs."

Kiernan did as instructed, his gloved hand at the ready as Claire slowly slid hers out. "Got it," he said, as he carefully but swiftly lifted the front of Sam's lower torso upwards.

With hands that were considerably larger than Claire's, it was an even tighter squeeze as he concentrated on maintaining the slight yet still sufficient space that would release pressure from the umbilical cord.

With his right shoulder pointed downward at an uncomfortable angle, and Claire pushing up against his stomach as she moved in closer for better positioning, he felt like he was in a medical practitioners' version of the game Twister. A cramp caught him hard in the side, and he cursed under his breath.

Claire looked up at him, her forehead creased as if to say, *What are you bellyaching about?*

"Sorry, I just… I moved the wrong way."

Her face softened slightly, and she nodded before getting back to the task at hand. With her palm pressing down on Sam's lower back, Claire rotated his trunk to the left, then slid her right hand into the vaginal opening, gently looping her fingers around his right leg and pulling it through. Without pause, she moved to the left side and repeated the action with his left leg.

It wasn't until Kiernan saw both legs freed and the rest of Sam's body beginning to inch out that he realized he had been holding his breath the whole time.

"You're doing great, Margaret," Claire called out. Moving her hand next to Kiernan's forearm, she quietly added, "Okay, I'll take it from here."

The exchange of hands was seamless—a feat in itself, given the circumstances, Kiernan thought. He stepped back slightly to give Claire more room. Another contraction sent Sam further out into the world.

"Here come his arms and shoulders," Claire said.

Knowing that they, too, could have become trapped like Sam's legs, Kiernan felt relief that another hurdle had been cleared. All that was left was for his head to emerge.

Clenching his jaw, Kiernan silently encouraged Sam.
You can do it. You're almost there.

It seemed like many minutes passed while Kiernan repeated the silent mantra, though he knew it couldn't have been more than thirty seconds.

From her crouched position, Claire looked up at him. "His head is trapped," she said in a low voice, so as not to alarm

Margaret. "I'm going to need a towel…something that I can fold and wrap around his torso."

Kiernan quickly scanned the ambulance interior, then rifled through several supply bins on the left. "Okay, ready when you are," he said, stepping back with a folded towel in his hand.

After placing her right forearm underneath the length of Sam's body, Claire looked up at him. It was the only cue he needed to slide the folded towel between her arm and Sam's torso, lifting him up at an angle that allowed Claire to slide her hand in further.

"I have his jaw…"

Several seconds ticked by. Kiernan knew that she was attempting to place her fingers in Sam's mouth, so that she could better position his head for the next step of the procedure.

"I got it," Claire said, an expression of relief flooding over her face. She slid her left hand over Sam's back and into the vaginal opening, nodding as she said, "I'm flexing his head downwards. It's coming…"

Without looking up, she instructed Kiernan to push above Margaret's pubic bone with his free hand.

As Sam's head emerged, Kiernan wondered if he had ever witnessed a more wondrous sight. Yes, he was a surgeon. The jack-of-all-trades type, as he was fond of saying whenever anyone asked if he had a specialty. With advanced training and certifications there weren't many surgical areas that he hadn't delved into. Heart bypasses, cancer surgery, joint replacements—he'd done it all. But he had to admit there was something especially poignant about bringing a new life into the world.

Kiernan watched closely, still sending words of encouragement to Sam in his thoughts. The baby boy had officially arrived, but he wasn't fully out of the woods yet. At least not until he took that crucial first breath on his own.

"Betadine," Claire said, her left arm outstretched as Kiernan once again began searching through the supply bins.

"The one on top," the EMT called out.

"Left or right?" Kiernan asked.

"Left."

Kiernan quickly extracted the antibacterial solution and some gauze. Anticipating that Claire would next be asking for clamps and scissors, he grabbed those as well.

Claire wiped the cord with Betadine, then placed two clamps several inches apart. She turned to Kiernan, meeting his eyes. "Do you want to cut the cord?"

She didn't have to ask twice. Snipping the section between the clamps, Kiernan held his own breath as he waited for Sam to take his first. His eyes met Claire's once again, and though no words were said, he knew she was thinking the same dreaded thought.

Had they delivered Sam in time?

"Can I have another towel?" Claire asked urgently.

Kiernan quickly complied, and Claire began vigorously rubbing it over Sam's body.

And then the most glorious sound that Kiernan could ever imagine filled the ambulance.

"I never thought I would be so happy to hear a baby cry," Kiernan said quietly.

A wistful smile crossed Claire's face. "Welcome to the world of obstetrics, where every day is a miracle."

Kiernan couldn't help but notice how she seemed to have momentarily stepped into another time and place, her eyes unblinking, yet focused on nothing in particular, until another surge of sound caused her to snap out of it.

"Sam!" Margaret called out, her voice shaky but unmistakably joyous.

"He's beautiful, Margaret," Claire said, taking the stethoscope that Kiernan had just handed to her.

She placed it over his tiny chest, then looked up at Kiernan and smiled as she nodded. Wrapping Sam in the towel, she lifted him up to Margaret.

"He has a great set of lungs on him, that's for sure," she said as Sam wailed even louder. But once placed in Margaret's arms, he immediately stopped crying.

"He knows where he belongs," the EMT said.

Claire looked up from the mother and baby, nodding to Kiernan with the hint of a smile. It was as if she was silently acknowledging that the two of them had helped make this moment a reality. He smiled and nodded back.

Ten minutes later, the ambulance pulled up to the emergency entrance at West Mercy Hospital. Kiernan hopped out of the vehicle, then turned and offered his hand to Claire as she was about to disembark. She glanced at it before meeting his eyes momentarily. He tried to read the expression on her face. Surprise? Hesitancy? A little of both?

"Thanks," she said, but instead she braced her hand against the open door before stepping carefully out onto the pavement. Given that she hadn't accepted his assistance, he couldn't be sure what she was thanking him for.

As the EMTs rolled the stretcher holding Margaret and Sam toward the entrance, Ted bounded out of the passenger side of the ambulance and ran toward them. Seeing Margaret clutching their tiny newborn son in her arms, he froze in place.

"Oh, my God. Oh, my God. *Oh, my God!*" he exclaimed, his body unlocking as he ran over to the stretcher. "He's beautiful," he said quietly with awe as he beamed down at Sam.

"He certainly is," Margaret said, mustering up the strength to turn her head toward Kiernan and Claire. "And these wonderful doctors saved his life."

Ted turned to Kiernan and Claire. "I don't know how to thank you. This is just...this is the happiest day of my life."

Kiernan smiled and reached out to shake Ted's hand. "Congratulations."

The poor guy is a bundle of nerves, Kiernan thought as Ted continued to shake his hand vigorously, like a wind-up doll with no "off" button.

As smoothly as possible, Kiernan pulled back his hand. He looked over at Claire, knowing that she, too, must be beaming with joy over such a hard-earned happy ending.

Except...she wasn't. Kiernan's own smile faltered as he saw the angst etched on her face. But why? Was it a delayed reaction to the heightened adrenaline and uncertainty that had earlier prevailed, up until the very moment that Sam had been safely delivered? He had seen that sort of thing before with colleagues, after a particularly grueling surgery—even those with miraculous outcomes.

But this felt different.

As though suddenly realizing she was being watched, Claire looked over at him, her eyes meeting his for only a few seconds before she looked away.

Any further contemplation of her strange reaction was cut short by a *swoosh* as the large glass entrance doors swung open. Out strode Lucy, head nurse at West Mercy and Kiernan's right-hand...well, *everything*, given her uncanny ability to stay two steps ahead of his packed daily agenda. And today's unpredictable rollercoaster was no exception.

With a small team of medical professionals behind her, Lucy looked down at the stretcher, her eyes popping open when they landed upon not one, but two occupants.

"We had a bit of an eventful drive on our way over here," Kiernan said, in what he knew could be construed as the understatement of the year.

"I guess so," Lucy said wholeheartedly, a deep smile forming on her lips as she peered down at the new mother and baby. "I would imagine this is one ambulance ride you'll remember for the rest of your life," she said to Margaret.

"I definitely will," Margaret replied with a smile.

"Lucy," Kiernan began, "I'd like you to meet Dr. Claire Delaney. She's visiting from the US and, luckily for Margaret and Sam, she was in the right place at the right time when Margaret went into labor."

"So nice to meet you," Lucy said as she extended her hand.

Claire shook her hand and smiled graciously. "Same here."

Lucy rested both hands on her hips as she turned back to Margaret. "Well, Dr. Preshad is scrubbing in as we speak, expecting that he was going to be performing an emergency C-section. But I'm sure he'll be delighted to know that nature took its course on the way here, and both of you came through with flying colors."

A low rumble of laughter emanated from her team, with Kiernan adding a subdued grin. He wasn't quite at the point where he could look back on the stressful events of the morning and chuckle, but maybe with time. A *lot* of time.

"You've no doubt been through a lot," Lucy continued, "so let's get you inside and settled in."

"Thank you, Doctors," Margaret called out to Kiernan and Claire as two staff members began to wheel the stretcher toward the hospital doors, with Ted close behind.

"Yes, thank you again," Ted called out, before disappearing with the others from view.

Kiernan turned to Claire. "I need to chime in with my huge thanks as well. You truly saved their lives."

"I couldn't have done it without your help."

Though he was tempted to point out that he'd done little more than hand her medical supplies, Kiernan instead smiled and accepted the compliment. "I'm just glad we were both at the right place, at the right time."

"Me too."

"Say, while you're here, I'd love to show you around our new neonatal wing. It's scheduled to be fully up and running in another month. It might not have all the bells and whistles that you're used to at a big-city hospital like Boston General, but it's close. In fact, one of our longer-range goals is to offer cutting-edge neonatal care and the latest treatment options that aren't widely available. And I don't just mean for this region, but for the entire country."

Claire smiled.

Finally, Kiernan thought.

"That's sounds wonderful. And certainly ambitious." She paused, and there was a distinct look of pain in her eyes. "But I have to leave now."

It was not the answer Kiernan had expected, and he wasn't prepared to reply. Finally, he managed to utter, "Oh?"

"Yes, sorry. I have to…there's…um… I have to be somewhere."

Kiernan studied the stunning but increasingly mysterious woman before him. He didn't believe for a second that she had to be somewhere else. An incredibly talented doctor? Yes. But a convincing actress? Not so much.

"Well, I'm not sure how long you're staying in Ireland, but I'd be happy to give you a tour another time."

Kiernan creased his brow as he waited for her reply.

Why is she looking at me like I'm asking her to tour a room full of rattlesnakes and tarantulas?

"That's nice of you to offer. But I'm not sure I'll have time while I'm here."

"I understand," Kiernan said, although nothing could be further from the truth. "No problem."

Claire slid her phone from the back pocket of her jeans and tapped on the screen. "I did a search before coming here about whether there are Ubers in Ireland…" She looked up at Kiernan. "The answer was yes, but they're actual taxis—not drivers in their personal cars. Kind of defeats the purpose of an Uber," she added with a nervous laugh.

"Look, I'm heading back to Ballyledge myself. Why don't you ride with me? It's the least I can do after you saved the day like you did. The hospital has a small fleet of cars that are used for patient transport. I'll have one of my staff take us back."

Claire's smile vanished faster than the flipping of a light switch. She looked down at her phone. "Actually, it looks like I have a ride that's two minutes out."

Kiernan forced a smile. There was no point suggesting that she cancel the taxi and ride back with him instead. For whatever reason—despite what he felt had been a connection between them as they'd worked together to save Margaret and Sam—she wanted nothing more to do with him.

"That was fast," Claire said just over a minute and a half later as she waved to a taxi heading toward them. As the taxi came to a stop, she turned to Kiernan. "It was nice meeting you. And thank you for helping me with the delivery. I really couldn't have done it without you."

Kiernan was about to insist otherwise, but stopped himself. She was merely trying to be polite, so no need to point out that he'd done little more than hold a folded towel and grab some supplies. Not when she had made it clear that she wanted to leave as soon as possible.

Opening the taxi passenger door, he waited for her to be seated before saying, "Take care of yourself. And enjoy your stay in Ireland."

Another skittish smile. "I will. Thank you."

As Kiernan watched the taxi drive away, he heard footsteps approach from behind. Dr. Sebastian Kincaid, an anesthesiologist and one of Kiernan's best friends since medical school, swaggered up to him.

"*Who* was *that*?"

Kiernan rolled his eyes—a reaction he didn't in the least

bit bother to hide from Sebastian. Known as a real-life Dr. McDreamy by half of the female staff at West Mercy who regularly ogled him for his perpetually tanned skin, thick sandy-blonde hair and gym-aficionado physique, he had also earned the moniker of Dr. McDouchebag from the other half who'd had the misfortune of actually dating him at one time or another.

"That's Claire Delaney. She's an American doctor who happened to be walking nearby when the patient we just brought in went into labor. And a breech presentation, no less. She was pretty amazing delivering the baby. I'll tell you that."

"Pretty amazing, huh? I'm sure she was," Sebastian noted with his usual lack of subtlety. A pained grunt followed as Kiernan elbowed him sharply in the ribs. "What's that for?"

Kiernan grinned. "For you being you."

Sebastian straightened himself up, still rubbing his side. "So, how long is she here for?"

"I have no idea."

"Seriously? You didn't get her number or anything? What— are you losing your touch?"

Kiernan sighed exasperatedly as he raised an eyebrow. "Yes, well… I decided to hold off hitting on her while she was delivering a breech baby in the back of a bumpy ambulance." He paused for full dramatic effect. "I'm silly like that."

Sebastian shook his head, but with a smirk and a twinkle in his eyes. "You know, I really thought once you made chief of surgery you'd finally loosen up and realize that there's more to life than work."

"And why would you think that?"

"You're at the top of the food chain now. Which means it's time to enjoy some of the fruits of your labor. So to speak."

As Sebastian winked and wiggled his eyebrows, Kiernan reluctantly grinned.

"You've got the goods, mate," Sebastian continued. "You just need to show more of your authentic self, that's all."

Kiernan was beginning to lose patience. Fast. *"What?"*

"Remember that speaker we had here a few months ago, who talked about how to avoid career burnout? She mentioned the importance of bringing our authentic selves to work. You know—being real human beings and not just the series of medical credentials after our names. No one—besides myself, of course—feels like they really know you. That's all. A little banter here and there, some joking around, sharing your weekend plans—or at least pretending you have some... Things like that could go a long way."

Kiernan stared at him hard. "Remind me again why we're friends?"

Sebastian smiled, revealing teeth so white that Kiernan wondered if he should don sunglasses.

"Because you need me. I'm the best wingman you'll ever have—even though you refuse to take advantage of my services."

"I'm head of the surgery department. I see people whose lives are at stake, day in and day out. I don't have time to mollycoddle my colleagues."

Sebastian stared at him, his mouth twisted to one side. "Right. If you say so," he finally said, this time slapping Kiernan on the other shoulder. He looked at his watch. "Well, I'm off to prep for a gallbladder removal."

He took a few steps in the direction of the hospital entrance, and then he stopped and swiveled around.

"And by the way... No one says 'mollycoddle' anymore. Other than time travelers from the nineteenth century."

He flashed a smile and gave a thumbs-up before turning on his heels and continuing on his way.

Kiernan sighed, then shook his head and managed a weary smile.

Bring your authentic self to work. Who comes up with this stuff, anyway?

And yet...

His thoughts turned to Claire, and the incredibly intense turn of events that had brought them so briefly together. Two complete strangers, working in tandem to save the lives of a mother and her newborn baby.

It doesn't get any more real than that, he thought.

But as he replayed their parting of ways in his mind, he was faced with another reality, and this one left a sting in its wake.

She couldn't get away from me fast enough.

Claire watched silently from the back passenger window of the taxi as rolling green fields, stone walls and the occasional grazing sheep whizzed past. Ten minutes ago they had left the city limits of Galway, and viewing the quiet countryside was like a calming elixir for her soul. Which was something she certainly needed right now.

Another patchwork of green fields, this time grazing goats, and Claire turned away from the window, leaning back against the headrest. She closed her eyes and breathed in deeply, feeling as though it was her first full breath since the moment she had knelt down on the ground beside Margaret.

Slowly, she shook her head. Was the universe trying to mess with her mind? She had come to Ireland for a reprieve from her life as a baby doctor, and only days in she'd been thrown back into it in the most unexpected and harrowing way.

Dabbing at her moist eyes with the sleeve of her cardigan, she caught the driver glancing at her through the rearview mirror. She hoped he would look away, and was relieved when he finally did.

It will pass, she told herself.

Not the pain that she still felt from losing Ariana, but the tears that flowed every time a situation triggered her emotions into overdrive.

Still... As she thought of the exhausted but overjoyed Margaret, holding tiny Sam in her arms, she couldn't help but think that maybe the universe knew what it was doing after all. Yes, a yet to be fully healed wound in her heart had been tugged open. But now there was a very happy new mom and a healthy baby boy who might not have had the same outcome if it hadn't been for her and a chief of surgery who had also been in the right place at the right time.

Her mind wandered again. And this time she didn't call it back. Not when it had settled upon a handsome doctor with a rugged build and kind brown eyes. Kiernan O'Rourke. Now, *that* was an Irish name, she mused to herself. Her emerging smile halted as she thought about how earlier she had cut him off at the knees. He was just trying to be friendly by offering a hospital tour, one doctor to another, and she had abruptly declined.

I have to be somewhere.

She rolled her eyes at what must have come across as the lamest excuse ever.

In another day or two he'll forget all about it, Claire told herself.

At least that was what she hoped. The last thing she would ever want to do was hurt another person's feelings. And something told her that was especially true of the attractive Irish doctor who had just helped her bring a new life into the world.

CHAPTER THREE

CLAIRE PLOPPED DOWN on the small couch with its lopsided cushions in her quaint two-room rental cottage. It was early Tuesday evening, three days since that whirlwind of medical drama had left her spinning on every level.

She had arrived in Ireland with no game plan other than to engage in some much-needed soul-searching. But, even so, she recognized that her tendency to withdraw from others when dealing with a personal issue was not doing her any favors right now. Perhaps it was time to switch things up. No one had to know the real reason she was in Ireland for an extended stay. So why not seek out some group activities…like a guided tour of castles?

Great idea, she thought as she proceeded to search for local attractions on her phone.

A notification icon popped up on her screen and she stared at it for several seconds. If there was one sound piece of advice that had come out of her therapy sessions, it was to stay off social media as much as possible. The algorithms had a way of knowing what was on your mind and only feeding you more of it—whether "it" was something good or bad. She had long ago removed her ex-husband Mark from any social media friends list but, both being doctors, they had so many mutual acquaintances in the medical world that she couldn't be certain he wouldn't pop up in someone else's post when least expected.

Still, what was the harm in tapping on one update? Maybe it would be a fun kitten or puppy video—always guaranteed to bring a smile.

She opened the notification…and her heart stopped.

Staring back at her was a photo of Mark, cradling an infant in his arms. *Daddy celebrates three months of diaper duty and butterfly kisses with his little girl!* the caption read, followed by hearts and smiles emojis.

Furiously scanning the post, Claire quickly discovered it had originated on the page of Christine White, a physician assistant at Mark's internal medicine practice. Just as she had been warned, Christine's post had found its way onto her phone as a "people you may know" notification.

She closed her eyes, somehow managing to do the math in her head that confirmed Christine had been pregnant with Mark's child when he had walked out on her and Ariana. She shouldn't be surprised. She *wasn't* surprised. And yet the revelation still cut like a knife.

The blade went even deeper as she recalled how Mark had been contacted by the hospital when she was about to have labor induced for the stillbirth of Ariana. He couldn't be bothered to come. The depths of his cold indifference to his own flesh and blood were almost inconceivable…but he had started a new family, and had already rendered her and Ariana inconsequential.

A few more moments of pained disbelief and then Claire shook her head, as though she could physically dislodge all of the distressing thoughts.

Time to pull yourself up by the bootstraps, she instructed herself.

She hadn't traveled three thousand miles just to sit in a

small cottage and brood, now, had she? Well, maybe she had, but that was about to change.

When in Rome...

Okay, she was in Ballyledge, which most certainly wasn't Rome, but it had more than its share of charm and possibilities.

Rising from the couch and walking several steps to a side window, she looked out onto the purplish-orange sky as dusk set in. Her mind flashed back to a cute little pub that had caught her eye the previous day, while she'd been picking up groceries in the village. Overlooking the water, and with an outdoor terrace softly lit by string lights, it had just the right vibe to help ease her out of her slump. Or so she hoped.

Before she had a chance to talk herself out of her sudden plan, Claire headed to the bathroom to brush her hair, put on some clear lip gloss, then stare in the mirror as she declared, "You. Can. Do. This."

Twenty minutes later she was seated at a small wooden table on the outside terrace of Gilroy's Pub, watching the rising moon cast an ethereal glow over the inland bay. The low hum of conversation around her was just enough of a reminder that she was not alone. But that all changed in an instant as a loud, rambunctious group of men tumbled onto the terrace.

I might as well be in an American sports bar, Claire thought as she turned to look at the sweaty, disheveled men.

Their blue and white shorts and matching shirts were streaked with dirt and mud, and their metal-cleated shoes sounded like a herd of horses galloping to the barn for their oats. Not exactly the ambiance she was expecting at the pub, but then again, was it really so bad to witness a group of guys having some rabble-rousing fun?

Nope, Claire concluded, but she still turned away and refocused her gaze on the shimmering bay.

"Dr. Delaney?"

Claire swung her head around, then did a double-take as her eyes landed on Dr. Kiernan O'Rourke.

"I thought that was you," he said, briefly glancing at the chair across from her.

It was more than enough of a cue for her to ask him to have a seat. As he pulled up the chair, Claire's mouth was still slightly agape. Whether it was from the overall surprise of seeing him again, or the fact that West Mercy's chief of surgery was now sitting across from her with a patch of dirt caked on one cheek and a nasty scratch etched across the other, she couldn't be sure.

"This is quite the surprise, Dr. O— Mr. O'Rourke." Suddenly remembering that Irish surgeons use honorific titles, Claire caught herself just in time.

"Please, call me Kiernan. With all we went through the other day, at the very least we should be on a first-name basis."

Claire dipped her head as she smiled, then added, "Claire. Nice to meet you—again." After a slight pause, she shook her head and laughed quietly.

Kiernan cocked his head. "I'd ask if you were laughing *with* me, except I haven't told a joke."

"I'm sorry. It's just that… Well, the first time I saw you, I thought you looked like a professional rugby player."

"Ahh." Kiernan appeared almost relieved. "And then you discovered I'm just the boring chief of surgery at West Mercy Hospital."

Claire smirked. "No—it's not like that at all. More like, what are the chances that I'd see you again and you really *do* play rugby. At least I think that's a rugby uniform you're wearing. Or is it soccer?" She tapped her hand to her mouth. "Oops, I mean football."

"You saved yourself just in time," Kiernan joked. "In fact, I'm not sure if the word 'soccer' is officially banned from Ireland, but it should be."

Claire chuckled. "Point taken."

"But, yes, I play in a local rugby league. We usually have a match every Tuesday night from spring to late autumn."

"So you live in the area?"

"I do. I have a house about five miles from here. Up on a high bluff and overlooking the ocean—just in case I ever decide to take up cliff-diving in the spare time that I don't have." He paused. "You look surprised."

"That you might take up cliff-diving?" Claire replied, gamely playing along.

He grinned. "That I live in town."

"I guess I am...sort of. Working at the hospital in Galway—I would have figured you lived in the city."

Kiernan nodded his head from side to side, as though weighing her observation, his thick dark hair bobbing back and forth in unison. "That's a reasonable assumption. And I did live there for a few years."

"Oh?"

"I came back because I grew up in Ballyledge, and I may be biased, but I don't think there are many more pristine spots in the country."

"The scenery is breathtaking, that's for sure," Claire agreed.

"Plus, it helps keep me grounded. I'm sure I don't have to tell you that working in a hospital—especially on difficult cases when lives are in the balance—is like a constant adrenaline rush that can be hard to come down from. But here..." he nodded toward the water "...the sound of the waves crashing up against the rocks, with no one around other than some egrets and a few seals—it helps put things in perspective."

Claire gestured appreciatively. "Poetically said."

Kiernan took a sizeable sip of beer. "I kind of surprised myself with that one." As Claire laughed, he added, "Okay, now it's your turn."

Claire's laughter quickly petered out. "My turn?" she asked, wide-eyed. Her mind raced as she tried to think of what to say.

Keep it light. And happy. And...

"I didn't mean to put you on the spot," Kiernan said, viewing her through perplexed eyes.

It took some effort, but Claire found her smile once more. "No—that's fine. I was just trying to think of something that might be remotely interesting."

Kiernan raised an eyebrow, his expression equal parts surprised and amused. "I just spent two hours on a muddy field listening to nothing but grunts, burps and the splat of projectile spits. So trust me when I say *anything* you'd like to share about yourself right now will be infinitely more fascinating by comparison."

Claire snickered, feeling her guard drop a notch, not just emotionally, but physically as well. The release of tension in her neck and shoulders was a welcome respite. "Okay, well... I always wanted to visit Ireland, and here I am." She paused, debating whether to go one step further. "For a month."

Slow down there, girl, she chided herself inwardly.

"Now, see? *That* was interesting." Kiernan studied her closely, as if trying to discern more through sheer will.

Good luck with that, she thought.

"Did you come here with others?"

As Claire shook her head, she could almost see the intrigue growing in his eyes.

"Did you come here to visit someone, then?"

"Nope."

Kiernan sat back in his chair, crossing his arms and grinning at the same time, as though relishing the challenge before him. "So, why Ireland?"

"It's an Irish American thing, I guess. We all want to visit the motherland, so to speak, at some point in our lives."

"Delaney," Kiernan said with a nod. "Of course. And the hospital is okay with you being away for a whole month?"

Claire swallowed hard, her heart momentarily surging in her chest before quieting down. She needed to steer the conversation away from her career—which ultimately led back to babies—and fast.

"Boston General's good about encouraging us to take time off as needed."

"I see. That's great." He paused, another grin emerging. "I feel like I'm on one of those game shows where I'm trying to guess someone's back story with limited clues."

Claire smirked, realizing she was about to let her guard down a teeny-weeny bit more, but was surprisingly okay with that. "Go ahead—give it your best shot."

"All right, then." Kiernan glanced down at her unadorned wedding ring finger, then back up at her, his warm brown eyes latching onto her own. "You're here alone, so either there's no husband or kids at home, or you decided you needed a bit of a break from them, too."

Her smile faltered for a fraction of a second, but she managed to recover it. "No husband or kids."

He cocked his head to the side. "Hmm…the plot thickens. So you came here in the hopes of meeting some strapping Irishman who looks like he stepped off the set of a commercial?"

Claire had just taken a sip of wine, and in short order choked on it as Kiernan unknowingly voiced her silent assessment of him at their first meeting.

Kiernan chuckled. "I think I'm on to something. Ten points for contestant number three."

Claire waved him away as she coughed some more. "I just swallowed the wrong way, that's all."

"Right…" he said, clearly unconvinced.

She laughed, perplexed at the high level of comfort she felt around Kiernan, but determined to go with the flow.

"Okay," Kiernan began. "I've put you on the hot seat long enough. Now it's your turn to ask me a question."

Claire ran her index finger over the rim of her wine glass as she stalled for time. So many possible questions, but best to keep it light. "Did the hospital make you take out an insurance policy on your hands when they heard you were playing a rough contact sport on the side?"

Kiernan laughed, then held up his hands in mock examination. Claire felt a swish of butterflies in her stomach as she admired their obvious strength and masculinity. Not what she would normally picture as "surgeon's hands," but she certainly had no complaints about the view.

"No, but they did suggest I trade in rugby for badminton."

Claire chuckled. "Somehow I can't picture you daintily prancing up to a badminton net."

Kiernan laughed heartily. "You got that right."

"Let's see… You live high up on a bluff, but no cliff-diving as of yet?"

"Correct. I'm waiting for the cliffs to shrink to the size of ant hills."

Claire grinned. "Do you live alone?"

"I do."

"Is that a good thing or a bad thing?"

Kiernan teetered his head back and forth, as though weighing his answer. "I would say it's a good thing."

"Just a man in his castle?"

Kiernan looked amused. "Something like that."

"So, no wife and kids in your future, or you just haven't met the right woman?"

Careful, Claire…

"I suppose the latter—although some might say I'm married to my profession."

There were so many possible replies to that—some humorous, some cutting—but Claire chose instead to safely change the subject. Except that no alternative subject immediately came to mind.

Keep it happy, she reminded herself once again. *Nothing too deep...*

"Which is probably just as well," he went on. "Since I don't foresee any children in my future."

It took a few moments for Claire to realize that her face must have frozen into a mask of shock. How else to explain why Kiernan's smile had instantly faded, and his forehead visibly tensed as he attempted to explain himself further.

"I only mention that because you asked."

"Yes... Right... Not everyone wants kids. Nor should everyone have them, based on some of the horrors I've seen as a doctor. And you, too, I'm sure."

"Unfortunately, yes. But for me personally, it's more like I've learned from the mistakes of my own father. He was a surgeon, too. A *brilliant* surgeon, I should add. He helped pioneer some of the first organ laparoscopic surgeries. But he was a lousy father. I know it sounds crass to say that about one's own parent, but he'd probably be the first to admit it himself if he were still here."

"He's passed away?" Claire asked as delicately as possible, still reeling from Kiernan's unexpected revelation, but doing her best to hide that fact.

Kiernan nodded. "Three years ago. In the last five years of his life, we actually forged some semblance of a relationship. Although it was more like a friendship based on a shared interest in medicine rather than a father-and-son kind of thing. He did finally acknowledge that he'd been an absentee father for most of my life. I think that's why he felt it important to advise me not to have kids if I truly wanted to be the best surgeon I could possibly be."

"Hmm… That's interesting."

Kiernan cocked his head slightly to one side, a look of curiosity in his eyes. "What's interesting?"

"That instead of telling you not to make the mistake of putting career over family, he essentially told you the opposite."

Kiernan was silent for a moment. "I never really looked at it like that, but I suppose you're right."

"And your mom?"

Kiernan's face brightened. "My mum is doing great. She lives about a half-hour from here in an independent living community. I don't think she realized how much she was living in my dad's shadow until he passed away. Now, she's made new friends, has taken up gardening as a hobby, and to be honest, I don't think I've ever seen her happier."

"Well, I've obviously never met your mom, but I'm glad to hear that."

She had never met his father, either, but she sure was getting a picture of an overbearing man who may have been a genius with a scalpel, but couldn't quite cut it as a father or a husband.

"And what about your family?" Kiernan asked.

"I lost my dad, too, also three years ago. We were very close, so it was hard. Still is, some days. My mom lives in one of those nice little New England towns outside of Boston. You know—the kind that have old historical houses with placards that say, *Paul Revere rode past here to warn colonists about approaching British troops*."

That observation elicited a chuckle from Kiernan, prompting Claire to laugh as well.

"I have a younger brother who works in finance and lives in New York, still doing the bachelor thing despite my mom's matchmaking attempts. And I have a sister, Grace, who works in real estate and is two years older than me. She moved to Pennsylvania recently, when my brother-in-law relocated for a job promotion, and she has two young sons. They're great kids and I love being an aunt."

Kiernan smiled. "Well, I think I know you better now than I know most of my colleagues."

Was he joking? Claire couldn't be sure. She had certainly known her share of doctors who were all business while on duty, but Kiernan didn't strike her as the uptight, humorless type. Then again, they weren't in a hospital environment at the moment. Perhaps he felt the need to maintain a measure of personal detachment from his colleagues as chief of surgery—and, given the monumental responsibility of the role, that was understandable.

But before she could contemplate things further, Kiernan's rugby teammates came barreling over, surrounding their table and kicking up an aromatic cloud of sweat, dirt and beer.

"Is he bothering you?" a gargantuan man with hands the size of baseball mitts slurred, as he tried to focus through red-tinged eyes.

"Not at all," Claire replied with a wink in Kiernan's direction.

"He's a great catch, this one, you know," another teammate said with a wallop on Kiernan's back that nearly shook the table. "He's a surgery bigwig. Which is good—because he'd never make it as a professional rugby player."

As the teammate topped off this observation with a hard knock of his knuckles on Kiernan's skull, Claire winced. "Oh...careful! That had to hurt."

Kiernan chuckled—but not before slugging his buddy hard in the thigh from where he sat.

"Eh... I've been punched harder by my ninety-year-old grandmother," the teammate said, though his bulging eyes and creased forehead suggested otherwise.

Kiernan backed up his chair a bit. "Well, I'd love to continue this scintillating conversation with you brutes, but...*no*. You can leave now."

He pointed to the terrace bar—not that they needed directions on how to return to their temporary watering hole.

After some good-natured grumblings and a few rounds of friendly slaps and punches, the group retreated to the other side of the pub.

"Wow!" Claire exclaimed, before breaking into laughter.

"Not the most subtle bunch, huh?" Kiernan replied as he shook his head, a half-smile on his lips.

"Last orders!" the bartender boomed from behind the counter.

Claire glanced at her watch. "Geez, that went by fast."

"Can I get you another glass of wine?" Kiernan asked as he nodded toward her empty glass.

The word "sure" was about to roll off her lips. And then... reality set in, bringing with it a slew of blinking red caution lights. She would be leaving Ireland in less than a month.

He doesn't want kids!

Even though she knew he was simply being polite in asking if she wanted a drink at last call, she couldn't deny that she felt a growing attraction to him. So why tempt herself with a situation that could never be? She might be putting the cart before the horse, but it was for her own good. She had come to Ireland to find clarity and to heal—not to muddy the waters with a strong but dead-end attraction.

Claire slowly pushed back her chair and stood up. "Thanks, but I think I'm going to head back to my cottage now. I must still be grappling with some jet lag, because I feel like it's three in the morning!"

Really, Claire, another lame excuse?

She could tell by his pinched expression that Kiernan wasn't buying her explanation for a second. And the fact that this pinched face was still one of the most handsome she had ever encountered… Well, that was reason alone to conclude that she was doing the right thing.

Kiernan stood up from his chair. "Did you walk here?"

"I did. It only took me fifteen minutes. I'm staying at one of the pink cottages about a mile that way," she said, pointing west.

"Ah, the pink cottages—which used to be white, by the way," Kiernan noted. "There's a rumor that the owner refurbished them while on an acid trip, but you didn't hear that from me."

Claire snickered. "I did wonder about the color…not going to lie. But they're cute, and it's sort of the perfect little home-away-from-home while I'm here."

"Well, let me at least walk you back."

Claire forced a smile to mask the discomfort that was expanding inside. "I'm fine, really. It's not like walking back through some dark Boston alley. In fact, I went for a walk last night along the pier and it was really quite beautiful." She looked up at the sky. "The moon and stars were out in full force, just like tonight."

Kiernan watched her silently for several moments, his lips pressed tightly together. Finally, he nodded and managed a smile. "Well, if you get bored and want someone to talk to over the next few weeks I'm here every Tuesday evening with my fellow louts. I'm occasionally here on late Sunday afternoons, too. There's a team practice that I join when I can, and we usually wind down afterwards with a pint or two."

"I'll keep that in mind," Claire said, truly appreciative of his offer.

Kiernan's lips curved into a slight grin. "Oh—and one more thing. If you decide to hit up the usual tourist spots, you might want to spray the Blarney Stone with a strong antiseptic before kissing it. Just saying…"

Claire chuckled quietly. "That's good advice."

"By the way, how are you getting around? Do you have a car?"

"I rented a Mini. A little red one. Goes perfectly with the pink house."

Kiernan smiled and nodded. "Good choice. Well, you take care."

"You, too."

As Claire walked past him, unable to fully divert her eyes away from his muscular body as it pressed against his taut athletic shirt, it was as if something grabbed hard at her stomach.

Once outside, she took a deep breath and allowed the cool night air to seep into her lungs. For a split second she questioned her decision to close the door—no, make that *slam* the door—on any further interaction with Kiernan. But she had no choice. She had come to Ireland to make a difficult decision that could potentially alter the course of her life from hereon in. The last thing she needed was to tempt another complication that would only create more heartache. She had had enough of that for a lifetime already.

Kiernan walked into the still-dark kitchen of his home and tossed his keys onto the counter. Switching on the light, he felt as though he could hear the emptiness that surrounded him. There were plenty of inanimate objects in view, of course, and some, like the refrigerator, emitted a low-level hum that could pass for a sign of life, albeit an electronic one.

But no human voices. No greeting from a loving partner, no joyful screeches of an excited child.

Not even a bark or a meow.

And although he had once toyed with the idea of getting a couple of goldfish, even that had fallen by the wayside when he'd considered the possibility that his fairly frequent one, two or even three-nighters at the hospital meant potentially coming home to fish that were floating belly-up in a tank.

The irony that he could save lives in the direst of situations as a surgeon but couldn't sustain a pet goldfish—or even a companion plant—was not lost on Kiernan.

He grimaced as he opened a bottle of electrolyte-infused water, staring blankly at the bland, cream-colored wall as he took several long sips. He was used to being met by silence upon returning home—found comfort in it, actually—but tonight something felt different.

He wondered if his reaction had been spawned by the look on Claire's face when he had mentioned his intention to live a child-free life. She had seemed surprised by his revelation, if not momentarily disturbed, but should she have been? How could any doctor at the top of their game feel differently?

He placed the bottle on the counter and sighed, knowing well the answer to his own question.

Because not every doctor had a father like you.

Which, depending on how he looked at it, was both a blessing and a curse.

The blessing was that he'd inherited his father's innate ability to excel as a surgeon—a combination of empirical knowledge, think-outside-the-box innovation and exceptional dexterity that had turned his hands into lifesaving instruments.

The curse was…well, it was the very same thing. Because—just like his father—he had an unrelenting desire to constantly improve. And continually expanding his skillset and saving more lives didn't just happen on its own. It required devotion to a singular purpose. Day in and day out. *Year* in and *year* out.

His father had made the mistake of thinking that if he cut back from one hundred percent devotion to his career to ninety-five percent, and directed the remaining five percent to his family, it would be enough. How wrong he had been. Those sparse breadcrumbs had been no substitute for his presence at the primary school play or the secondary school rugby game.

Even career advice had been more aptly dispensed by the

school's advisor than his own father. When Kiernan had told his father that he was applying to the School of Medicine at Trinity College—his father's alma mater—the detached reply had been: "Don't expect to coast on my coattails if you get in." Not *I'm so proud of you* or *You'll make a great surgeon*.

His dad had relayed one more nugget of advice that Kiernan had taken to heart, though: "You'd better not entertain trying out for the Trinity rugby team if you do get in. You need to devote one thousand percent to your studies, otherwise you'll never make it."

Kiernan smiled wistfully as he recalled one of his first actions upon starting his freshers year. Not only had he tried out for Trinity's football team, but he'd been the star inside center up until graduation. Had it been a safe act of rebellion on his part? Perhaps. But he couldn't have rebelled by choosing an alternative profession—that would have only hurt him, not his dad.

He was doing what he was meant to do. And he had learned from his father's mistakes. He would forgo having a family of his own not because he was cold inside, or because he had no affinity for children, but because he *did*. And he would never want them to suffer the loneliness and insecurity that he had felt as a young boy, growing up with a father who was a parent in name only.

Kiernan shuddered as he pulled himself back to the present. That was then, and this was now. Yes, there had been more than a few romantic relationships that had skidded to a halt once the topic of children had been broached, but better to know upfront that his priorities were a deal-breaker for someone. The simple fact was that most women wanted a family of their own—and he would never want to deny them that source of joy and fulfillment.

Perhaps he was destined to sail through life unattached, and he was okay with that. Well, it was more like he had come to accept that this was his fate. It was a choice he'd made know-ingly and willingly—career over commitment—and he had yet to regret his decision.

His thoughts turned to Claire, her face coming into sharp focus in his mind. The pale but piercing green eyes, the full, pillowy lips and rich chestnut hair. What was her real story, anyway? Why was she taking a whole month off from her critical role as an ob-gyn at a major Boston hospital? Why had she come to Ireland all alone? Was it some sort of American thing? She certainly didn't strike him as the flighty type—quite the opposite, actually—but something just didn't add up.

Not that he would ever get answers to his questions. Unless Claire decided to deliberately show up at the pub when he was there—and he highly doubted she would—he was never going to see her again. She had disappeared into the darkness of the night like Cinderella, leaving him with no means to contact her. Instead of a glass slipper, he needed…what? A hospital-grade clog to try and track her down?

Perhaps it was just as well, Kiernan thought. Something told him he could fall hard for the intriguing American doctor who had suddenly appeared in his life. And that, quite simply, did not fit in with his ultimate plan.

CHAPTER FOUR

"THERE YOU ARE," Lucy said to Kiernan as he looked up from his tablet.

Though he would admit it to no one, he sometimes longed for the days—not so far in the past—when he could rifle through physical charts rather than be tapping ad nauseam on a digital screen.

"What is it with this thing?" Kiernan said impatiently as he pressed on "lab results" and up popped a list of the patient's current medications instead. "Are my fingers too fat or something?"

Lucy twisted her mouth to one side. "No, I'm sure it's just that the tabs are too small."

Placing the tablet onto the nurses' station counter with an exasperated sigh, he turned to Lucy. "Nice try."

"I do my best."

"Were you looking for me?"

"I was. It's about Jan Reddy—her ultrasound last week showed fetal spina bifida."

"Yes…right. I haven't met with her personally, but her case came up in the weekly staff meeting."

Lucy nodded. "She's here for more tests this morning, and I was wondering if maybe you'd be able to talk to her. She's having a hard time dealing with the diagnosis, especially since her surgery options are still up in the air."

"Of course. I'll swing by and see her. I thought we had our scheduling staff looking into fetal surgery availability at other hospitals?"

"They are, but no luck as of yet."

Kiernan grimaced. It was not the news he wanted to hear. Fetal surgery for spina bifida offered hope for babies that were developing in the womb with an open gap in their spinal cord. But it was an extremely complex surgery that only certain hospitals were equipped to offer, and West Mercy wasn't one of them.

Kiernan hoped that this would change once the new neonatal wing was up and running, but even then it would most likely be some way down the road. It took a very gifted surgeon to perform this delicate operation, and although he had many exceptional surgeons on his staff, none were trained in this type of procedure. All of which meant Jan would have to find another hospital that could schedule the surgery in time, and even if that was possible it would mean significant personal expense and possibly traveling away from her two young children.

"Okay, keep me posted. I'll probably touch base with Dr. Fleming first," he said, referring to Jan's obstetrician, "but I'll check in on Jan right after."

"Great, thanks," Lucy replied. She nodded toward the tablet on the counter. "Don't forget to take your friend with you on your travels. As of last count, it's been brought to a nurses' station on every floor and designated as 'lost' no less than a dozen times."

Kiernan shot an annoyed glance at the device. "Yeah, well... I guess subconsciously I keep hoping that it won't find its way back to me."

Lucy smirked. "Progress, Mr. O'Rourke. It's a good thing, I promise."

Once Lucy had departed, Kiernan took a moment to organize his thoughts. Per usual, he had a busy day ahead, but he preferred to map it out in his mind rather than record it on the tablet.

"Hey, hey, hey, my man!" Sebastian exclaimed as he suddenly inserted himself in front of Kiernan like a photo-bombing squirrel.

"Not you again," Kiernan replied with a mixture of annoyance and friendly affection.

"Listen, that hot American doctor from the other day... I got the goods on her."

Now *this* had Kiernan's attention. "What do you mean?"

"I discovered she's got quite the resume back at Boston General."

Kiernan's voice grew sharper. "And how exactly did you find this out?"

Sebastian let loose with a crocodile smile. "Simple. You told me her name..." The smile grew impossibly wider. "And Google is my friend."

Kiernan slid the tablet off the counter and tucked it under his arm. "Good, because you don't have any others."

Like all of Kiernan's pretend insults, this one rolled off Sebastian like water off a duck. "My, my, we're touchy today. I was certain you'd want to know that she's considered an expert in high-risk pregnancies and cutting-edge fetal surgery. And she's got quite the list of awards and distinctions."

"I'm not surprised," Kiernan said. "I saw firsthand what she's capable of."

Sebastian ran his fingers through his perfectly coiffed hair, then leaned his elbow on the counter. "You think she's still in the area? I bet I could find out where she's staying. I've never played tour guide before, but for her I'd make an exception."

Kiernan viewed him through narrowed eyes. "And I've never punched a colleague before, but I'm about to make an exception as well."

Sebastian raised his hands in mock surrender. "Take it easy, sunshine. I was just joking around."

Kiernan swung his arm in Sebastian's direction, prompting him to lurch back from the counter with a high-pitched yelp.

Instead of landing a punch, Kiernan patted him on the shoulder. "You're awfully jumpy today. Might want to cut back on your morning caffeine fix."

With a wink, Kiernan headed off for a quick chat with Dr. Fleming.

Jan Reddy was lying down on the treatment table when Kiernan entered the room. Her face was turned away as she stared at the far wall, but upon hearing the door swing open, she immediately looked over.

"Hello, Jan, I'm Mr. O'Rourke," Kiernan said as he walked up to her and shook her hand. "I'm the chief of surgery here at West Mercy." He pulled up a chair and seated himself close to the head of the table. "My staff have been keeping me up to date on your case, but I wanted to meet and talk to you personally, if that's okay."

Her tense face softened into a smile. "Yes, of course."

"I know these past few days since the spina bifida diagnosis haven't been easy."

She shook her head. "They haven't. You read about this sort of thing happening to other women, and you never think it's going to happen to you. Especially since my other two pregnancies were perfectly healthy."

"Unfortunately, that's how it is sometimes with birth defects. There's no rhyme or reason to it. I reviewed your case history, and you have none of the risk factors."

"That's what Dr. Fleming said. She's so nice… But things like diabetes, and I think she said folate deficiency was another factor—they don't apply to me."

Kiernan pressed his lips together and nodded. At times

like this, when there was nothing he could do in the moment to instantly fix something, he could only offer a genuine gesture of understanding.

"So, I know Dr. Fleming has talked to you about fetal surgery to repair the spinal opening…"

"She has. And I know the surgery can't be done here."

"Believe me when I say I wish that weren't the case. We're working hard to get to a point where we can offer fetal surgeries for spina bifida and other congenital anomalies. In the meantime, we're hoping we can find a spot for you at another hospital that can perform this procedure. I spoke to Dr. Fleming a little while ago, and she said that even if we can, you have some concerns about whether to move forward with the surgery."

"I do. And I know this probably won't make any sense, but when I found out that I was a candidate for fetal surgery, I wished for a second that I wasn't. Because that way I wouldn't have to make a decision that could possibly lead to the death of my baby." She paused and swallowed hard. "Or me. And I want you to know that I would do anything to save my baby's life—even if it meant losing mine. But I have two other children who need me. And a husband, too." She rolled her eyes, topped off with a half-smile. "You know how most men are just big babies themselves."

Kiernan laughed quietly. "So I've heard."

He truly felt for Jan. She was facing a dilemma that he wouldn't wish on anyone. It was true that not all mothers-to-be facing her predicament fulfilled the criteria needed to move forward with the surgery. From the mother's past medical history to a current BMI, and even the presence of a support person, there were a number of boxes that needed to be checked off before the green light could be given for the procedure. Additionally, the anomaly had to be discovered early enough for the surgery to be performed—in the twenty-second to twenty-fifth week of pregnancy. In Jan's case, it had been discovered during her second trimester scan at twenty-one weeks. Which meant the clock was ticking...and the pressure was on.

As a surgeon, Kiernan didn't believe in sugarcoating the risks to a patient. In his mind, it was ultimately a disservice to them. Instead, he believed they should have all the facts they needed to make an informed decision, and he would always fully support them in whatever they chose to do.

"Jan, I know this is not an easy decision. I'm sure Dr. Fleming went over this with you, but there's always the option of post-delivery surgery. This would typically be within the first twenty-four to forty-eight hours after birth. It's less risky but, since spina bifida is a progressive condition, it won't halt progression within the womb like fetal surgery can do, so your baby will most likely experience more complications down the road. That being said, I've seen it lessen considerably the severity of spina bifida in the handful of patients that we've treated here."

"And you can perform this surgery here?"

"Yes."

"But it won't fix the defect to the same degree that fetal surgery can?"

"Unfortunately, no."

Jan stared up at the ceiling and sighed. "I wish I could talk to someone who's actually performed fetal surgery for spina bifida and can personally share with me the good and bad of how it turned out." She gasped, then sat up on her elbows. "I'm sorry, Mr. O'Rourke! I didn't mean to imply that talking to you isn't helpful, because it is..."

Kiernan smiled. "No need to apologize. I totally understand where you're coming from. I'm still hopeful that we'll be able to line you up with a surgeon at another hospital, and once we do, I'm sure they'll be more than happy to answer any of your questions."

She squeezed her lips together as though doing her best to smile through her anxious thoughts. "Thank you for coming by."

"Of course." Kiernan stood up. "And I know you're in good hands with Dr. Fleming and the rest of her team, but I'm here if you need anything."

This time her smile was full width. "I appreciate that."

As Kiernan started down the hospital corridor, he tried to organize the tidal wave of thoughts that were cresting all at once in his mind. Hearing Jan speak firsthand about the treatment options for her baby's condition only strengthened his resolve to ensure West Mercy's new neonatal wing would one day be fully equipped to offer cutting-edge fetal surgery—and more.

But that wasn't going to help Jan now. His temples throbbed with the realization that, no matter how lofty his ambitions to go all in and give one hundred and ten percent on behalf of his patients, there were still obstacles that he had no control over. All he could do was plow ahead, knowing that progress was inevitable, but often on its own timetable.

And then another thought hit him like a bolt of lightning. He paused and rifled through the pocket of his lab coat, extracting his phone and instantly initiating a search. Tapping on a search results link, his eyes widened…and then widened some more.

"Thank you, Sebastian," he said under his breath. "You're a pain in the ass, but sometimes a *helpful* pain in the ass."

Claire tossed some breadcrumbs into the water and laughed as a small flock of ducks pounced on the treats, slurping them up within seconds. She threw out another handful, then announced, "That's all I got, guys!"

Yesterday, she had followed the path from her cottage down over a slight hill, through thickened brush and finally an opening that revealed the shallow, rocky shoreline of the bay. She had been instantly captivated by the colorful waterfowl, chirping birds and myriad wildflowers, and today was no different.

Despite her vow a few days ago to get out and mingle with other people, she was finding the quiet serenity of nature to be a much greater draw. Spotting a large boulder to sit on, she pulled up her knees and rested her forearms and chin on top of them. There was no doubt in her mind that this peaceful solitude would be a better facilitator than loud tourist spots for the monumental career decision that she needed to make. And yet she felt no closer to a resolution than when she had first arrived in the country.

Closing her eyes, she replayed all that had already transpired in less than a week. An emergency breech delivery. An unexpected but powerful attraction to a fellow doctor. No wonder she was no further along in sorting out a difficult professional dilemma.

Reopening her eyes and staring out at the gently shimmering waters, her thoughts were pulled like a magnet back to her encounter with Kiernan at the pub. Since the end of her marriage, and the loss of Ariana, she had not felt even the slightest spark of interest toward another man. Not those who had approached her during occasional social outings with friends, a drink in one hand and a "How *you* doing?" tumbling out of their mouths, nor the male colleagues who had been circling the waters upon news of her divorce.

Her therapist and her friends had more than once suggested that maybe she was protecting her heart after Mark's betrayal and Ariana's death. But if that were true, it was on an unconscious level, rather than a deliberate decision to squash any attraction. She simply hadn't *felt* anything, either physically or emotionally, toward another man. And, given that she hadn't been in the right headspace to open her heart up to someone else, it was probably just as well.

And yet, with seemingly no effort on his part, Kiernan had drawn her in and reawakened a yearning in her that she had come to believe was gone for good. Perhaps it was the easy rapport they shared. The kind brown eyes and disarming smile. The sexily tousled hair—oh, heck, the sexy *everything*. She smiled at the deliciousness of her thoughts—until reminding herself that although daydreaming about Kiernan was an enjoyable pastime, it was also a distraction that she couldn't afford right now. Not when her career hung in the balance, and her time would be best spent engaging in some serious soul-searching.

With that in mind, Claire forced herself to redirect her thoughts. But a sudden, familiar voice stopped them dead in their tracks.

"Claire!"

Swinging her head around, Claire watched, mouth slightly agape, as Kiernan spread aside the end of a thicket patch with both hands and emerged out into the open.

What in the...?

She stood up from the boulder, both happy to see him and wishing she could feel otherwise. "How in the world did you know where to find me?"

Kiernan grinned, the sun catching golden flecks in his brown eyes. "Well, I knocked on every pink cottage door, and only strangers answered. Then I came to your cottage, and no one was home. But I saw fresh footprints that looked to be your size on the path behind the cottage and decided to follow them."

"For real," she insisted, with a *Yeah, right* expression etched across her face.

"Okay, the red Mini parked outside gave it away."

Claire tapped her head with her hand as if to say, *Of course*.

"I know this is a surprise..." Kiernan said, taking a few more steps to close the gap between them.

"You could say that."

Kiernan stared into her eyes. "I have a favor to ask you. Actually, if you could magnify the word 'favor' by about ten thousand, then that's what I'm about to ask."

"Okay, now you're starting to scare me," Claire said, only half kidding.

"I don't mean to scare you," Kiernan said, as he briefly touched her forearm.

Perhaps the gesture was meant to calm her, but the electricity that shot through her had the opposite effect. Coupled with the intense physical attraction she felt for the hunky surgeon just inches away from her, the surge caught her off guard. But as she regained her breath and looked into his eyes, she allowed herself to settle into the feeling his touch provoked. And it felt good.

"I met with a patient today whose unborn baby was recently diagnosed with spina bifida."

Kiernan's words quickly put a damper on the opening she had allowed herself. She wasn't sure if it was her chest or her stomach that tightened first, but either way a sense of dread was building.

"She's been ruled as a candidate for fetal surgery, and we're trying to set her up with a hospital that offers the procedure. But she's worried about the outcome if she goes through with it. She has two young children, and she doesn't want to leave them without a mother if something goes wrong."

"There's always a risk," Claire conceded, "but the odds would still be in her favor."

"I think knowing that would help her make the right decision for her baby and her family."

"You mean no doctors at West Mercy have explained the risks and benefits of the surgery to her?"

"They have. But I really think it would help if she heard it from someone who's actually performed the procedure."

Claire felt her heart quicken—no small feat given that her chest was now tighter than a drum. "Wait—do you mean *me*?"

Kiernan nodded, his eyes eager with anticipation.

"What makes you think I've even performed this surgery?"

"It came up in a Google search."

"You *Googled* me?" Claire asked, her voice rising.

"It's not as bad as it sounds," Kiernan replied, his face tight as though he were talking on eggshells, never mind walking on them.

"After meeting with the patient this morning—her name is Jan—I got to wondering if maybe you'd done this sort of surgery yourself. It was just a hunch. In fact, I wasn't expecting anything to turn up in my search when I entered your name, but quite a bit did." He paused, his face softening as he added, "It's not my fault you're an exceptionally talented doctor."

Claire *almost* smiled.

"You've performed close to a dozen successful spina bifida fetal surgeries. I mean, I can't imagine anyone more qualified to talk to Jan about what to expect if she moves forward with the surgery." He paused, the silence between them peppered with the sound of birdsong and water gently lapping up against rocks. "I know you're here on vacation, and I shouldn't even be asking you. But if you're up for this, it would just be an hour at most of your time. A consultation, that's all."

Claire stared down at the ground as she ran through the scenario in her head.

A woman has discovered she's carrying a baby with a condition that could significantly compromise the quality of his or her life. She's devastated. She's scared. She wants to do the right thing for her unborn baby and the two children she already has. How can I not do what I can to help her make that decision?

Claire knew very well that she couldn't answer this question without first placing it within a greater context. After all, if there were two things that were *not* on her Ireland travel itinerary, they were entering a hospital and meeting with a patient. Especially when her whole reason for being here was to figure out whether she could resume that life. But there was a flipside to every coin, and an argument could just as easily be made that the only way to determine this would be to walk the walk. Which in this case meant meeting Jan and talking through the treatment options that were best for her and her unborn baby.

Trial by fire. Or, better yet, trial by *controlled* fire.

Claire looked back up at Kiernan, silently catching her breath as his handsome face greeted her with a smile. There was something in that moment between them that told her she could do this. Something about *him* that made her feel safe and infused with inner strength.

"Okay," she said, a smile slowly emerging. "I'll do it."

"Thank you," Kiernan said breathlessly. "Thank you so much."

"No need to thank me."

"Would tomorrow work for you?" he asked. "Say at around eleven a.m.?"

"Yes, I can do that."

"Great! I'll pick you up at—"

"I'll drive to the hospital myself," Claire interjected, softening her tone when she noticed how Kiernan flinched at her unintended harshness.

It was difficult enough pushing past her fears and agreeing to the consultation. No need to add to the stomach butterflies she'd be feeling tomorrow by sitting oh-so-close to Kiernan on the drive in.

"After all, I've got this cute little Mini, so I might as well put it to use."

Kiernan chuckled. "Yes, good idea."

Ten silent seconds passed by as slow as molasses. Claire

smiled and widened her eyes—her go-to expression when she was feeling uneasy or awkward. There was a nonverbal exchange of...*something*...between them, and it pulled at every fiber of her being in a way that she hadn't felt in a very long time.

"So I'll see you and Jan tomorrow at eleven?" she asked, feeling the need to fill in the silence.

Kiernan smiled and nodded—then jolted slightly as though suddenly remembering something. He pulled his phone from a side pocket in his scrub pants. "Should we exchange phone numbers? Just in case there's an emergency or I need to adjust the time?"

Claire hesitated momentarily. It was a reasonable request, but also one more swing of the sledgehammer into the barrier she had built around herself. But maybe she should let go of a brick or two. For Kiernan, she could do that.

"My phone is in the cottage, but call my number and I'll have yours as well." She quickly recited the numbers, and he punched them into his phone.

"Great. Well, I've got two surgeries scheduled this afternoon, so I'd better be heading back to the hospital." He started to leave, then stopped. "Oh, and don't forget. We drive on the left side of the road here."

Claire grinned. "Thanks for the reminder."

Trudging through the dense thicket that lined the midsection of the path on the way back to his car, Kiernan felt elated. Not even the thorns that were catching on his shirt or the burrs sticking to his hair were enough to deter his ear-to-ear smile. He had successfully convinced Claire to meet with Jan and fully trusted that she would help Jan better understand the risks and benefits of spina bifida fetal surgery so that she could make the best possible decision for her and her family.

But his smile soon wavered as he replayed the look in

Claire's eyes as he had awaited her answer. Granted, he hadn't expected her to jump for joy at the prospect of taking time out of her vacation to consult on a patient. Or...maybe he kind of had. She was a dedicated doctor and a confident, highly skilled surgeon, and this was an opportunity to weigh in on a potential surgical outcome that could significantly better the lives of a mother and her unborn child. Plus, shouldn't she be even mildly curious to see how West Mercy was positioning itself to eventually offer innovative neonatal surgeries? So why the unmistakable hesitancy on her part?

His hand resting on the door handle of his SUV, Kiernan stood immobile as he pondered the question further. Finally, he shook his head and opened the door. Perhaps he was overthinking things. His question had caught Claire by surprise, and understandably so. Tomorrow it would all work out. Jan would get the consultation she had hoped for. And he would once again have the chance to bask in Claire's presence. And, oh, what a presence it was. Beauty, intelligence, empathy and compassion—all wrapped into one somewhat mysterious but altogether magnetic package.

His thoughts were steamrollering through his head—until an obvious buzzkill slammed on the brakes. In less than a month Claire would be returning to her life in the States. Which meant time was of the essence if he was going to act on his undeniable attraction to her. Perhaps Sebastian was right—painful as that was to admit. He should savor the present moment—nothing more, nothing less. And the good thing about the present moment? It was already here.

CHAPTER FIVE

CLAIRE FELT HER tight grip on the steering wheel relax as late-morning sunshine filtered in through the Mini's windshield and side windows. The fact that she had butterflies in her stomach was more than apropos, given that springtime was on the verge of full bloom in the early-May countryside.

The serene landscape of lush fields and colorful wildflowers helped calm her nerves, but didn't erase them altogether. Not that anything could totally put her at ease. After all, she was on her way to West Mercy Hospital, where she would be meeting with a worried mother to help her make a momentous decision about her unborn baby.

You can do this, Claire told herself, slowly drawing in a breath of air and holding it for several moments as she inwardly repeated the mantra. *It's a one-time consultation, that's all.*

She needed to remind herself of this as well, given that it was a far cry from her normal interaction with patients. She was accustomed to getting to know them and their families well—especially those who were dealing with difficult medical situations.

The importance of maintaining an emotional detachment had been instilled in her since day one of medical school. But even though she had been an overachiever in all of her classes, this was one area where she didn't mind falling short if it meant allowing herself to care about her patients. She celebrated their joys and grieved their losses. Only now did she realize how doing so had made it more difficult to put her own pain aside when she had resumed her physician duties after losing Ariana.

Driving into the West Mercy parking lot, she pulled into the nearest open space, turned off the engine, then closed her eyes and reminded herself that she needed to hide her vulnerability not just from Jan, but from Kiernan, too. Neither of them needed to know that she felt like a walking open wound. Or that just speaking the word "baby" was enough to grab at her gut with a pain that she actually felt on a physical level.

The good news was there could be a happy ending to all of this. As a onetime consultant on Jan's condition, she would be playing the most minor of roles in such a miracle, but it was still something.

Walking up to the main entrance a short time later, Claire suddenly stopped in her tracks and viewed the multi-building complex before her. Seen from the front, the hospital was much larger than she had expected, prompting inevitable reminders of Boston General. Her earlier resolve to push past potential triggers was facing its first severe test, and she had to quickly recover before all was lost.

Deep breaths. Deep breaths.

Pinching her palm with her nails, she temporarily dispersed the distressing thoughts and memories that were tumbling forth. A few more seconds, another deep breath, and she was fully back in the present.

Once inside the entrance, Claire realized she hadn't locked down the details of where exactly to meet Kiernan. But as she approached the main nurses' station, she recognized a familiar friendly face.

"Hello, Dr. Delaney," Lucy said with a warm smile as she walked out from behind the station counter. "Mr. O'Rourke has just finished with a patient and is on his way down." Glancing over her shoulder, she added, "Speak of the devil."

"Are you calling me the devil?" Kiernan asked with amusement as he seemingly materialized from out of the blue.

Or maybe Claire's slightly dizzy reaction upon seeing him once again just made it feel that way. It was a brief but altogether enjoyable distraction from her nerves.

Lucy flashed a side grin. "Of course not. You're nothing short of angelic, Mr. O'Rourke. And I know your patients would all agree."

"Good save." There was a twinkle in Kiernan's eyes that grew in intensity as he shifted his gaze to Claire. "How was the drive in?" he asked, his dark brown hair imperfectly...yet perfectly...tousled.

Claire's next breath caught in her throat. If ever there was an *I'm a brilliant surgeon too busy to brush my hair, but I'm still sexy as heck* vibe, then this had to be it. Not that Kiernan deliberately sent out those signals. Up to this point, everything in his demeanor had convinced Claire that he had no idea how attractive he was. Or, if he did, it fell so low on his list of important virtues that he simply couldn't care less.

She forced herself to exhale, then smiled. "It was fine. I have to say I really like that little Mini. I'm not sure how it would fare during a Boston winter, but I think I'm going to look into getting one when I'm back in the States."

Kiernan's smile momentarily faltered, as though the reminder of the temporary nature of her stay had triggered a somber moment. Or maybe she was just projecting her own suddenly mixed feelings on the subject.

Stepping off the elevator several minutes later, Kiernan turned to Claire. "Before you talk to Jan, I thought you might want to look over her case notes and test results."

Claire nodded. "Sure, that's a good idea."

"My office is just down this hall," he said.

Upon entering the smallish but neat and well-lit room, Claire's eyes were drawn to the barrage of diplomas and certificates, along with a handful of framed photos, that lined the wall behind his desk. "I can see you're quite the under-achiever," she observed wryly.

Kiernan grinned slightly, but said nothing as he rifled through a pile of folders on his expansive desk.

"Wait—is that Bono?" Claire asked incredulously as she homed in on a photo of Kiernan hugging shoulders with the Irish rocker.

Kiernan looked up from a thick folder that he had just extracted from the pile. "Ah, yes. That's from a hospital charity event last year. Quite an interesting chap—and very gener-ous, too."

Claire eyed Kiernan curiously, amused by his rather non-chalant reply.

There was a knock on the partially open door, and she and Kiernan turned as a young male nurse in light green scrubs began to enter the room. Realizing that Kiernan wasn't alone, he stopped mid-step.

"Sorry, I'll come back," he said, slowly retreating back-wards.

"No, come on in," Kiernan said. "Did you hear back from UCLH?"

The man frowned, as though dreading his own reply. "I did. Mr. Ferguson dislocated his shoulder during a golf match over the weekend. He's out of commission for at least the next month."

"Damn," Kiernan muttered under his breath. "We're run-ning out of options. And that one was looking like a sure thing." He sighed heavily, then turned back to the nurse. "What about Manchester General?"

"Still waiting to hear back."

"Okay, keep me posted."

"I will," the nurse said, before exiting the room.

Claire didn't want to pry about what was clearly distressing news for Kiernan, but she did wonder if it could possibly have something to do with Jan. She didn't have to guess for long.

"That was University College Hospital in London," Kiernan explained. "We were told a few days ago that they might be able to do Jan's surgery in two weeks. I haven't told her yet, because we were waiting for final confirmation, and it's a good thing I didn't. And I get grief for risking injury while playing rugby... Who knew putting a tiny white ball around in starched checked trousers was more dangerous than being face-deep in mud at the bottom of a rugby pileup?"

"Wild," Claire said quietly, viscerally feeling Kiernan's frustration. "But fetal surgery is more common now than, say, even ten years ago. Granted, not every hospital is equipped to perform some of the procedures, or has the right team in place, but it seems like there should be more options if you're expanding your search outside the country."

"There are. But one of the issues is red tape—something I'm sure you deal with back in America as well."

Claire rolled her eyes almost instinctively. "I have more experience with that than I'd like to admit. But I thought it would be a bit less so here, given the exchange between countries within Europe. Not that I fully understand how that might work."

"Unfortunately, red tape is red tape—especially when it comes to scheduling a complex surgery in another country at short notice." He grimaced, then gave a slight nod of the head as though trying to snap himself out of negative thoughts. "Here," he said, his voice softening as he handed the folder to Claire. "This should have all of Jan's records."

"Thanks," Claire replied, the hefty stack of papers landing in her hands like a solid brick. Or two. "You don't have digital records here at the hospital?"

"We do. But I like to have a hard copy of cases I'm working on as well." He paused, a half-smirk slowly emerging. "Call me old school."

Claire grinned. "Nothing wrong with that."

She leafed through the numerous documents in the folder, pausing at the ultrasound report. It confirmed what she'd expected with considerable apprehension: Jan's baby had the most severe form of spina bifida, myelomeningocele, in which part of the spine protruded from the back in a fluid-filled sac. It meant the surgery would be that much more difficult—and a positive outcome would be that much more life-enhancing. She then viewed the surgery criteria notes, a checklist of close to two dozen "must-haves" in order for the surgery to move forward. No history of placenta previa or hypertension...ability to adhere to a follow-up requirements...*check, check, check*....

It was only when she was three-quarters through the checklist that she realized she had been reviewing the notes without the stomach-churning anxiety she had tried to prepare for. Could it be because she was in a new hospital, and not at Boston General, which had triggers at every turn? It was a possible revelation that she'd need to ruminate on further. But right now she had to concentrate on Jan's prognosis.

Finishing her review, Claire looked up to find that Kiernan had been watching her intently, as though taking his next breath was contingent upon receiving her thumbs-up. She wasn't about to disappoint him.

"Jan's a textbook candidate for this surgery."

He pursed his lips together and nodded. "That's my team's assessment as well. But I wanted to hear it from the expert."

There was the slightest teasing edge to Kiernan's voice, but Claire didn't mind. She knew he respected her exceptional knowledge and experience on this matter—just as she respected his immense know-how in...well, no doubt in everything related to surgery and hospital leadership.

"Shall we go and talk to Jan?" Kiernan asked as he opened the door to the hallway and gestured for Claire to exit first.

Claire smiled, masking her inner turmoil. As she started down the hallway, with Kiernan by her side, there were only two thoughts in her mind:

Stay strong for Jan. And for her baby.

Kiernan ushered Claire into a tastefully decorated consultation room that more closely resembled a cozy parlor.

A petite woman in a white lab coat with a short black bob and ice-blue eyes immediately stood up from one of several thick-cushioned chairs and came over.

"I'm Dr. Fleming, senior doctor ob-gyn," she said, shaking Claire's hand. "Mr. O'Rourke has filled me in on everything, and I really appreciate you taking the time to talk to Jan about fetal surgery."

"Nice to meet you," Claire said.

As Dr. Fleming resumed her seat, Kiernan introduced Claire to Jan, who sat on the adjacent couch.

"Hi," she said, managing a weak smile. "Thank you for being here. Mr. O'Rourke said you're an expert at spina bifida fetal surgery."

Now seated between Dr. Fleming and Kiernan, Claire silently took note of the dark circles under Jan's eyes, the hollow cheeks and raspy voice. There was no doubt that the immense worry about her unborn baby's condition was taking its toll.

"I'm glad to be here," Claire replied. "I know Mr. O'Rourke and Dr. Fleming have talked to you about the benefits of fetal surgery for your baby, and I'm sure you have lots of questions."

"I do. But the two main ones are, will it work? And is there a possibility I won't survive the surgery?" Jan's voice cracked as she added, "I'm not asking about survival for myself. I'm asking for the sake of my other two children."

Claire gripped the armrest of her chair as the air seemed to suddenly evaporate from the room. She wanted so badly to be fully present for Jan, to calm her fears and help her make the right choice for *all* her children. But first she needed to push past her own lingering trauma.

From the corner of her eye, she could see Kiernan's forehead crease as he glanced down at her white-knuckled grasp of the chair-arm. She had to rein in her emotions, or the situation would quickly spiral downwards.

Focus, Claire, focus...

Pulling herself back to the present, Claire explained to Jan that the rigorous screening process would help ensure the surgery's safety and success. And with each additional question Jan posed, Claire dug deep within herself to stay in the moment. By the time Jan got around to asking whether her previous spina bifida surgeries had been successful nearly twenty minutes had passed, and Claire's anxiety was almost fully in check.

"Here," Claire said after scrolling briefly through her phone and pulling up a picture. She quickly showed the image to Kiernan and Dr. Fleming before walking over to Jan. "This is Samantha. Her mom sent me this picture a few months ago, when Samantha turned five. She was one of my first fetal surgery patients, and she's doing great. Her mom said she started school last fall, and is keeping right up with the other kids."

Jan leaned in further to get a closer look at the young girl with blonde pigtails, freckles and an ear-to-ear smile. "And if she hadn't had the surgery it might have been a different outcome—right?"

Claire reluctantly nodded. Her whole purpose for coming here today was to help steer Jan in the direction that she truly felt was best for her and her unborn child. But if no hospital was available to do the surgery in time, then what was the point? She'd be doing little more than confirming to Jan that her best option was unobtainable. Without the surgery, Jan's unborn baby faced a host of potential health issues, including incontinence, paralysis and cognitive impairment.

Claire turned to Kiernan, meeting his eyes and feeling that he somehow understood her dilemma. He quickly stepped in and reassured Jan that they were doing everything they could to schedule the surgery at an appropriate facility. But would it happen in time? Claire wanted to stay optimistic, but doubt was setting in. She was used to preparing herself for the possibility that a treatment option might fall short of the desired outcome, especially for a high-risk pregnancy. But to not even have the chance to get a life-enhancing surgery off the ground?

That possibility brought with it a new sense of helplessness that she wasn't accustomed to.

"That seemed to go well," Kiernan said later, as he and Claire walked down the hospital corridor after the consultation had ended.

Claire nodded, but couldn't quite muster up a smile.

Kiernan eyed her sideways as they turned onto another corridor. "You're not saying much."

"Sorry. I think it went well, too. But unfortunately, I feel like maybe all I did was get her hopes up for a surgery that she might not be able to get in time."

Kiernan sighed. "I know. I was kind of fighting that thought as well. She did say she'd be willing to travel further than she initially indicated, so I'm going to tell my team to expand their search outside of Ireland and the UK Or I should say outside of the UK It's already been confirmed nothing can be scheduled in time at the few facilities equipped for this surgery in Ireland."

"But it's not just the surgery—there's all the follow-up, too. And it could mean being away from her children for quite some time."

"I thought of that as well. But Dr. Fleming is getting her

team up to speed on post-surgery care for Jan. She thinks it can be handled here, especially with the neonatal unit fully operational."

"I thought you said it wasn't open yet?"

"Not officially. But construction is completed, and the operating theaters and patient wards are equipped and ready to go." He turned to Claire as they continued their walk. "You know how hospital boards are. They want the opening to be big on publicity and fanfare."

"Is that what you want?"

"Personally, I couldn't care less about all that stuff." As they came to a large sliding glass door at the end of the corridor, Kiernan slowed to a halt, with Claire following his lead. "I just want to start offering cutting-edge neonatal care here, so we don't have to scramble to find other options for patients like Jan. But I'm also pragmatic enough to realize that we need to get the word out on as large a scale as possible to make this new undertaking a success. We can't help women with high-risk pregnancies if they're not being sent here for treatment. And that will only happen when we start forging a reputation for top-tier neonatal care."

"Good point."

Claire wondered if the intense effort behind her smile was obvious to Kiernan. She hoped it wasn't. In another time and place she'd be excited to talk about advanced treatment options for high-risk pregnancies. Heck, it was the type of conversation that she herself once typically initiated with colleagues. But that had been before the subject matter had become inextricably tied to personal loss and pain.

Kiernan turned and swiped his badge along the reader. The glass doors swiftly opened, and he gestured to Claire to enter first.

She wrinkled her nose slightly as they started down the corridor. "It almost has that new car smell in here."

Kiernan eyed her curiously from the side. "Funny you picked up on that. It's because everything *is* new in here. This is the neonatal wing I've been talking your ear off about."

Claire's breath caught in her throat, her rapid walk quickly decelerating.

Kiernan slowed down with her, his face perplexed. "Are you okay?"

Claire inwardly scrambled to salvage the situation. With every fiber of her being she wanted to avoid being pulled further back into the world of pregnancies and babies. Yes, she was at West Mercy today by choice. But she had never intended for her visit to extend beyond her consultation with Jan.

Still…could she reframe this moment? See it as an opportunity to witness a hospital making major progress for women's health and that of their newborn babies? Confirm to Kiernan that he was doing a commendable thing by driving this progress? He deserved no less. And perhaps at the same time she could begin to see glimpses of the joy and satisfaction she had once derived from playing an integral role in the health and wellness of mothers and their babies.

She looked up at him. His eyes were still searching hers. "I'm okay," she finally replied, conjuring up a smile as she gestured to the corridor before them. "Lead the way."

Kiernan appeared more than happy to oblige. Weaving through the main areas of the wing with Claire at his side, he paused at intervals to get her input on a particular process or piece of medical apparatus, as though wanting to ensure no stone had been left unturned in his quest for the most advanced neonatal center possible.

Entering the neonatal intensive care unit, Claire braced herself for an onslaught of emotion. A startled technician turned from the incubator that he had been testing with a biomedical analyzer. As Kiernan engaged him in a friendly conversation Claire held her breath, wondering if an anxiety episode was about to burst forth. But instead, the tightness in her chest dissipated, and she found herself peering more closely at the state-of-the-art equipment.

Could it be because the memories of her last moments with Ariana were confined to a birthing room and had never progressed to the NICU? Possibly. She only knew that she felt a sense of relief to have made it this far without any significant emotional fallout.

"And that concludes your personalized tour of the new West Mercy neonatal wing," Kiernan said twenty minutes later as they circled back to their starting point. "I hope you've enjoyed this sneak peek of our soon-to-open cutting-edge unit, and please come back again soon."

Her initial raw nerves had now dialed down several notches, and Claire couldn't help but snicker at Kiernan's pitch-perfect flight attendant voice.

"Well done," she conceded. "I can see why you're proud of this unit. Everything is state of the art, and once your team is certified in some of the specialized neonatal and fetal surgery techniques, I can't imagine West Mercy won't make a name for itself in neonatal medicine."

"I'm glad you think so," Kiernan said, looking pleased. "Yours is a highly coveted opinion."

The line was delivered with both sincerity and a touch of humor, and Claire laughed in return.

A door opened behind Kiernan and an electrician emerged, with a flashlight in one hand and a workbag in the other. He pulled the *Do Not Enter* sign off the door, then addressed Kiernan.

"All set, sir. There was some loose wiring in one of the walls, but I reconnected it and everything's good to go."

"Great," Kiernan said, turning to Claire. "The birthing suites are down this way. I didn't think I'd be able to show you, since there's been some electrical issues and we closed off the area out of an abundance of caution, but it looks like we've got the green light."

Before Claire could come up with an excuse to pass on this final and most potentially triggering leg of the tour, Kiernan swung open the door.

"You first."

Moments later they were standing inside a spacious yet cozy birthing suite. Soothing rays of natural light filtered in through floor-to-ceiling windows, dancing off the earth-toned walls and casting an iridescent glow over vast paintings of pastoral landscapes.

The scene was eerily familiar, and as Claire's eyes darted around the room a heavy sadness descended upon her.

Five and a half months into her pregnancy, she and Mark had stood in a nearly identical room during a birthing suite tour at Boston General, admiring the suite's calming color scheme and expansive windows.

Or, at least, *she* had viewed the surroundings with awe. Mark, on the other hand, had seemed distant and distracted. She recalled the unease she had felt at his I-want-to-be-any-where-but-here vibe, chalking it up at the time to the jitters of impending fatherhood.

But even then, something in the pit of her stomach told her there was more at play. Unable to fathom that her suspicions could possibly be true, she had squelched her snowballing doubts.

When they had solidified into reality less than a month later with his abrupt departure, the snowballs had turned into an avalanche of disbelief.

Needing something to grab on to, Claire searched for the nearest solid object. *Kiernan.* No, she was not going to grasp his arm, regardless of how muscular and strong it appeared to be. He might be wearing a lab coat now, but a form-fitting rugby shirt hid no secrets, and she wasn't about to forget *that* earlier image anytime soon.

Really? You're thinking about Kiernan's hunk of a build now?

Mind racing, Claire tried to reason with herself, but crazy thoughts had a way of quickly multiplying. Sweat beads broke out on her forehead. She had almost made it through the tour unscathed. *Almost.* If only the electrician's exit had been delayed a few more minutes. Then she and Kiernan would have moved on from the area and....

"Claire?" Kiernan said, alarm in his voice.

She peered up at him, wondering if she looked like a deer in the headlights, ready to bolt. That was certainly how she felt.

"You're awfully pale. Sit down," he said, nodding to a plump-pillowed chair against the wall. "Let me get you some water."

"I think I... I just need some air."

Making a beeline for the door, Claire was only half aware that Kiernan was right on her heels. But when he jumped in front of her out in the hallway, she could no longer pretend she was unraveling sight unseen. Kiernan had a front row seat to her meltdown, and her humiliation was only equaled by her desire to be instantly transported off the hospital grounds.

Wrapping his arm around her shoulder, Kiernan began to steer her diagonally toward a door on the other side of the corridor. With her fight-or-flight response switched on—emphasis on flight—Claire wanted to run for the nearest exit. But Kiernan's strong, protective grip was like a weighted blanket cocooned around her, and her rapid shallow breathing began to slow down a notch.

Once inside the empty exam room, Kiernan gently helped Claire onto a chair, then pulled another chair up beside her. He placed her hand over the palm side of his wrist, then draped his other hand on top of it.

"Just breathe and feel my pulse, and let yours sync to it."

Thump...thump...thump...

Claire closed her eyes and allowed Kiernan's slow, steady heartbeat to seep deeply into her very being. She felt her shoulders drop, and for the first time became aware that her feet were touching the ground. It was as if his strong but calm heartbeat was telling her own rapid-fire pulse: *Just follow me and everything will be okay.*

When she finally opened her eyes and looked up at Kiernan, she couldn't be sure how much time had passed. She only knew that his kind brown eyes were gazing deeply into own.

"I think we need to trade hearts," she quipped, her weakened voice cracking slightly.

The earlier adrenaline coursing through her body had been the equivalent of running a marathon, but at least she had crossed the finish line—and all thanks to the handsome surgeon just inches away from her.

"There's nothing wrong with your heart at all," Kiernan replied, with such decisiveness that she couldn't help but feel he wasn't just referring to its physical aspects.

Mr. O'Rourke, please report to Room 247 for a consultation.

Claire looked up at the intercom box above the doorway, then back at Kiernan.

He shook his head. "It can wait. You're my patient now."

A smile slowly emerged, and he squeezed her hand just tightly enough for her heart to skip a beat. He sure had a way of making her heart do unexpected things.

"I'm feeling much better," she finally managed to say. "Thank you."

"No need to thank me."

"I should let you get back to work."

"I'm not leaving until I'm certain you're okay." He cocked his head slightly to one side, as if wondering whether to say more. "Is there anything you want to talk about? My colleagues like to call me a grump behind my back—and sometimes to my face, for that matter—but truth be told, I'm a really good listener."

Claire smirked. "I'm sure you are. But I'm okay—really. I should have mentioned that I can be sensitive to a lot of environmental things. I probably just had a reaction to the new paint or the carpets in the suite."

She could tell by Kiernan's narrowed eyes that he wasn't buying her excuse for a second. But that didn't stop her from doubling down.

"Besides, you know how we doctors make the worst patients. Once I'm outside and get some fresh air, I'll be good as new."

"Well, let me at least walk you out to your car."

"That's not necessary—"

"I insist," Kiernan interjected, his sternness offset by the twinkle in his eye. "Besides, I'm going to be checking your stride. Any wobbliness and you'll be confined to quarters."

"Confined to quarters?" Claire repeated with a touch of amusement in her voice. "Is this a hospital or a military institution?"

Kiernan let out a mock sigh. "Sometimes it feels like a little of both."

The rejuvenating midday sun felt good on Claire's face as she walked through the parking lot to her car, with Kiernan close by her side.

"Are you sure you're okay?" he asked as she seated herself in the Mini and rolled down the window.

She smiled. "I'm sure."

"Thank you again for talking to Jan."

"Happy to do so."

After an exchange of goodbyes, Claire watched as Kiernan strode confidently across the parking lot, waiting for him to disappear from view before leaning her head back against the seat and taking a deep breath. She closed her eyes, wishing more than anything that his hand could still be clasping her own as her heartbeat synched with his. How he had turned the feeling of a pulse—normally just a routine diagnostic tool—into something so...*intimate* was something she'd be pondering for days to come.

But it was more than that. He had stayed with her, offering to talk about what had triggered her reaction and refusing to leave her side until he was convinced she was okay. And the kicker to all of this? Not once had he made her feel like he was doing so out of medical obligation.

Compare that to Mark, who hadn't even made the effort to be present during the loss of their daughter....

Claire shook her head. *Don't go there.* A few more deep breaths. *Focus on the positive.*

It was easy enough to do. She just had to think of Kiernan, and the way she was starting to feel whenever he was near.

Up in the third-floor cafeteria, which offered the most expansive view of the parking lot below, Kiernan stared out of the floor-to-ceiling window, his eyes glued to Claire's red Mini. Though ten minutes had passed, it had yet to leave its parking spot, and he decided to give it one more minute before heading back outside to check on her.

Another twenty seconds and the Mini backed out and headed toward the exit. Kiernan stared at the empty spot for several moments, trying to wrap his head around what had just transpired. He had previously toyed with the possibility that there was more to Claire's story than her *I'm just taking a month-long vacation* declaration. But now his suspicions were deepening.

"Mr. O'Rourke to Theater Three, STAT."

The intercom announcement pulled him back to the present. With a possible emergency unfolding, he had to put those thoughts on hold. Although something told him they'd return soon enough…

CHAPTER SIX

KIERNAN KNOCKED BRIEFLY on the hospital room door, then entered while scanning patient notes on his tablet. Yesterday, his concerned speculation over a possible trauma in Claire's past had been cut short when he'd been summoned to the operating theater for a woman—Darla—who had just been admitted with a burst appendix. Always a perilous situation, the risk had been magnified tenfold because Darla was six months pregnant.

Fortunately, Darla's surgery had gone well, and she was now resting comfortably with her husband at her bedside, along with their two adolescent daughters.

"I just wanted to check in to see how you're doing," Kiernan said now, as Darla and her husband smiled appreciatively.

A few more minutes of friendly small talk and then Kiernan wished Darla a speedy recovery back home, knowing she'd be discharged later in the afternoon.

Exiting the room, he glanced back at the family once more, wincing slightly as he tried to suppress the wave of poignancy that descended over him. There was something eerily familiar about the scene, and he didn't have to dig deep within his memories to make the connection.

Twenty years ago, the heavily pregnant woman with a perforated appendix had been none other than his mother. He recalled his aunt bringing him and his younger sister Colleen to visit her during an extended hospital stay due to complications. And his father? He'd been nowhere to be found. Actually... that wasn't true. He'd been in the same hospital as Kiernan's mother, but too tied up with his patients to check in on the most important patient...the most important *person*...of all.

It was probably just as well, Kiernan thought now, eyes narrowing and jaw clenching as he quickened his pace down the corridor. It wasn't like his father had been known for his bedside manner—though for the patients whose lives he had saved, forgoing the warm fuzzies was probably considered a small price to pay.

Still, Kiernan had never forgotten the excuses his mother had made for his father's cruel absence when she'd needed him most. "Your father's busy saving other lives," she had said at the time, struggling to form a smile with parched lips nearly as pale as her anemic skin.

And she had been right. His father *had* been saving other lives. Which would have been all fine and dandy if he'd had no family of his own that needed him, too.

Perhaps that explained Kiernan's actions when his mother had been hospitalized at West Mercy with double pneumonia, just over a year ago. Though she hadn't been a surgical patient, he had popped into her room at every opportunity, plumping up her pillows, double-checking her meds and fussing over her like only a loving son-slash-doctor could.

"I'll say one thing," his mum had said during one such occasion, when his doting had been in full overdrive. "Maybe it's because I'm your mother, but you most definitely have much more of a bedside manner than your father ever did." She had paused, in part to take more air into her healing lungs but also to flash a rueful smile. "Thank goodness for that."

So at least he'd got that part right—and without any real effort, given that he truly cared about his patients. They were actual people, with hopes and dreams and loved ones, not merely a list of symptoms and diagnoses. But sidestepping his father's other major flaw... That required more deliberation on his part.

Throw himself into his career as a surgeon dedicated to saving lives? *Check.* Avoid serious personal relationships that would make that first goal impossible? *Check.* Because the two had to go together—right? Even his mother had seemed to think so. She'd never actually *said* this to him...rather it was more about what she hadn't said.

Once, several years ago, she had asked him when he was planning to settle down and start a family.

"You mean so I can be an absentee husband and father like Dad?" he had replied pointedly.

She had silently looked back at him, understanding and regret in her eyes. And she'd never asked again.

Back in his office, Kiernan stared at the wall as thoughts of Claire incessantly flooded his mind. Ever since they had parted ways yesterday, he had not been able to stop thinking about her. He had texted her last night, to see how she was feeling, and had been at least mildly relieved when she had replied that she was fine. But he wasn't fully convinced.

He closed his eyes, reliving each second that had ticked by when she had tuned in to his pulse, her hand delicately placed on his wrist and her beautiful face just inches away from him. Only now did he realize how lucky he had been that his heart rate hadn't surged with her touch. He had felt it quicken, and only through sheer willpower had he slowed it down so that she, too, would begin to relax.

With a loud sigh, Kiernan swung his chair around to stare at the other equally bland wall. What he wouldn't give to see her again. As in *now*.

Extracting his phone from his white coat, he stared at the screen, then quickly typed out a text before he could talk himself out of it.

There's a great little garden tea shop that serves lunch halfway between the hospital and your cottage. Fancy taking out the Mini to meet me there at noon?

Kiernan wasn't aware that he was holding his breath while waiting for the beep of a text reply from Claire. It was only when his screen lit up with the word Sure that he sputtered and realized he was probably turning blue.

Wonderful. I'll text you the address shortly.

Leaning back in his chair, Kiernan replenished his oxygen supply with some deep breaths, then shook his head slightly, perplexed by his own actions. Lunch—if he even paused long enough to have it—was typically a couple of power bars eaten while on the move from one patient or operating theater to the next. And now he was taking a chunk of time out of his busy schedule to meet Claire? And not just at any restaurant, mind you. By choosing a quaint little tea shop nestled within carefully manicured gardens of tulips, daffodils and roses, he was fully setting the scene for... Well, it couldn't be romance...could it?

"That's crazy talk," he muttered aloud to his own thoughts.

But as he launched himself out of the chair he felt nearly giddy at the thought of soon seeing Claire. It was a state of mind that was new to him. But what the heck.

I might as well go with it.

Kiernan waved to Claire as she approached the small white wrought-iron table on the outside patio of the Gilded Petal Tea Shop. He stood up and pulled out her chair, his nerve-endings on fire as her shiny chestnut hair fluttered against his forearm while he helped push her chair back in.

"You dressed for the occasion," he said, admiring the gauzy flowered dress that clung to her taut curves. Or maybe it was the curves themselves that he was admiring. He cleared his throat at the distinction.

Claire smirked as she nodded toward him. "And I see you didn't."

He glanced down at his green scrubs—an unfashionable necessity given he was squeezing in lunch between surgeries. "You never know when a wilted tulip is going to need medical intervention."

Claire's lilting laughter filtered through him like a soul-soothing elixir. It was a relief to find that the sparkle had returned to her eyes and the peachy glow to her cheeks. Perhaps he had prematurely jumped to conclusions about her puzzling reaction in the birthing suite.

"It's good to see you," he said. "Even though you said you felt okay when you left yesterday, you still had me worried."

Claire twisted her mouth to one side. "Like I said...doctors make the worst patients."

He grinned. "Well, I can't say I disagree with that."

A waitress came by and poured two cups of tea, placing a pot on the table and handing small, folded menus to each of them.

"I should have known this was one of those finger sandwich kinds of places," Kiernan said with mock resignation in his voice as he skimmed the short list of options.

Claire chuckled. "I figured you'd been here before."

Kiernan glanced up from the menu. "To be honest, I've driven by it and admired the flowers, but never stopped in."

"I got to say...you don't strike me as a cucumber sandwich kind of guy."

Kiernan laughed heartily. "Looks like I'm going to have to be today." He perused the limited choices once more. "Or a tomato sandwich guy."

"Let's splurge and get a platter of both."

"Deal."

He placed the menu down and raised a tea toast to Claire, who obliged with a clink of porcelain.

"So, what are some of your favorite spots back home?" Kiernan asked after the waitress had come by to take their order. "There must be an award-winning cucumber sandwich shop back in Boston?"

Claire chuckled. "I'm sure there is. But favorite spots? Hmm… There's a park on the outskirts of the city that I go to whenever I can. It has some nice walking paths. And a pond— with ducks. You might have noticed I really like ducks."

Kiernan laughed as she pondered some more.

"There's also a quirky little bookshop in my town that I really love. It's been family-owned for years—not one of those big chain bookstores. Whenever I go there Marge, one of the owners, will have some hand-picked books put aside for me."

"That sounds wonderful. And what of kind of books do you like to read?"

"Lately, I've been into cozy mysteries."

"Ah, you mean like the little ol' British grandmother who solves crimes while tending to her rose garden?"

Claire snickered. "Sounds like the plot of the last one I read." As Kiernan raised his teacup for another toast, she obliged and said, "Your turn."

"I should have known that was coming…"

"Come on. Favorite places. Spill."

"Well, I think you've already seen both." As Claire raised her eyebrows he added, "The hospital and Gilroy's Pub. Although I guess I should add any rugby field within a sixty-mile radius."

"The hospital is your favorite spot?" she asked curiously.

"Kind of. It's where I spend most of my time."

"All the more reason you need different favorite spots."

"Huh…" Kiernan ruminated on her observation for several moments. "I think I misunderstood the question."

"Nice try."

Kiernan laughed. He was squirming in the hot seat, but just seeing Claire's easy grin was worth the discomfort.

Four finger sandwiches and three cups of sweetened tea later, Kiernan leaned back in his chair and admired the even sweeter view from not so afar. Just across from him, Claire and her serene beauty were nothing short of mesmerizing—and if duty hadn't been calling, he knew he could have got lost in that vision all day. But with a tonsillectomy scheduled for two p.m., he had to get back to the hospital soon.

"Thanks," Kiernan said a few minutes later as the waitress handed him back his bank card. He turned to Claire. "Well, back to the hospital for me—and hopefully back to something enjoyable for you. Have you been doing any fun touristy things?"

"How can I?" Claire replied with a mischievous twinkle in her eye. "You keep interrupting my vacation."

"Ouch." Kiernan chuckled, and when his phone buzzed in his pocket, he was fully prepared to ignore it.

Except medical emergencies had a way of following him.

He pulled out the phone and grimaced. "I'm sorry—this is the hospital."

Silently reading the text message, he felt his jaw and neck instantly tense.

Manchester Gen is out and team confirmed we can't cut thru red tape in time for surgery outside of UK. We're out of options. But wanted to get OK from you before telling Jan.

Kiernan sighed deeply and placed the phone on the table with the screen facing down, unable to pull the trigger that would end Jan's dream of giving birth to a healthy baby.

With a creased forehead and concerned eyes, Claire asked, "Is everything okay?"

"Not really. The last few potential hospitals that could do Jan's surgery in time are no-gos. It looks like we're at the end of the road."

Claire's shoulders dropped, her pale green eyes mirroring the deep disappointment that Kiernan now felt. Silence passed between them, the upbeat atmosphere of a few seconds ago now fully deflated and somber.

Suddenly, a thought sprang into Kiernan's mind. And it was a doozy. As he looked up at Claire she lurched back slightly, as though reverberating with the energy that was bouncing off him.

"I have an idea. A *crazy* idea. But… Okay, just hear me out. If I can get permission from the hospital and make everything else fall into place, would you be able to perform Jan's surgery? The hospital will pay you, of course, and I can't imagine they'd turn down the proposition, knowing how much they want West Mercy to make a name for itself in this sort of surgery. Plus, it would be an amazing experience for my team to learn from someone of your caliber."

Claire appeared stricken as she stared back at him. Her reaction was enough to drop his stomach to his knees.

"Believe me, I know this is a lot to ask." He paused, waiting for her to reply. And waiting some more. "I'm sorry—it was an impulsive thought. I should never have suggested it."

"I… I um…."

Claire's head dropped downwards as she stared at the table. Kiernan didn't need to be a doctor to see that her breathing had accelerated and the color was draining from her face.

Finally, she looked up. "Can I just…? Can I think about it, please? I'll give you an answer by tomorrow. I promise."

"Yes. Yes, of course."

As she started to stand up from the chair, Kiernan stood

up as well, quickly stepping over and gently grabbing her arm as she braced her other arm unsteadily against the table. Her skin was soft, but slightly clammy, and as she locked eyes with him, he saw fear bordering on panic. It was the same look he'd seen yesterday.

But why?

Had something happened back at Boston General? Had there been a failed surgery that had been so devastating she'd taken a leave of absence for a month? Not every surgery was successful—no matter how gifted the surgeon. Or perhaps she had become too emotionally involved in a case and the outcome had pushed her over the edge.

Kiernan tightened his jaw, knowing he needed to reel in his suspicions. He was grasping at straws, wanting to understand. But unless she opened up to him, he was blindly guessing at best.

"Thank you for lunch," Claire said. "If I ever crave a mean cucumber sandwich again, I know where to go."

There was a slight quiver in her smile, and the sheer effort to hide her discomfort was almost palpable.

Kiernan watched as Claire headed out of the dining patio, frozen in place until a wave of heightened resolve swept over him. No. *No!* He was *not* going to let her run off like this in such a clearly distressed state of mind. He pulled his phone out of his pocket and waited for the call to be answered.

"Hello, Mr. O'—"

"Lucy," he urgently interjected. "I have a personal matter to attend to and I need you to put Mr. Ramsey on my two p.m. tonsillectomy."

"Yes, I'll let him know right away." There was a brief pause. Then, "Is everything okay?"

He knew why Lucy was asking. If there were two words she had never heard him utter in succession, they were "personal" and "matter."

"Yes," he said, his voice clipped. "I'll touch base with you when I'm back."

Bounding out to the parking lot, he spotted Claire just as she was about to get into her car. "Claire! Wait!"

She swung around, eyes widened.

She was still holding on to the door handle when he caught up with her. "I can't let you leave like this. Please—can we sit and talk for a bit?"

It took several moments for Claire to find her voice. "I'm not sure what you mean..."

"I've upset you."

"No, I'm fine...really."

Kiernan shook his head. "You're not fine."

Her eyes met his and, surprisingly, she didn't push back on his assessment. He turned and nodded to a cobblestoned path lined with several benches that cut through the flowered grounds.

"Walk with me? Please?"

Perhaps it was the pleading quality to his voice, but Claire slowly closed the car door and together they headed out of the parking lot and onto the path. Several minutes later they were seated on a wooden bench, surrounded by the heady aroma of tulips, daffodils and roses.

"Wait—what about your tonsillectomy?" Claire asked, before Kiernan had a chance to initiate conversation.

"I already called the hospital and another surgeon is filling in for me." He flashed the hint of a smile. "It's one of the advantages of being chief of surgery. I can pass off a procedure to someone else and no one will say anything."

Claire's tense face relaxed slightly as her lips curved upward. But the smile was short-lived. "If this is about Jan's surgery—your question caught me off guard, that's all."

"I don't care about Jan's surgery," Kiernan replied forcefully. He shook his head and looked briefly up at the sky. "That didn't come out right. Of course I care. But right now my concern is you. I don't mean to pry, Claire, and maybe it's none of my business, but I can't help feeling there's something you're not telling me—something that caused you to react the way you did in the birthing suite yesterday, and now this. Whatever it is, you can talk to me. Maybe I can help. Or I'll just be quiet and listen."

She stared intently into his eyes for what seemed like an eternity, as though debating inwardly whether to open up to him.

"You're right," she said finally. "I haven't been entirely upfront with you as to why I took a leave of absence to come here." She paused, her eyes now glossy and pained. "Seven months ago, I gave birth to a stillborn daughter. Her name was Ariana."

Kiernan flinched, feeling as though an unseen hand had slapped him across the cheek. He had not seen this coming. Not by a longshot. "Claire, I'm so sorry."

Claire blinked several times to push back tears. She started to speak again, but nothing came out.

"You don't have to say any more," Kiernan said quietly.

She took in a deep breath, as if re-energized with resolve. "I want to. You see, I came to Ireland for a month to figure out if I can continue in my career as an ob-gyn. I know I'm not the first obstetrician to lose a child, and I really thought I would be able to separate my personal pain from my professional life. But I can't. Every time I witness the birth of a healthy baby, I'm glad for the parents, but I also wonder why I didn't have the same happy ending with Ariana. And every miscarriage or stillbirth…it's like reliving her death all over again." Claire's voice cracked, but she pushed herself to finish. "I'm no good to my patients like this. They deserve better. But I just don't know how to get past it all."

Kiernan looked up at the bright afternoon sky, his chest

tightening as the unintended repercussions of his actions grew clearer. "And then you come here and right from the start..."

He shook his head, unable to say more. An emergency breech delivery. A consultation on fetal surgery for a serious birth defect. And—the ultimate stab in the heart—being asked to perform complex, high-risk surgery to correct that anomaly in an unborn child. Everything she had been trying to get away from he had been unwittingly throwing her way since her arrival.

"Claire, I'm so sorry that I've caused you pain."

She placed a hand over his, and her soft, warm touch momentarily disrupted his focus.

"None of this is your fault. There was no way you could have known."

So many thoughts and emotions were swirling around in Kiernan's mind. Not to mention more questions. Such as who and where was Ariana's father? But he wasn't about to ask. The last thing he wanted to do was potentially add salt to a wound whose depths he could not even begin to imagine.

"In case you're wondering, Ariana's father is no longer in the picture."

Kiernan gulped silently. Had Claire just read his mind? "I'm sorry to hear that."

"It's okay. I mean, better to have found out the kind of person he really is now than even further down the road. The CliffsNotes version is that we met in medical school, married after graduation, and he left when I was six months pregnant with Ariana. It turns out he was having an affair with someone at his practice and she recently gave birth to a daughter."

Kiernan narrowed his eyes. "That's despicable."

He wanted to punch the man, surgeon's hands be damned. The satisfaction of inflicting upon him even a fraction of the pain he had caused Claire would be worth a broken knuckle or two.

"Whew!" Claire exclaimed, dabbing at her moistened eyes. "I'm a real joy to be around, huh?"

"You are—and then some," he said quietly, looking into her eyes. "And I never would have asked you to perform Jan's surgery if I had known what you've been going through."

"Believe me, I know that. But my earlier answer hasn't changed. I just need the rest of the day to think everything over."

Kiernan shook his head. "No, I don't think this is a good idea."

Claire squeezed his hand, her reddened eyes offset by a growing smile. "Too late. You already asked me."

Kiernan clenched his jaw as he tried to wrangle a swirl of conflicting emotions. Maybe *he* needed the day to reexamine his thoughts, too. His first instinct was to protect Claire from further pain and trauma. But at the same time she had come to Ireland to determine whether she could reengage in her profession as an ob-gyn. Could successfully performing Jan's surgery, and at a hospital without all the painful memories of Boston General, provide the definitive answer she needed?

He turned to her, nearly overwhelmed by a sudden desire to lean in and kiss her. She stared into his eyes in a way that made him think she, too, might feel the same. And yet he resisted.

Never had he thought twice about seizing the moment when it came to a kiss. But never had anyone revealed something so deeply personal to him. He had sensed from the get-go that Claire was a private person. You weren't going to find her announcing her every thought and action on social media—if you found her there at all. She had made herself vulnerable by sharing with him her loss of Ariana, and he did not take her trust in him lightly. It was a trust he would safeguard at all costs, and the last thing he wanted to do was misconstrue her willingness to open up to him.

Claire briefly looked out over the flowered landscape, a

kaleidoscope of colors swaying slightly in the breeze, before turning back to him. "I would imagine you need to get back to the hospital soon."

"I'm in no rush," Kiernan replied—an answer that previously would never have left his lips. This was certainly turning out to be a day of firsts for him.

"Do you mind if we just sit here for a bit?" she asked.

That was an easy question to answer.

"I wouldn't want to be anywhere else."

Claire sat on her now favorite rock by the water as she tossed cracked corn onto the ground. In short order, the chopped golden kernels were gobbled up by the boisterous flock of ducks before her.

Quack-quack-quack. Quack-quack-quack.

"Slow down, guys," she said with an affectionate smile as she tossed more corn their way.

It was a brief respite from the whirlwind of emotions that she was still trying to navigate.

After returning home from the tea shop a half-hour ago, Claire had immediately headed down to the water. Mother Nature had an unfailing way of providing clarity when she needed it most, and today that figurative mother had her work cut out for her.

She had been surprised to receive Kiernan's spur-of-the-moment lunch invite, and even more surprised at how readily she had accepted it. But the reasons had been simple—she'd wanted to see him again, her earlier blinking red caution lights be damned, and it would be an opportunity to make up for her skittish behavior the day before. That objective hadn't gone exactly as planned...but maybe that was good thing.

Claire thought back to a nugget of advice dispensed during one of her post-stillbirth therapy sessions. Holding on to a secret gave it power. And if the secret was a source of pain and grief…well, it would only cause more of the same.

Opening up to Kiernan had profoundly changed something inside of her. She could feel it like a heavy weight lifted not only from her shoulders, but from the deepest corners of her mind. His reaction to her revelation had made it clear that he was fully and unequivocally looking out for her. And though he had pulled back on his suggestion that she perform Jan's surgery, they both knew the stakes. There were no more options left for this mother and her unborn child. She was it.

Claire turned her gaze onto several fluffy yellow ducklings as they waddled close behind their mom. When one lost its balance and tumbled over, the mother turned away from the cracked corn she was just about to devour, and used her beak to nudge him back up.

It was a gesture that grabbed at her heart. But that was what all mothers did, regardless of species. They put their children first. And being part of that beautiful dynamic was one of the reasons she loved being an ob-gyn. Or she had.

Claire stood up from the rock and began walking along the water's edge. Could she get that love back again? It was a question she still couldn't answer—although inside she now felt a fluidity where before there had been only rigidity.

But perhaps she was projecting too far ahead. She could make a difference for Jan and her baby *now*. Kiernan had thrown that opportunity into her lap, and she had to…she *wanted* to…give them every chance for the best outcome possible. And with Kiernan by her side, she could do it.

She cupped a hand over her eyes as the afternoon sun glistened on the water. Slowly, a smile emerged. It was accompanied by a flutter of nerves, but that was okay—big decisions could be disconcerting at first. And the fact that this one came easier—and quicker—than expected only solidified to her that it was the right decision to make.

Claire reached into the pocket of her windbreaker to get her phone, then thought better of it. Knowing Kiernan, if she texted him now instead of in the morning, as planned, he'd think she was jumping the gun.

Knowing Kiernan?

Had she really crossed that invisible line from regarding him as a professional associate, kept at arm's length, to someone she was beginning to connect with on a much deeper level?

She closed her eyes, knowing very well the answer to that.

Kiernan entered the kitchen of his home and tossed his keys on the counter. He was greeted by silence save for the hum of the refrigerator.

Nothing he could say to himself—certainly not *What a day!* or similar—could come close to sufficing as a recap of the past twelve hours. His spur-of-the-moment lunch with Claire had set off a chain reaction of events and revelations, all of which he was still trying to process.

As his eyes scanned the room—the spotless counters and perfectly lined-up canisters, the sparkling stainless-steel appliances and the neat stack of mail in its designated tray—one word came to mind: *sterile*. Which, if this were an operating theater, would be more than appropriate.

But this was his home, his personal oasis. And suddenly, it all just seemed…strange.

He shook his head, wondering why he had never really noticed this before. Could it be because there was little, if any, distinction between his professional and personal life? That was a *duh* question, he surmised silently.

An image of Claire flashed in his mind, and he wondered what it would be like to come home to the feeling that he had whenever she was near. It was a feeling that he craved, but one that also scared him. If he gave in to it, then he'd need to reevaluate his whole approach to life—the "must-haves" versus the "can-live-withouts." Full devotion to his career, at the expense of everything else, had always been a must-have. But the more his feelings for Claire were beginning to grow, the more tiny fissures were forming in these notions that had been set in stone.

He'd had a glimpse of one those fissures earlier in the day, when he'd bowed out of performing a surgery so that he could stay with Claire and make sure she was okay. He thought back to the day when his father had passed away. He had been prepping for a coronary artery bypass surgery when he had taken an urgent call from his mother. His father's death from a sudden heart attack had been both unexpected and shocking. But both he and his mother had known the drill all too well. After all, it was his father who had pounded it into him.

Personal matters and relationships came second. *Always.*

And the one thing he had thought that day, as he'd suppressed his emotions and walked into the operating theater without so much as a mention of his loss, feeling the disbelieving eyes of colleagues who had heard the news upon him? *Dad would be proud of me.* Which meant he had been proud of himself.

Only now did he realize how misguided his priorities might have been at that moment.

Realizing he needed some air, Kiernan headed out on the back deck that overlooked the ocean, peering into the darkness. With just a sliver of moonlight, he couldn't see the water, but he could hear every wave that crashed against the cliffs below and smell the brine that brought on an instant head rush.

As a sharp ocean breeze whipped through his hair, Kiernan grabbed the rail of the deck with both hands. He needed to steady himself, because everything around him was churning like a cyclone.

Get a hold of yourself.

He was reeling from Claire's unexpected and deeply personal revelation, and the possibility that she might take on Jan's surgery. That was all this was. *Right?* A lot of raw emotion packed into a short span of time.

Of course, if that was the case, then he'd be on edge every time he came out of a difficult surgery that had been touch-and-go until the final successful moments. He always felt relief for both the patients and their families in those situations, but it had never spurred him to come home and question why the damn refrigerator was the closest thing he had to a significant other after a long day at the hospital.

No, this was about Claire. Of that, he was sure. Seeing her heartache as she'd told him about Ariana…

Could performing Jan's surgery be the catalyst she needed to reengage in her career as an ob-gyn?

The question nearly cut off his air supply, and he took in a deep breath of salty ocean air. He needed to be careful. This was not one medical professional concerned about the career of a peer. For him, at least, it was already so much more. And he couldn't have that in the life he had mapped out for himself.

Unless, of course, he redrew the map.

It was a thought that hit him harder than a tidal wave.

CHAPTER SEVEN

KIERNAN ENTERED THE café on the second floor of the hospital, immediately spotting Claire at a small table in the furthest, most quiet corner. Earlier in the morning she had texted him to say that she wanted to move forward with Jan's surgery, but that alone wasn't enough to convince him. He needed to see her in person, to read her body language and look into her eyes to be certain that *she* was certain.

After all, it was in her nature to want to help others, but he couldn't let that be at the expense of her own well-being.

"Thanks for meeting me here," he said as he sat down next to her.

Dressed in casual jeans and a light pink sweater, she looked downright gorgeous. Then again, Kiernan thought, she could don a burlap sack and still put a designer-clad supermodel to shame. He'd take natural, unfettered beauty over an artificially enhanced appearance any day of the week—and Claire had that in spades.

She smiled, her eyes bright but anxious. "So, you said you wanted to talk to me in person about the surgery. Are you thinking the hospital won't sign off on it?"

"No, that's not why I asked you to come by…" As Claire's smile began to wilt, he knew he couldn't drag out his concerns any longer. "Claire, you don't have to do this."

"I know. But I want to. Look, I don't know what the future

holds for me as far as my career goes. I still have a lot to think through. But one thing I know for sure is that I can make a difference for Jan and her baby. And it's the only chance they have at this point. That alone is enough for me to pull it together. I *want* to do this. Besides, we've already proved that we're a pretty good team in an operating room."

Kiernan grinned. "You mean in the back of a bumpy ambulance?"

"Right." She smirked, but then her face grew more serious. "The thing is, after telling you about Ariana…you know my secret now. And somehow…just opening up to you… I feel like it's lessened its hold on me."

Kiernan wanted to believe she was right. For Jan and her baby, yes. But also for Claire's own healing. Her previous reaction in the birthing suite and at yesterday's lunch clearly indicated she was still in the throes of pain and grief over losing Ariana. Could sharing her loss really have changed all that? Silently, he tossed the question around in his mind, his face tense with concern.

"What's wrong?" Claire asked, picking up on his doubts.

"I'm just worried that you might not be ready to take on this surgery. You've been through so much. How do you know you won't be triggered by something that happens in Theater? I'm afraid it might be too much, too soon."

"Believe me, I've thought about this. I'd never put Jan and her baby at risk. I'm not going into this surgery thinking it will help me decide once and for all what to do about my career. That would be putting too much pressure on myself. But I do know that right here, right now, I'm fully committed to doing everything I can to help them. And knowing you'll be with me in the operating room…"

Her voice trailed off, but Kiernan knew what she was implying—that his presence would have a stabilizing effect on her should a potential trigger arise. He wanted to believe that was true, but wasn't entirely sold on the notion.

Once again, Claire seemed to home in on his doubts.

"You know how people sometimes hold a paper clip when they're giving a speech to calm their nerves? Well, you'll be my paper clip in the operating room."

He raised an amused eyebrow. "You mean like a surgical lucky charm?"

It wasn't his intention to make light of a serious situation, only to help put her at ease. And himself, too, for that matter.

"Something like that, yes." She snickered slightly, then grew more serious. "So, given that Jan's surgery needs to happen very soon, we do need to go over some specifics. I'm sure you already know this, but this is an all hands on deck procedure. I'll need every specialist in every discipline that you've got. Cardiology, neurology, pediatrics—and they'll need to get up to speed on the surgery itself. I mean, is all of that even possible on such short notice?"

"I'll *make* it possible," Kiernan replied, pulling confidence out of thin air given all that needed to fall into place—and fast. "I'm going to call an emergency meeting with the board. It's probably too short notice to get everyone together today, but I should be able to set something up for first thing tomorrow morning. And I'll have my surgery coordinator get to work on putting together a comprehensive team."

"Will you wait to get the okay before telling Jan?"

"I think that would be best. The last thing I want to do is falsely get her hopes up. I don't think there'll be any major roadblocks to moving forward with the surgery, but best to be sure first."

Claire nodded, her face visibly relaxing. "Good."

"So, now that that's settled, I have some doctor's orders for you."

She raised an eyebrow. "Oh?"

Kiernan extracted a prescription pad from the pocket of his white coat, scribbled away for a few moments, then tore off a piece of paper and handed it to her.

Claire twisted her mouth to one side with amusement before reading it out loud: *"You are to spend the next twenty-four hours playing with ducks, reading a cozy mystery, exploring a castle and eating cucumber sandwiches to your heart's desire. Unlimited refills."*

"Don't be one of those patients who refuses to take good advice," Kiernan said with a twinkle in his eyes.

Claire laughed. "I'll do my best."

Claire tapped her fingers on the black-lacquered chair-arm and stared at the TV screen in front of her. A football game was in full swing, and though the half-dozen other occupants in the room sat glued to the action, her eyes—and thoughts—wandered as she waited in vain for time to speed up.

More than twenty-four hours had passed since she had met with Kiernan in the café and, like a *partially* dutiful patient, she had played with the ducks and toured a local castle. But the cozy mystery book would have to wait. And the cucumber sandwiches...? Those would have to wait, too. Perhaps indefinitely....

With a silent sigh, she once again glanced at the large digital clock on the adjacent wall of one of West Mercy's smaller waiting rooms. The original plan had been for Kiernan to call her as soon as the board meeting ended, but sitting at the cottage to await such a pivotal decision had made her so antsy that she'd been ready to go search for a sand hill.

Instead, she had texted Kiernan to say that she was on her way to the hospital so that she could hear the good news in person. Of course, that presumed that there would *be* good news. But she had to hold on to hope.

Suddenly, she caught a flash of movement out of the corner of her eye. Kiernan swept into the waiting room, his commanding presence prompting those around her to instinctively sit up straighter in their chairs. His serious face was devoid of a smile, and Claire's shoulders sank as her own smile faded in response.

And then a thumb shot up as a Cheshire cat grin spread from ear to ear. "We're on," he said as Claire sprang from her chair.

She caught herself just short of pouncing on him with hug-ready arms. Clearing her throat, she tucked several loose locks of hair behind her ear, dropped her arms woodenly to her sides, and said, in a measured, low-key voice, "That's fantastic news."

Kiernan was still viewing her through widened eyes, as though he was fully prepared for and looking forward to being tackled, and seemed disappointed that she'd reversed course at the last second.

"Did you get any pushback?" Claire asked, hoping the inquiry would erase the awkward moment she had created between them.

"They had a lot of questions, of course. And there are still some logistics to work out. But they also understand that time is of the essence. They're looking at it as a major milestone for West Mercy. But I think you'll agree with me that the biggest win is for Jan and her baby."

"Absolutely. When do you plan to tell her?"

"*We* can tell her right now. She had a follow-up ultrasound appointment today, and I told the technician to let her know that I wanted to touch base with her before she left. I wasn't sure we'd have good news to share, but I hedged my bets and now we actually do."

Twenty minutes later, Claire and Kiernan exited the consultation room after sharing the good news with Jan. As expected, she was equal parts ecstatic and nervous—a completely normal reaction in the face of surgery that held the highest hopes for her unborn baby, yet was far from routine and simple.

At one point, Jan had shared the fact that she and her husband had decided to learn the sex of the baby, and had named their daughter Rhianna. The similar ring to Ariana had caught Claire by surprise, but one glance in Kiernan's direction, his expression both knowing and understanding, and she had quickly been pulled back to the present. That she could acknowledge her pain without being instantly transported back to a very dark place was testament to the healing power of sharing her secret. And not with just anyone, of course, but with Kiernan, whom she was trusting more and more.

As they continued down the corridor a flurry of thoughts vied for Claire's attention. She always felt as though she was balancing on a tightrope when reassuring patients about the outcome of a complex surgery. She believed in her skills, and all of her previous spina bifida fetal surgeries to date had been successful. But that didn't mean complications couldn't arise. And to be performing this procedure at an unfamiliar hospital, with an inexperienced team as far as fetal surgery was concerned... Well, she'd have to be in deep denial not to realize the risk factor was far from non-existent.

"I know it's a lot of pressure to perform this surgery under such unusual circumstances," Kiernan said, perhaps picking up on her concern. "But I want to assure you that we're doing everything at our end to be fully prepared by Monday. You said this is an all hands on deck situation, and I have nearly two dozen surgeons and specialists coming in this weekend to go over everything ahead of time. They might not all need to be present for the surgery on Monday, but we're covering all ground just in case."

"I should be there," Claire said, wondering why she hadn't thought to offer before.

"I don't think that will be necessary. You came to Ireland

to get away from it all, and I don't want you to be pulled back into the medical world any more than necessary."

"I think it's a little too late for that," Claire said, with a touch of humor in her voice.

Kiernan half grinned. "I know. But I've found some great training videos from the hospital that pioneered this procedure, and they're about as thorough as you can get. We'll all study everything over the weekend, and on Monday we'll get an early start so you can address the team and take any last-minute questions. If something comes up during the training this weekend that requires your input, I'll give you a call." He slowed his pace and turned to her. "Does that sound like a plan?"

She smiled. "Yes, that sounds like a plan."

Suddenly, he came to a halt. "Actually, there *is* a bit of bad news that I should have mentioned earlier."

Claire felt her stomach sink.

"The board is haggling about appropriate payment for the surgery and, knowing how slow this sort of thing moves through the system, I think it might be another week or two before the money can be transferred to you."

Claire breathed a sigh of relief. "Oh—that! I should have mentioned this earlier as well. I'm not looking to get paid for the surgery."

Kiernan nearly balked. "That's hugely generous of you, but I can't let you perform such a time-intensive, complex surgery for free. Let the hospital cough something up to compensate you fairly—as well they should."

"How about you let them figure out what they think my services are worth, and whatever it is, I'll donate it to a worthy cause. You can choose what that should be, since I'm not familiar with local organizations. But maybe something like a women's shelter, or a women's health educational program?"

Kiernan stared at her in near-disbelief. "Have I told you lately that you're amazing?"

Claire felt her face flush, and an appreciative smile was the only reply she could manage.

They resumed walking, but took only a few steps before Kiernan stopped and turned to her. "Actually, if you're not going to accept payment, then I have a counteroffer."

"Which is…?" Claire asked, equal parts cautious and intrigued.

"Let me cook dinner for you tomorrow night at my place."

Claire gulped silently. "Dinner?" Another silent gulp. "At your place?"

"It's not a dungeon, I swear," Kiernan replied, prompting a slightly nervous smile from Claire. "Plus, remember how I failed at your question about my favorite spots?"

"Miserably, as I recall."

Kiernan grinned. "Well, this is a chance for me to amend my answer. I have an outdoor deck that virtually dangles over the cliffs and looks out onto the ocean. I might be biased, but it's one of the most magnificent views on the West Coast of Ireland."

Claire grimaced apprehensively. "'Dangles over the cliffs'? You need to work on your sales pitch."

Kiernan laughed. "It's one hundred percent safe and secure, I promise."

"Mr. O'Rourke! Mr. O'Rourke!"

Kiernan and Claire turned in the direction of the eager voice, watching as a young boy ran toward them while his mother tried to keep pace close behind.

"Henry!" Kiernan exclaimed, returning the boy's high five before giving his carrot-red hair an affectionate tousle. "What a wonderful surprise!" He looked up at the boy's mother. "Catherine, how are you?"

"Hello, Mr. O'Rourke. I'm doing great." She smiled from ear to ear. "And, more importantly, *Henry's* doing great."

"I'm on the school rugby team now!" Henry exclaimed.

Kiernan's eyes widened. "Fantastic! What position?"

"Inside center—just like you."

"Best position there is," Kiernan said with a wink.

He turned to Claire and commenced introductions, summing up his history with Henry as being one of many West Mercy doctors who'd banded together to treat the young boy after a life-threatening car accident four years ago.

"Mr. O'Rourke is being far too modest," Catherine said to Claire. "He headed up a team that not only saved Henry's life, but saved his leg—which at one point wasn't a certainty." She looked down at her son, beaming with pride. "And now he's playing rugby on the school team. If that's not a miracle, I don't know what is."

"Were you in today for a recheck?" Kiernan asked.

Catherine nodded. "We had an annual appointment with Mr. O'Leary to make sure everything is working as it should with Henry's leg. Although after Henry bounded into the room and more or less catapulted himself onto the table, Mr. O'Leary said he probably doesn't need to see him again—at least not in an official capacity."

"With an entrance like that, who needs X-rays, right?" Kiernan observed to all-around laughter.

Claire discreetly stepped back. Not only to give Kiernan and Henry some room for their boisterous reunion, but also to make sure her eyes—and ears—weren't playing tricks on her. Because if she hadn't known better, she'd have thought Kiernan—he of the "I don't see children in my future" mantra—was carrying on in a downright paternal manner. Which meant that suddenly, and quite unexpectedly, she could see him as a father. And not just as *any* father, but the kind she would want for her own children.

Whoa, whoa, whoa!

Claire took another step back—but this time because she had just jumped so far out in front of herself. In the span of a few seconds she'd started to see Kiernan in a whole new light—one that made him even more attractive than before, if that was possible. And for the first time since losing Ariana, the thought of having another child had entered her mind.

"Claire?"

Claire jerked her head up just in time to see Henry and his mother departing down the corridor.

"They said goodbye to you, but I don't think you heard them."

Slightly dazed, Claire steadied herself and smiled. "Sorry, I...um... I got distracted."

He cocked his head to one side. "You okay?"

"Yes." Another smile...this time with less effort needed.

"Good. Well, before you head out let's settle on a time for dinner tomorrow. How about if I pick you about seven p.m.?" As Claire's eyes widened, he added, "I know...you love your Mini. But my place is rather remote and tricky to find, and this will just make it easier."

She allowed herself to breathe again. "Yes, of course. That makes sense."

As Claire walked through the parking lot to her car, a short time later, she tried to wrap her head around the dizzying speed at which everything seemed to be swirling around her. Hadn't she come to Ireland to slow things down and mull over her future? Instead, she was about to dive headfirst back into the high-stakes medical world that she had put on hold. And, even more confounding, although romance had been the last thing on her mind when she'd arrived here, the universe seemed to have other ideas.

How else to explain why someone like Kiernan had almost

instantly landed in the midst of everything and every moment spent with him since had been nothing short of magical?

Cupping her hand over her eyes, she looked up at the bright sky, quietly saying out loud, "You're either one very smart universe…" She paused, knowing full well that her time with Kiernan was limited. "Or the joke's on me."

CHAPTER EIGHT

CLAIRE TOOK ONE final look at her reflection in the bathroom mirror, sighed deeply, then headed to the main room in her cottage to wait for Kiernan. The fact that she had changed her outfit three times, segued from a hair-twist to a sleek ponytail and finally loose tresses, told her one thing.

This is not good.

Her attraction to Kiernan had gone beyond the point where she could convince herself that it was simply admiration for his surgical prowess. There was the way he'd been so understanding when she'd opened up to him about Ariana. His supportive concern about her own well-being if she were to perform Jan's high-stakes surgery, which in turn had infused her with the courage she needed to step back into the world of obstetrics.

And can we talk about that thick, run-your-fingers-through-it dark hair and that muscular rugby build?

Claire took a deep breath and reminded herself that this wasn't a date...or was it? Kiernan might have tried to frame the dinner as a substitute payment for her doing the surgery, but she'd have been remiss not to have seen the anticipation in his eyes when he'd made the offer. Especially since it had matched her own.

Just be yourself.

That was all she could do, right? Real date or sort-of date— this was still the first date of *any* kind since her marriage to

Mark had ended. And that alone had her alternating between nervousness and excitement.

A knock at the door brought Claire's racing thoughts to a halt. At least temporarily. They came flooding back as soon as she opened the door.

It should have dawned on her that any man who was a feast for the eyes in drab scrubs would be impossible to look away from in dressier clothes. Which in this case were crisp jeans and a light gray casual sports coat over a form-fitting black T-shirt. Mouth slightly agape, her mind drew a blank as it searched for a standard greeting.

Kiernan smiled, and as his lips curved upwards, her knees buckled downwards. "Hi."

Oh, that's the word.

"Hi," she replied.

"You look beautiful."

"So do you."

As they shared a laugh at her awkward comment, Claire inwardly admonished herself.

Don't be a dork. Please.

A short time later she was seated in the passenger seat of Kiernan's silver hybrid SUV as it effortlessly climbed a steep, winding road framed on both sides by lush green fields.

"I guess you weren't kidding about living in a remote area," Claire observed five more miles into the journey, as the off-the-grid scenery grew increasingly breathtaking.

He turned to her and grinned. "It gets even better."

When she stepped out of the SUV fifteen minutes later, it was with a sense of awe. She walked with Kiernan up the short driveway and viewed the modern, eco-friendly dwelling before her. With more glass than solid walls, its presence was considerable, despite its relatively modest size.

"I was expecting a stone cottage, but this is…wow."

"Thanks. I fell in love with this spot, but there weren't any existing homes. So I bought a parcel of land and had this one built five years ago."

Once inside, Kiernan commenced a brief tour, and Claire couldn't help but notice the tidy, everything-in-its-place décor. She was about to ask jokingly if he sterilized his eating utensils with the same autoclaving method of surgical instrument sanitization, when she spotted a vase of vibrant blue flowers on the kitchen counter that could easily double as a "what doesn't belong here?" picture riddle.

"They're beautiful," she said as she leaned over to smell them. "Did you pick them yourself?"

"I did—from the side of a cliff."

Claire did a double-take. "I never realized flower-gathering could be such a high-risk endeavor."

Kiernan smiled, and when he answered there was a tinge of pride in his voice. "Nothing that some spiked shoes and a sturdy rope couldn't solve. I thought you might like them. It was either the flowers or some ducks, and I figured the flowers would be easier to maintain indoors."

Claire laughed, touched that he'd gone to such extremes on her behalf. She didn't want to read *too* much into the gesture...but it was hard not to conclude that he wouldn't have done this for just anyone.

"Let's head outside."

Kiernan led Claire out to the cedar deck attached to the back of the house.

"Holy moly, Kiernan! This view is unbelievable," Claire said breathlessly as she looked out onto the ocean. "I can see why it's a favorite spot."

"Just don't look down."

"Too late," Claire said as she grasped the deck railing with both hands. "You really *are* dangling off a cliff!"

"More like a highly engineered teetering," Kiernan observed wryly as he opened the bottle of wine that rested in the center of a wrought-iron table, complete with two fancy place settings. He then joined Claire, and together they leaned their folded arms on the railing and looked out onto the waves as they crashed against the cliff.

"Is the water always this turbulent?" Claire asked curiously.

Kiernan nodded. "Enough so that on the rare day when things are relatively still, I start to worry that there's an earthquake or something in store."

They silently appreciated the view for another minute, then Kiernan turned to her.

"I hope you're hungry?"

"That depends on how good the chef is," Claire teased.

"I'll have you know my deep-dish, three-cheese lasagna has been a hit at every West Mercy staff summer picnic for the past six years."

"I'm impressed. So what's on the menu tonight?"

Kiernan's left cheek creased with a one-sided smile. "Deep-dish, three-cheese lasagna."

Claire chuckled. "Ah, so you're a one-trick pony?"

"I beg your pardon?" Kiernan replied, feigning insult. "More like a prize steed that knows enough to stick to a winning formula."

Claire laughed.

"I thought we could dine out here."

Kiernan walked over to a stone-encased fire pit and lit the aromatic wood inside. As if on cue, the string of dusk-to-dawn automatic lights that spanned the surrounding deck rail blinked on.

"Look at this…" Claire scanned the softly glowing deck. "It's like Gilroy's Pub after dark—minus the drunken rugby players and the smell of stale beer."

"My teammates are just a phone call away if you'd prefer the full Gilroy's experience."

Claire grinned. "Thanks, I'm good."

"I was hoping you'd say that." Kiernan pulled out a chair at the table and waited for Claire to be seated. "I was looking forward to dinner just the two of us."

Claire wondered if Kiernan could actually hear her gulp.

Yup, I think this is a date.

With considerable effort, she corralled the butterflies in her stomach that had been set off by a rush of adrenaline.

Just go with the flow, she reminded herself, though it was easier said than done.

"I'm going to go check on my fan favorite lasagna. Be back in a minute."

Claire nodded and smiled. He could serve her a baked hockey puck and she'd probably think it was a culinary masterpiece. Not that he needed to know that, of course.

Twenty minutes later, Claire placed her fork and knife together on her empty plate and pushed it slightly forward, more than pleasantly surprised. "That was delicious. My compliments to the chef."

"You mean the one-trick pony?"

Claire grinned. "All joking aside, you're a great cook. I'm surprised."

Kiernan pretended to choke on her comment. "I'm not *too* insulted."

"Ha! I just mean I'm surprised you find the time to cook with your schedule."

"You did catch the part where I told you I have one recipe in my arsenal, right?"

"Well, it's a winner."

"Glad it wasn't awful. More wine?"

"Please."

Her glass replenished, she glanced over at the fire pit, her eyes lingering on the dancing flames for longer than she had intended. Perhaps because they were a metaphor for the question that was burning inside of her. She turned back to Kiernan. Dare she ask him? A few more seconds of contemplation, and then impulse took over.

"So, I'm curious about something..." she began.

Kiernan cocked his head slightly to one side. "Go on."

"At the hospital yesterday, when you were talking with Henry, I couldn't help but notice how...natural...you were around him. In fact, if I didn't know any better, I'd say you actually *like* children."

Kiernan's expression changed from one of intrigue to confusion. "I *do* like children. What makes you think I don't?"

"Well, you said before that you don't want children."

"I said I don't think I can fully devote myself to my career and children at the same time. One or the other would have to give. It's just the way it is. And my decision to put my career first has nothing to do with any imagined prestige of being chief of surgery. It's that I get to save lives. I mean, *you* know what that feeling is like. It's a huge responsibility and one that I don't take lightly. And it's because I *do* like children that I'd never subject them to the type of childhood I had with an absentee father."

Claire managed a faint nod. "I get it."

She could leave it at that. She *should* leave it at that. Except...

"But on the other hand, I can think of a number of colleagues back home—both men and women—who are very involved with their children and are still top-notch doctors who give one hundred percent to their patients."

Kiernan pursed his lips together and stared at Claire, as though trying to discern why she was grilling him on this matter. "I don't know," he finally replied. "Maybe some doctors can strike that perfect balance. I suppose it depends what field of medicine they're in. Some are more demanding than others." He paused. "And I've never shied away from admitting my views have been shaped in large part by the fact that my father was a very dedicated surgeon, but an incredibly inattentive father."

"And that realization isn't enough to make you wonder if there might be another way?"

As soon as the question left Claire's mouth, she knew she had to stop. She was pushing Kiernan too far—raising questions that might be appropriate if they had just embarked on a relationship, but not as very temporary colleagues. It didn't matter if there was a part of her that yearned for more with him.

Did I just admit that?

It was not something that could ever be. Soon, there would be three thousand miles between them. And did she really need to remind herself about their conflicting views on parenthood yet again?

She could see in Kiernan's eyes that he was struggling to form an answer to her question. So she decided to make it easy for him. Perhaps for them both.

"I don't think we've had an official toast yet." She raised her glass of wine. "Here's to a successful surgery for Jan and Rhianna."

Kiernan's tense face softened, and he raised his glass as well. "I will happily drink to that."

Claire smiled, then took a sip of wine. It was a mellow Merlot that initially tasted sweet on her lips, but quickly morphed into bitterness. Funny how it mirrored her growing feelings for Kiernan, she thought. A dream that was so enticing, and a reality that cut like a knife.

"Hard to believe I'm halfway through my stay here," she said pensively.

Kiernan's smile was cut short, though it soon reemerged with what appeared to be some effort. "It seems like just yesterday we were strangers who met on a hillside during a medical crisis," he said.

"It does…" An uncomfortable silence filled the air, and Claire scrambled to break its hold. "So, I guess I have some catching up to do if I'm going to play tourist for the remainder of my time here. Any suggestions?"

Kiernan's face instantly lit up. "What you really need is a good tourist guide. Someone who knows Ireland like the back of his hand."

"Hmm… Do you have anyone in mind?"

"I do. He's a great conversationalist and he knows all the hidden gems that the big tour companies miss. Plus, I heard that for certain individuals—make that certain *very special* individuals—his services are free."

Claire had been gamely playing along with what she assumed was a playful ruse until she saw the look of earnestness on Kiernan's face. "Wait, you're not serious…are you?"

"That I'm a great conversationalist? Gift of the Blarney here. I just happen to hide it well." He winked. "At least when I'm in surgeon mode."

"But how are you going to get time off from the hospital on such short notice?"

"Leave that up to me. I probably have about five years' worth of unused leave at this point."

"Why do I not find that hard to believe?"

Kiernan smirked. "So, what do you say?"

"Surgeon, restaurateur and now tour guide. You're quite the entrepreneur."

"The day I announce I'm a sheep herder, too—that's when you have to start worrying."

Claire snickered. "Duly noted."

She paused, grappling with a modified version of an angel on one shoulder, a devil on the other. In this instance it consisted of an angel on each side. On the left shoulder, the angel advised her to let down her protective guard and follow her heart. And on the right? Well, that angel had something to say about her heart, too.

This situation can't go anywhere. You'll only be hurt.

Both angels were looking out for her. But though she typically erred on the side of caution—especially with matters of the heart—in this moment, and with this man, she was willing to plunge into the unknown, consequences be damned.

She took a deep breath, silently acknowledging that such a cavalier attitude could come back to bite her. But Kiernan was both smart and perceptive. He had to know as well as she did that there was no future for them beyond the next two weeks. Perhaps he *did* just want to show her some interesting sights off the beaten path. There was no harm in that...right?

"So, when does my personalized tour begin?" Claire asked, her voice a tad too flirty for her own liking. "Given that we first have a very major surgery to get through on Monday."

Kiernan pulled his phone out of his pants pocket and scrolled through his calendar. "How does Tuesday sound? I have a carotid endarterectomy in the morning, and an afternoon of administrative work that I'll be more than happy to push to another day."

"Tuesday works. And is there a particular dress code for whatever you have in store?"

As thoughts of a bare-chested Kiernan in an Irish kilt flooded her mind—a most enticing dress code for *him*—she did her best to keep her eyes from popping out of her head.

"Well, I know you like being outdoors—especially when there are ducks around." As Claire laughed, he added, "So let's plan on a countryside walkabout. I have just the place in mind."

"I'll toast to that," she said, clinking her wine glass against his.

She took a sip and swallowed it down, doing her best to shut out the inner whispers of warning from the angel on her right shoulder.

It was that very same shoulder that Kiernan looked past as he pointed behind her. "The moon's just starting to come up. This is the best time of the night—when it's still partially dusk and the light of the moon hits the water." He stood up and offered his hand. "Let's go take a look."

Claire's breath caught in her throat as he took her hand and helped her up from the chair. As he stared into her eyes she felt as though she might melt into the deck boards. Even the brief stroll to the railing felt like a dream. Had she walked there, or floated? She couldn't be sure...

As they leaned over the railing and looked down onto the foamy waves that shimmered with moonlight, a strong breeze came up from the ocean, whipping Claire's hair around her face and shoulders.

"It's chilly, isn't it?" Kiernan asked, turning to her.

In the diminishing light of dusk, his normally light brown eyes were a shade of dark espresso, but the kindness behind them was unaltered.

Claire crossed her arms tightly in front of her. "Woo! It's like a twenty-degree temperature-drop here."

Wrapping his arm around her side, Kiernan pulled her in close, the warmth of his muscular body seeping into her skin. Now she was *really* melting into the ground... And as he looked into her eyes, she knew he wanted to kiss her. And she wanted to kiss him, too.

He brushed a wayward lock of hair from her cheek, moving his face closer to hers...closer...closer...and then he stopped.

Claire held her breath for several moments. A kiss hadn't passed between them, but in those last seconds, as their eyes locked, an understanding had. Because even though she couldn't imagine a more perfect and atmospheric backdrop to her first kiss with Kiernan, this wasn't the right time.

Her attraction to him was growing exponentially and, as such, it was occupying a huge space in her thoughts and emotions. But right now that space needed to be devoted to one thing above all else: walking back into an operating room on Monday, a path still strewn with trauma from the past, and successfully completing a complex surgery that might also help decide the fate of her career.

And after the surgery? Hopefully there would still be time to pick up where they had just left off. But with her return to Boston imminent, that time was ticking by fast.

No wonder the angel on her right shoulder was whispering in her ear: *Don't get too attached, Claire.*

One, two, three, four, five... Er...yeah, I think that makes six...

Later that night, with his eyes closed, Kiernan counted the number of opportunities he had had over the course of the evening to take Claire into his arms and kiss her. Fully. Passionately. Deeply. There were probably some more adjectives he could add into the mix, but three was enough to get the point across.

He was able to recall each instance with vivid detail, as though they were playing out in real time in his mind.

Leaning closely over her shoulder as he poured her another glass of wine.

Taking her hand and helping her up from her chair.

Standing side by side at the deck railing after dinner as they gazed out into the moonlit sky—*ugh, I* really *blew that one*—the waves crashing below them.

Walking her up to her cottage door at the end of the evening to make sure she got safely inside.

And not even then?

Truth be told, he couldn't recall ever struggling to get up the nerve to kiss someone when the circumstances seemed right. But the situation with Claire was different. And the reason was simple, really. He didn't want to scare Claire off before he had a chance to show her...well, *what?* That he was the perfect man for her, despite the fact that they lived thousands of miles apart and had incompatible views on children?

And then there was the matter of Monday's surgery. The last thing he'd wanted to do was to complicate things by throwing a kiss into the mix. There was so much riding on this procedure. For Jan and Rhianna, of course. But for Claire as well. In fact, her very future as an ob-gyn might depend on how everything turned out. Which meant it was imperative that extra distractions be barred from the operating room.

Keep it professional.

At least until after the surgery. And then, if he got the chance to kiss her again— No, wait... *When* he got the chance to kiss her again, he would make up for lost time.

Time. That was another complicating factor that he had to push from his mind. Soon—make that *very* soon—Claire would be heading back to the States for good. And his earlier resolve to just enjoy the now?

What had initially been a *problem solved* solution, was now one that filled him with a growing sense of unease.

CHAPTER NINE

CLAIRE'S PHONE ALARM went off at precisely four a.m. on Monday, as planned, but she was already awake, eyes fixated on the dark ceiling above her. Today, she would be altering the course of life for a mother and her unborn child. She wouldn't blame anyone for thinking she was full of herself to reach such a heady conclusion, but it was true. And it had nothing to do with a biased self-assessment of her skills. If everything went as planned, Rhianna would have as normal a life as possible for a child with a spina bifida birth defect. She had seen—and been the catalyst for—such miracles firsthand in the past.

But if complications arose....

Claire sat up in bed and rested on her elbows for several moments. She wasn't going to go there. Only positive thoughts. She was a firm believer that they could make a difference in the operating room and in life in general. But sometimes, in the latter instance, it was easier said than done—especially in light of personal loss.

But today wasn't about her. It was about Jan and Rhianna, about Jan's husband Dave, and their other two children, Melody and Sean. She had to be strong for them.

Claire reminded herself that Kiernan would be by her side throughout the procedure and instantly felt calmer. He had texted her several times to check in and let her know that the weekend-long intense training session with his team had gone well. They were ready to go. And so was she.

The sun was just beginning to rise as she pulled into the West Mercy staff parking lot. The security guards knew to expect her arrival, and ushered her in after viewing her Boston General photo ID. From the side entrance, it was a three-minute walk to the new neonatal wing, but with the weight of what lay ahead, it felt more like thirty.

After Ariana's death, walking to the OR for a scheduled surgery had felt like trudging through a black cloud. But now? She felt a fluttering of nerves mixed with the anticipated joy and relief of a successful outcome. An unsuccessful outcome, and that black cloud would be back and ten times thicker.

Think only good thoughts, Claire inwardly reminded herself. *Just be fully in the moment for Jan and Rhianna.*

Kiernan and a handful of his colleagues were conversing by the nurses' station as she entered the wing. He turned to her as she approached the group and she quietly caught her breath. Could everyone see how she was looking at him not only as a fellow doctor, but also as the man whose desirable lips had nearly touched her own several nights ago?

She hoped not. Just because *she* had thought about that near-kiss all weekend long, it didn't mean anyone else—other than Kiernan, of course—had any inkling of their dinner together. And she preferred it to stay that way. Effectively leading a new team through a complex surgery required being seen as a top-notch professional in their eyes. And fantasizing about locking lips with the hunky chief of surgery didn't exactly cater to that image.

"Good morning, Dr. Delaney."

The smile on Kiernan's face seemed overly calm—and also quite familiar. It was the "pre-surgery smile" that Claire had come to perfect herself over the years, an almost Zen-like state of mind that descended upon her as she readied for a grueling surgery. The only difference was that his smile was accompanied by a twinkle in his eye. Perhaps he was reminiscing about their almost-kiss, too?

Turning back to the small group, Kiernan said, "If you'll excuse me for a few minutes," then gestured to Claire to follow him.

After a short walk down the hall, he opened a door and peered inside, then switched on the lights. Once they were both inside, he closed the door and turned his full attention on Claire.

"How are you feeling?" he asked, eyes gazing steadily into hers.

Over the years, she had been privy to countless one-on-one interactions with fellow doctors in the privacy of a hospital room or staff quarters...and none had ever made her feel weak in the knees like she did at this moment.

It's pre-surgery jitters, that's all.

If ever she'd needed that Zen mindset, it was now. There was so much riding on this surgery—the most obvious being the best possible outcome for Jan and Rhianna. But there was much at stake on a personal level as well. She needed to stay one hundred percent objective before, during and immediately after the complex procedure—a feat that was easier said than done. Letting even a tiny fraction of her personal pain and angst seep into her performance in the operating room could have devastating consequences.

Would she be able to keep a tight lid on her emotions? She wouldn't have agreed to take on the surgery if she hadn't believed that she could. But now that the moment of reckoning was imminent....

"Claire?"

Kiernan's voice cut into her thoughts, and not a moment too soon. It was time to focus on one thing and one thing only: a successful fetal surgery.

"Sorry," she finally managed to say. "I'm okay. Just giving myself an inner pep talk, that's all."

"You've got this, Claire. I know you do."

He reached over and clasped both her hands. His hands were warm and strong, and his touch sent her brain and body to places that they didn't need to go right now.

"You're going to come through this with flying colors. And you know why?"

Claire was too breathless to answer.

"Because once you do, a special outing awaits with a devastatingly handsome surgeon from West Mercy who moonlights as a tour guide. Or so I've heard…"

In an instant, Claire's flailing nerves were flattened on the spot, and she shook her head and grinned. "I'll keep that in mind."

He squeezed her hands tighter. "All kidding aside, I know how strong you are. But I know this surgery is bringing up a lot of personal issues for you as well. Let's just get in that operating theater and give Jan and Rhianna the happy ending they deserve. Then we'll deal with the other stuff."

We? Did he say "we"?

Claire swallowed hard, reminding herself that now was not the time to read too much into anything that Kiernan might say. He was merely helping her double down on her earlier silent pep talk, and for that she was grateful.

Her resolve now cemented, she looked back up into Kiernan's eyes. "Let's do this."

He smiled and slowly let go of her hands, as though reluctant to break the connection, then opened the door and held it for her to pass through.

There was no turning back now.

As promised, Kiernan assembled the large team just outside the OR for a pre-surgery pep talk. With all eyes focused on her—eager eyes, at that—there was little that Claire needed to say. It was clear that everyone understood the gravity of the situation, but also the miraculous possibilities. And they would all be part of that miracle now.

Once in the OR, Jan was wheeled in, groggy from the IV anesthesia medication that had been started in the pre-surgery area, but still cognizant enough to squeeze Claire's hand as she assured her that they were going to take good care of her and Rhianna.

Sebastian placed a face mask over Jan's nose and mouth, administering the gases that would send her into a deep sedation.

Scalpel in hand, Claire briefly looked up at Kiernan where he stood directly across the operating table. With his surgical mask in place, she could only see his eyes, but they spoke volumes.

You can do this. And I'm right here with you.

She waited as one of the OR nurses swabbed Jan's belly with antiseptic, then performed a laparotomy across her abdomen. With Jan's uterus exposed, Dr. Fleming moved in and began performing an ultrasound to determine Rhianna's position. All eyes were on the ultrasound monitor as her tiny body came into view.

"We'll need to rotate her slightly to gain full access to the spinal opening," Claire said, carefully but firmly placing her gloved hands on each side of Rhianna's body and exerting pressure on the left. This prompted Rhianna to roll slightly to the right—enough of a shift to reposition her spinal opening.

Claire looked to her left at Dr. Fleming who, without needing to be asked, stepped over to confirm the repositioning through ultrasound. This seamless communication—with no actual words needed—was so important in a surgery such as this, with so many moving parts, and Claire appreciated the doctor's diligence.

"Perfect," Claire said quietly as she viewed the spinal defect on the monitor, in the exact spot where it needed to be.

A surgical nurse handed her a uterine stapling device.

"You did a great job prepping your team," Claire said as she looked up at Kiernan.

"We had a very productive weekend," he said. "Saturday was chock-full of training videos, and Sunday was a simulated run-through of the surgery. Make that *many* run-throughs."

"It shows."

She nodded her appreciation in every direction, her eyes creased at the corners as her hidden lips curved upwards. Every doctor who had ever donned a surgical mask knew that this was the OR equivalent of a smile. But there was one doctor in particular whose silent encouragement she needed most. Looking across the operating table, she locked eyes with Kiernan and held his gaze for several moments. The exchange was silent, but the message was the same.

You can do this. I'm right here with you.

After a slight nod of acknowledgement, Claire took a deep breath, then cut into Jan's uterus with the stapling device. She flipped the attachment arm of her microscope glasses downward, instantly revealing a detailed closeup of the myelomeningocele sac, a thin, bluish, fluid-containing membrane about an inch and a half long that protruded from the opening in Rhianna's back.

Here we go.

Her breathing calm and her hands steady, she carefully excised the sac and placed it into a pan. A critical part of the surgery was now complete, but the time-intensive delicate closing of the spinal opening remained. Knowing that this multilayer closing was normally performed in tandem by a fetal surgeon and a neurosurgeon, she turned to the neurosurgeon to her left.

"Mr. Siwa, would you like to assist?"

"Absolutely," he declared as he moved in closer.

Once the spinal defect was fully repaired, it was time to close up the uterus. This, too, required the suturing of multiple layers—a more standard procedure than closing the spinal opening, but one that still required intense focus. Claire welcomed the task at hand, for it meant they were that much closer to completing a successful surgery.

There was an air of calmness in the OR as she and Mr. Siwa began stitching up the first uterine layer. It was as if everyone was breathing a collective sigh of relief now that the most critical part of the surgery was now behind them.

Suddenly Dr. McAdams, the cardiologist who had quietly been monitoring Rhianna's heart through echocardiology, called out. "Fetal heart rate is dropping."

Claire jerked her head up as Kiernan asked, "What is it?"

"One-oh-five. Still dropping."

Claire knew that a normal fetal heart rate was one-ten to one-sixty. If it continued to drop steadily, Rhianna would be heading fast to bradycardia. They could lose her.

For a split second, Claire closed her eyes.

"Doctor!" she heard someone exclaim urgently.

Given that the title covered half of the OR team, she couldn't be sure who it was directed to, but it didn't matter at this point. Rhianna's life—perhaps even Jan's—was in her hands now.

"We're in bradycardia," the cardiologist announced, his booming voice momentarily drowning out all the mechanical beeps and hurried voices in the room.

Claire swung her head from the direction of the cardiologist's voice to Kiernan. They locked eyes for a fraction of a second, and in that moment time stood still for Claire. There was no sound, no movement—no anything.

And then…it all came crashing back.

"Increase maternal oxygen," Claire instructed, knowing that doing so would improve Rhianna's oxygen levels as well.

As Sebastian adjusted Jan's oxygen levels, Kiernan asked, "What's her blood pressure?"

"One-ten over eighty," replied the nurse monitoring vital signs.

If the pressure was low, they could increase it through IV fluids and ephedrine, which in turn would improve blood flow to Rhianna. But it was within normal range.

She shared a look with Kiernan, and knew he was thinking the same thing as her. Aggressive intervention was needed to save Rhianna, and they didn't have a boatload of options.

Though fetal surgery had been inching its way into a viable solution for a growing list of congenital disorders, it was—as Claire's fetal surgery mentor at Boston General, Dr. Eugene Martin, would often say—"Still in its infancy, if you'll pardon the pun."

"Start a fetal IV of point-zero-one milligrams epinephrine," Claire said, shutting off the part of her mind that was one step short of inwardly screaming, *Hurry!*

"An IV?" the closest nurse to her asked.

Rather than be annoyed by the question in the midst of an emergency, Claire replied with a simple, "Yes."

She understood the need for confirmation. To say that she was navigating through uncharted waters was an understatement. Fetal bradycardia was a relatively rare complication during open fetal surgery, but it had been known to happen. Still, there was no definitive protocol in place.

Releasing some of the stiches to pull Rhianna's tiny forearm through, Claire inserted the IV needle and held her breath as Dr. Fleming administered the medication through the IV line. Thirty seconds went by—or was it thirty minutes? Claire knew it was the former, but with Rhianna's life in the balance, it felt like an eternity.

She turned to the cardiologist, who shook his head. "Still dropping. Eighty-seven."

"Atropine?" Kiernan suggested, just as Claire was about to call for it.

She nodded. "I need point-zero-zero-five milligrams atropine."

Dr. Fleming quickly administered the medication. Now all they could do was wait an agonizing minute to see if it worked.

Tick-tick-tick...

"No response!" the cardiologist said, just short of a shout.

Kiernan's ability to remain coolly detached through the most dire of surgical circumstances was being severely tested as the unthinkable began to unfold before him.

They couldn't lose Rhianna. They just couldn't.

It had been his idea to do this surgery here, and Rhianna's death would be on him. Not only would he be responsible for Jan losing her baby, but the loss would destroy Claire—a realization that nearly rendered him immobile. But now was not the time to freeze up. If ever he'd needed to shut off his emotions and focus solely on averting disaster, it was now.

"I'm going to start chest compressions," he said as he leaned over Jan's abdomen.

Across the table, Claire squeezed a hand into the reopened uterus and lifted Rhianna up so that her chest was well into view. But it wasn't enough.

"I'm going to lift her out," Claire said as she pulled Rhianna's head and chest through, leaving the rest of her body inside the womb.

Using his forefinger and middle finger, Kiernan began gently but rapidly compressing the center of Rhianna's chest at a rate of one hundred and twenty compressions per minute. At the sixty-second mark, he swung his head in the direction of Dr. McAdams.

Without needing to be asked, the cardiologist blurted out, "Eighty-five."

Kiernan couldn't see Claire's face beneath the mask, but he knew her grave expression matched his.

"Give another point-zero-one milligrams of epinephrine," she said urgently.

Kiernan halted compressions as Dr. Fleming administered the medication.

"We're still at eighty-five," Dr. McAdams called out twenty seconds later.

"Atropine?" Dr. Fleming asked, a syringe at the ready.

"Yes—point-zero-zero-five milligrams."

Tick-tick-tick...

"Eighty!" came the cardiologist's one-word update.

"Start compressions again," Claire said to Kiernan.

He quickly complied, with a laser-sharp focus, as he strived to deliver the precise amount of pressure.

"Heart rate is increasing. Ninety-eight," said the cardiologist.

Another ten compressions.

"One-twenty."

Kiernan's hand froze as he waited, desperately hoping that Rhianna's heart rate would stabilize.

"One-thirty-seven." Another ten seconds passed. "Heart rate is holding."

"Let's give it another minute to be sure before we start re-closing the uterus," Claire said, her voice a steady beacon in the quiet chaos of the operating theater.

Turning back to Kiernan, she gave a brief nod, as if to say, *I think we got through it.*

Forty-five minutes later Jan was wheeled out into Recovery, all of her vital signs, and Rhianna's, holding steady.

Kiernan watched as Claire walked over to the far side of the room, leaning up against the wall and removing her mask to take a deep and unfiltered breath of air.

"You were amazing," Kiernan said as he walked up beside her.

Claire looked up, her expression exhausted and yet exhilarated at the same time. "So were you. You saved Rhianna's life."

"*We* saved her life."

Claire smiled wearily. "Listen to us. We're debating over who did more to save Rhianna. It was a team effort all the way."

Kiernan's smile was as tired as Claire's, but also as genuine. "You're right. What matters most is that Jan and her baby are both safe and it truly was the best possible outcome."

He paused, wanting so badly to brush back the loose lock of silky chestnut hair that had spilled out of Claire's surgeon's cap. Fighting the urge, he forced himself to briefly look away. But wait… It was officially after the surgery, right? Which meant his self-imposed *don't touch* rule had expired.

He turned back to Claire just as she was pulling off her cap, her hair tumbling perfectly around her shoulders. *Really?* Every lock of hair had just fallen into exactly the right place, with nothing for him to brush aside?

She tilted her head, eyes perplexed. "What's wrong?"

Kiernan mustered up a smile. "Nothing. I was just going to suggest we go and talk to Jan's husband."

"Yes—good idea. I'm sure he'll be relieved… I can only imagine how worried he must have been this whole time."

And with good reason, Kiernan wanted to say as the earlier emergency played out in quick snippets in his mind.

After sharing the good news with Dave and Jan's two children in the waiting room, Kiernan escorted Claire back into the corridor.

"That is one happy father-to-be," he noted.

Claire smiled. "It feels good, being part of that happiness."

He wanted to probe further, to ask if the successful surgery had shifted anything for her career-wise, but he knew it was way too soon.

Claire bent her neck from side to side, then rubbed her shoulder. "Well, I think I'm going to head back to the cottage and take a nice, long, celebratory hot shower."

Kiernan was *so* tempted to offer to help loofah her back, and pretty much every other square inch of her beautiful, soft skin… But instead he cleared his throat and looked back at her with widened eyes that he did his best to minimize.

"That sounds like a good idea."

"I'll see you tomorrow for our country walkabout. Oh— and please tell Jan's care team to call me if there are any issues. Everything's looking good, and I'm not expecting any complications to crop up, but just in case."

"Will do."

She started down the corridor, turning back briefly to wave and flash an ear-to-ear smile.

"Enjoy your shower!" Kiernan called out, before cringing to himself.

Geez, did I just say that?

As Claire disappeared from view Kiernan had a sinking feeling in the pit of his stomach. He would see her again—for the time being. But the day was coming fast when that would no longer be the case.

And the feeling that was welling up inside him…the almost desperate realization that one day soon she'd be out of his life… Where was it coming from?

Because it wasn't anything he had ever felt for a woman before.

CHAPTER TEN

CLAIRE GLANCED AT her watch as Kiernan's SUV rolled up to her cottage. It was eleven fifty-nine a.m.

One minute early, she mused to herself as their "country walkabout"—destination still unknown—was about to commence.

The digital screen on her watch flashed as the display shifted to twelve p.m.

Or not.

So now she could add "punctual" to the list of Kiernan's attributes, which so far included "talented, brilliant, handsome, athletic, humorous and caring" among others. Although... could someone who was truly caring opt to live a life with no family of his own?

She frowned at her own line of thinking. It was a silly and unfair question. Some people opted to be married to their job, and in Kiernan's case the job entailed helping others—and often saving lives. So wasn't that a type of extended family? Kind of? Sort of?

"Hi."

Claire closed the cottage door behind her and greeted Kiernan. Standing by the SUV passenger door, a casual smile on his face, he looked both unassuming and ruggedly smoldering at the same time.

Claire's next breath caught in her throat.

Whew! Is it getting hot out here?

"What do you know?" Kiernan said, breaking into a smile. "We're twinning."

Claire's eyes had been so laser-focused on Kiernan that she hadn't seen the forest for the trees. Or, more precisely, she hadn't actually noticed what he was wearing. A closer inspection, and she began to laugh.

"You're right," she said as she took note of his jeans, white T-shirt, navy windbreaker and hiking shoes—all of which matched her own attire. "Great minds think alike."

"And dress alike, too," he said with a wink as he held the passenger door open for her.

As their drive got underway, Claire asked the question that had been uppermost in her mind. "How is Jan doing?"

"I checked in on her before leaving the hospital today. She's doing quite well, all things considered. She said Dave and the kids had come by to see her in the morning and were heading back for evening visiting hours."

"That's great to hear."

"She asked about you."

Claire did a double-take. "She did?"

Kiernan turned to her briefly before focusing back on the road. "You seem surprised. She's very grateful that you took on this surgery and wants to make sure you know this."

Claire was genuinely touched. "Please tell her I'm so happy to hear she and Rhianna are doing well."

Kiernan cleared his throat, hesitating for a moment before continuing, "You could come by the hospital and tell her yourself—if you're comfortable with that. I'm sure she'd be thrilled to see you."

Claire looked out the passenger window to collect her thoughts. "It's not that I don't want to see Jan. But I don't want to encroach on Dr. Fleming and her team. I'm sure they're all doing a wonderful job with postoperative care. They deserve credit, too."

She wondered if Kiernan could see through her explanation, which was half truthful and half flimsy excuse. The half that was truth was that she was afraid to get further involved in Jan's journey. Everything was headed in the right direction, and that was how she wanted to remember the experience. The more positives she could build on, the more she might be willing to fully step back into that world someday.

"Are you sure that's all it is?" Kiernan turned to her, seemingly holding his breath for several moments. "I know you came here to try to figure out if you can recommit to your career. If the reason you don't want to come by to see Jan is because you're still grappling with that, I can understand. Although I'm not going to lie... Seeing how happy you were after the surgery was successful, I just thought..."

His voice trailed off, but Claire knew where he was headed. "I know. You thought I'd finally got over the hurdle that's been holding me back." She paused. "I wish I could say it was that easy. And maybe it did help being in a different hospital and in a whole other country. There are so many memories back in Boston."

"I'm sorry. I shouldn't pressure you like this." Another short but meaningful sideways glance. "It's just that you're such an amazing doctor, and I know you still have so much to give. But ultimately I just want for you whatever will make you happiest."

"Me, too," Claire said quietly. "And I feel like I'm on the cusp of figuring it all out." She conjured up a smile as he briefly turned to her once more, his kind brown eyes locking onto hers. "I'm working on it, I promise."

Twenty-five minutes later, Kiernan pulled into the Connemara National Park visitors' center. "We're not visiting the center," he said with a wink. "We're hiking on the Diamond

Hill Trail. It's one of the most popular hiking spots in the country." As they exited the SUV, he added, "But we'll be veering off the beaten path in pursuit of one of those hidden gems I mentioned earlier."

Claire raised an eyebrow. "A hidden gem? I'm intrigued."

Kiernan grinned, then stepped around the back of the SUV and lifted up the hatch door. He pulled out two walking sticks, handing one to Claire.

"You can't go for a walkabout in Ireland without a shillelagh. I carved it myself."

Claire's eyes lit up as she ran her hand over the smooth exterior. Some women got excited over expensive jewelry, but not her.

Give me a genuine shillelagh, hand-carved by a dreamboat surgeon, and I'm the richest woman on the planet.

Looking up at Kiernan, she asked, "What are you—some kind of Renaissance man?"

He chuckled. "I've been called worse." Reaching again into the back of the SUV, he pulled out a large olive-green backpack. "I forgot to tell you to save room for lunch."

"I ate an energy bar just before you picked me up, but don't worry. I always work up an appetite when I'm out moving around in fresh air."

A thick lock of dark hair tumbled over Kiernan's left eye as he dipped down slightly to strap the backpack in place. "Good," he replied as he straightened back up with a mischievous twinkle in his eye. "That could come in handy."

Did he mean...?

Claire grinned, their earlier near-kiss front and center in her mind.

Ten minutes later they were on their way down a path that twisted and turned like a slate-gray version of the yellow brick road.

"There aren't many people here," Claire observed as she looked as far ahead as her vision allowed.

She could see several moving specks that she assumed were fellow hikers, but other than that they had the wide-open trail to themselves.

"It's a weekday, and still a bit early in the season," Kiernan said. "I've been here on weekends in late June and the trail entrance is like the starting gate at a horse race."

Claire wrinkled her nose. "Nothing against other humans, but I'd rather hike alone. Present company the exception, of course."

Kiernan smirked at her comment, adding, "I second that."

Another thing they had in common, Claire thought as they fell into an easy stride. Though the early-spring air held a faint chill, the afternoon sun was warm on her cheeks. She took a deep breath and soaked in her surroundings, and the panoramic view of gently sloping moors dotted with boulders and low mountains in the distance covered in mist.

Thump, step, thump, step, thump, step....

"You know, I've never actually used a walking stick before, but I have to say this really does help you get into a rhythm."

"And you thought Guinness was Ireland's most coveted contribution to the masses."

Claire chuckled. "You do have a way with words." Anticipating his reply, she beat him to the punch. "I know—it's the Gift of the Blarney."

Amused, Kiernan glanced sideways at her. "Matching outfits and now you're reading my mind. Should I be worried?"

Claire wanted to joke back, except his observation had hit a little too close to the mark. More likely the question was, should *she* be worried that she was enjoying his company so much?

The rapport that she shared with Kiernan was so natural, and so real, that it prompted her to rethink her entire relationship with Mark. Yes, he had turned into someone she no longer recognized, and it still haunted her knowing he had managed to pull the wool over her eyes for so long, shattering her trust in the process. But even before that, back when she'd *thought* they had something good together, it had still never been at this level, nor as easy and effortless.

But soon you'll be out of each other's lives.

The inevitable reminder left a pang in Claire's side, and it was one that she needed to heed. Her mind raced for a way to quickly change the subject, and there was one that was literally in hand.

"What kind of wood is this?" she asked as she held up her shillelagh.

"Blackthorn."

"Sounds prickly."

"It is. The shoots have thorns that can grow up to four inches. Let's just say I practically had to wear an iron hazmat suit when I cut off the branches."

"You definitely are a study in contradictions."

Kiernan glanced at her curiously. "How's that?"

She shrugged. "I haven't known many surgeons who play rugby and carve walking sticks."

"There must be an American equivalent. Surgeons who play tag football and carve pumpkins?"

Claire snickered. "I suppose."

Fifteen minutes later, Kiernan slowed down and pointed to the left. "Here's where we branch off the main path."

Claire cupped her eyes and looked out onto the western landscape. There was nothing obvious that set it apart from the terrain ahead if they stayed on the official trail, but Claire trusted that Kiernan had his reasons for the diversion. Plus, it added to the spirit of adventure, and that could only be a good thing.

They continued on, this time with no words, each taking

in the breathtaking scenery as they navigated the slightly uneven terrain.

Another ten minutes passed before Claire broke the silence. "I can see why you choose to live out here in the country, rather than in the city."

Kiernan turned to her. "What about you? I know you work in Boston, but is that where you live as well?"

"I live in Wayland, which is a suburb just west of Boston. It's pretty built up, but there are some pockets of nature here and there."

"That's good."

The conversation dropped off as they continued their climb, and Claire wondered if it was in part due to the subject matter. *You live here. I live there.*

Strip away the niceties, and that was what was left. A reminder that they came from two different worlds. And soon she would be returning to hers.

She winced as this reality sank in. The fact that she'd resume her life in Boston after a month in Ireland had always been a given. But then, she hadn't planned on meeting someone like Kiernan.

She turned to him, wondering if he could possibly know that being in his presence made her feel more blissfully alive… and far less tethered to the hurtful past…than she had in a very long time. His eyes were cast downward as he scanned the uneven ground for safe footing, but when he suddenly looked over at her, she blurted out a question to segue from her own thoughts.

"So, you mentioned you grew up in Ballyledge. Did your dad work at West Mercy as well?"

"No, he worked at St. Joseph's Hospital in Dublin."

"That sounds like quite a commute."

"He had an apartment in Dublin."

"Oh..." Claire grimaced, thinking that something in this equation wasn't adding up.

Kiernan turned to her in mid-stride. "You're wondering if he was living a double life of sorts."

"I am?"

Of course she was—not that it felt appropriate to admit as much.

"Well, that's what I'd be wondering if someone told me their father had his own apartment two hundred kilometers away. Which wouldn't necessarily raise red flags if he was divorced from my mother, but that wasn't the case."

"She didn't mind the arrangement?"

"I don't think she felt like she had a say in the matter."

Claire balked, failing to hide her displeasure at this latest revelation. "Sorry," she said quietly.

"Don't be. My mother deserved better, for sure. As to whether my father had a secret second family in Dublin— I honestly don't think so. At least I hope not, given that he couldn't live up to his responsibilities as a husband and father with his first family. And the crazy part—or maybe not so crazy—was that his father, my grandfather, was cut from the same cloth."

"He was a surgeon, too?"

"Yup. And an absentee husband and father."

Claire slowed to a stop.

It was only when Kiernan was several steps ahead of her that he realized she was no longer by his side. He swiveled around, an expression of slight alarm on his face. "Are you okay?"

"You can break the cycle, you know."

Confusion replaced alarm. "What?"

Claire bit her lower lip.

It's now or never. Say what you need to say.

A few moments passed as she tried to muster up some courage. Scanning the immediate vicinity, her gaze landed on a large, flattish boulder that seemed almost too perfect a find. Perhaps the universe was conspiring with her.

"Come sit with me for a minute," she said to Kiernan, before nodding toward the boulder.

Before he could reply, Claire took a seat, leaving plenty of room for Kiernan to join her. He slowly sat down beside her, leaving only the hint of a gap between them. She could feel the warmth of his body and smell his spicy aftershave. Not exactly helpful as she tried to concentrate on the point she needed to make.

"Thanks," she said. "I needed a break."

"No, you didn't," Kiernan said, squinting as he sized her up with the sun in his eyes. "In fact, I'm beginning to think you might be a secret marathoner. I'm feeling slightly winded climbing this hill, and your respiratory rate is on a par with a sloth's."

"You know, I could take offense at that." Claire laughed nonetheless.

Kiernan grinned. "Don't. I meant it in the best possible way."

A cloud must have covered part of the sun, because suddenly his face was partially shaded. No longer squinting, his eyes now displayed the hint of a twinkle.

"So, you were saying that I could break the cycle. Meaning, I suppose, that I can be the first surgeon in my family to not be a selfish jerk."

Claire was taken aback by his blunt assessment, both figuratively and literally. She pulled her torso forward so that she was once again sitting fully upright. "That's not what I meant at all."

"And, for the record, it's only selfish if a man chooses to have a family knowing that he can't give them what they deserve."

Claire widened her eyes at Kiernan's attempted clarification. He was digging his heels in, that was for sure.

"All I meant was, just because both your father and grandfather took the same approach to career versus family, you might think you can't possibly do things differently. But you can."

Kiernan studied Claire closely, his eyes burning into hers. "The old nature versus nurture argument. Is it something genetic that made them both brilliant surgeons but lousy husbands and fathers? Or did my father learn it from his dad, who learned it from who knows who?" He momentarily looked up at the sky in thought. "Come to think of it, my great-great-grandfather was a doctor, too, although I can't vouch for his parenting skills—or lack thereof."

"I just don't want to see you sell yourself short, that's all. Or go through life settling for less than you can have."

Kiernan nodded, and was silent for several moments. Then, "So you always knew you wanted a family, despite what I would imagine is a fairly grueling career as an ob-gyn at a major hospital like Boston General?"

Claire inwardly winced.

Breathe. You prodded him to get this opening. Now make the most of it.

"Yes and no. As in yes, I knew I wanted a family, but no, I wasn't certain I could be fully engaged in my career and also be there for a child in the way that I'd want to be."

As Kiernan pursed his lips together, Claire could almost see the wheels turning in his mind.

"So what made you decide that you could, in fact, do both?"

"When you work with mothers and babies, you see a lot of miracles. And to be a part of making those miracles happen is just the best feeling in the world. But there were times when I'd watch one of these happy endings play out in front of my eyes and it would suddenly dawn on me... Was it right to deny myself that same kind of happiness in order to help bring it to others? You can't go into medicine at a high level, like we have, and not sacrifice something for your career. But was it too great a sacrifice? That's the question I kept asking myself. And ultimately I decided that it was."

"Did you start to approach your career differently once you'd made that decision?"

"I suppose I did—but not in any way that would negatively impact my patients." A slight smile formed on Claire's lips. "Basically, I learned to say no."

Kiernan raised a curious eyebrow. "Oh?"

"No, I'm not going to be regularly putting in twelve-plus-hour days. No, I'm not going to be answering emails at midnight. No, I'm not going to spend *all* my free time at medical conferences or adding more credentials after my name—unless it's something I specifically need to better treat my patients."

She paused for a moment of self-reflection.

"Maybe I couldn't have taken that stance as a resident. But once I paid my dues, I had to rethink my boundaries. And, truth be told, I'm a better doctor for it."

Kiernan half smiled. "Happy doctor, happy patient?"

Claire grinned. "Exactly."

Kiernan looked out onto the rocky yet still lush landscape, his eyes seemingly fixated on a distant object. Was he weighing her take on balancing career and family? She hoped he was at least considering that there were other possibilities besides the one he was so rigidly holding on to.

"I'm glad you shared this," he said quietly. "And I know you'll have another child when the time is right. You have so much love to give."

"Be sure to mention that to the future father—whoever he may be. I want to make sure I don't unknowingly blow him off before things have a chance to get off the ground."

Claire briefly smirked at her own comment, but it was clear that Kiernan didn't share her amusement. His forehead was creased, his eyes pained. Perhaps he knew her seeming irreverence was an attempt to mask her discomfort.

"That was a stupid thing to say," she said quietly. She waited for his reply, but none was forthcoming. "Well, should we get back on the trail?" she asked, after more silence ensued.

"There's no trail where we're headed, remember?" Kiernan replied with a slight chuckle.

But he had to know that she was deliberately diverting the conversation, and Claire was glad that he knowingly went along with it. As he turned to check his backpack, his shoulder brushed against hers. It felt as strong and as solid as Claire had imagined it would—courtesy, no doubt, of rough-and-tumble rugby rather than the lifting of a scalpel.

"Come on," Kiernan said as he rose from the boulder. "Let's cover some more ground and then we can break for lunch. I have the perfect spot in mind."

No more proselytizing, Claire silently instructed herself.

Today was supposed to be a carefree, take-your-temporary-colleague-on-a-tour day. Couldn't she just go with the flow and enjoy herself?

As she clasped Kiernan's outstretched hand and hopped off the boulder, she had her answer. His grip, firm yet gentle—oxymoron though that might be—was enough to send a jolt through the length of her body. She couldn't be sure what the future held. Not for Kiernan, nor for herself. But she unequivocally knew that in this moment there was no one she would rather be with than the man standing before her now.

You can break the cycle.

Kiernan played the words over again and again in his head, grateful that in a world where it seemed every thought and action were documented in some form of social media, his brain was still a safe haven for every idea and emotion that passed through.

Was he in fact merely repeating what he *assumed* to be true? That dedicated surgeons couldn't successfully split their focus between their career and a family?

Looking back, he couldn't recall a time when he had ever felt differently. And the pushback that had inevitably cropped up in past romantic relationships, the "but of course you can do both" refrains? They had gone in one ear and out the other, accompanied in short order with his own refrain:

I don't think this relationship is going to work.

Done. End of story.

Of course he was exaggerating to himself to think that he had been able to cut all ties so easily. He was human, after all, and he did have a heart—though he sometimes kept that fact well hidden. But what *was* entirely accurate was that no one had ever made him truly question his beliefs. That was until now.

He turned to look at Claire as they forged ahead. With her eyes intently focused on the uneven grassy terrain beneath their feet, she was oblivious to his stare. Which was good. The last thing he wanted to do was unnerve her with his secret rapt attention.

In the late midday sun, Claire's chestnut hair took on redder tones, and her fair complexion was virtually translucent. She possessed a physical beauty that, quite literally, took his breath away. But it was so much more than that. To know everything she had been through, and see her willingness to potentially invite more personal pain through selflessly taking on Jan's surgery...now *that* was a thing of beauty.

"Is something wrong?" Claire asked, startling Kiernan and dismantling his thoughts.

"No—why do you ask?"

She smiled a bit nervously. "You're looking at me like I have two heads."

Kiernan squashed a wide-eyed grimace before it could fully

take hold. "Sorry about that. I was…um…just thinking about something and I guess I was staring without realizing it."

Lame, lame, lame, he silently scolded himself.

"I do the same thing," she said casually, prompting an equally silent *phew.*

"The spot I had in mind for a lunch break is just over that next hill," he said, eager to change the subject.

"Sounds good."

"Your shillelagh holding up okay?"

Claire smiled. "It sure is. In fact, I don't think I'll ever hike again without one."

"Awesome. And, by the way, if you look down near the bottom, you'll see a little something that I carved into the wood for you."

Claire halted and lifted up the bottom of the stick. She twisted it clockwise until the small carved lettering came into view. "'To Claire,'" she read aloud. "'One step at a time. Kiernan.'" She turned to him, momentarily speechless. "Thank you," she said finally, her voice both soft and sincere. "Words to live by, for sure."

Kiernan pursed his lips together and nodded. "You're very welcome."

He had added the message earlier in the morning, before picking up Claire, an idea that had only partially been on a whim. The desire to leave something with Claire that she could always remember him by had been percolating in his mind for several days. That it would be a message on a walking stick had been a last-minute choice, but it had felt so right when it came to him that he hadn't second-guessed the decision.

"Whew!" Claire declared fifteen minutes later, when they had nearly finished descending the final hill before lunch. She removed her windbreaker and tied it around her waist. "The sun is really starting to throw some heat."

"I know," Kiernan agreed. "It feels good."

He scanned the area once they were back on level ground, looking for familiar landmarks. It didn't take long to spot them. A heavy concentration of large boulders lining another hill about one hundred meters ahead and to the left, thick brush to the right, and a narrow grassy passageway in between.

He pointed to a stone ledge at the start of the rocky hill. "We can lunch there."

It was a short climb to the naturally formed perch, and he wasted no time sliding the backpack off his shoulders.

"Heavy?" Claire asked.

"Heavy enough," he replied with a rueful smile, stretching his neck to both sides to work out some of the kinks.

"Let me guess… Deep-dish, three-cheese lasagna?" Claire quipped as he unzipped the backpack.

Kiernan chuckled. "Even better. I decided to ditch my usual lunch of greasy sausage and chips for something healthier."

Claire grimaced. "Sausage and chips? Seriously? That's probably what brought your carotid endarterectomy patient into the OR today."

"Be quiet, you."

Claire smirked. "Just saying. And by the way—how did the surgery go?"

"It was fairly routine and by the book. He'll be back home tomorrow, and hopefully he will start following some of the healthy eating guidelines that one of our dieticians will be going over with him."

"You mean the ones you don't follow yourself?"

Kiernan feigned insult—not easy to do, given that he was actually quite amused. "I don't think I've seen this feisty side to you before."

"That's what happens when I'm hungry. I get a little obnoxious."

"Remind me to carry snacks around at all times," Kiernan quipped as he extracted two brown bags out of the backpack.

"One for me and one for you. Chickpea spread sandwiches with baked—not fried—crisps. And don't blame me if the sandwich tastes like…"

"Chickpeas?" Claire offered teasingly.

"I was going to say chalk."

"I love chickpeas. Good choice. And definitely a step above cucumbers."

Kiernan chuckled as he handed her a bottle of seltzer water and then leaned back, with a boulder behind him doubling as a backrest. He scanned the thicket across the way, looking for any sign that a certain four-legged dweller was still in the area. Suddenly, a swatch of white flashed within the twisted tangles of brown vegetation.

Kiernan gently grabbed Claire's forearm and pointed with his other hand. "There. Do you see her?"

Claire strained to view the area, then gasped. "Yes…yes, I see her! She's beautiful!" She turned to Kiernan, eyes wide with wonder. "I didn't realize there were white foxes in Ireland."

"There aren't. Well, not as a species. She's albino. I first spotted her two springs ago and I thought the same thing, too. White foxes in Ireland? But I did a little research and, though it's extremely rare, there is such a thing as an albino red fox."

As Claire leaned in slightly and squinted, Kiernan quietly pulled a pair of binoculars from the backpack. "I brought them just in case."

Claire peered into them for several moments. "I see two babies with her. Not white."

She handed the binoculars to Kiernan, and he confirmed her observation.

"She has a burrow somewhere in the thicket. To be honest, when I first spotted her two years ago, I never thought I'd see her the following year."

"You mean because she can't blend into her surroundings?"

"Exactly. She's even more vulnerable to predators than a normal fox. But since that first time I've had five sightings in total, the last one being in November."

"Her ears just pricked up," Claire said as she peered through the binoculars. "Oh—she's looking right at me."

"I'd say she can smell the chickpea sandwich, but I'm sure she'd prefer chips and sausages."

Claire smiled at the comment. "She's turning around now. There she goes—back with her babies into the brush."

"Her den's in there and she's being a protective mum."

Claire nodded and rested the binoculars beside her. "Not a bad thing."

"Nope. Safety first."

Claire looked earnestly into his eyes, and this time he held her gaze. "Thank you for bringing me here. You're right—it's a hidden gem."

"I'm glad you think so."

Claire wasn't looking away, and neither was he. His eyes fell to her pillowy lips...those same luscious lips he had come so close to kissing under a moonlit sky as ocean breezes danced around them. He had thought *that* had been the perfect, albeit missed, moment. But being this close to Claire...seeing the desire in her eyes that matched his own...feeling a connection to her that was deeper than he had ever felt for a woman...*this* was the perfect moment. And he was going to make it last.

Every. Spine-tingling. Second.

As he slowly moved in closer, she met him halfway. Their lips touched, and he felt as though he had been waiting for this kiss his whole life. Perhaps he had. Which was why he had no intention of rushing through it. He savored every exquisite sensation: the sweet softness of her lips, the silky luster of her hair as he ran his fingers through it, the warmth of her breath on his cheek as they slowly pulled back, only to reengage...

It was deeper and longer and more satiating than he had

imagined their kiss could be. And he had been imagining it from almost the first time he had laid eyes on Claire.

Moments—no, make that minutes...*many* minutes later, they reluctantly parted lips and leaned back on the rock.

"Wow," Claire said, looking slightly dazed but altogether pleased.

"I second that," Kiernan said.

And third and fourth...

"Are you sure you weren't just trying to get me to work up an appetite for that chickpea sandwich?"

Kiernan chuckled. "Am I that transparent?"

Claire leaned over and grabbed one of the sandwiches, then delicately took a bite as Kiernan watched.

"Well?" he asked.

She shrugged her shoulders. "Eh...maybe I'm just not hungry right now."

An impish grin gave away her ruse, and he placed a hand just above her knee as he pulled himself closer again. "Then you give me no choice but to work more on that appetite."

"If you insist."

As he caressed her back and pulled her close, Kiernan replied, "I most certainly do."

It was still light outside but heading toward dusk as Kiernan pulled up to Claire's cottage. She turned to him while remaining seated. "Thanks. I had a great time. Make that a *really* great time."

"Me, too."

"And I love the shillelagh. I might need to book its own seat on the flight home, but it's well worth it."

Though Kiernan grinned at her joke, this reminder of the transient nature of her stay was anything but amusing.

Seeing her hand on the door handle, he quickly changed the subject. "Despite my insistence that I could take time off during the week, it's not looking like I can break away from the hospital for another outing before the weekend. One of my general surgeons broke his ankle stepping in a rabbit hole."

"Don't tell me—he was playing golf?"

Kiernan rolled his eyes. "He was. And now I have to fill in for some of his surgeries. But I'm free this Saturday, if you're up for another adventure. No chickpea sandwiches, I promise."

"Sounds like a plan." She stepped out of the SUV and turned back. "Call or text me about when you plan to come by, and I'll see you then."

"Wait—I think you're forgetting something."

Her quizzical expression quickly eased into a smile. Leaning back into the car, she readily kissed him before finally pulling away to exit the vehicle once more.

As Kiernan watched her walk to the cottage he briefly closed his eyes. He had never been one to jump on the *life can be so unfair* bandwagon, but it sure as heck felt like the universe was conspiring against him. How else to explain that he had met a woman who took his breath away on every level, but soon she'd be out of his life for good?

He opened his eyes just in time to see Claire wave to him before disappearing into the cottage. With a deep sigh, he put the SUV in "drive." It was equipped with a GPS that had never led him astray. If only he had the equivalent of such a device for his heart. Because that earlier directive of "just enjoy the moment while she's here?" It no longer felt like a viable destination.

CHAPTER ELEVEN

CLAIRE STARED OUT the cottage window as she leaned over the back of the couch, her phone plastered against her ear. Only two rings into the call, her sister promptly answered.

"Claire—it's so good to hear from you! How's it going over there? Meet any hunky Irishmen?"

Claire managed to crack a smile as she shook her head. "No comment."

Her sister was quick to reply. "Whoa—that means yes!"

Claire turned back from the window, her thoughts very much on a particular hunky Irishman. If there were others in existence she didn't know, and quite frankly didn't care.

"Well?" Grace asked, disrupting Claire's *very* enjoyable thoughts.

Grace was not only her sister, but also her best friend. At home, they talked on the phone, often with video, at least four or five times a week. But before coming to Ireland, Claire had made a pledge to herself that she would limit her calls with Grace to no more than a few in total. She had come here to break free of the past and to contemplate her future—and doing so meant uncoupling from reminders of home. Even those reminders that she cared about. Their only previous call had been on the day she'd landed, to say that she had arrived safely. Which meant there was a whole lot of ground to cover.

Taking a deep breath, Claire fully dove in and filled Grace

in on Margaret and Kiernan, and Jan and Kiernan…and Kiernan and Kiernan and Kiernan.

"Oh, my gosh," Grace said breathlessly. "Here I was joking around, but you really *did* meet a hunky Irishman. And another doctor, no less."

"Surgeon," Claire corrected.

"There's a difference?"

Claire smiled ruefully. "According to most surgeons, yes."

"I have so many questions that I don't even know where to begin. Let me start with the obvious one."

"Okay, I'll bite. What's the obvious question?"

"Is he a good kisser?"

Claire laughed while simultaneously feeling her cheeks grow hot. "No."

"Really?"

"He's better than good. But that's all I'm going to tell you."

"Oh, come on, now! I've been married for about a gazillion years—I need some vicarious thrills."

Claire snickered softly, but she was too caught up in her thoughts to answer. Grace's question had sent her right back to that moment when Kiernan had looked deeply into her eyes, pulled her close, and kissed her in a way that had made every previous kiss in her life a pale second at best. Or was it more like a pale tenth? Um…a pale *hundredth*?

"Claire?"

"Huh?"

"I asked you if you thought it was possible that things with Kiernan could develop into something more?"

Claire's smile quickly evaporated. Harsh reality had a way of making smiles doing that. "I don't see how, given that we live in different countries. And I told you he doesn't want to have kids."

"Yeah, that's a deal-breaker, for sure. Although maybe you could change his mind."

"Grace, you know what four words have led to the most disappointment in relationships since the beginning of time? *I can change him.* Or, for that matter, *I can change her.*"

Grace sighed. "I know... I know. It's just that when you talk about him I can hear in your voice how happy you are. And I don't think I've heard that in a very long time."

Claire stared at the floor as she contemplated her sister's observation. It was true that Kiernan had a way of making her feel more alive, and it was a feeling that grew every time she was with him. But that didn't mean they could possibly have a future together. Not when the insurmountable obstacles of living in two different countries, with opposing views on having children, were stacked against them.

"Well, I'm actually on my way to see the man of the hour."

"Kiernan?"

Claire tempered a roll of her eyes with a grin. "No, a leprechaun."

"Ha-ha. Well, good for you. And Claire...?"

After a few moments of silence, Claire spoke. "Were you going to ask me something?"

"I was just wondering if you've made any headway on your decision about your career."

Claire sighed. "Headway, yes. But any definitive game plan of what to do next...not exactly. I came here expecting some quiet time alone to contemplate things. But it's been a crazy whirlwind from the start."

"What about the breech delivery and the fetal surgery, though? You must have felt good about helping those mothers and their babies."

"Of course! I don't think that part of the job ever changes. But it's not always a happy ending like that." She paused. "Maybe I just need to start fresh somewhere else."

"You mean leave Boston General? You love that hospital!"

"I know. I have great colleagues, and I've made some really

good friends over the years. But it's hard to separate that from some of the bad feelings I get when I think about the hospital. There are just so many memories there."

Claire knew she didn't have to point out to her sister exactly what she meant. After graduating medical school, both she and Mark had completed their residency at Boston General, with Mark then moving on to private practice. But it still held three years of memories of one of the most exciting times of her life as she'd fully realized her dream of becoming an ob-gyn.

And then, four years later...in Room 471 on the fourth floor in the obstetrics wing...she'd said goodbye to Ariana.

"Well, if you do decide to move on from Boston General, you'll have no problem landing somewhere else, that's for sure," said Grace. "In fact, they'll be lining up to sign you on."

Claire pulled her lips into a tight smile. "Thanks, Sis. But I'm a long way from making such a big decision. One step at a time, I guess."

Her own words momentarily startled her. Whether consciously or not, she had just repeated the message on her walking stick. As if on cue, she heard Kiernan's SUV roll to a stop outside the cottage.

After promising Grace they'd talk again soon, Claire closed the cottage door behind her, then turned to greet Kiernan as he stood by the passenger door. But instead of saying hi, the only word that came out of her mouth was a loud gasp. It was quickly followed by a blink of her eyes—just to make sure they weren't playing tricks on her.

"That is *not* a kilt you're wearing."

Had he read her mind the other night at his place?

Kiernan peered down at the green and black plaid tartan skirt, then back up at Claire. "Huh. I could have sworn I put trousers on this morning."

Claire's laughter bordered on a giggle.

"Do you like it?" Kiernan asked as he jokingly twirled

around, his rugged body the equivalent of a bull pirouetting in a china shop.

It was a spectacle that promoted even more laughter from Claire.

"I do," she conceded, though she couldn't be sure if she was complimenting the kilt or the black-socked muscular calves that were fully on display. "So, is there a reason for this catchy ensemble?"

"As a matter of fact, there is." He opened the passenger door. "Step inside, lass, and you'll find out soon enough."

Twenty minutes later, the SUV turned off the main road, slowly passed through an open wrought-iron gate, then continued up a narrow paved path. At the top of a hill, a one-tower castle loomed over the lavish landscape.

Claire strained her neck to get a better view from the passenger seat. "What castle is this?"

"Rockminster Castle. Built in 1547 by my great-great-great-great-grandfather on my mother's side. Wait—did I say five greats, or four?"

"I wasn't counting, but I think four."

"Should be five." He turned to Claire, a half-smile on his face. "It was a long time ago."

"Your family has a *castle*? Any other secrets I should know about?"

Kiernan chuckled. "Don't get too excited. It's a small castle. Kind of the equivalent of a studio apartment in the sixteenth century."

"It looks way bigger than a studio apartment," Claire observed as they drew closer to the structure. "Is it open to the public?"

"Not in any official capacity. My uncle, who lives in town, takes care of the upkeep. He'll rent it out for the occasional photo shoot or tea party on the grounds. That sort of thing... There's some interesting history in the walls of this castle, too."

As they exited the SUV, Claire scanned the postcard-worthy grounds with awe. "So, let's hear about some of that interesting history. Ours doesn't go back nearly as far in America."

Kiernan extracted a key from his pocket and unlocked the deadbolt on the large wooden door at the castle entrance. The air was chilled and musty as they made their way inside.

"Better yet, I'll take you right to the scene where it all happened."

As Claire followed Kiernan, she couldn't imagine a sexier history guide. At the top of a short flight of stairs they entered a small room with a wooden bed against one wall, and a dresser with a wash pan on the other side. A single window with metal bars looked out onto the front grounds. It was hard not to feel claustrophobic in such cramped surroundings, although Claire wondered if more was at play.

Kiernan, on the other hand, seemed unfazed as he began to fill her in on some of the castle's secrets. "Legend has it that at the turn of the seventeenth century, during the Nine Years War with England, the daughter of one of my ancestors fell in love with a British soldier."

"Uh-oh…"

Kiernan grimaced. "Exactly. When her father found out, he had her locked up in this very room, fully intending to keep her here until the war ended and the soldier departed. Or died in battle, I suppose—whichever came first."

Whether real or imaginary, Claire felt a sudden breeze rustle past her, and she wrapped her arms close to her chest in a protective stance.

"Am I scaring you?" Kiernan asked, stepping closer until there was little space between them. "I don't mean to."

"More like I'm scaring myself." She forced a brave smile, but the goosebumps on her arms remained. "So what happened?"

"Well, the daughter—her name was Bronagh—didn't take

too well to being locked away. One night, when a castle guard was shoving a plate of food under the door, she asked if she could open the door to speak to him. Of course he said no, but she must have said something to charm him into complying, because he did open the door."

Wide-eyed, Claire blurted out, "And...?"

"She pushed past the guard and ran upstairs onto the watch-tower, where she jumped to her death."

Claire flinched, her breath momentarily caught in her throat. "I think I now have goosebumps on top of my goosebumps."

"You might be feeling the presence of her ghost."

Claire bared her teeth. "Okay, now you're just messing with me."

Kiernan chuckled. "No, it's the truth. Over the years there's been a number of sightings of a young woman in a white frock, gazing out of this window." He pointed just behind Claire. "She stares back...then evaporates into thin air."

"Have you ever seen her?"

"No, but my mum saw her when she was a kid. It scared her so much she's rarely been back here. And my uncle has, on at least half a dozen occasions—including up on the tower where she jumped from. It's up the stairs outside this room. One of the previous groundskeepers saw her there, too."

"Can we go up the tower?" Claire asked, hoping Kiernan would reply quickly, before she lost her nerve.

Kiernan raised an eyebrow. "Are you sure you want to?"

"Are you calling me a scaredy cat?"

Kiernan grinned. "Nope, not me." He nodded to the door.

With Kiernan just behind her, Claire made her way up the narrow stone stairs, which coiled upwards in a clockwise fash-ion like a tightly wound snake.

"I can see why they didn't need elliptical machines back then," Claire said as she felt the lactic acid building up in her leg muscles with each additional step. "They got a workout just from getting from point A to point B in the castle."

"True," Kiernan replied, though Claire was quite certain *his* legs were finding the laborious climb a breeze.

Finally, a ray of sun broke through the darkness and illuminated the stairs just above her. "I think we're almost there."

A few more steps, and they were at the top of the watchtower. Unlike the small, bar-covered window in the previous room, the tower's windows were much larger and free of any hindrance. It made sense, though morbidly so, that Bronagh had chosen this spot to cast herself to the ground.

Kiernan walked up beside Claire, and together they looked out onto the sun-drenched grounds. "It almost looks too idyllic, considering what happened here," she said quietly.

"I know. Although I've been here on overcast days and you really do feel a different energy." Still staring straight ahead, he said, "And by the way...the name Bronagh means sorrow."

"Wow," Claire said softly. "It's like the plot for a tragic romance—except it really happened. I wonder why she felt she had to go to that extreme. The war wasn't going to last forever, so she had to know that someday she'd be free again."

"I don't know..." Kiernan's gaze remained fixed on the horizon. "I guess people do crazy things for love."

He slowly turned to Claire, his dark eyes melting into her own. She felt her breath catch first, and then her heart.

Stepping in closer, he brushed his fingers along her cheek, then pulled her in until their bodies touched. Without hesitation, he caressed her lips with his own, and time seemed to stand still as the kiss grew deeper and more passionate.

Claire no longer needed to fantasize about the rugby-primed chest beneath his shirt. She could feel each taut muscle as it pushed against her breasts, and the friction of their clothing sent waves of pleasure throughout her body. His lingering kisses along the length of her neck made her weak in the knees, and as Kiernan swept her off her feet and up into his powerful arms all she could do…all she *wanted* to do…was fully melt into the moment.

She closed her eyes and tipped back her head, but as Kiernan determinedly strode back to the staircase, like a man on a mission, she reluctantly popped one eye back open.

"Kiernan," she said breathlessly. "You can't carry me down these crazy stairs."

He playfully brushed his lips against her bottom lip. "Aye, I can. Leave it to me, lass."

Claire wasn't sure whether to laugh at his comment, brace herself for a fall, or kiss him passionately for good luck. So she did all three.

With his body of a bull that had somehow merged with the gracefulness of a gazelle, Kiernan descended the twisting staircase in record time. Entering the small room from where they had started their climb, he gently placed Claire on the bed, but there was a fire in his eyes that she knew was about to engulf them both.

Clothing came off…slowly at first, then at a feverish pitch. And as the timeworn wooden bed creaked Claire wondered if it might snap in half.

Go ahead. Break.

It was easy not to have a care in the world when every nerve-ending quivered with desire…

Kiernan was every bit the incredible lover she had imagined he'd be. And, yes, she had been imagining it a *lot* leading up to this moment. He was attentive, generous, and fully attuned to her on a level that seemed to go far beyond the physical. Every kiss, every whisper, every touch seemed solely designed to bring her pleasure, and she fully responded in kind.

As their lovemaking climaxed into a glorious release she felt something deep inside her shift, as though her healing had reached another apex. Lying quietly together, still wrapped in each other's arms, she could only conclude one thing: the power of love was real.

Later, as they walked in the flower-filled castle grounds, Kiernan reached over and took Claire's hand, their fingers effortlessly interlocking.

"How's Jan doing?" she asked suddenly.

The question caught Kiernan by surprise. Was she trying to deflect the conversation away from the two of them, knowing that the closeness and passion they'd just shared had opened an exhilarating door that would soon be slammed shut? It was a sobering realization that hovered in the back of his own mind, so he couldn't blame her for possibly feeling the same.

"She's doing great," he replied. "In fact, she'll be discharged from the hospital on Tuesday. Her C-section has been scheduled, so it's just a matter of her taking it easy at home for the remainder of the pregnancy."

"Do you think I could see her before she leaves?"

Given Claire's previous reluctance to see Jan again, the question shocked Kiernan—but in the best possible way. Still, knowing that literally jumping for joy in his kilt might not only make her change her mind, but also possibly put the family jewels on full display—*ahem*—he tamped down his outward enthusiasm.

"Of course. Do you want to come by on Monday? Say late morning or early afternoon? That way, I'll be able to pop in for the visit as well." He paused. "Unless you'd rather I didn't?"

Claire grinned. "Of course I want you to be there. And Dr. Fleming, too, if she's available. We were all in this together, and it would be nice to have a little reunion post-surgery."

Hoo, boy! This was progress!

Kiernan discreetly took a deep breath, but there was no hiding his ear-to-ear smile. Not only was he basking in the glow of the intimacy they had just shared, but Claire was taking another step in a career-reengaging direction, and he simply couldn't be happier.

Except....

Kiernan clenched his jaw tight as the other half of this equation revealed itself. Resuming her career meant her returning to Boston General. Which certainly was not a new revelation. But now...no, *especially* now, the thought of Claire leaving Ireland stung. And it stung hard.

Be happy for her, he told himself.

And he was. But that didn't mean he wouldn't miss her for the rest of his life.

Claire and Dr. Fleming were standing by Jan's bedside late on Monday morning when Kiernan entered the room. "I'm sorry I'm late. My last surgery went over a bit," he said hurriedly, his rapid breath screeching to a halt as Claire looked up at him, her green eyes sparkling in the brightly lit room.

"No worries," Dr. Fleming replied. "We've just been chatting with Jan about some of the best online stores for baby girls' clothing. My personal favorite is Tiny Frills. And Claire likes the handmade clothes on Etsy."

Uh-oh. Kiernan felt the muscles in his jaw and neck clench. Of course Dr. Fleming could have no idea how much discomfort this discussion would trigger in Claire. Still, though there was a tightness evident in her smile, Claire seemed to be taking it all in stride.

"Jan is being discharged at ten a.m. tomorrow," Dr. Fleming said. "Then it's home to be with her family until her scheduled C-section at thirty-seven weeks."

"Don't forget I have to take bedrest," Jan said, with an understandable lack of enthusiasm in her voice.

"I know it can seem daunting," Claire replied empathetically. "But I have a feeling the time will fly by."

"And then, before you know it," Dr. Fleming added, "you'll be holding Rhianna in your arms."

Seeing Claire's smile waver for a fleeting second, Kiernan quickly jumped in. "So, have you thought about what your first home-cooked meal will be?"

Claire met his eyes, as if silently thanking him for his not so thinly veiled attempt to change the subject.

"That depends on who's doing the cooking," Jan replied wryly. "I assume it won't be me, so that leaves either Dave or my mum, who's going to be staying with us until Rhianna arrives. Let's just say I know who I *hope* will be playing chef. Don't get me wrong—my husband's good at sharing the chores at home. But he can't properly boil an egg, never mind make an edible meal."

Laughter sounded through the room, and after another ten minutes of easy banter between Jan and the doctors the conversation came to a natural standstill. Finally, Claire filled in the silence.

"Well, Jan, I want to wish you the best with everything. I can now leave Ireland knowing you're in good hands here, with Dr. Fleming and her team."

"Thank you for everything," Jan said earnestly. "And I'd love to send you a picture of Rhianna when she's born."

"That would be wonderful."

Ten minutes later, the visit wound down, and Kiernan and Claire exited the room.

"I'm glad I came by," Claire said, in buoyant spirits at least as far as Kiernan could discern.

"I'm glad you did, too. It was good to get that closure with Jan." He slowed to a halt in the corridor, with Claire following suit. "So, have you thought about how you'll spend your last days here?"

He'd dreaded asking the question, but posed it in the hopes that she might say she had extended her leave.

"I'm not sure. Maybe I'll take a drive up the coast…stay in a bed-and-breakfast for a night."

As a sharp pang of disappointment gripped him, he pivoted to the thought of asking if there might be room for two. But before he could get the words out a door several feet away flew open and a young, cherub-faced nurse with reddened eyes nearly stumbled out of the room.

Kiernan froze in his steps. "What's wrong?" he asked urgently.

The nurse glanced at his nametag, her cheeks now reddening as much as her eyes. "I'm sorry, sir," she said, her voice cracking with emotion.

An older nurse exited the room and gently closed the door behind her.

"Is everything okay, Carol?" Kiernan asked.

She nodded, then placed a comforting hand on the younger nurse's shoulder. "This is Amy's first week…she's fresh out of nursing school," she explained. Turning to her younger colleague, she added, "It never gets easy, seeing something like this, but with time you'll be able to keep your emotions in check."

"What happened?" Claire asked, a hint of dread in her voice.

"A stillborn girl at thirty-four weeks. Dr. O'Conner induced labor nearly forty minutes ago, and both parents have been cradling her ever since. It's quite an emotional scene, as you can imagine." She looked back at the closed door, her forehead creased. "I've told them to take all the time they need. Everyone's different. Sometimes, the parents can't bear to do more than kiss their baby goodbye. Others find it hard to let go."

Kiernan turned to Claire, a sense of disbelief seeping into him that such a positive visit with Jan could be instantly counteracted in the worst possible way.

Instead of meeting his eyes, she stared at the door, and all he could do was hold his breath.

* * *

Claire looked at the small square window on the door. Everything told her to remain where she was, that nothing good would come out of peering inside the room. And that was on top of the fact that doing so would be a tremendous invasion of privacy for the grieving parents. But the compulsion building inside her had a mind of its own.

Turning back to Kiernan, she saw the deep concern etched on his face. She smiled and nodded to him as a signal that she was okay, then waited for him to be reluctantly pulled into a conversation with Carol. With his head now turned away from her, Claire discreetly stepped toward the door.

Her glance inside the window could not have lasted more than five seconds. But it was still long enough to imprint the scene on her mind. A couple, presumably husband and wife, clutching each other and sobbing together.

Stepping away from the window, Claire saw Kiernan do a double-take as he glanced back over at her. Had he read the distress on her face? It would have been hard not to at this point. Though she couldn't hear the exact conversation between Kiernan and the two nurses, it was clear from both the inflection of his voice and his fidgety stance that he was trying to wrap things up as quickly as possible.

As the nurses departed, Kiernan was immediately at Claire's side. "Are you okay?"

"Yes. It's just that…" She paused, shaking her head. "I shouldn't have looked in the room."

"I'm sure it brought back painful memories," Kiernan said quietly.

"The husband was holding his wife, and they were both crying. When I lost Ariana, Mark was nowhere to be found. I remember holding her for what seemed like forever, not wanting the doctor to come take her away. And Mark didn't even care."

Kiernan's eyes narrowed, like daggers aimed at an invisible Mark. "Did he know you were in the hospital?"

"I didn't contact him, but one of the nurses did. She really had no right to do that, but she was friends with him. She told me later that he acted all annoyed when she told him that Ariana was about to be stillborn and they were inducing labor. 'Like he couldn't be bothered' was the way she described it to me. She vowed never to talk to him again after that."

Kiernan clenched his jaw. "I'm so sorry you went through this alone. That never should have happened."

Alone. She hadn't really thought much before about how deeply Mark's complete disregard for the loss of their child had affected her, but now she couldn't unsee the connection. Watching that couple grieve together, simultaneously cradling each other and their tiny stillborn daughter—that was how it *should* be. If Mark had been the man she'd initially thought he was—if they'd had a strong marriage and if he had grieved the death of their baby as a loving husband and father should—then perhaps she would have been better equipped to move past the active stage of a trauma that had never fully resolved.

Kiernan wouldn't have left me alone.

That her thoughts had even gone there was almost shocking to Claire. But should it have been, knowing how he had so resolutely stayed by her side through several emotional upheavals?

"Are you okay?" Kiernan asked again, eyeing her intently.

It took several moments for her to nod. "I wasn't expecting this…especially after everything went so well with Jan's visit…but I'm okay. Really."

Less than a month ago she would never have been able to

say this. But that had been before Kiernan. Their time together, though counted only in weeks, had impacted her enough for a lifetime, and given her a renewed strength that she'd thought she had lost forever.

But Kiernan appeared less than convinced by her reply.

"Do you want to go to the café, and we can sit and talk for a bit?"

Claire hesitated as she weighed the offer. Though she had just successfully ridden out the surge of emotions prompted by peering into the stillbirth room, something was still niggling at her.

"I think I'm going to head back to the cottage for some duck therapy," she replied finally.

Kiernan smiled, though it didn't completely erase the concern in his eyes. "Can I see you tonight?"

She held his gaze, unable to answer. There was that niggling again, like a tapping against her brain that said, *Yoo-hoo, there's something we need to discuss.*

"I think I'm just going to lay low tonight. But I'll be in touch."

Kiernan pursed his lips together and nodded. He didn't say anything...nor did he have to. The disappointment in his eyes spoke loud and clear.

Later that night, as she stared up at the dark ceiling from her bed, Claire finally acknowledged what had been chipping away at her subconscious since earlier that day. From their initial chance meeting during a high-stakes baby delivery, and culminating in their better-than-she-could-have-imagined tryst in the castle, she had shared an emotional and physical connection with Kiernan unlike any she had ever known.

But today she'd had an unexpected gut-check. And what

had it taken for the bubble to finally burst? The fantasy to be replaced with reality? It had been seeing the couple at the hospital who had just lost their baby, and knowing that Kiernan would be the kind of husband and father who'd be there for her if she'd been that grieving mother...

Except for one little thing. He wanted nothing to do with either role. Which was his prerogative, right? Just as it was hers to decide to cut her losses before her heart was further crushed. And that meant telling him goodbye. Not on her last day here. Not at the airport. *Now.*

Claire abruptly turned on her side, as though she could dislodge her distressing thoughts, but they clung to her too tightly. She had known from the get-go that her time in Ireland was temporary and any attachment to Kiernan would be a mistake. But somewhere along the way she'd forgotten—or perhaps willfully ignored—her own warning. It was as if she had started to believe that *this* was her life now. Living in the beautiful Irish countryside, working side by side with Kiernan, her love for him growing every second of every day...

Yes... I said it. My love for him.

Never in a million years had she thought she'd fall so head-over-heels in love during her brief stint in Ireland.

But the heart wants what it wants. Even when it can't have what it wants.

Just shy of a week from now she would again be staring at a dark ceiling—but it would be in the bedroom of her condo just outside of Boston. Somehow, some way, she'd resume her previous life—though it now seemed inevitable that Boston General would not be part of that reunion.

It will all work out, she told herself.

More than once in the past those words had gotten her through the toughest of times. But not so much now. Maybe because the mantra implied that something good could come out of saying goodbye to Kiernan forever. And that, quite frankly, just didn't seem possible.

CHAPTER TWELVE

KIERNAN DUCKED AS a sledgehammer swung precariously close to his head. The fact that it came complete with human fingers and was attached to the gargantuan shoulder of a rugby teammate named Angus did little to alter Kiernan's perception that he was being swiped at with a block of iron on a stick.

"Hey, take it easy," he said as Angus swung out again, this time smacking him hard on the shoulder.

In his boisterous teammate's defense, he realized Angus probably thought he was just giving him a friendly post-game pat—not setting him up for future joint replacement surgery.

"Aye! I'm just a little pumped-up about our win."

Angus grabbed Kiernan in a bear hug, landing a couple of knuckle-knocks on the head for good measure. When he finally broke free, Kiernan laughed at his friend's shenanigans, then joined the rest of the rambunctious group as they tumbled into the main room of Gilroy's Pub.

Almost immediately, he spotted Claire sitting alone at a nearby table.

She waved discreetly, and he wasted no time in heading over.

"This is a pleasant surprise," he said as he pulled out a chair, smiling so deeply that he felt his cheeks would burst.

After their downcast parting of ways at the hospital yesterday, this unexpected reunion was a special treat. Actually, that could be said about *any* time he was in her presence. Which begged the question…was it possible he could find a way to stay in her presence more permanently?

I know… I know…she's leaving soon.

Knowing it wasn't the right time to grapple with such thoughts, Kiernan pushed them aside and focused on the beautiful face in front of him.

Claire smiled, but not with her usual verve. "I wasn't sure if you'd still be playing today, with all the rain we had earlier," she said.

"Are you kidding? Rain means mud, and I swear some of the guys—make that most—prefer a soggy field. It's easier to squash someone's face into the ground."

Claire snickered, but her amusement was short-lived. The smile evaporated and her eyes flashed with angst.

"Are you okay?" he asked gingerly.

"I came here hoping that we could talk."

Coupled with her troubled demeanor, the announcement left Kiernan reeling with dread.

"Yes, of course," he managed to say, as evenly as possible.

She scanned the loud and crowded pub. "It was raining pretty hard when I got here a half-hour ago. Is it still raining now?"

"No, just a light mist."

"Can we take a walk on the pier?"

"Sure."

As they walked along the pier several minutes later, Claire stopped abruptly and turned to him. "Kiernan, what I'm about to say is not easy for me. As you know, I came here seeking clarity about my career—something that I felt I was never going to find back home, where there are still so many reminders of painful things. But what I didn't expect to happen…"

She paused, visibly swallowing twice, as though pushing back emotions. "What I didn't expect was meeting someone I'd develop very strong feelings for."

Only the sound of waves lapping against the pier could be heard as she stared into his eyes. Kiernan wanted to stay silent as he waited for her to resume talking, but he couldn't.

"Claire, I wasn't expecting this either. But is it so bad that we *did* meet each other, and that we *do* have these feelings?"

"For me, yes."

Her reply was like a one-two gut-punch. "I see," was all that he could manage to say.

"I can't be the only one realizing that this can't go anywhere. We don't want the same things, Kiernan. I mean, many things, we do—but not the one thing that I can't compromise on."

"A child," he said quietly.

She nodded. "And I know that I'm getting too far ahead of myself here by even bringing this up. It's not like we're even in a relationship—right?"

Kiernan wasn't sure if this was a genuine or rhetorical question, but he was unable to answer either way.

"And you know what kills me about all of this, what I just can't wrap my head around, is how you insist that you're someone you're not."

What?

Kiernan's head was now officially spinning. He had told Claire why he wouldn't put a child in the position his father had put him in. He'd been honest with her about that.

"I'm not sure what you mean."

"Yesterday, when I looked into that room and saw the husband consoling his wife… Mark wasn't that kind of husband and father. But Kiernan, *you* are."

"But—"

"I know," Claire quickly interjected. "What the heck am I talking about, right? You're not a husband or a father, nor do you want to be. But that's what I can't understand. Because the Kiernan I know is kind and compassionate. He's someone who goes the extra mile for his patients, but he also cares about the people in his life. Think about how you cancelled a surgery to stay with me when you knew I was upset. Or how you wouldn't let me leave the hospital and comforted me when I had an anxiety attack after visiting the birthing suite."

Claire's words had nearly knocked Kiernan backwards, but she wasn't finished.

"You're not your father, Kiernan. Yet for some inexplicable reason, you seem convinced that you are. And you know what the saddest part of all this is?"

Kiernan wasn't sure, but he was pretty damn certain that Claire was about to tell him.

"The person you're hurting the most is yourself. Because I *know* you would be an amazing father and husband. And if you could only get past whatever it is that has you convinced otherwise, I know you'd find happiness in committing to more than just your career. And I mean a different kind of happiness—not the one you can find in your work, no matter how dedicated you are or how many lives you save."

It was only the sensation of raindrops on his bottom lip that made Kiernan realize his mouth was slightly agape. He swallowed to close it.

"I think I'm having one of those sorry-not-sorry moments," Claire said sheepishly, as though she, too, was shocked by her own words. "I wasn't actually planning to say all of that. It just kind of came out."

It took several moments for Kiernan to reply, "That's okay." He knew how insufficient those two words were at a moment like this, but was too paralyzed to say anything more.

As Claire reached over and clasped his hand he shuddered at her touch—and at the thought that he might never feel the warmth of her skin again.

"What I *did* come here to say is that I think it's best if we say goodbye now…before it gets even harder to do so. At least harder for me."

"Claire…"

She stared at him, clearly waiting for him to say more. But as the world around him seemingly came to a halt, he could only pose two questions in his mind. Could this be it? Was it the last time he would ever look into her eyes? He'd known this day was coming—but not here…not in this very moment.

Say something!

His directive fell on deaf ears—*his* deaf ears. No, that wasn't quite right. He heard himself, loud and clear, but what could he say? That she was right and he *was* missing out on the joy of having a partner in life and children? *Was* she right?

His breath choked in his throat. It was all too much to take in at this moment. Still, there was something he needed to know.

"Will you be going back to Boston General?"

Claire briefly looked down at the ground, but not before he saw disappointment in her eyes. Was she hoping that he'd tell her she was right, rather than ask about her career decision? He had only asked because he desperately wanted her to continue the work she was meant to do.

Claire looked back up at him. "I might not return to the hospital itself, given that I think a fresh start somewhere else will probably be better for me. But I also think I've come to realize over the last few weeks that making a difference in the lives of mothers and their babies is the work that I'm meant to do." She stared earnestly into Kiernan's eyes. "And I have you to thank for that."

"Claire—"

She squeezed his hand. "I'm not sure what the medical equivalent is of getting back in the saddle…"

A half-smile emerged on Kiernan's lips. "Getting back into the scrubs?"

She grinned. "Something like that. But without your encouragement and support I never would have been able to do it."

"You're an incredible doctor—all I did was open the door. You're the one who willingly walked through it, despite what I know had to be immense difficulty in doing so. I'm just so grateful and proud of you that you did."

With a surge of wind, the drizzle turned into steady rain that began to drum down upon them. Kiernan looked up at the sky, only to be immediately pelted in the eyes.

Claire looked up as well. "Where's an umbrella when you need one?"

Kiernan studied her closely through the raindrops that were pooling on his eyelashes. Even with her hair plastered against the sides of her face and rivulets of water running down her nose and cheeks, she was exquisitely beautiful, both inside and out.

"Come on," he said. "Let's go inside."

"Actually, I think I'll go back to my cottage."

Right, Kiernan thought, his stomach sinking. And it wasn't alone. His heart also plunged as reality set in. *This is the end of the road for us. And it's my doing.*

"Let me at least drive you back."

He hoped beyond hope that she'd take up his offer—if for no other reason than to avoid the rain. At least he would have another ten minutes in her presence.

"No—I'm fine. It's not a long walk. And, believe it or not, I sometimes like being out in the rain."

There it was again. The streak of stubbornness and independence that drove him crazy, but also garnered his admiration.

"Take care of yourself, Kiernan," Claire said, her voice subdued and yet almost echoing against the roar of the rain. "I'll never forget the time that we spent together."

One more long, lingering look his way, and then she turned and walked away from him along the pier. He was still watching intently as she turned left onto the perpendicular portion of the platform that led back to the shore, knowing she would then take the paved path beside the road that led to her cottage.

Soon she disappeared from view. And still, he stayed.

Another ten minutes passed—or was it more like fifteen? Kiernan couldn't be sure. He continued to stare off into the distance, only vaguely aware of the slightly swaying pier beneath his feet the storm-provoked winds and waves kicked into overdrive.

Apparently he must like the rain, too, he thought. Because here he was, soaked to the bone and then some, and still he couldn't step away from the last spot where he had held Claire's hands and stared into her eyes.

Back at his home, later that night, Kiernan leaned up against the deck railing and stared outwards. He usually did his best thinking when it was just him and the endless expanse of ocean, but now its powers of insight seemed to be on hold. Never in a million years had he thought he'd be facing such a seemingly insurmountable impasse...

But *was* it insurmountable?

Since his early teens, he'd had his whole life mapped out before him. Perhaps it had been a way to assert control when everything else around him at the time had seemed to be about as stable and solid as quicksand. And there was no doubt that this steely resolve had served him well over the years. It had got him through medical school when his own father had cast doubts on his ability to succeed. And it had kept him rising up the ranks as a surgeon, culminating in a position that would allow him to have the greatest impact on patients in need of potentially life-saving care.

But at what cost?

Kiernan shook his head, dumbfounded by his own question. He had never dared ask himself this before—simply because it was a non-issue.

Meeting Claire had changed all of that.

Like a kaleidoscope of images, every moment spent with Claire played out in his mind. From performing a high-risk delivery together, as two strangers in the back of an ambulance, to their passionate encounter in the castle and everything in between... In less than a month she had managed to capture his heart in a way that no other woman ever had. And now he was losing her. Not only to her inevitable return to America, but to his rigid insistence that children were not part of his life plan.

You can break the cycle, you know.

Claire's earlier words echoed in his mind. Was it possible that he had been denying himself the joy and fulfillment of having a family of his own all because of his negative experiences as the son of a negligent father? It couldn't be that simple—a textbook case of unintentionally sabotaging his own ultimate happiness due to the misdeeds of his dad.

It just couldn't.

Or...could it?

"I am not my father," he said quietly into the wind.

It whistled back, as though reassuring him that his thoughts were the key to his salvation.

Nothing would make him happier than seeing Claire with the child that she so desperately wanted. A child that would help heal the wounds of her past loss. A child that she would love with the endless compassion that was so much a part of who she was.

There was only one problem. He couldn't imagine her sharing that joy with anyone but him.

The revelation frightened him—but not because it meant

upending a life plan that up until very recently had been set in immovable stone. No, the fear was that it was too late to reverse course. Claire was leaving the country on Saturday. That gave him three days to do...*something*. And it had to be big.

His mind whirled and whirled and whirled.

Yes...yes...uh-huh...right.

Another nod as a plan emerged out of thin air and began to take shape in his thoughts.

It was crazy. *He* was crazy.

The formerly logical, even-keeled, uber-grounded surgeon was about to go off the deep end, and he had zero regrets. His only regret would be if he waited another second and ended up being too late.

It was time to set his plan in motion.

CHAPTER THIRTEEN

CLAIRE TOSSED SOME cracked corn to the ducks as she walked along the shoreline behind her cottage. Earlier in the day she had started to pack for her inevitable flight home tomorrow, but hadn't got any further than throwing a pair of jeans and two tops into the suitcase.

She didn't have to look deep within herself to know that her heart wasn't fully on board with returning to Boston. Nor did she have to question why. Or, more precisely, the *who* behind the why.

Still, she didn't regret a single second that she had spent with Kiernan. *Not one.* In so many ways he had helped her heal from a loss that had previously seemed insurmountable. She would never, ever forget precious Ariana, but the thoughts were no longer paralyzing to her very soul like they had been before. Plus, she was ready to reengage in her career as an ob-gyn—another step forward that only a month ago had seemed impossible.

And he showed you that you can fall in love again.

Claire winced. If ever there was a positive that came with an equally weighted negative, this had to be it. Yes, she now knew she could love again. But she could love *Kiernan*—a distinction that was non-negotiable. And now, she had to leave him.

Even if you stayed, you'd still have to say goodbye.

Claire pressed her lips together, jaw tightened. Did she really need to remind herself of the obvious?

Just be glad for the time you had together, she told herself.

Not *too* much of cliché, she thought, but it was a notion she was going to hold on to...because right now it was all she had.

"I thought I might find you here."

Claire gasped and whirled around, her eyes wide with disbelief as she saw Kiernan standing barely ten feet away from her. He wore a grin that suited his handsome face in the same way that his dark jeans and long-sleeved burgundy T-shirt suited his muscular body.

It took a few moments for Claire to process what was happening. She had told Kiernan no more goodbyes. But, damn, was she ever happy that he had ignored her request.

"I had to see you again," he said as he walked over and took both her hands in his. "So please don't get mad at me for defying your orders."

She couldn't help but laugh quietly at his cheekiness. "That's okay. I'm supposed to be packing to leave, but as you can see, I've been procrastinating." As he squeezed her hands and pulled her in closer, she could feel the electricity surge between them. "And I can think of worse diversions than seeing you again."

He smiled, but then his face grew serious. "Claire, I couldn't let you leave without telling you something."

She waited for him to continue, suddenly aware that she was holding her breath.

"I love you," he said softly. "And in a way that I've never loved anyone before. You are the most gifted, caring, beautiful...*amazing* woman, and you've made me see things that no one else ever has. Or ever could. Being with you has made me a better person. Which I know probably sounds crazy, given that we've only known each other a month. But it's been a month that's completely changed my life."

Claire caught her breath just in time before it escaped her once more. "I love you, too," she said quietly. "Which is why saying goodbye is so hard…"

"But what if we didn't have to say goodbye?"

Her forehead creased in confusion. They had been over this before. Surely he knew why they had to part ways.

Realizing there was no point in repeating their conflicting views on family, she could only look at him with questioning eyes.

"I've been doing a lot of thinking over the past few days," he said. "*A lot*. You said something to me that day we went hiking. How I could be the one to break the cycle. At the time I knew what you meant on an intellectual level, but I couldn't truly *feel* it, if you know what I mean. But I do now. My desire not to have kids totally stemmed from my father's inadequacies. I thought that being the best surgeon I could be meant forgoing a family, or else being an absentee husband and father like him. But it's simply not true. Being with you…it's made me see what really matters in life. The work that we both do as doctors—yes, that is important. It can even save lives. But it's not the be-all and end-all. I want to spend the rest of my life with you. And to have a family together."

He looked up at the sky, shaking his head and nearly laughing, as though he couldn't comprehend how some of his core beliefs had suddenly been turned upside down.

"All of my life I've wanted to steer clear of anything that remotely hinted at having a family of my own. And now… because of you…it's like I suddenly can't think about anything else."

"Kiernan… I…"

Was this really happening?

She swallowed hard, reminding herself that she needed to stay grounded in reality. "You do know that I'm flying back to Boston tomorrow."

"I know. But I also know that you probably won't be going back to Boston General—at least that's what you shared with me. So I hope you don't mind that I took the liberty of making a few inquiries."

Claire arched an eyebrow. "A few inquiries...?"

"I've been in talks with the hospital board and the CEO, and they all agree. There's no one more qualified to lead West Mercy's new neonatal wing than you. They're still hammering out the fine print, but if you're interested they're prepared to offer you a contract that will give you full control over the direction of this new program. Fetal surgeries, treatments for high-risk mothers—all of it."

Claire didn't think her jaw could fall any further, but with this most unexpected announcement, it found a way. Her mind, though spinning, travelled back to a recent wish...a seemingly *impossible* wish...that she was living in the beautiful Irish countryside and working with the love of her life, who just so happened to be gazing into her eyes at this very moment.

And now Kiernan was pledging his love to her and sharing his desire for them to have a family together. Which meant that in the span of a single minute—two at tops—he had just made all her dreams come true.

"I know this is a lot to throw at you all at once," he said. "And I don't want you to feel in any way pressured to make a decision now. Take whatever time you need. Go home, like you planned, and talk to your family about it if that helps." He paused. "Oh—and I should mention that the contract comes with a very important rider."

Seeing the glint of a twinkle in his eye, Claire grinned cautiously as she asked, "Which is...?"

"Twenty-four-seven access to the chief of surgery, who is fully invested in the goal of making you the happiest woman on earth."

"You've already done that," Claire said softly as Kiernan leaned in and kissed her passionately.

"Like I said before," Kiernan said, once they both had a chance to breathe again. "No pressure... But while you're tossing around the pros and cons of my offer, how about we go inside the cottage and I'll show you some of the exclusive benefits you'll get with that contract rider?"

Claire grinned. She already knew what her answer would be, but there was no need to let the chief of surgery know just yet. "Okay... But just so you know—I'm very much on the fence about this offer, so you'll really need to persuade me."

His eyes flashed with desire as they gazed into hers. "Oh, I will... I can promise you that."

Claire had no doubt Kiernan would keep his promise. He was just that kind of man.

EPILOGUE

CLAIRE PROPPED HERSELF up on both elbows as she lay down on a soft blanket covering an equally cushiony carpet of grass. The early-afternoon sun felt good on her face, and with her eyes closed, she tipped her head back.

"Nothing like getting some vitamin D the good, old-fashioned way."

Kiernan leaned over and kissed her on the forehead. "Hard to believe that exactly one year ago we met at this precise spot."

Claire opened her eyes and smiled. "I know. I sometimes wonder…what if I'd come here for a walk twenty minutes sooner, or you'd gone for a run twenty minutes later. Chances are we never would have met."

"Or been at the right place, at the right time, to help deliver Sam."

"Exactly."

"So, are you saying you believe in fate?" Kiernan asked, with a teasing quality to his voice.

Claire smiled wistfully. "Either that or extremely good luck."

Kiernan scanned the grass that lined the border of the blanket, then plucked a four-leaf clover. He offered it to Claire, placing his other hand on her belly. "Well, I can personally vouch for the fact that I'm the luckiest man alive."

She placed her hand over his. At four and a half months pregnant, she had just started to experience Caitlin's kicks, and her smile widened as one poked her just under her ribcage.

"Did you feel that?" she asked excitedly.

Kiernan nodded, his face beaming with pride. "I think we have a star football player in the making. Or, better yet, a rugby player."

A ringing phone interrupted Claire's laughter.

"Who is it?" she asked as Kiernan glanced down at his phone screen.

"It's Craig," he replied, rolling his eyes.

Two more rings, and the call stopped.

"You can call him back. I don't mind."

"It's nothing that can't wait."

"Are you sure about that? You don't want the hospital CEO labeling you a slacker." She paused. "And I'm only half kidding, by the way, knowing how he expects twenty-four-seven access."

"It's a beautiful Saturday afternoon, and I'm here with my even more beautiful wife. If it were a medical emergency, I'd take the call. But administrative stuff—that can wait until Monday."

"You really have become quite the slouch, Mr. O'Rourke."

Kiernan grinned. "If it means spending more time with you and our daughter, then I'll gladly own up to that."

"I love you," she said, at the exact moment Kiernan uttered the same three words.

They both laughed at the unintended perfect timing.

"And I can't wait to meet you, little Caitlin," Kiernan said as he leaned over and kissed her belly.

Claire lifted the four-leaf clover that she had been twirling between her thumb and forefinger and studied it for a moment. There had to be some truth to its powers of good fortune. Because she was, indeed, the luckiest woman in the world.

* * * * *

MEDICAL

Life and love in the world
of modern medicine.

Available Next Month

Best Friend To Husband? Louisa Heaton
Finding A Family Next Door Louisa Heaton

....

The GP's Seaside Reunion Annie Claydon
A Kiss With The Irish Surgeon Kristine Lynn

....

Nurse's Baby Bombshell Charlotte Hawkes
The Single Dad's Secret Zoey Gomez

Keep reading for an excerpt of a new title
from the Romantic Suspense series,
LETHAL WILDERNESS TRAP by Susan Furlong

Chapter One

Ava Burke sat cross-legged on the crest of the hill, propped against the trunk of a sugar maple amid the tombstones of generations of Burkes and the freshly placed sod of her own husband's grave. Behind her loomed Burke House, three stories of red brick and white columns with rows of mullioned windows gaping over the churning waters of Lake Superior and what she knew to be the dark island beyond.

Long fingerlike clouds drifted overhead, carried on a cold breeze. Ava shivered and pulled the hood of her sweatshirt tight, tucking in a few long brown curls beneath the fabric as her gaze settled on the cross etched in Kevin's gravestone.

Kevin had passed in late January, when the ground in the Upper Peninsula of Michigan had been frozen and piled with snow and burial on the family land impossible. The past few months, while she'd waited to lay her husband to rest, had been dark and still. The only light in that gloom had been Rose, their six-year-old daughter. But since Kevin's death, Rose had slipped into sullenness, turning inward, rarely speaking and never smiling.

"How will I raise her without Kevin?" But even as she whispered the words, she knew that God had already given her part of that answer. Not long after Kevin's death, her father-in-law, Mac, had reached out and invited her and Rosie to live with him here in Sculpin Bay. She was grateful for Mac's generosity. He had a special way with Rose, and even though the lakeside village of Sculpin Bay seemed a million miles from their old home in Detroit, Ava had welcomed the change.

She stood and headed back to the house, her mind wandering to supper and what she might fix. As she neared the barn, she opted for a shortcut and ducked under the pasture fence. A promise Mac had made to Rose earlier popped into her mind: a pony. What was he thinking? She was too young.

Ava waded through the pasture's knee-high weeds toward the barn. It was a small, tired stable with only two stalls, weathered clapboard siding and a leftward list, but the stone foundation looked solid. Could it be fixed up for a pony? She pictured Rose sitting in the swayed back of a sturdy pony, her hands entangled in its shaggy main, her face all smiles. Maybe Mac was right. Maybe a pony was just what Rose needed—a friend, something to bring her out of her shell. Ava would do anything to see her little girl's smile again.

Another breeze kicked up, and Ava's gaze was drawn to the barn's patchy roof where a rusty iron weather vane creaked as it spun on top of the cupola. Out of nowhere, a large black bird appeared, paused on the roof's pitch and slipped through a jagged opening in the patchy shingles. Another bird followed and did the same thing. From inside the barn came the hollow knocking of their beating wings.

A shadow swung over Ava's head: a vulture. It, too, landed on the roof, likely attracted by the commotion of the other birds' raucous calls inside. But it spied her and lifted off to the sky as she moved forward. She sighed. Likely another dead mouse inside the barn—something common here. But if a pony was in their future, she might as well see what they'd need to repair or replace.

Ava headed into the barn, passing through the narrow opening between the doorjamb and the boarded door, careful not to catch her shirt on the splintered wood.

She blinked against the dim light, her eyes adjusting as she spied the two birds hunched on a pile of fallen timbers. They'd caught sight of her, cocked their heads and, in a flurry, careened into each other, feathers flying, before taking flight. Her gaze traced their ascent through a large hole in the roof. Well, roof and timbers could be fixed, though keeping out vermin would always be an issue, she supposed.

Then her gaze fell back to the wood pile, and she caught sight of a snatch of brightly colored fabric under one of the timbers. She stepped closer, suddenly wary.

As she neared, dank air crept up her nostrils, coating her throat and making her stomach gurgle. There, lodged between the boards, a woman's body lay, whitish blond hair splayed out around her head like a halo, arms outstretched, her body twisted and contorted, and her milky eyes fixed in a rheumy stare.

Seconds ticked by as Ava's shocked mind absorbed the scene. Then her skin prickled. Her eyes swept the shadows as fear washed over her, and she turned and bolted to the house, bursting inside the back door. Mac stood in the kitchen stirring something on the stove. Her panic-filled gaze searched the room, landing on the table and her purse.

"There you are," Mac said. "Decided to make spaghetti tonight—it's Jane's favorite. Forgot to tell you she's coming over to… What's wrong?"

"Where's Rose?" Ava gasped, her breath ragged as she tore through her bag, searching for her phone.

Mac nodded toward the other room. "In there, watching a show. Why—what's going on?" He set down the spoon, his brow furrowed.

Ava pulled out her phone and peeked on Rose, relieved at the sight of her daughter's small body hunched in front of the television.

Mac turned off the stove. "What happened? Are you okay?"

Ava shook her head, her shaky fingers pushing 911. A dispatcher answered, and Ava recited the address over the line. "Please send the police. A woman's been hurt... She's...she's dead."

Mac came to her side. "A dead woman?" he hissed. "Are you sure? Where?"

Ava's voice wavered, and her mind flashed back to the scene. "It's horrible... She was..." She couldn't finish. Didn't need to. Mac enveloped her in his arms and pulled her close while she relayed what she knew to the dispatcher. She disconnected, exhaled and leaned into him, her body trembling from the aftershock.

He pulled back and held her at arm's length. "The barn, you said?"

Ava nodded.

"Stay here with Rose while I go take a look."

"No. Don't. Wait for the police."

"I have to make sure she's not just hurt and in need of medical attention."

Ava grabbed his arm. "She's dead, Mac. I'm sure of it." But there was no convincing him. She knew Mac took care of things himself, handled pressure well and would need to check if there was any chance the woman was alive. Much like Kevin, caring and capable and... Mac gently shook off her grip and headed outside.

She watched him go, clasping her arms around her midsection to hold herself together. "Stay calm," she told herself, for Rose's sake.

"Rosie," she called out gently to keep the tremor from her voice, turning to the family room. "What are you watching, bug? Can Mommy—"

Rose was gone.

A small gasp escaped her lips. *Rosie?*

"Rosie? Rosie!"

Ava rushed to the small bathroom off the kitchen; had she slipped past them? But she wasn't there. Back through the kitchen to the dining room, where Rose and Mac had started a puzzle. But no Rose.

"Rosie? Rosie!"

A chill stillness stung the house, a silence filled with pure panic. Ava turned toward the stairs and took the steps two at a time to the second floor, murmuring her child's name— *Rosie, Rosie, Rosie*—telling herself not to frighten her daughter with her own anxiety. At the top of the stairs, she called out for Rose again and threw open the door to her bedroom. A pink bedspread, play kitchen, crayons and books strewed over a floral print rug, but no Rose. And she wasn't in Ava's room or Mac's room or the spare room at the end of the hall.

Ava stopped and spun in all directions. *She was just here. Just here! Where could she have... The attic!* Ava turned her attention to a narrow set of rickety stairs and noticed the attic door was ajar.

"Rosie? Are you in here?" Ava mounted the steps and pushed through stacked boxes and years of discarded household items. The attic was empty.

Fear pounded in her chest. *My baby. Where's my—* Her breath caught and she strode toward the window and pressed her face against the dirty pane.

"Oh no!" Rose was climbing through the fence, heading for the barn. She must have seen Mac going that way and decided to follow. Ava shuddered. The woman's body and...the birds! She'd be scarred forever.

Ava flew down the attic steps, through the house and launched herself outside, calling after Rose. Halfway across the yard, she bent over, relieved at the sight; Mac had heard her calls and come out of the barn and found Rose.

Sirens wailed as Ava made her way, composed as she could, to where Mac was crouched down, speaking gently to Rose. They both looked up as Ava approached.

"Look who followed me," Mac said, his voice calm, although Ava saw the tightness in his features.

The sirens sounded close. "I see that. Rosie, you know better than to go outside without telling me."

Rose's eyes grew wide.

"Easy now," Mac said. "No need to get upset with her. Bet she was coming out to look for that pony we've been talking about. Was that it, Rosie girl?"

Rose shook her head.

Mac looked surprised. "No? Well, she's my little shadow, this one is."

They turned as the first of the police vehicles made it up the drive. Next to her, Rose stiffened. This wasn't good—not at all. The last time Rose had seen police officers was when one came to the door to give them the bad news about Kevin.

"Come with me," Ava said, tugging at her arm. "We can color for a while or play cards, or... I know, we could cook something special for Grandpa. Cookies, maybe? Do you want to help me make sugar cookies?"

The first of the officers was out of his car and coming their way, Rosie's wide eyes on him, not hearing anything her mother had said.

Ava plucked at the girl's arm. "Rose, please. Come inside with Mommy."

Mac gave her a gentle nudge. "Go on now, pumpkin. Do as your mother says." But Rose remained still, her eyes fixated on the approaching officer.

"Rose." Mac's voice was stern. "Go with your mother now."

"But what about the lady?"

Mac and Ava exchanged a look. Rose rarely spoke anymore, and her voice was so faint, Ava wasn't sure she'd heard her correctly. She stooped down and looked her daughter in the eye. "What was that, bug?"

Rose pointed a finger toward the barn. "The lady that got shot?"